the girl
who fell

the girl who fell

THE CHESS RAVEN CHRONICLES: BOOK ONE

VIOLET GRACE

NERO

Published by Nero,
an imprint of Schwartz Publishing Pty Ltd
Level 1, 221 Drummond Street
Carlton VIC 3053, Australia
enquiries@blackincbooks.com
www.nerobooks.com

 A catalogue record for this
book is available from the
National Library of Australia

9781760640248 (paperback)
9781743820353 (ebook)

Cover design by Design by Committee
Text design and typesetting by Tristan Main
Cover image © aleshin

To Violet and Ivy. Find your power.

FACT

The Luck of Edenhall is a glass cup from the fourteenth century, currently part of the collection at the Victoria and Albert Museum in London. The cup once belonged to the Musgrave family of Edenhall in Cumberland, and was said to have brought them great luck. In 1791 *The Gentleman's Magazine* speculated that a butler from the Musgrave estate had stolen the Luck of Edenhall from fairies.

FACT

The unicorn was added to the royal coat of arms of the United Kingdom in 1603 when James I of England ascended to the throne.

chapter 1

'A criminal has no place in the Victoria and Albert Museum,' Janine the Labeller screeches into her phone, loud enough for everyone in the office to hear.

Her name isn't really Janine the Labeller. It's just Janine. I added 'the Labeller' on my first day of work, when I noticed that she'd stuck a sticky name label on her tape dispenser. And her hole puncher. And her scissors. And pretty much everything else on her desk. I'm not sure if she's always been a labeller or if she took up the habit when she found out she'd be working with a criminal.

That would be me.

It isn't just my criminal record that Janine objects to. She also has issues with the way I dress. On my second day she studied my scuffed commando boots and baby-doll dress with a thin-lipped smile. 'Ms Raven,' she said stiffly, 'your clothes violate the Victoria and Albert Museum's expectations of staff attire. Even for back-of-house roles.' She refuses to call the museum 'the V&A' like everyone else does. It's always 'the Victoria and Albert Museum', as if Queen Victoria and her husband, Albert, were personal friends of hers.

I'm used to people not wanting me around. It's just that they usually manage to be a touch more subtle about it.

I catch my reflection in the screen of my computer. Ethereal – that's how people sometimes describe me. And not always as a compliment. But when I look at myself I just think I look, well, unfinished. Even when I make an effort, I look incomplete. Something's missing, and I've never been able to figure out what. This morning I took extra care when I got ready, but I still came up short. Okay, so I didn't polish my boots. But I did wash and blow-dry my long auburn hair. And even rimmed my green eyes with some eyeliner. It's not every day you turn sixteen.

A calendar alert pops up on my screen, reminding me that I'm meeting Marshall Musgrave in five minutes. It's our regular fortnightly catch-up, where he pretends to be concerned about my welfare and I pretend to believe him, until such time that I can leave without causing offence.

I mumble to Janine that I'm taking my lunch break. Still on the phone, she responds with a raised eyebrow and twisted bottom lip that conveys seething contempt more effectively than words ever could.

In some ways, I don't blame her. I'm also baffled why one of England's richest and most powerful businessmen kept me out of jail after I got done for stealing.

Let me rewind a bit.

The first thing you need to understand is that working in data entry at the V&A Museum isn't my choice. I'm only here by the grace of Her Majesty's government's Second Chances program to keep delinquents like me out of prison. Of course, they don't use words like 'delinquents' anymore. They prefer 'youth at risk' or 'young offenders', as if thieving is a medical condition you have the misfortune to catch or a stage of life you eventually grow out of.

Usually the Second Chances program involves some sort of rehabilitation, which is code for spending months bored out of your brain, picking up rubbish from the side of the M6 highway and attending regular meetings with a sponsor who's considered to be an upstanding member of the community. The sponsor's good influence is supposed to inspire us to stick to the straight and narrow, and to go back to school – once we've paid our debt to society and perfected our rubbish collection skills.

Marshall Musgrave is my sponsor. He's also on the Board of Trustees at the V&A. So not only did he arrange to get me out of the lock-up and into the program, he also pulled some strings so I could do my time entering data here instead of breathing in fumes on the side of a busy motorway.

The second thing you need to know – and this is where things get really awkward – is that Marshall is also the 'victim' of my 'crime'. It's hard for me to imagine one of the richest men in England, with a reputation as a hard-arsed businessman, being a victim of anything, let alone anything I could do to him. He was named *Time* magazine's Person of the Year last year because of all the power he wields from his drug company, power plant and telecommunications and internet businesses. He's also on first-name basis with everyone from Elon Musk to the Pope. You don't build an empire like that by being a pussycat. But there it is: Marshall is the victim of my criminal ways.

Showing remorse was a prerequisite for acceptance into the Second Chances program. But I faked it. The truth is, I don't regret stealing from him one little bit. It was the only way to save Gladys's life and I'd happily do it again.

Gladys is my landlord and the closest I've ever come to having a friend. I started renting the apartment above Gladys's laundromat when I was fourteen. My foster father, Larry, was long dead by the time I moved out, and my foster mother, Sue, was happy to see the back of me – so long as she and whichever boyfriend she had at the time still got to pocket the welfare payments. We had a deal: Sue would keep quiet about me moving out before reaching adulthood and I wouldn't mention that she was taking money for nothing.

It was a sweet deal for everyone concerned. The only person who didn't do so well out of the arrangement was Gladys. Because when I say 'rent', I mean that she lets me live there for free. All she asks in return is that I service and repair the machines and help out with the ironing and steaming when things get busy. She would probably do better finding a tenant who could pay in actual cash, but for some reason she's always had a soft spot for me.

I have no idea how old Gladys is. It's not the sort of question I ever felt I could ask. She was ancient when I first started visiting her after school and she's even more ancient now, a decade later. When I was a kid I'd delay going home for as long as possible, sitting at her kitchen table either doing my homework or helping her fold washing, and listening to her sing the same bizarre songs over and over. She has an atonal voice that sounds a lot like a dying cat, but somehow I find it comforting.

A year back, Gladys was diagnosed with a potentially fatal blood disorder. She tried to hide it from me, but she was getting tireder and tireder, and then one day she could barely get up and I forced her to tell me what was the matter. Her only hope was a kidney transplant or a new, very expensive, class of drugs called hemotenes.

It just so happens that hemotenes were developed by one of Marshall's companies. We couldn't have afforded the drugs in a million years and I wasn't about to stand by and watch Gladys die. So I used the only real skill I have.

Hacking.

I've always been better with machines than with people. Computers don't lie to you; they have no hidden agenda. When I was growing up I spent all my spare time playing around on an old laptop a social worker had given me. It was a piece of junk but I liked it better than any person I knew. I guess that tells you all you need to know about my people skills.

When Gladys got sick I hacked into Musgrave Pharmaceuticals and flagged a small batch of drugs that was scheduled to be delivered to a pharmacy and rerouted them to the laundromat instead. I hid my tracks, using a different pharmacy and a different courier company each month.

And it all went like clockwork. The drugs were delivered, Gladys was looking better. And we weren't paying a cent.

Until one day the police came knocking. They read me my rights, took my fingerprints, and then faster than you can say 'youth custody' I had a criminal record.

Fortunately for me, Marshall Musgrave was one of the business leaders closely associated with the Second Chances program. It would've looked bad for him and the program if I'd gone to prison after I was convicted. Just imagine the tabloid headlines about the billionaire do-gooder who put a young offender behind bars.

But credit where it's due: Marshall not only made sure I stayed out of prison, he also ensured Gladys got a regular supply of the drugs. And he kept all of it, even his good deeds, out of the papers. He'd probably hate his business competitors to know that underneath the tough-guy image he has a good heart.

So here I am, well on my way to becoming a functional member of society. That is, of course, if you define a bored-out-of-her-brains data-entry clerk a functional member of society. But as much as I hate the mindlessness of entering visitor feedback surveys into a database, I know I'd hate rubbish duty a lot more, so I will forever be in Marshall's debt.

As I walk down the corridor towards my preferred meeting spot with Marshall, I hear yelling from the lawn outside. Peering out the window, I see two police officers evicting Neville from the area. Neville is the resident homeless man. I've shared many of my homemade ham and cheese sandwiches with him in the five months I've been trapped here. I like how he throws back his head and laughs a deep belly laugh, showing off all the missed opportunities for the dental industry.

Like Neville, I know what it's like to be hungry. The pittance social services paid to my foster parents was only rarely spent on me. I was an income stream for them – and not a particularly good one. Unlike Neville, I escaped my predicament. But I'll never forget the aching stomach and shivering body, the feeling of not knowing if or when I would eat again.

'But … but … where'm I s'pos' to go?' Neville stammers as he clings to the rusty trolley containing his worldly possessions.

One of the police officers assumes that menacing stance that all male law enforcers seem to have mastered – legs wide, hips thrust forward, as if they think their dick is a sword. To be honest, he's not nearly as convincing as he thinks he is. He's tall but scrawny, and has a weak chin. I bet his email password is something like 'stud' or 'champ'. The other one is built like a bulldog and looks like he could squash Neville like a bug. Far more convincing.

I hate police. And social workers. And counsellors and doctors. No doubt the endless parade of professional do-gooders who've case-managed me over the years would say I have 'trust issues'. And they'd probably be right. But in my experience, the people who are supposed to care are usually the first to let you down.

I decide to help Neville as a matter of principle. I whip

out my heavily modified phone and fire up a little app I put together to slip in the back door of CADMIS. For the uninitiated, that's the Computer-Aided Dispatch Management Information System – the secure computer network the police use to send officers to jobs.

Yes, yes. I know. Breaching computer systems is how I got here in the first place. But I don't have many talents, and a girl's got to use what she has.

I see on CADMIS that there's been a serious car accident in Chelsea, so with a few quick strokes on my phone I send a notification to all available officers to attend the scene immediately. A couple of seconds later Officer Bulldog lifts his radio and listens, while Constable Weak Chin tries to maintain a threatening stance towards Neville.

Come on, I will them.

Bulldog signals to Weak Chin and turns back towards their car. Weak Chin says something to Neville – a parting warning to save face, I'll bet – then heads to the car too. A satisfied smile creeps across my face as Neville flips Weak Chin the bird and settles back down onto the grass beside the water fountain. I decide to bring him a coffee on my way back. Maybe I'll splurge on a cupcake for us to share for my birthday.

But Marshall first.

The Medieval and Renaissance Room is mostly empty today: just Tony, the security guard who nods at me when I enter; a few schoolkids with sketchpads and pencils; and a portly old man wearing a peacock-blue suit with five enormous, gold-rimmed buttons and a gold cravat, holding a walking stick that seems more decorative than functional. Even from across the room I can see that every one of his fingers is adorned with jewel-encrusted gold rings. I feel his gaze on me so I look away, at the ornate glass objects and what appear to be old treasure chests.

Marshall isn't here yet, so I sit down to wait on one of the benches along the wall. As I sit, a sense of deja vu washes over me. Not from being in the room – I've come into this room dozens of times since I began the Second Chances program – but from sitting on this bench seat.

I've sat in this exact spot before, I know it. The feeling is intense, and it spills into a memory.

A lady.

I think harder, but I can't summon her face. All I can remember are her shoes. She wore high heels, the kind that *click-clacked* on the marble floor. We came into the V&A through one of the side doors. More than once. She'd ask me to help her find something, but I never knew what. It was like she wanted to play hide-and-seek, only with the fun part taken out. And she wanted me to hold a cup. It looked more like a vase to me, but she always called it a cup. It was beautiful, colourful and fancy. Occasionally she'd buy me something to eat afterwards and I'd try to eat it slowly. I didn't want her to know how hungry I was. I wanted to please her. But she always seemed angry, disappointed in me.

As the memory fades I realise the very same cup – the one from my childhood – is in this room.

In fact, it's right in front of me.

chapter 2

The rest of the room falls away. The cup's elegant swirls of blue, green, red and white enamel draw me in. I must have walked through this room a dozen times. Why have I never noticed it before now? A knot of unease tightens in my stomach as I stand and move towards it. I have to get a closer look. I want to hold it, touch it. At the same time, I sense that I shouldn't. That it's dangerous.

It's smaller than I remember, roughly the size of a pint glass. When I was a kid it seemed enormous. As I near it, my path is blocked by a group of hungover twenty-somethings who've wandered into the room. Most are wearing crumpled t-shirts emblazoned with logos from the US's finest cultural institutions: Harvard, Yale, Abercrombie & Fitch.

A tour guide's voice echoes off the arched ceilings and magnificently carved pillars. 'Gather round. I'm going to tell you a story,' she says, holding up a yellow flag that matches the sunflowers on her dress. Twenty or so pairs of Birkenstocked and sneakered feet shuffle around the cabinet that contains the glass cup.

'The cup you see before you is the Luck of Edenhall,' says the guide, trying to imbue each word with an air of mystery. This lady has a bad case of Frustrated Actor Syndrome. 'Historians tell us that it's most likely of Egyptian or Syrian provenance, dating from the middle of the fourteenth century. But not everyone is so sure.' Her voice lowers to a conspiratorial whisper as she glances around theatrically. 'Some people say it was actually made by ...' she pauses for effect, a big smile on her face '... fairies!'

Her revelation is met with a solitary cough from the wholly underwhelmed crowd. She ploughs on, oblivious. 'The cup was owned by the rich and powerful Musgrave family of Edenhall – that's in Cumberland – before it found its way to the museum.'

My ears prick up. Musgrave? She has to be talking about Marshall's family. I edge forward through the crowd, staring at the guide. From what I've pieced together from Wikipedia and the *Time* article, Marshall's family lived on the Cumberland estate for generations until they hit hard times and were forced to sell up.

'Legend has it that a butler in the Musgrave household stole the cup from the Fae, as the fairy folk are called, who were drinking from it by St Cuthbert's Well,' the guide continues. 'It's believed that the cup is enchanted with magical properties and brought the owners great fortune and prosperity. That's why it's known as the *Luck* of Edenhall. By some accounts, the fairies called out to the butler as he scurried away: "If this cup should break or fall, farewell the Luck of Edenhall!"'

The tour guide beams at her audience, either unaware of or unconcerned by their total lack of interest. I, on the other hand, am enthralled. I silently will her to continue with her story.

'As you can see, the cup is quite intact, but alas, not so the Musgrave family fortune,' she says gravely, as if personally affected by the fate of one of England's upper-class families. 'The Luck of Edenhall, it seems, eventually ran out of luck. Like so many other families, the Musgrave family was bankrupted by the Great Depression after a succession of disastrous investment decisions throughout the 1920s. Their family estate of Edenhall was demolished in 1934. The family loaned the glass to the V&A in 1926 and it was eventually acquired in 1958. The moral of the story? If you mess with fairies, you'll pay the price … eventually.'

She erupts with a cackle, then waves her yellow flag and leads the group away. I make a beeline for the display case. The coincidence makes me uneasy. What are the chances of me being brought as a child to see the very same cup that used to belong to my sponsor?

I trace my index finger along the corner of the glass case and instantly feel a tremor. I draw my hand back and look around to see if anyone else has noticed. But everyone seems to be distracted – except, perhaps, the weird guy with the cane and the cravat. He's studying a marble sculpture, but I swear I can feel his attention on me.

I assure myself that I'm not doing anything wrong as I place my hand on the case again. The vibration feels stronger; a frisson of energy faintly pulses out from it, tingling my fingertips. It's like the cup is trying to communicate with me but I can't hear it properly. Or perhaps I don't know its language.

I look around again. The old guy is still staring at the statue. I flatten my palm gently against the glass to see if I can absorb more of a sensation. My fingers tingle and my whole body shivers, as if a trail of ants just scurried down my spine. My chest tightens. I rip my hand away.

The tingle in my fingers subsides. I check my hand to see if it has left any physical trace. *Get a grip*, I tell myself. *It's just a stupid old cup in a glass case.*

Embarrassed to have been sucked in by the tour guide's bad acting, I take a deep breath and let it out slowly, worried that the anxiety I'm feeling is about to morph into a full-blown panic attack. I'm no stranger to panic attacks, although usually they're triggered by people, not museum pieces. I take a few more deep breaths and the fingers of dread release their grip on my chest.

I'm still slightly on edge as Marshall strides into the room. Every woman in the room surreptitiously glances in his direction. And, I notice, so does the man with the cravat and the cane. He's staring straight at Marshall, not bothering to conceal his interest. A strange look comes over the man's face, but I don't get time to decipher it before he scuffles for the exit.

Marshall commands the room as if it were a stage. Fittingly, *Time*'s cover had shown him positioned with one hand in the pocket of his Zegna suit jacket, those unreadable but somehow welcoming eyes framed by his thick boyish hair, greying at the temples. He's probably pushing fifty, but he's not bad looking – for an old guy. The article detailed his various businesses and the property portfolio that spanned the globe's most exclusive neighbourhoods: London's Bloomsbury, Shanghai's Xuhui District, Pollock's Path in Hong Kong, Singapore's Paterson's Hill. He even owns an island somewhere.

This must be our tenth meeting but Marshall and I are still at that awkward stage where we haven't yet worked out appropriate greeting etiquette. He leans in to peck my cheek. It's not creepy but it is so unexpected that I flinch. His kiss lands on my ear and I somehow find myself patting his shoulder instead of shaking his hand. As we break apart, I notice that Marshall is looking as embarrassed as I feel. I sense that he's trying to position himself less as my mentor and more as my friend. Or worse, a father figure. He probably read something about it in the Second Chances manual under the heading 'Building Rapport'.

'Happy birthday, Chess,' he says, regaining his composure. 'I thought we'd celebrate with lunch.'

My eyebrows shoot up in surprise. I wasn't expecting anyone to remember my birthday, certainly not Marshall. He's probably in the process of negotiating the purchase of a small country and he's about to put it on hold to celebrate my birthday?

'It's in your file,' he says. 'Your birthday.'

I have to admit that I woke up this morning and thought how different my life would be if my parents were here.

14

I miss them all the time, but birthdays are the worst. And Christmas. My dad was supposedly a brilliant physicist. As for my mother, I know almost nothing about her. I have some hazy memories, but I can't tell if they're real or if I dreamed them up.

I've tried searching for information about my parents, but even with my ability to access computer networks I've turned up next to nothing. Just a few mentions in obscure government databases that haven't led me anywhere. Over the years I've heard ridiculous whispers and gossip from social workers and other bureaucrats that, as far as I can piece together, amount to my parents being abducted by the Russians. Or the Chinese. Some hostile foreign government, anyway. They snuck right up the Thames in a submarine and snatched my parents off a boat, apparently. I don't believe a word of it.

The only reliable information I have is a brief newspaper article about my parents being reported missing in a boating accident and then, about a week later, a follow-up report saying that extensive sea and air searches had found no trace of them. 'Missing, presumed drowned' was the official finding.

I was three when they died, and any photos, mementos, assets or money I inherited were lost during the next three years, as I was shuffled from one temporary home to another. It wasn't until I was six that I went to live with Larry and Sue, who became my permanent foster parents. But by that stage all my belongings had disappeared and any memories of my parents were long forgotten.

As Marshall ushers me across the courtyard on the way to the cafe, I suck in the cool spring air, trying to slow my breathing and ignore the tightening knot that has returned to my gut. The idea of sitting across a table making small talk with my sponsor, who's posher than Harrods, will do that to a girl. But I relax as soon as I step into the cafe. All the faces painted in the blue and white tiles of the Poynter Room help to put me at ease. They always do.

The Poynter Room in the cafe is my favourite place in the whole V&A building. The soft light streaming through the stained-glass windows kisses my skin and – I know it sounds nutty – I can't shake the feeling that I'm being watched by the people in the tiles. Not in a predatory or threatening way; it's like they're watching over me, the way I've seen proud parents watch over their little ones. I keep catching glimpses of the goddess Venus in my peripheral vision, waving and pointing at me, but when I turn to look at the painting she's as still and lifeless as you'd expect. I'm not sure if these delusions make me insane or just really lonely. Either way, I figure it's best that I don't mention them to Marshall – or anyone else for that matter.

Marshall catches the eye of a waitress and, rather than ordering at the counter like everyone else, gives his order directly to her. I'm pretty sure she's about to tell him there's no table service, but then she recognises him and produces an old receipt from her back pocket and scribbles his order. Before I have time to read the menu, Marshall orders a toasted panini for me.

'I hope you don't mind,' he says breezily as the waitress hurries away. 'I don't have long.'

I do mind, but I don't say anything. All my life people have been making decisions for me. They always say they have my 'best interests' in mind, but in my experience that was almost never the case. And now that I'm sixteen I figure it's time I started making my own decisions. But I've also learned the hard way that picking fights can make things worse. I'm in Marshall's debt too, so I'm not about to cause a scene over a sandwich and get reassigned to rubbish duty.

'Thank you,' I say, leaving it at that. And then, partly to fill the silence that's fast becoming awkward, and partly to hide my annoyance at being treated like a child, I blurt, 'I just saw the Luck of Edenhall.'

'Ah,' he says carefully. 'What did you make of it?' He's doing his best to sound casual. And if you hadn't spent hours watching videos of Marshall on the internet when you were supposed to be doing data entry, you'd miss that his jaw just clenched ever so slightly.

It's not an option to tell him my memories of the cup. There is no way to explain it that makes sense, even to me. So I just say, 'It's pretty.'

He raises one thick eyebrow. 'That's all?'

'Yep.'

His pupils contract for a tiny instant and his boyish face turns almost reptilian. I blink and his features have returned to normal.

'The Musgrave family owned that once,' he says.

'According to the story I just heard,' I tease, trying to lighten the mood, 'your family's butler stole it from fairies. Technically that puts the question of ownership in doubt.' I'm about to say how rude the guide had been about the fate of his family's fortune, when Marshall levels me with a cool stare. He's trying to be calm, but his hand strangling his glass says otherwise.

'It wasn't stolen. They gave it up. Willingly. The fools.'

They? Did one of the most powerful men in England just let slip that he believes in fairytales? If I didn't know better I'd assume he was having me on. Marshall clearly has many excellent qualities: Hard-working. Check. Focused. Check. Extraordinary business acumen. Check. Kind, considerate and generous. Check, check and check. But a sense of the absurd definitely isn't on the list.

I stare at him, unsure what to say. And then I make the mistake of letting out an awkward laugh. 'Marshall, you don't actually believe in fantasy stories, do you?'

'Of course not,' he says. His cool anger tells me I've hit a nerve. 'I hardly need explain to *you* that I'm not talking about children's stories. I'm talking about ... What I'm talking about are real people with real lives, robbed of their legacy without a second thought.'

I don't know where to go with this. I'm not even sure if we're still talking about the Luck of Edenhall or if he's talking about something else entirely.

'Well, it's just a silly story anyway,' I say, trying to close down the conflict.

Now it's Marshall's turn to look surprised and I realise

that I've gone too far. I can't afford to upset my sponsor. He sits back in his seat, and with his hands planted on the table, studies me as if he's not sure if I'm a fool or a liar.

'Chess, you're sixteen now. Don't you think it's time you stopped playing games?'

It was a light-hearted bit of teasing, I want to protest. Am I supposed to give up joking around now that I've had a birthday? I say nothing and make a mental note never to mention Marshall's family again. Ever.

I sense that he wants me to say or do something but I have no idea what. And this worries me. Marshall holds the key to my life for the next seven months. If he decides that I'm not committed to my rehabilitation, I could end up wearing an ugly jumpsuit and a tamper-proof ankle bracelet every day for anywhere between eighteen months and five years.

Or worse, he could stop Gladys's supply of medication.

Just as the waiter arrives with our food, Marshall's phone buzzes on the table. He checks the message.

'I've just got to …' he says, distracted by the screen. 'I was hoping this would be more straightforward. And that I didn't have to do this on your birthday, but time is of the essence.' He stands and leans across the table to brush his cheek against mine and then, before he leaves, he says, 'I just want you to be who you are. When the time comes, I'll be there.'

chapter 3

I just want you to be who you are. Who does he think I am? And what does he want to talk about 'when the time comes'?

The lunchtime crowd bustles around me as I remain in the cafe, trying to piece together what just happened. I'd like to think Marshall is just a rich eccentric. Who knows? Eton and Oxford with just the right twist of bonkers might be the secret formula for success in the world of business. Or maybe it was just one of those social worker type of things rich people say because they haven't got a clue. As if they imagine that all the problems in the world can be solved through a pep talk and a spot of personal development, because they've never been poor, or had nowhere to sleep, or felt unsafe.

But I have a feeling there's more going on here. There was meaning in his words that he expects me to decipher. Which just pisses me off. Why does everyone have to talk in riddles? Social workers, child-protection workers, doctors, magistrates – the whole lot of them. They couldn't put together a straight sentence to save themselves. All my life, it's been like this. I'm always the last one to know what's going on.

I finish my panini and start eating Marshall's untouched food. The *Time* article said that Marshall's family had struggled financially until he restored the Musgrave wealth. I'd like to know the writer's definition of 'struggle'. If Marshall's childhood was anything like mine, there is no way he could walk away from food the way he just did.

My thoughts are interrupted by a dull thud on the stained-glass window just above where I'm seated.

The cafe goes quiet. I look around. Every pair of eyes in the cafe looks warily in my direction, at the source of the sound. Maybe a bird hit the window. A large bird. A moment passes in silence, then the buzz of conversation returns. Half a minute later there's another thud. Then another, hard enough to rattle the window in its frame. I wince at the force of it, scared the window might shatter above me. I push my chair back and prepare to leave. Time to get that cupcake for Neville.

Someone lets out a yelp as yet another thud triggers a shower of plaster onto the tables. Other people begin gathering their belongings. The woman behind the counter picks up a phone, her eyes fixed on the window. I'm guessing she's calling maintenance or security – or both.

There's another thud against the window and I freeze in fright. Soon there are slams against all the windows and they're coming at such regular intervals that it sounds like thunder, or the continuous roar of a heavy hailstorm.

Above the noise I hear a high-pitched screech. At first it's like a ringing in my ears, but soon it grows to a chorus of what sounds like thousands of demonic seagulls. Looks of horror pass between the remaining diners. The Poynter Room plunges into darkness, as every window is blocked by thick curtains of swarming blackness, pierced by red pinpricks of light.

That's when the screaming begins. Glass and china smash all around me, knocked to the ground by the stampede of panicked bodies rushing towards the exits.

I can't move. Raw fear bolts me to the spot.

The windows finally give out against the continual blows, exploding into the room. Glass shards rain down on me, followed by a rancid stench. Hundreds, maybe thousands of – what? Ravens? – swarm into the room. A squadron of razor-sharp beaks manoeuvre around people and objects, zooming directly towards me. I suck in a breath and cover my face with my trembling hands as I realise that I am their target, their prey. Inky black wings, flapping manically, smother me. I swing my arms and legs furiously, connecting with their putrid bodies.

There are too many for me to fend off. As I hit the ground rolling, I feel ravens crush under me. Curling into a ball, I cover my face again. The ravens' claws graze the skin on my legs and pull on my dress. I scream, struggling to free myself, but the more I move, the tighter their claws grip onto me. Each time I manage to kick one of the vile creatures away, it's immediately replaced by another. I'm suffocating in a churning, shrieking cloud of vile darkness.

A flash of searing white light fills the room, followed by an explosion that vibrates through me. My ears pop, and my head fills with static. Speckled white light dances in my eyes. Scrambling, I try to stand, but the blast has knocked out all my senses. The ravens' claws seem to have gone, replaced by what feel like long bony fingers, grabbing at my body and dragging me across the room. I thrash and kick through a haze of fear and confusion, trying to get away. I blink, struggling for a clearer look.

Four walking carcasses. Blistering and pus-covered skin stretches across sinewy muscle and skeletal frames, complete with tangled hair and Neanderthal feet. One grips my leg. Another has my arm in a bony vice grip. The other two walk alongside in some kind of formation, carrying sticks that look like short spears. And they smell as bad as they look. I gag as my nostrils fill with a stench that's somewhere between rotting flesh and an open sewer. Whatever these things are, would it kill them to bathe?

'Get off!' I scream, scrambling and swatting my free arm at one of the creatures walking alongside me, before freeing my foot and launching a kick across my body at the groin of another. I connect and it doubles over with a groan, but quickly recovers and grips my free arm. My stomach fills with terror. 'What do you want?!'

It just continues, snarling and grunting, to drag me along the ground of ... of ... a ruin. The V&A has been completely trashed. The floor is covered in mud and grime. Shards of broken tiles dig into my back and sides and my head bounces on clumps of weeds and overgrown vegetation that somehow seem to be sprouting *inside* the Poynter Room.

There is a bolt of golden light from somewhere behind me. I let out an involuntary scream. That's when I notice the grip of the creature on one side weaken and then release. The creature shrieks and hisses before exploding in a cloud of dust, leaving behind the smell of burnt barbeque.

It happens so fast I'm too shocked to do anything.

The remaining creatures stop and pivot in a slow arc, like particularly nasty dogs turning on their prey. The one dragging me by the leg lets out a low, rumbling snarl and I thrash even more feverishly. I don't want to be anywhere near this thing when it's pissed off.

I turn my head to see who or what managed to annoy these creatures and probably make this whole situation worse. I make out the silhouette of a … a woman?

She strides towards the creatures through the rubble. The brown leather outfit she's poured into looks like armour. Narrow grooves snake up the legs and the bodice, so that she resembles one of those pictures in anatomy books that shows exposed muscle fibres. She's close enough now that I can see a round golden brooch of a unicorn insignia pinned above her left breast. Her dark brown hair is cropped close, and she has what I'm guessing are bird guts smeared on her black motorcycle boots. Her movements are precise and practised.

Police or military? Whatever she is, she's trained.

Mid-stride she raises her gloved hand, adorned with silver knuckledusters, and levels it at the creature holding my leg. I clamp my eyes shut, anticipating another blast. A whimper escapes me as another explosion rocks the room. The air sizzles and I open my eyes to see a plume of dust that used to be the creature.

The woman locks eyes with the third walking carcass, who's now forgotten me, snarling and leaping towards her with its spear outstretched. Looking completely unfazed, she raises her arm in a single fluid movement and obliterates it with another burst of light, before turning to the remaining creature.

'Last chance,' she says to it, but it's closing in on her, stupidly defiant. 'Too late,' she mutters, and it disintegrates before me.

I clamber to my feet and scan the room for more danger. The table and chairs from the cafe are gone. The distinctive black and red tiles of the Poynter Room floor are cracked, chipped or else smashed entirely, replaced by small craters where dirty water has pooled. The stained-glass windows are all shattered, and shards of faded coloured glass litter the floor. The woman remains in place, watching me silently, as if deliberately keeping her distance. She doesn't seem at all surprised by any of this. I'm not sure I'm any safer with this assassin, but at least she's not covered in pus and rot.

Looking up, I see a branch from a giant oak tree poking through where the roof used to be. Half a wall has gone, leaving bricks exposed like jagged teeth. I can see directly outside, into what should be a courtyard for the tourists to sit. But the grassy areas are overgrown with foliage and flowers in every colour. The pond is filled with slimy water, overgrown lily pads and felled masonry. As far as I can make out, the rest of the V&A is in a similar state of disrepair. All around, thick vines and flowers are strangling the brick walls, claiming the buildings. The air is thick and heavy with moisture, brimming with the harmonic chirps of crickets and songbirds.

I spin around in a trance, disoriented. This damage didn't happen from the blast a few minutes ago. It's years, even decades, old. I rub my hands through my hair, feeling for bumps. Perhaps I've sustained more serious injuries than I thought.

I spot a motorbike. Vintage, by the looks of it. It's shiny and black with a heavy bronze trim and oversized exhausts. It looks out of place among the chaotic jungle.

The woman clears her throat behind me and I whirl around, letting out a yelp as I come face to face with her. I'm about to run, when I realise that she's transformed from bad-arse assassin to looking, well, hesitant. Shy even. In fact, now that I can see her face properly, I'm surprised to discover she looks not much older than me.

With one fluid movement she drops her knee to a moss-covered tile, rests a forearm on her front leg and bows her head. A moment passes as I watch her. She doesn't move an inch, just stares fixedly at the ground as if lost in prayer, or waiting for me to talk. My heart's pounding and I can't think of a single thing to say. I just stand there, staring down at the top of her head like a complete idiot, wondering what to do.

The silence drags on and it appears that if I don't break it, I could be standing here for the rest of my life.

'What is going on?' I say in a voice I wish wasn't so shaky.

She lifts her head. 'Please, Your Highness, it's not safe here.'

Your Highness?

'They were just an advance party,' she continues. 'Reinforcements will be on the way.' Her voice is unexpectedly soft, given what I just saw she's capable of.

'Who is *they*?'

'I cannot say for sure, Your Highness,' she says. 'What I am certain of is who they serve. He will not be satisfied with this outcome. Allow me to escort you.' And then, a little too fast, as if she might have caused offence, she adds, 'It's your decision, of course. But the Chancellor will know what to do. I must take you to him.'

Her voice is so quiet that it takes me a minute to register what she has said. The Chancellor? *What is this?*

Again I consider running, but figure it would be futile. I couldn't outrun the bike. And I'm a little worried about what's poking out the top of her boot. It could be a knife. Or the handle of a gun. And I've already seen what she can do with those knuckledusters.

Goosebumps sprout along my arms as the sun disappears behind the canopy of trees above us. A breeze whispers through the broken building. The woman doesn't seem to want to hurt me. In fact, I'm pretty sure she just saved me.

'I think there's been some mistake,' I say.

'Yes, Your Highness. We did not anticipate that events would move so quickly. There was only time to send me. And I should have detected the predators before they attacked. I will detail my error in full in my report.'

Again with 'Your Highness'.

She bows her head towards the ground as if expecting me to berate her.

'Um, that's not what I meant,' I say. 'I'm really glad you came along when you did and saved me from those ... those things.' I wait for her to look up but she doesn't. 'Who are you and why do you keep calling me "Your Highness"? And where am I?'

Even with her eyes fixed on the ground, I can see her brow furrow in puzzlement.

'Trinovantum.' She says it slowly, as if the answer is so obvious that I must be asking a trick question. 'I am First Officer Jules of the Protectorate,' she continues, now with clipped military intonation. 'I am your escort —'

'Can we talk like normal people?' I interrupt. 'It's just too weird talking to the top of someone's head.'

'Of course, Your Highness.' She rises deferentially, but still doesn't look me in the eye.

'And where exactly is "Trinovantum"?' I say.

First Officer Jules looks even more confused, as if I've just asked what shape blue is, or how tall is the number seven.

'Never mind,' I say. 'Can you tell me how to get back home?'

She brightens a little. 'Yes, Your Highness. Of course, Your Highness.'

I let out an exasperated sigh and plant my hands on my hips. 'Why do you keep calling me that?'

Uncertainty, or perhaps fear, returns to her face. 'Forgive me, Your Highness. My answers are unsatisfactory. The Chancellor will know the proper answers.' She regards me warily. I'm clearly not who – or what – she was expecting.

Before I can ask another question, the gentle breeze suddenly builds, growling to life as a blustering wind. It's cold and has a quality that I've never felt in wind before. I'd swear it's hissing around me specifically, enclosing me and menacing me. The force is so strong that I stumble forward, almost losing my balance. The giant tree branches above us quake and creak. The songbirds' chirps turn to squawks before the flock flees.

First Officer Jules springs into some kind of ninja stance. She looks back towards me, her confusion replaced with purpose.

'Your Highness, my counsel is that we leave,' she says, sniffing the air. 'Now. Another pack won't be far off. And if I'm correct, they'll come in number.'

A hundred questions flood my mind, but before I can ask any of them, First Officer Jules is ushering me through the ruins of the V&A towards the motorbike. I don't want to take my chances with those other creatures and, considering I don't have any other options, I follow. The force of the wind is now so great that I feel like we're in a wind tunnel, each step deliberate and exaggerated as my whole body pushes against the wind.

'What's happening?' I shout as we navigate broken bricks and tiles and step through murky puddles. She just pushes me forward, then produces a second helmet from the side of the bike and hands it to me.

I grapple with the helmet clasp, finally forcing it on. It does little to drown out the howling wind, which has grown even more ferocious. Giant trees whip around as if they're saplings. Swarms of petals are loosed from flowers, creating mini-cyclones of colour. Enormous butterflies with wings the size of dinner plates struggle against the wind.

Jules slings her leg over the bike, and signals for me to climb aboard. Reaching around, she grabs my hand, pulling me in close and indicating for me to hang on. The engine thunders to life and I tentatively place my hands on the grooved brown leather of this strange woman's bodysuit.

Behind me, I feel a presence, dark and wrong. A shard of ice slivers down my spine.

As we speed away, I whip my head back over my shoulder. Another pack of the pus-faced creatures is marauding through the ruins in our direction, leaping off walls and through broken windows. I see a tall figure in among them, more a man than a creature. He's wearing a leather kilt and a studded leather jacket. I can't make out his features, but I'm certain that I can feel his eyes boring directly into my soul.

chapter 4

The bike screams through the rubble of the V&A, and I take in the extent of the damage. Every room has been wrecked and ruined by whatever disaster happened here. Sculpture and paintings litter the floor. Walls and roofs have collapsed.

Jules takes a sharp right, barely slowing as we cascade down the broken stairs and out onto the street outside. The bike gathers speed as we head north towards Kensington Gardens.

The wind has gone. London's weather is inclement, but these abrupt shifts are ridiculous.

Perched on the back of the bike, I gasp. Once-familiar streets look alien. Giant oaks tower above us, silent sentinels whose hulking branches form an expansive canopy, dwarfing the buildings below and making the road ahead darker and more ominous. Flowers bloom in an orderly chaos below the trees, in blues, pinks, yellows and oranges. Even through the helmet, the air is dense with the succulent fragrance of blossoms.

London never smelled so good.

The buildings are kind of the same as they should be; they're a similar shape and height, but it's as if the concrete and steel have been carefully taken out and replaced with smoothed stones and polished woods. Thick glass, the kind that distorts and takes on a green tinge, is in every window. Celtic symbols adorn the doors.

Beneath the lichen and ivy covering the buildings and framing every window are scars of war. Chipped walls and broken roofs surround us. Every so often, a building has been smashed beyond repair, leaving nothing but a pile of rubble. The Albert Hall's domed roof is gone. Through its majestic arch entrance, I see long grass and shrubbery claiming it. The roads are cratered with potholes, which Jules expertly swerves to avoid.

At this time of the day the London streets should be teeming with shoppers and workers on their lunch breaks. But every street we pass is deserted. Or at least, they become deserted as we approach. I catch glimpses of people in twos and threes scurrying like mice down alleys and into buildings as we approach. Even from a distance, the people look tired and desperate. Doors shut quietly as we go by. Curtains are drawn. Blinds are pulled. And yet, I swear we're being watched. I can sense eyes on me. But it feels different from the man in the leather kilt and jacket who was staring at me at the V&A. These eyes are looking *at* me. The man was looking *into* me.

I don't have a clue who that man is and what he wants. And I really hope I never find out.

Closer to Kensington Gardens, my reality is officially knocked sideways. Again.

Draped from the top of a hotel – or at least, what used to be a hotel – near Kensington Palace is a huge painting of a girl who bears a striking resemblance to me.

More than a resemblance. It *is* me. My eyes, my face, my hair.

For a moment, the strangeness of this world sinks into the background as I stare, agog, at my face plastered on the side of a building.

In the banner, I'm looking straight ahead, defiant, strong, but with the faintest of smiles on my face. I am groomed to perfection. It's something you'd expect to see in North Korea or on one of those banners they hang outside the front of museums advertising the latest exhibition. It's glossy and new, completely at odds with the devastated streets and buildings around us. Under the portrait, written in huge bold letters, are the words, 'THE RESTORATION'.

Restoration? Who do these people think I am?

How they were able to paint my portrait, I have no idea. I've never posed for a portrait, or even had a photo like that taken. This girl must be my twin – no, my doppelganger. Has Jules mistaken me for her?

Or else it's a parallel universe. Maybe those physicists are right – the ones who claim that the universe splits when we make choices. That the choices we make take shape, while the other choices branch off into some other version of reality. But if this is another version of me and some of my choices have branched off into this reality, how did London – my London – come to look like a bombsite?

Jules revs the bike as we thread between two pillars. Atop one sits a stone unicorn. I tighten my grip on her. I don't like being this close to anyone – certainly not a stranger – but it's either that or fly off the back of the bike.

Kensington Palace doesn't look how it's supposed to either. The magisterial red-brick building still commands respect but it's dwarfed by the trees and flowers in the surrounding gardens. Guards, dressed the same as Jules, stand shoulder to shoulder around the perimeter, parting with mechanical precision as we approach. We speed through the gates and towards the main entrance. Jules swings us up the pebble driveway and I see more portraits of the girl who is the spitting image of me. There are two massive banners unfurled on either side of the main entrance. Under these portraits is written: 'SHE IS COMING'.

We screech to a halt in front of the palace, loose gravel flying up around us. Jules kills the engine and dismounts in one fluid movement, lifting her leg over the fuel tank. More guards ring the palace. It's free of the damage that's hit the rest of London. The building is neat and the grounds manicured. I clamber off the bike and try not to look at the banners. They're freaking me out.

'Isn't this William and Kate's house?' I say to Jules as she removes her helmet and hangs it on her handlebars.

'I'm sorry, Your Highness, I'm not familiar with either William or Kate,' she says, as uncertainty reigns on her face. 'But I can make enquiries.'

'What rock have you been liv—' I say, but trail off as I get the strangest feeling that I've been here before. I have stood right here. I have no conscious memory of it, just the unshakable knowledge that I've been in this exact spot before.

For a moment I consider the possibility that the person on the banners is me after all. But I immediately dismiss the thought; my confusion is probably the result of the explosion back at the V&A. Maybe the trauma has reset my emotional state to my last strong response, which was the deja vu I felt when I saw the Luck of Edenhall. I've never even been in the grounds of Kensington Palace before. Not even for a school excursion. The schools I went to didn't do excursions. And I'm pretty sure this part of the palace would not be open to the general public anyway.

Jules starts apologising and reprimanding herself for putting me in danger back at the V&A.

'... tender my resignation immediately, Your Highness,' I hear her say.

I look at her in surprise. Her brown eyes are a mixture of fear and remorse. 'What?'

'I put Your Highness in danger. The Chancellor ... If he hears about ... No, no, I must be disciplined and resign.'

'You didn't put me in danger,' I say. 'You got me out of it. You're fine, I'm fine, end of story.'

If she thinks she's in trouble over some ravens and rotten freaky things, how much trouble is she going to be in when it's discovered that she's wasted her time rescuing a nobody when she should, presumably, be looking after 'Her Highness'?

Jules stares at me in disbelief. 'But, that would … that would breach security protocols. Strictly out of … out of the … No, no, there must be consequences.'

I don't want her to lose her job because of me. And besides, she saved me from those creatures, so I owe her. Sure, she thought she was saving someone else, but she was the one who got those flying rodents and rotting corpses off me. And I might need a friend, or at least someone who's friendly, when this Chancellor person realises I'm not the girl they're after.

I try another approach to get her to calm down. 'I'm "Your Highness", right?'

Jules nods emphatically.

'So, if I say you have to do something, that means you have to do it. Right?'

She nods again, this time less certainly.

'Okay. I command you to not resign.'

'But, I —'

'Uh-uh,' I say, starting to enjoy issuing a decree for what I'm sure will be the first and last time. 'First Officer Jules of the – um, what was it again?'

'Protectorate, Your Highness.'

'First Officer Jules of the Protectorate, I command you to retain your position and put this, um, situation behind you.'

'As you wish, Your Highness. Thank you, Your Highness,' Jules says, relief creeping into her features. Whoever she thinks I am apparently isn't the sort of person who shows mercy. 'We must go now.' She straightens up and ushers me through the entrance. 'He will be waiting for us.'

As we climb marble stairs to a grand hall, I wrap my arms around my body, trying to still my shaking hands. I don't know how to play the meeting with the Chancellor. Do I tell him straight out that while there's an uncanny resemblance between me and the girl on the banners we're not the same person? Or do I play along, bide my time and make a break for it when I can? *If* I can. I begin counting all the guards I've seen standing between me and freedom and stop when it becomes hard to breathe. If I'm not careful I could end up being blasted into dust like those pus-faced creatures.

Two more women dressed in the same skin-tight brown leather armour as Jules approach us as we enter the building. The sunlight catches their knuckledusters and reminds me just how much trouble I'm in. I notice the same seal on their bodysuits: a circle encasing a unicorn in raised gold. They drop to one knee and bow their heads the same way Jules did.

'Your Highness,' they chorus.

I look behind me to see who they are bowing to before realising it's me. Again.

'Um. You can get up,' I mumble, embarrassed.

The two women exchange uncertain glances.

'You can stand,' I say, more loudly.

They rise, step to the side and flank Jules and me as we continue through the palace. I scan the ceiling and walls for CCTV cameras that I may need to avoid on my way out of here. But I don't see any signs of surveillance equipment, which only adds to my anxiety. I can't dodge it if I can't see it. At regular intervals, I'm met by more guards dressed the same way; each stiffens and bows as we pass.

Surrounded by all these guards, I figure that making a run for it is out of the question. I could hide, because this place is enormous. The ceiling looks like something from the Vatican, but instead of angels, or Adam reaching for the hand of God, the ceiling is adorned with a pack of unicorns, all of them bowing before a woman clothed only in her flowing red hair. I stare at the woman's face. She looks like me, but older. And stronger. Her green eyes sparkle with power and determination.

We enter another room with another domed, painted ceiling. The two women flanking us peel off, pulling the doors shut, leaving Jules and me standing in a cavernous space, empty but for some fancy tapestries hanging on the walls. Compared to what I've seen of the rest of London, this building is an oasis of order and luxury.

I wipe my sweaty palms down the sides of my dress. My mind conjures every worst-case scenario of what's going to happen to me when this Chancellor guy arrives and works out they've made a right royal stuff-up and got a fake 'Her Highness' by mistake. Jules must sense my rising panic because her expression changes from rigid detachment to curious assessment. Her head tilts slightly as if she's not just looking at me, but listening to me too. She opens her mouth to speak and then closes it.

I try to calm my breathing by focusing on the painting on the ceiling. It's the woman from the other painting, with the green eyes and long red hair. But this time she has wings – huge iridescent wings that stretch out on either side of her. And in her arms she cradles a baby.

A door at the far end of the room clicks open and a man waddles in and bows. It's not a full-body bow like the others have done, more an exaggerated nod of the head and a sweep of his arm.

I look at the man and then at Jules, and then, as recognition dawns, my head whips back to the man. My mouth is dry and I'm too confused to speak. I've seen him before.

'Your Highness, what a great honour it is to see you,' he says. 'Again.'

chapter 5

'The museum. This morning,' I say, placing him.

It's the weird old guy who was staring at me in the Medieval and Renaissance Room. He's changed his outfit to something even more flamboyant than before, but he's quite obviously the same person. He looks ridiculous, swishing his long black cloak against his knee-length britches as he approaches. His embroidered coat is so unnecessarily puffy it wouldn't be out of place in the court of King Henry VIII.

'Are you stalking me?' I'm surprised by the anger in my voice.

'Stalking?' he asks, his jowls wobbling. 'In a sense, yes, I suppose I have been stalking you. But that's an altogether too sinister way of putting it.' His face softens as he regards me with a mixture of puzzlement and pity – and, if I'm not mistaken, a hint of pride. His smile spreads like warm butter on hot toast and I'm amazed to see it reaches all the way to his eyes.

'I was at the V&A this morning to personally oversee

your extraction. After all, I have known you since you were born. You even vomited on me once after a feed, right here on my left shoulder.' He chuckles fondly.

A lump of longing forms in my throat. He's obviously mistaken and is reminiscing about someone else. Still, I find myself wishing that it were me. Nobody's ever told stories about me as a baby. I've come to terms with my past, but sometimes I still fight back tears when I think about my parents and what could have been.

'I am the Chancellor,' he says, as if he's in a pantomime.

I get the feeling that not only am I supposed to know who he is, I am also expected to understand that he's important. I'm going to have to disappoint him on both counts.

He dismisses Jules with scarcely a glance. 'Leave us.'

Jules nods in acknowledgement and turns to leave.

'She stays,' I blurt. I'm not sure why, but I don't want to be left alone with this guy. Admittedly, I don't know much about Jules either, but I figure at least she does what I ask. And once the Chancellor works out he's got the wrong girl, I may need Jules – and her bike – to get out of here.

Jules looks unsure about the consequences of defying the Chancellor's orders. The Chancellor's eyes also widen. Clearly he's used to getting what he wants.

'As you wish, Your Highness,' he says. He smiles obligingly, but I sense a wariness that wasn't there before.

Interesting. Whoever they think I am, clearly she has the authority to overrule the Chancellor.

I relax a little. 'Why have you brought me here?'

'Because you are in great danger,' he says simply.

A shiver surges up my spine as the icy feeling of darkness I experienced on the bike hits me again.

'Please. Sit.' He gestures to a chair that I swear was not there a moment ago. It's covered in royal-blue velvet, punctuated by bronze studs that make little balloons in the fabric. Its arms are stuffed so full it looks like they are reaching out to hug me.

The Chancellor lifts his cane, flicks it, and golden light shoots out from the top. A table and two other chairs materialise before my eyes.

A yelp escapes me and I end up half-cowering behind the chair.

Lightning fast, Jules is at my side, taking my arm with a look of concern. 'Your Highness?'

A shimmer of sparkling dust hovers around the furniture for a moment and then dissipates. On the table is a crystal vase with the most enormous peonies I've ever seen. Each flower is about the size of my face, overshadowing the pitcher of water and a set of tumblers at the other end of the table.

I can't trust or comprehend what I'm seeing.

Jules ushers me to my chair and I all but fall into it, sinking deep down into the cushioned base. Despite its comfort, I'm on edge – and not just because it's not the sort of chair you can spring out of to make a quick getaway.

Jules pours water into one of the tall tumblers, hands it to me and then returns to standing to attention at the side of the table. I try to regain my composure, still staring at the table, trying to work out if it's real and how it got there. I run my fingers around the top of the glass. Yep, real crystal. As solid in my hand as any other glass I've held.

The Chancellor wears an amused smile.

'You said I was danger,' I say, slightly breathless. 'From what?'

'It's not so much a what as a who,' he says gravely, all trace of amusement gone. 'To properly answer your question, Your Highness, you first need to know some background that I am beginning to suspect you have forgotten. You are in Trinovantum.'

Huh? I reach into my pocket for my phone, keen to see what Google Maps has to say about this Trinovantum place. But my pocket is empty. My phone must be back at the V&A.

'Trinovantum is a city in Iridesca, realm of the Fae,' the Chancellor explains as he wedges himself into the chair on the opposite side of the table.

'The Fae?'

'Fairies, unicorns and what humans patronisingly refer to as "enchanted folk",' the Chancellor explains.

'Hold on a tick,' I say, unable to keep a smirk from my face. 'You're saying I'm in fairyland? And fairyland just happens to look the same as London? Well, aside from the trees. And all the buildings do look … funny.'

'Funny?' says the Chancellor, raising his eyebrows. 'It's quite true that Iridesca and the city you know as London are similar – very similar indeed. But the world you think of as yours is of a different realm, one that has many names, but which we call Volgaris. The physical environ of humans. You might say that London Iridesca, which we call Trinovantum, and London Volgaris parallel one another, sharing the same longitude and latitude, as well as the same atmosphere. But they overlay one another as a glove fits a hand. And just like a glove and a hand, they are similar, but also quite distinct. One is far more intricate and sophisticated than the other.'

I'm in no doubt as to which the Chancellor thinks is more sophisticated. His smugness seems a bit rich to me, given that we – in 'Volgaris' – haven't blasted our museums into rubble.

'For the most part,' he goes on, 'Iridesca is replicated entirely in Volgaris, but it has different, how shall we say, aspects.'

I look towards Jules, searching for some crack, some inconsistency in what sounds like the ravings of a New Age mystic. But her face is impassive. The Chancellor might as well have been observing that the sky is blue for all she gives away.

'All three worlds are interdependent —'

'Three?' I say, hoping I've just caught an inconsistency in his story.

'Transcendence,' he clarifies. 'That's the other one. The Shining Realm. It's where we are only consciousness, unburdened by our corporeal bodies and any physical pain or constraint. Transcendence is our playground, a place of spiritual enlightenment. Humans can journey into

Transcendence, but only with great discipline of mind.' He smirks as if having a private joke with himself. 'Humans are not known for their discipline of mind.'

I remain silent. I've never had much time for religion or spiritual stuff. It always seemed like a luxury I couldn't afford. Spirituality wasn't going to fill my aching belly or keep me safe at night. I've never even considered the idea of other worlds. That parallel worlds exist just does my head in. What the Chancellor is telling me makes about as much sense as anything else – which is to say, none at all.

I take a sip of my water and taste raspberries and honey. On reflex, I spit it out onto the shining oak tabletop.

'It's not poison,' the Chancellor says, chuckling. He dries the table with a flick of his walking stick. 'You have been away from us for too long, my dear.'

'Away?' I take another sip of the drink and swallow it as a gesture of goodwill.

'You were born in Iridesca, my dear child, but were taken to live in Volgaris when you were a girl of three,' says the Chancellor. 'Many moons gone, Queen Cordelia, the ruler of Albion in Iridesca —'

'Albion?'

'It's the name we give here in Iridesca to the land you know as Great Britain,' he explains, before getting on with his story. 'Queen Cordelia fell in love with a human. A scientist who, some would say, was too clever for his own good. Or should that be, too clever for *our* own good.' He chuckles at his own joke and his eyebrow cocks expectantly, as if I'll start laughing too.

I just stare at him blankly, my jaw slightly dropped. I don't see much to laugh about right now and I can't bring myself to fake it.

'While the Fae have always loved between the veil of the worlds, it is strictly forbidden to enter a more permanent union,' he continues, regaining his composure. 'The Queen did not simply wish to take Samuel Maxwell as her lover. Her wish was unprecedented, and the consequences far-reaching. Her Majesty Queen Cordelia believed that love should not be decided by committee and she defied the Order by marrying the human scientist.

'The Queen's union caused much disquiet. Most hoped that this relationship was just a dalliance of a young queen, that it would run its natural course and that in time a more suitable union could be made.'

He pours himself a glass of the weird water, but he doesn't drink it. 'Two years later, a child was born from the union.' The Chancellor stops again, like he's waiting for me to say something. I don't. Despite the bizarreness of his story, or perhaps because of it, I find myself engrossed, eager for him to continue.

'Naturally, many Fae were enraged by the birth of the child. The Queen's firstborn daughter, Francesca' – he looks at me as if that name should mean something – 'would be next in line to the Fae throne of Albion, but with a human father, her blood would not be pure. Some believed the throne should not pass to a mongrel child —'

Out of the corner of my eye I notice Jules's hands curl into fists.

The Chancellor smiles at me. '"Mongrel child" is the rebels' term, not mine. Alas, the Queen's enemies led a rebellion against the Royal House.' He lets out a deep sigh, seemingly lost in the tragedy of it all. 'And your parents' lives were lost.'

Parents? *Your* parents?

It finally dawns on me. He – they – think I'm Francesca.

My doppelganger on the banners outside must be Francesca. I feel like I'm trespassing on someone else's life, someone else's pain. I need to put a stop to this little charade before things get even more out of hand.

'Whoa, whoa,' I say. 'There's been a mistake. I'm not who you think I am. My parents died when I was three. A boating accident. I've seen their death certificates and the reports from the newspapers.'

The Chancellor looks at me, and then at Jules, as if considering his next move. I don't know who's in more trouble: Jules for getting the wrong girl or me for being the wrong girl.

He lets out a sigh, more of resignation than of frustration or anger. 'I was hoping that bringing you here and telling you all this would awaken your memory. The stories you heard about your parents? All fabricated, I'm afraid. A necessary precaution to hide your whereabouts.'

He doesn't pause long enough for me to respond.

'Despite your mother's marital ... unorthodoxy, the Order – those of us who remain loyal to Queen Cordelia and her family, at any rate – feared the rebels would never be content with the removal of the Queen. We feared they would also come after you, so they could secure the throne for … one of their own.'

I'm pretty sure he was about to say someone's name but then thought better of it. Which is crazy, because it's not like I'd know anybody he's talking about anyway.

'In the midst of the rebel attack, I spirited you from Iridesca and into hiding among the humans in Volgaris. For the last thirteen years we have allowed you to grow up a human, but now that you have come of age, you have a claim to your mother's throne. And not a moment too soon. We can wait no longer for your return. The restoration is afoot.'

It's suddenly hard to breathe. I need to get out of here and away from these crazy people. I try to stand and run but my legs aren't cooperating.

'Your birth name is Francesca. You are Francesca, daughter of Cordelia,' he says solemnly.

'No, no … There's been a mistake. My name is Chess,' I protest, my voice raw and unsteady. I've forgotten so much of my childhood, but I wouldn't have forgotten that. 'The girl you're looking for – we look exactly the same. But I've never been here.'

'You are Francesca,' the Chancellor insists. 'When we hid you, we changed your name to Chess. That's what your father used to call you. But we kept your surname on your fabricated birth records. Raven. You are Francesca of House Raven. A Raven is a protector, and a bringer of great magic,' he adds, as if this somehow makes everything okay.

'I thought it was the bird of death.'

'That too,' he says quietly. 'A forewarning of war.'

The corners of my mouth tighten and I feel my throat heave as if I've just swallowed a sock. Nausea and light-headedness wash over me. My parents' death has been the one fixed point in my life, the bedrock upon which every-thing, no matter how much it sucked, made some kind of sense. To have my past rewritten by a complete stranger with terrible dress sense who claims to know me better than I know myself infuriates me.

None of it can be true. Fairies don't exist.

Do they?

No. Fairies can't exist.

I take another sip of my drink and try to work out how to get out of this place. The sweetness and tang tickles my tongue. I wonder if it's the water that's affecting me, if they've spiked it with something.

'Time is running out. For all of us.' The Chancellor's words come through a thick fog in my head. 'War is coming, a war that will consume the realms. We have reports that rebel forces are growing daily. Even those who sided with the Order, who remained loyal to House Raven, are beginning to talk of appeasement. Unless you return to Iridesca to cement your claim as the Queen in the Ascendant and unify the Fae of Albion, I fear – for us all.'

The Chancellor levels me with a piercing stare. 'And so, Your Highness, we have brought you back to do your duty as heir to the Fae throne. Welcome home.'

Silence.

The dull sound of a clock chiming in the distance.

The hum of air circulating in the high ceiling of the room.

The crash of shattering crystal as my drink slips from my trembling hand.

I stare at him, consumed by disgust. I don't know why he's trying to manipulate me. Or how he could do it in such a vile and despicable manner.

He must know that this is every foster kid's fantasy: that one day somebody realises that it's all been a terrible mistake. You go from the aching emptiness of being nobody to suddenly becoming somebody. You matter, you're not alone anymore, and for the first time in your life the frosty hole at the centre of your being is plugged.

How dare he use the pain of my childhood to twist my emotions. I taste blood in my mouth and realise I've bitten the inside of my cheek. But I can't release my jaw. Mute fury courses through every muscle in my body. My fingers dig into the blue velvet so deeply that I can feel the wooden frame beneath.

I'm burning up with such rage that it physically hurts. I'm trembling, sweating.

'Screw. You,' I spit, willing back the hot tears pooling in my eyes.

The Chancellor inches back into his chair, sitting upright, his eyes wide in shock. I feel Jules glance uncertainly in my direction.

Clearly, neither of them expected this.

'I have no idea who you are, where I am, or what you've given me,' I say, gesturing at the remnants of the glass on the floor. 'But I'm not going to sit here and be told who I am by a complete stranger with an overactive imagination.' I lever myself out of the chair, unsteady on my feet. 'I told you: *my parents died in an accident!* I'm not going to save you or anyone else. I've got enough problems already; I don't care about yours. If I don't get back home soon, I'm going to be fired and then probably sent to prison.'

Silence envelops the room once more.

After a moment, the Chancellor speaks. 'Before you make a decision, have a look at that painting.'

I grasp the back of the chair to steady myself, staring at the Chancellor, a fresh batch of anger rushing from the knot in my stomach. He points to the ceiling.

'Queen Cordelia,' he says. 'Rather a striking resemblance, wouldn't you say?'

'To who?' I snap. Sure, we have the same colouring and frame, but I couldn't hope to possess her combination of serenity and strength. 'That may be *Francesca's* mother but she's not mine.'

I can barely see the painting through the tears pricking my eyes. If that woman really is my mother, then that baby would be me. But it can't be. That look on her face, the way she is staring at the baby with pure love … If someone had ever looked at me like that, I would remember.

'Francesca, listen to me,' the Chancellor starts again, and this time there's the barest hint of desperation in his voice. The painting on the ceiling, it seems, was his trump card.

'Don't call me that.'

He reaches across the table and grabs my arm, his teeth bared. 'This isn't a game, Francesca. You are the only one standing between the rebels and the throne. If they find you, there's no telling what they might do.'

'*Get your hands off*—' I hear myself scream as I rip away my arm. There's a scorching spark of blue light, like a camera flash, then darkness.

chapter 6

I'm balanced on the edge of pain.

My head's foggy. Drugs – I must be on painkillers. But drugs can only mask pain, not erase it. Dull aches throb throughout my body, punctuated by the occasional stab. I can tell that I'm covered in bruises without even looking.

As a kid I woke to this feeling too many times to count, after Larry had had too much to drink the night before. Or not enough. It was the bruises on my face that used to upset me the most – the ones I couldn't hide. Did I fall down the stairs again, or walk into a doorframe? After a while it didn't matter because people stopped asking.

My left temple is stinging, and I know I'm cut. My hand prickles from the drip inserted into the vein. I want to rip it out but I don't, reluctant to do without the pain meds. I move my hand to my temple to assess the damage.

'Don't touch,' comes a stern voice. There's a guy wearing green hospital scrubs standing by the foot of my bed, staring at a chart in a blue plastic ring-binder. 'Six stitches. That's what's under that bandage and it will heal a lot quicker if you stop poking at it.' He delivers this in clipped tones without looking up, giving me the distinct impression that he'd rather be anywhere but here.

'Where am I?' I take in my surrounds: white walls, white ceiling, a double window to my right with a curtain in the familiar shade of neglect. I peer out the window, searching for damaged buildings and overgrown trees. But I see soft afternoon sunlight glinting off car windscreens. As far as I can tell, it looks like a normal car park and street. I hope this means that I'm back from … whatever that was.

'Hospital,' the guy says flatly, still studying the folder.

I'd already worked that out. The beeping machines and all-pervasive smell of industrial bleach were a dead give-away. What I really want to know is whether I'm back home, or if I'm still stuck wherever I was before – that Iridesca place. The trouble is, I don't know how to ask without being whisked off to the psych ward.

He hasn't called me 'Your Highness' yet, so that's a good sign.

In one enormous stride the doctor moves to the boxes of latex gloves mounted on the wall. He takes one out of the box marked 'Large' and forces his hand into it. I shudder at the sight of his gloved hand. I hate doctors.

One more step and he's at my bedside, running his gloved finger softly along the edge of the bandage on my face. He still hasn't looked me directly in the eyes.

'It's a deep cut but it'll heal nicely,' he says, more to himself than to me. 'The stitches will dissolve in a couple of weeks but you'll need to keep the wound dry for a day or two.'

His rigid manner makes it easier for me to overlook his ridiculously large blue eyes. And his blond spiky mane of hair. Not to mention the tiny indent in the centre of each of his cheeks. And he's so rude that I don't even find myself musing that he'd have dimples if he ever smiled – a rare occurrence, I'm sure. In fact, I'm finding it easy to overlook the fact that he is, without a doubt, the most beautiful person I've ever set eyes on.

Snap out of it, I tell myself.

He's also the youngest-looking doctor I've ever seen. He looks only a few years older than me, but that can't be right. If he's that young, he surely wouldn't have finished medical school yet. He would have barely started.

But that's not why I'm staring at him.

It's something else, but I can't think what. A memory? A dream?

Or maybe it's my first-ever hormone rush?

'Who are you?' I ask. My mouth and throat are as parched as sandpaper.

'Tom Williams,' he says, finally looking at me. He pauses for a moment, as if gauging my reaction. There's a flicker of warmth, concern even, in his eyes. A beat later it's gone. He whips the glove off, rolls it in a ball and tosses it into the rubbish bin, where it lands perfectly without touching the sides.

'You're a bit young to be a doctor, aren't you?' I say.

'I get that a lot,' he says, only half listening. He looks at the plastic bag of fluid above my bed, which is slowly dripping down the tube and into my hand.

'You are a real doctor, aren't you?' I say, feeling greater unease.

'I *have* done this before,' he replies, not even trying to conceal the irritation in his voice. He slips a penlight out of his top pocket and shines it into my eyes.

I'm about to look away, but find I can't tear my eyes from his face. I'm staring at him like a complete idiot. I shake my head, trying to break the trance.

'Hold still,' he says.

'What am I doing here?'

He ignores my question. I knock his hand away and feel a sharp tingle on my finger where it touches his. I might be projecting, but the flash in his eyes tells me he felt it too.

'Just tell me why I'm here,' I say, rubbing my tingling hand.

He raises an eyebrow, as if asking for information is totally unreasonable. Clicking off the penlight and letting out a sigh, he folds his arms across his broad torso.

'You were found lying in the middle of Kensington High Street earlier today. You were unconscious, so you were brought here.' There's that look again – a tiny hint of something warm through his cold detachment. And then it vanishes once more. 'Your possessions were gone, so I'm guessing they got away.'

'Who got away?' I ask, digging for some evidence of the Chancellor and the woman on the bike. Jules, her name was.

'Whoever mugged you.'

Ordinarily, I'd freak out at being told I was found unconscious. The fact that I'd been found on a street and without any of my stuff would make it even worse. Instead, relief washes over me. I must be home.

'Now, hold still,' he orders. 'I need to make sure you haven't suffered a concussion.'

Normally I wouldn't allow a doctor near me, much less one who looks barely old enough to vote. But I'm wondering, perhaps even hoping, that I do have concussion. At least that could explain what just happened to me with the Chancellor and those freaky pus creatures.

It might also explain this weird reaction I'm having to a complete stranger.

He resumes shining his torch in both my eyes and has me track the light from left to right and then up and down.

'What exactly do you remember?'

I open my mouth to answer but stop. Do I go with the mugging explanation? I have no clue how to articulate what happened, and even if I did I'm pretty sure I wouldn't be spilling it to Doctor Hot and Sour. If I mention ravens smashing windows, an alternative London that is a cross between a jungle and a war zone, being rescued by a woman on a motorbike, and meeting with some man calling himself 'the Chancellor', I'm not going to win any credibility awards. He'll think I'm using controlled substances and that's going to look really bad on my parole report. Since I evidently don't have concussion, part of me would like to write off the whole episode as a dream or a brain glitch.

But I can't. Because, whatever it was, I know it happened. It was real.

Or is that the definition of crazy: when you can no longer distinguish what's real from what's fantasy?

'It's not a trick question,' the doctor says in a frosty voice.

'I don't know what happened,' I say too quickly.

He flicks his white blond spiky fringe. 'Uh-huh', he says, but his face says 'Liar'.

He wraps a cuff around my arm to take my blood pressure. As it tightens, he looks down at the screen and I sneak a closer look at his face. His eyes, ice in both colour and temperature, are framed with such long, thick eyelashes that his face would look almost feminine if it weren't for the strong jaw. I can't decide if the spikes of his fringe, which look remarkably like icicles, are the result of hours in front a mirror or incredibly fortunate just-got-out-of-bed hair.

'Your blood pressure's low,' he says, removing the cuff from my arm. 'Too low. If I were you, I'd stay horizontal. You'll need to be here for a while.'

'I'm not staying here,' I say, feeling my stomach clench.

'You need to rest in order to recover.'

'I'll rest at home.'

'Chess,' he says in an authoritative doctor tone.

'How do you know my name?'

'It's on your chart.'

I don't believe him. I wonder if he knows me. Or if I know him but for some reason can't remember.

But how could I have forgotten a face like that?

'Have we met before?' I ask.

The doctor inhales so quickly I can hear it. His alabaster skin turns a whiter shade of pale. His eyes tilt upwards for a moment as if searching for a memory and then he sets his gaze on my face, boring into me as if expecting some kind of explanation.

'What?' I ask, a tad more defensively than I intend.

He swears under his breath as he runs his hand through his hair, and then backs away from me as if I'm contagious. Then he steadies himself, locks his eyes with mine and says, 'You don't know me,' as if it's a command rather than a simple statement of fact.

But memories flash through my mind, like someone just let off a hundred blinding flash bulbs. Each memory is crystal clear, as if it happened only yesterday. But it's like I'm seeing them for the first time.

chapter 7

I'm fighting for air but it's not enough.

A weight pushes down on my chest. Panic floods through me. My mind fills with an incoherent mass of images that can't be real.

'Can't breathe,' I hear myself wheeze. My lungs are on fire.

The doctor springs to action. All trace of the weirdness from before has disappeared as he takes my hand into his huge palm.

'You need to calm down,' he says firmly, but with unexpected warmth. 'Take a deep breath.'

I try to do as he says, but can't. The tips of my fingers begin tingling with pins and needles. He places his other hand on my forehead and sucks in a breath as if he's steeling himself for something. Through my blurred vision, he looks like he's grimacing, in pain maybe, before calm warmth suffuses my entire body. His face relaxes and his eyes become mesmerising, as if he's communicating with the innermost core of my being.

He's so close to me I can imbibe his musky saltiness.

More memories surface … but of what?

Somewhere deep inside, a door inches ajar.

And then I remember. A feeling. Or rather, what he's making me feel. The warmth, the calm and the peace. I've felt it before.

My heart stops racing, and my breathing returns to normal.

'You're okay,' the doctor says, and strangely, his command makes it so. 'It was a panic attack, but it's over now.'

It's hard to make sense of his expression. Fear? Terror even? But what could have him so worried?

'I'll, er … I'll get the registrar.' He sounds like someone desperate to find a reason to leave. My eyes follow him out of the room. He looks back over his shoulder and meets my gaze. It's not the careless glance of a stranger, or the clinical look of a doctor. His eyes are pools filled with unspoken meaning and there's something achingly familiar hiding beneath the surface. I can't look away until he slips completely out of view.

I want to follow him. I have a hundred questions to ask but every one of them would sound completely bonkers if I said it out loud. How can you ask someone how you know them when they've just told you that you don't? Particularly when you have no distinct memory of ever actually knowing them?

I push the questions from my mind. I must have imagined the familiarity, that connection. I guess it's a symptom of my head injury.

I must have fallen asleep because the next thing I know there's a nurse at my bedside carrying a tray with arid sandwiches, a cup of tea and a glass of juice. She places the tray on the table next to my bed and hands me the juice.

'Drink up, dear,' she says. 'It'll help with your blood pressure.' She collects the blue folder from the end of the bed and clicks her pen. 'I'm Bronwyn, honey. I'm going to need your name now.'

'Don't you already have it?'

'No, dear. You weren't coherent enough to supply it when you were brought in.'

'But that doctor – he knew my name. He read it off my chart.'

'Now what doctor would that be?' Bronwyn asks brightly.

I think for a moment to recall his name. 'Tom. Tom Williams.'

Nurse Bronwyn looks at me kindly. 'There's no Dr Williams working on this ward.' She pats my hand. 'Don't worry, dear, it's normal to feel a bit confused after an accident. You'll be right as rain soon enough.'

I give her my name and then she asks me if I know the year and the name of the prime minister. Once I prove that I'm coherent, we move on to my address and questions about allergies. She stands to leave, promising that a doctor will be along soon.

Alone in the cold, impersonal hospital room, I try to piece together what has happened. I catch my reflection in the glass of one of the machines I'm connected to. I don't see a fairy princess staring back. My hair is a grease slick and my eyes are bloodshot pools ringed with dark circles.

The street lights outside my window flicker to life as Nurse Bronwyn appears again at my bedside, wearing a sympathetic expression. 'Dear,' she begins, her voice troubled, 'there are two police officers here who'd like to have a word with you.'

The last thing I need right now is more law-enforcement personnel in my life. I need time to work out a story – one that's more convincing than 'I blacked out and I don't remember anything'.

But I don't have time. I gulp guiltily as Bronwyn ushers two men in, even though I'm pretty sure I'm innocent of whatever they're here to accuse of me of. They're not in uniform – at least, not in police uniform. One's wearing a nondescript suit. The other has the features of a basset hound – floppy skin and droopy eyes – and looks like he pulled his suit from a charity bin.

'Chess Raven?' asks the basset hound.

'Yes,' I answer, my muscles tensing with the anxiety of a person who's never been given the benefit of the doubt. I'm certain that both men notice as they approach my bed.

The basset hound introduces himself as Special Agent Weekes, and his colleague as Special Agent Westerfield.

Special Agent? What happened to Constable or Sergeant? This must be even more serious than I imagined.

Westerfield snarls in response to his name, making it

clear he's the pit bull to Weekes's basset hound. Both flash their badges and I spot the Home Office emblem. My breath catches in my chest. So, not police then. They must be from the Second Chances program. Jeez, these guys don't miss a thing.

I've seen enough cop dramas to notice the bulge at the back of both of their coats. Since when do office stiffs from the Home Office carry weapons?

Westerfield carefully picks up a teaspoon next to my teacup on the table beside my bed and moves it out of my reach.

'Wouldn't want you getting any ideas, now, would we?' he says.

What does he think I'm going to do with a teaspoon? Dig a hole through the floor and escape?

He picks up my watch and tosses it to his partner. Weekes takes out what looks like a barcode scanner from his inside jacket pocket. The device casts a thin red laser light, which he runs over the face and buckle of my watch. The machine makes three short, sharp beeps.

'It's clean,' Weekes says with a nod, tossing my watch back to Westerfield, who then returns it to the table as if nothing weird just happened.

'Who are you?' I say, trying to keep the nervousness from my voice. 'You're not police.'

Westerfield pulls a seat closer to my bed and sits down, crossing one spindly leg over the other.

'Things have gone well past the point of this being a police matter,' he says. 'It's time we had a little chat.'

I stiffen at his threatening tone and shuffle over to the very edge of my bed, putting as much distance between us as possible.

Weekes steps forward, his saggy face stretching out into a smile. 'We just have a few questions about your whereabouts in the past twenty-four hours.'

It's obvious they are good cop/bad copping me and I'm not stupid enough to fall for his fatherly tone.

'Before you answer,' Westerfield says, 'I'd like to remind you that if you're anything less than honest, you can kiss Second Chances goodbye.'

'I'm sure it won't come to that,' says Weekes lightly. 'We just need to know where you've been.'

'I'd like to help,' I begin, 'but I honestly don't know what happened. I was sitting in the cafe in the V&A and then, after that … it's, well … a blank.'

My words hang in the air for a moment like a frozen computer screen right before the system crashes and you lose everything, and I know that I've miscalculated. Of course the truth was never an option, but I should have come up with a more convincing lie. I stare at both the officers, trying to gauge exactly how much trouble I'm in. Both return my look with suspicion.

Weekes sighs and shakes his head as if to say 'There's no helping some people'. He gives Westerfield a barely perceptible nod, which is akin to letting him off his leash.

'I warned you not to lie to us,' says Westerfield, his voice rising and his lip curling back with contempt.

I sit bolt upright, desperate to make this right. Sharp

pain explodes in my head and shoots down my spine. They both flinch, drawing back as if they're scared of me.

Weekes looks towards the door, then whispers, 'We know you've been away with the fairies.'

My mouth drops open as Westerfield whips something out of his jacket and points it at my neck.

A shock of burning pain hits me and everything goes pitch black.

chapter 8

My head's heavy and my cheek's wet.

Drool. My drool. At least I hope it is.

I try to wipe it but I can't. My hands are stuck fast to the table in front of me with metal clamps that are digging into my wrists. A plaster strip covers the place on the back of my hand where the drip was. The dull pain in my temple remains.

I look down, relieved to see that I'm fully clothed. I don't want to think about who changed me out of my hospital gown, though. The two goons from the Home Office? *Ugh*.

Actually, I'm not fully dressed. My freezing-cold feet alert me to my missing boots. My belt's gone too.

Metal. They've taken care to remove anything made of metal. Or anything that might contain metal. I think back to how skittish they were about my watch and the spoon. What is it they think I can do with metal?

I take in my surroundings. Nothing but a table and three chairs. The chair I'm seated in wasn't built for comfort.

The other two are tucked under the opposite side of the table I'm clamped to.

My neck stings where Westerfield shot me. Or whatever he did to me. A taser, is my guess. I have no idea how long I've been out. Or where I am. The one thing I am sure of is that I'm not in the hospital anymore.

I push my body into the back of the chair and angle my head under the table to see how securely my cuffs are attached, and find something more interesting. A micro listening device. Interesting – and possibly useful.

It's planted just under the edge of the table. I crane my head further to read the serial number printed in little white letters on the top of the bug. I don't recognise the sequence. Probably military issue. I commit the serial number to memory as I attempt to dislodge the bug with my knee, but stop when I catch my reflection in the blackened glass window in front of me.

An interrogation room. They're probably watching me. Whoever 'they' are.

The door clicks behind me and I swing my head around. Westerfield and Weekes block the doorway so fully that I can't see what's behind them. Without a word, they each take a chair across from me.

'Where am I? Who are you?' I demand. I figure I've got nothing to lose.

Westerfield and Weekes look at one another for a moment, silently conferring.

Weekes sighs. 'We're from the Agency.'

'What agency?' I say, feeling a fresh batch of anxiety

well inside me. 'I thought you were Home Office.'

'Its official name is the Council for Inter-Realm Affairs,' Weekes continues. 'Don't bother googling us; you'll find nothing. Most of us just tell family and friends we work for this or that government agency. Hence 'the Agency'. Her Majesty's government has decided that we should reside within the Home Office.'

'But what do you do? And what has any of it got to do with me?'

'We'll ask the questions,' snarls Westerfield.

Weekes raises his hand, his basset hound jowls wobbling into a smile that I'm not prepared to believe is genuine.

'No, no, my friend,' he says to Westerfield. 'She has a right to know.'

Turning back to me, Weekes offers up his doggy smile again and says, 'The Agency was instituted under King James in the 1600s after he signed the Treaty between humans and the Fae.'

'Our job is to control you lot,' Westerfield jumps in. 'Fairies and unicorns, and the rest of you who haven't had the good grace to die out. Yet.'

I stare at his bulging eyes and the spit leaking out the corner of his mouth. He seriously looks insane. I'm having trouble getting my head around a whole department full of government officials who actually believe in fairies and unicorns and whatever else. I think back to Marshall's comments about fairies at the V&A. Maybe he's not so bonkers after all. He knew something, even if he didn't quite know the full extent of it. He wanted me to talk, I'm sure of that. With any luck he'll find out that I'm being held, and where. If anyone has the recourses and contacts to find me, it's Marshall.

'Don't pretend you don't know what I'm talking about. Having been where you've been and seen what you've seen.'

The sentence lingers in a way that implies that not only do they know all about my little trip into Iridesca, they also have knowledge of that world far beyond anything I could possibly tell them. But if they know all this already, then what do they want with me?

'Assuming what you say is true,' I say, 'why haven't I ever heard of fairies – outside storybooks, that is? Where are the serious history or science books about all your magical creatures? And your inter-realm thingy? You don't expect me to believe that you've been around for 400 years and no one's let slip that there are fairies and unicorns all over the place. Ever heard of WikiLeaks?'

'Oh, but they have.' Weekes smiles conspiratorially. 'You just said so yourself. We've all heard of fairytales. Every known language and culture has them. They're in all the earliest stories we tell our children. Why do you think that might be? Hmm?'

'But they're just stories,' I say, wondering who I'm trying to convince – them or myself.

'Only because we've done a sterling job discrediting them,' he says with wounded pride. 'We've singlehandedly convinced pretty much everyone that enchanted creatures are harmless, cute wee people who collect teeth and grant wishes to little girls. Anyone who says different outs themselves as mentally unstable.'

'Come on,' I scoff. 'You expect me to believe that you've fooled the whole world through Enid Blyton and Disney propaganda?'

'Have you ever wondered why there are unicorns all over this city?' Weekes says. 'Look closely, and everywhere you turn you'll see statues and images of unicorns. Royal palaces. The Houses of Westminster. Even the coat of arms. They probably told you in school that the unicorn on the coat of arms represents Scotland.'

If one of my history teachers did mention it, then I've forgotten – or else I skipped class that day.

'As if that would have appeased the Scots,' Westerfield mutters.

'Quite,' Weekes replies. 'Unicorns have nothing to do with Scotland. The unicorn was added to the coat of arms after the Treaty was signed, as a gesture of goodwill. Hiding in plain sight.'

'What treaty?' I ask.

But Weekes is on a roll. 'In fairytales, fairies and unicorns are mostly good,' he says, undeterred.

'Hmmph,' mutters Westerfield. 'Steal our young, kill our livestock and generally wreak havoc wherever they go. Interesting definition of "good" you've got there. Vindictive little bastards, that's what you are.' His face gets redder and redder as his rant continues. 'You lot haven't an ounce of morality. None of you gives a damn about the consequences of your actions. Not a care for anyone or anything but yourselves.'

71

I'd like to believe that he's railing against fairies because he's unhinged. But since I have no other explanation for the war-ravaged London I saw, or First Officer Jules, or the Chancellor, I don't think I can dismiss all of it as the ravings of a madman.

Weekes clears his throat, signalling for Westerfield to get himself under control. I wonder if they are still playing good cop/bad cop or if Westerfield just can't help himself.

Westerfield ignores the warning. 'The church had the right idea, burning you lot at the stake. That's something else you won't read about in your history books. It wasn't witches. It was Fae. Rounded up in their hundreds and burned alive —'

'That's quite enough history for now,' Weekes jumps in. 'After all, we don't want to detain *Your Highness* longer than we have to, do we?'

My eyes widen. Whatever rabbit hole I've fallen down, it seems I still have a way to go before I hit the bottom. I'm still royalty. But the venom in his partner's voice tells me that my regal status isn't going to do me any favours here. No one's going to obey me without question this time.

A sickening realisation dawns on me. Westerfield hates fairies, and he thinks I'm one. This can only end one way: badly. I shiver, suddenly cold all over.

'Can I have my shoes back, please?'

Weekes shakes his head sympathetically. 'Rules are rules. We are, of course, allies, but I'm sure you understand that we do have to take precautions.'

'Allies? Precautions for what?'

He looks at me quizzically. 'Magic, of course.'

I roll my eyes. How could they have got this so wrong? Even if I could do magic, what does that have to do with shoes?

Of course, when I was a kid I did try to do magic. But what kid doesn't? There was only that one time when I thought it actually worked. I had stared at Larry and willed him not to take another sip of his drink. When Larry got drunk, I inevitably suffered. I stood in the hallway, out of sight, and focused on his bottle of bourbon. Larry was slumped on the couch in his underwear, watching football on TV. The neck of the bottle was resting in one of his rough and callused hands, the other hand was tucked into the elastic of his Y-fronts. In my head I chanted over and over:

Do not drink, not another sip.
Don't raise that bottle to your lip.

After several minutes of chanting and focusing and hoping, the bottle exploded into shards of glass. Larry screamed and swore as the brown liquor mixed with the bloody glass cuts on his hand and leg. I was so freaked out by what I thought I had done I got a splitting headache and then passed out from the pain.

He didn't touch me that night, or for the next couple of weeks. His heavily bandaged hand saved me for a short while. I stupidly thought that I'd made that bottle explode through the sheer force of my will. But over time I became certain that it was a coincidence. I soon discovered that putting Sue's pills in Larry's bottles was a more effective and reliable way of stopping his drunken rampages anyway.

'Sorry to disappoint,' I say, 'but the only magic I know how to do is to get around Musgrave Industries' end-to-end multifactor encryption security. And look how well that worked out.' I gesture at the manacles bolting my hands to the table.

'For all of our sakes, I'm going to assume you're lying,' says Westerfield coolly. 'There's a war coming that could destroy both our worlds and, as much as it pains me to say it, you're the key to preventing it.'

I'm about to laugh. This is over-the-top dramatic and paranoid, even for Westerfield.

'People think that the biggest threat to humanity is terrorism or environmental disaster,' he goes on. 'They're wrong. There's no greater threat to our existence than your uncle, Damius.'

I sit up straighter in my chair. I don't have an uncle. And if I'd ever met anyone with a name like that I'm pretty sure I'd remember. This is just one more reason why I can't possibly be who they think I am.

'Our analysis shows your uncle has already amassed a level of power that could prove devastating,' Weekes says. 'That's why you must not give him any more – either intentionally or otherwise.'

'Huh?'

Westerfield's phone rings and he leaves the room. Weekes scrunches up his face into a smile that could even be heartfelt.

'You'll have to excuse my colleague. Our agents aren't hired for their people skills.'

'If he wants my help, you'd think he'd be a little more polite.'

'War – even the threat of war – can bring out the worst in people. And the best.' Weekes leans forward in his chair and says in an almost fatherly voice, 'We need you, Chess. We need you to make the right choice to save us all.'

I know that Weekes is trying to manipulate me but I want to believe him. I want to feel like I matter, that I'm not a nobody anymore. I'm not going to lie – even though I have no idea what choice he's talking about, the idea of being needed is incredibly seductive.

There's just one problem. They've got the wrong girl. There's nothing special or exceptional about me. The best I've ever hoped for is to be ordinary. And most of the time I have fallen way short of even that.

'I wish I could help,' I say. 'But I wasn't lying before. I'm not a princess and I'm certainly not magical.'

Behind me, the door bursts open with such force that both Weekes and I jolt in fright. Westerfield is standing in the door with two mean-looking security guards on either side of him.

'Change of plan,' he says. 'Orders from above.' He looks triumphant, as if he's just been granted permission to burn me at the stake along with all the witches he delighted in telling me about. Weekes, by contrast, looks scared. For me.

Westerfield turns to the guards and says with a smirk, 'Bring her.'

chapter 9

The cuffs click open and I take my chance.

I rock back on my chair and kick the table forward with all my weight.

The table flips, sending the chairs hurtling across the room, clattering against the wall and door. It's all the diversion I need. With Weekes and Westerfield momentarily distracted, I leap forward and bodyslam down onto the upturned table.

And that's as far as I get. But it's enough. I managed to get what I was after.

Rough hands clamp around the back of my neck and drag me to my feet.

Westerfield is laughing. 'Well, that was all rather pointless, wasn't it?' he mocks as he surveys the scattered furniture. 'You don't get to leave here until we say so.'

'Where are you taking me?' I demand.

One guard yanks my arms behind my back with unnecessary force while the other slaps metal handcuffs around my wrists.

'You'll find out when we get there,' says Westerfield, exchanging a dark look with Weekes.

'This is not what was agreed,' Weekes says under his breath. The unease in his voice makes my hands clammy and the nauseous feeling rushes back.

'She terminated our orders and decided on a different course of action,' Westerfield replies.

She? Who is *she*? What course of action?

'Harming her risks provoking retaliation,' Weekes says.

Westerfield just shrugs.

I start to sway. I'm not sure if it's the low blood pressure or the terror of imagining all the things they might do to me. Or both. One of the guards clamps his hand on my shoulder and pushes me from the room.

We walk along a windowless corridor that seems to go forever. Our footfalls echo off featureless concrete. The walls, ceiling and floor are a joyless, gun-metal grey.

Weekes and Westerfield shadow me, flanked by the two guards dressed in black paramilitary uniforms. It seems like overkill, given I'm restrained, untrained and should still be in a hospital bed. What are they going to do to me that requires four men?

No one says anything. Their shoes slap in time on the concrete, like a clock ticking down to my impending doom. The look of pity on Weekes's face has me peaking towards a full-blown anxiety attack, the sort where you actually can't breathe and fear you're going to suffocate and die. And I know there is no chance that one of these brutes would help me the way the intense and exasperating doctor, or whoever he was, did in the hospital.

One of the guards eyes me tentatively, and a realisation pulls me back from the precipice. The stiff posture. The twitching hand hovering above his weapon. The uneasy glances.

He's scared of me. They're all scared of me.

They're waiting for me to strike. Despite the handcuffs and the difference in our body sizes, all four of my captors seem just as terrified of me as I am of them. I can't imagine what they think I'm going to do, but their reticence calms me a little. Reality is often overrated. What matters more is perception. And the perception that I'm a threat may be something I can work with, even though it makes no sense.

Eventually we approach the end of the corridor. There's a single door painted in the same sad grey colour.

The guards draw their weapons. Westerfield grips the top of my arm with a vice-like pincer and pushes me towards the door. I can sense the gun barrels aiming at the back of my head. Weekes unlocks the handcuffs before opening the door.

I'm shoved into the room, the door slamming shut behind me. Plunged into complete darkness, I stumble to the floor.

Except, it's not a floor. It's bars. Cold, hard, metal bars, crisscrossing beneath me.

I frantically scramble around in the darkness trying to orientate myself or find a doorway or even something to use as a weapon. All I find are more bars.

My breath turns to rapid panting. There's a thrumming

in my ears. The dark emptiness closes in, crushing me, penetrating what defences I have left. I resist the overwhelming urge to curl up in a ball, and force myself to stand. But as soon as I'm on my feet the darkness disorients me and I lose my balance and collapse again, the bars digging into my knees.

A moment passes in the dark.

Banks of huge lights pop to life, blinding me again. I squint as my eyes adjust to the brightness.

A cage. I'm in a cage.

My mind fills with memories of the weeks I spent in custody waiting for my trial for stealing Gladys's meds: the oppressiveness of the space, the hopelessness in the air, not knowing how long I'd be stuck there for. I push the memories down. If I'm going to survive this, I need to stay in the present.

As far as I can make out, the cage is at one end of what looks like a huge abandoned warehouse. Or hangar. The place could fit a commercial jet – or three. There's polished concrete and nothing much else, except for a solitary folding chair placed in front of the cage. Behind me is another grey, featureless concrete wall and the door I came through.

I spot small black bubbles along the ceiling, the telltale sign of security cameras. I'd be willing to bet that they're all pointed straight at me.

And dust. The air is so thick with dust I can taste it.

I hear the creaking of a door opening, followed by a crisp clicking sound echoing around the hangar. I make out a compact woman at the far end. She doesn't look at me as she strides in her killer heels, all business-like, towards the chair. As she nears I notice a grey bob and an unhealthy relationship with hairspray. She's carrying a bright red folder with the word 'Sealed' stamped across it.

Her manner is as severe as her posture. Not the sort of person I should mess with. If I were going to stereotype I'd say she's one of those overachievers who has six degrees, speaks four languages fluently and practises martial arts in her spare time. She could bash the life out of me without chipping one of her manicured talons.

She sits on the solitary chair and slides the folder under it. Crossing her arms in front of her chest, she finally looks up at me.

'Francesca Raven. Haven't you grown?' she sneers.

I wrap my trembling fingers around the bars, levering myself into a standing position. My legs are unsteady but I try not to show it. With as much dignity as I can muster, I match her stare defiantly. She doesn't flinch or blink as her eyes bore into mine. I'm the first to break our eye lock as I lose my nerve and my eyes start to water.

She rises from the chair and walks towards me, a lion stalking its prey.

'You can call me Agent Eight. We've met before but you probably don't remember.'

I don't. 'Where am I?'

'Irrelevant,' she declares, like a computer I've entered the wrong command into.

'Are you going to kill me?' I blurt.

Her mouth twists at the corner and then straightens into a thin line again, as if she's about to laugh but then can't be bothered.

'You are more valuable to us alive. Killing you now would be a waste of a lengthy investment.' She removes a speck of lint from the shoulder of her suit jacket. 'No matter how much I'd like to,' she adds with disdain.

I try to soothe myself by slowing down my breathing, closing my eyes and silently chanting, *She's not going to kill me, she's not going to kill me.*

'You can try that all you like but those bars are graphite so you won't be able to do any of your little tricks in there.'

What tricks does she think I'm doing? What have I got myself mixed up in here? Somewhere along the line, somebody stuffed up big time. The Chancellor thinks I'm a superhero and the Agency seems to be worried I'm some kind of supervillain.

Still, mistaken identity or not, it's the only thing I have to work with at the moment, so I use it. I open my eyes and look pointedly around the cage.

'If you want to persuade me to help you, you should work on your hospitality.'

'I have no intention of being hospitable,' she snaps, spit flying out of her thin-lipped mouth. 'I have run out a patience for indulging you and asking nicely.'

She takes a step closer to the cage. I'm tempted to retreat to the far side but I hold my ground.

'If you harm me you'll jeopardise inter-realm relations,'

I say too quickly. I'm clutching at straws, hoping this might mean something to her, but my bluff backfires spectacularly.

She leans in towards the cage, angling her head to hide her mouth from the overhead cameras, and hisses through her teeth, 'I don't give a shit about the politics. Or you.'

Chills run through me. It's not so much what she said, but the fact that she meant those words for me, and me alone. Whatever this is, it's personal for her. She hates me. She really hates me.

Stepping back and resuming her normal voice, she says, 'Let's talk about the chalice. If you know what's good for you, you'll give me the location of the key.'

'Now I'm supposed to know something about a chalice and a key?' I say, exasperated.

'Enough!' she yells. 'You've tested my patience quite enough. I will not ask you for it again.'

Again?

As I watch her face turn an alarming shade of crimson, it suddenly all falls into place. She means the cup in the V&A. Marshall's family's old cup.

More memories escape from the vault. A long-forgotten door in my mind has been prised opened and is refusing to close. Childhood trips to the V&A. The black car with the cream leather seats. The woman with the click-clack shoes.

The same woman who's standing in front of me now. Her hair used to be brown and her face smoother, but those fierce eyes, which stare sharp enough to slice your skin, haven't changed a bit. She's been hounding me, monitoring me, occasionally pretending to be concerned with my welfare, for years.

'You've remembered,' she says, registering my realisation. 'Now here's what you're going to do. Tell me where the key is or you're going to disappear for a long time.'

'What? In some Black Ops site like Guantanamo?' I ask, trying to keep the fear from my voice as I'm overwhelmed by memories. The time I spent staring at the cup. The expectant looks from men and women in suits, waiting for me to do something. The air of disappointment when I failed.

How far will these people go?

'Oh, we don't need to be so dramatic. Just one of England's best correctional facilities. Maximum security, of course, but otherwise just a regular lock-up for regular scum.'

'You can't just fling people into prison for nothing,' I say, but as the words leave my mouth, I hear their naivety.

'I think you'll find that most magistrates don't view murder as "nothing",' Agent Eight says, inspecting her fingernails. 'But don't worry, your boyfriend will be incarcerated too.'

'What are you talking about?' I say, my voice cracking. 'I don't have a boyfriend and I definitely haven't killed anyone. And I don't know how else to tell you people this: you've got the wrong person.'

Slowly she turns and walks back to the chair. She picks up the folder from under the seat.

'Do you know what this is?' she asks, waving it at me as she returns to the cage. 'A police file. From a murder investigation. The victim is one Larry Goldsworthy. Remember Larry? Sure you do. Hard to forget, I imagine,' she says under her breath, a tight little grimace cutting across her face. 'He was your foster father, after all.'

I don't want to think about him, speak about him or know any other details about him, but I force myself to look at his file.

'I didn't kill Larry,' I say. 'Death by misadventure is what the cops called it.'

'You can stop with the lies!' she screeches. 'Remember who you're talking to. We know you killed him because we were the ones who covered it up for you and your boyfriend. We made sure the investigation never went any further.' She holds the file up to the cage. 'I can see you inherited your sense of morality from your mother's side of the family. Monsters, the lot of you.'

I peer down at her folder and see my name and other details about me: my address, date of birth, foster care number and another ID number I don't recognise. There's even a photo of me. I look about ten years old, with dirty hair and a look of hunger in my eyes. And there's another photo in the folder.

A boy.

I've seen him before. It's the same boy from those strange memories I had in the hospital. He was a friend when I had nothing and no one. We spent hours together, roaming. Free.

Or was it only a dream? Just a desperate wish to not be so alone?

I crane my neck to get a better look at the photo, but Agent Eight slams the folder shut. 'He thought he could outrun us with his little disappearing act, but that only works for a while,' she says. 'When I started monitoring you all those years ago I had no idea you'd hold out on me for so long. But your little games need to end. We know the Fae have made contact with you. And that can only mean one thing – that after all this time, you've finally decided to reveal the location of the key. So, where is it?'

I stare at her. 'You were watching me in foster care all that time?'

'I was kept appraised of your situation, yes,' she says officiously, but I detect a slight quiver of her lips. Her voice softens. 'We all want the same thing. It's what's best for everyone. You tell us about the key so we can all make this unpleasantness' – she nods at the file – 'go away.'

Anger wells within me. 'You knew what was happening to me but you left me there? You actually made the choice to leave me there and you question *my* morality?'

'My job was to get the key. Anything else was outside my brief. I'm not your mother, after all.'

Something snaps. An inferno erupts inside me as if molten lava is flowing through my veins. Fear and light-headedness are replaced by an all-consuming fury that is both foreign and welcome. I still have no idea what she's talking about or what any of this has to do with Larry's death. But none of that matters right now. All I can think about is how much I hate her. Raw, animal hate. Intensely satisfying and liberating.

I'm up against the bars, clenching them in my hands, screaming with unrestrained rage. 'You made my life hell and now you want me to help you? I'd rather die than do anything for you!'

My skin burns, my teeth grind; energy builds inside me. Then I'm moving. There's a force under my feet, propelling me upwards, fast. With a violent explosion, the cage rips apart as I catapult into the air like I've just been shot from a cannon. I hurtle past the jagged bars towards the warehouse ceiling. I close my eyes and cover my head with my hands in an attempt to protect myself from the impact.

When the impact doesn't come, I open my eyes and look down.

Air. Cool night air against my skin.

Below, I see light streaming out of the warehouse and a huge hole crowned by thorns of twisted metal and debris.

And then I'm falling back to earth, plummeting from the sky.

chapter 1o

My eyes flood with tears as the cool air lashes my face.

My back itches like crazy as a tightness and burning sensation rushes between my shoulder blades. Burns or cuts – I can't tell which – lace my body. Probably from being thrown through the ceiling.

The ground below races to meet me and I close my eyes again, twisting and clawing at the air to slow my fall and stop the burning in my back. A thousand thoughts rush through me. For the briefest moment I consider the possibility of there being a soft landing place – water or shrubbery – to break my fall, like in a cartoon.

But then I know with finality and certainty: I'm going to die.

I've spent a lot of my life wishing I was dead but now, faced with it actually happening, I want more than anything to live.

I hear fabric tearing and then a little popping noise and I'm no longer falling. I'm rising, sucked back up into the night sky. Opening my eyes again, I see the concrete below me retreating.

I'm hovering.

The itchiness and burning have gone. I gulp the cool night air down, confused.

Out of the corner of my eyes I spy movement. I flick my head to the side for a closer look, and I see … iridescent light shimmering from the tips of huge wings. Lustrous colours ripple down the wings as they scoop the night air. Golden capillaries form intricate swirling patterns, making me think of a giant butterfly. The top of the wings arch up to points and the bottoms finish with delicate coils.

They're flapping steadily, keeping me suspended above the tree line. The cool breeze tickles my face as I hover in the air, free and at peace. It reminds me of my favourite childhood dream, the one where I'm riding bareback on a flying horse over London, racing with owls, peering into birds' nests and looking down at the rooftops.

I reach around to touch the wings; they're silky, strong and about two metres in width. And they're connected to me. They're part of me. It's like I've suddenly sprouted new limbs.

And then it hits me.

I can fly.

I am Fae.

The sense of wonder is broken by a sharp pain that ricochets through my body. It's like barbed wire, stabbing me from the inside. I cry out in agony and terror. Blustering winds swirl around me. I'm spiralling madly downwards, past the treetops, past the tree trunks. My wings flail in the wind like sheets on a washing line during a cyclone. They

88

slow my descent, but not enough to stop me entirely. I'm losing altitude too fast.

For a moment there's no sound. I land with a thud, my wings breaking the worst of the fall as I manage a commando roll onto the rough ground, rocks and debris digging into my hands and knees. Razor-sharp pains shoot along my shins and a sick feeling lodges itself in the pit of my stomach as the air rushes out of my lungs.

Gasping for breath, I stare up at the stars. I'm drenched with sweat and shaking uncontrollably. The breeze licks sweat off my shivering skin. I can't focus. A daisy sprouting through the rocks, cold and wet with night air, tickles my nose.

With great difficulty, I roll onto my side and somehow scuff the side of my face on gravel. It takes all my strength to reach an arm around to my back to feel my wings. But they're gone. I feel nothing but smooth skin. No open wound, nor, so far as I can tell, even a scratch between my shoulder blades. But the tear in the back of my dress is all the proof I need to know that the wings – my wings – were real.

In the distance, men's angry shouts mix with the menacing howls of dogs readying for a hunt. They're joined by engines revving and the wail of sirens.

I need to get away. Far away.

I struggle up onto all fours and try to stand. My body aches, paralysed by exhaustion, but my mind races.

I am who they want. I am Francesca of House Raven.

The Agency wants me to give them a key to unlock something. The Luck of Edenhall? How do you unlock a cup? And what could possibly be inside an empty glass cup?

What's the point of finding a key for something that doesn't even have a lock? It makes no sense, yet they seem to want it badly. They've been after it ever since I was a kid.

And they think I murdered Larry.

I hated my foster father and I didn't shed a single tear when he died. But kill him? I think I'd remember something like that. Wouldn't I? Or is this just one more crucial piece of my life that I repressed? I wished him dead countless times. But wishes can't kill a person.

Or can they? I don't want to believe that I'm capable of murder, no matter what the circumstances. But I don't know what I'm capable of anymore. I'm not even sure who I am.

Perhaps I really am the monster Agent Eight thinks that I am.

I didn't feel like a monster when I was fluttering above the tree line with my wings unfurled. I felt love.

No, that's not it. It's more like I *was* love, as if I were connected to everything and restrained by nothing, all at once.

Whatever the case, I need to get away from here. If Agent Eight meant what she said – and she doesn't strike me as the type to muck around with idle threats – the file for Larry's murder investigation is open and I'm the number-one suspect. There goes my Second Chance – and every chance after that.

The barking dogs are nearer now. They're coming for me, I know it. I stagger to my feet, but my legs buckle. As I crumple back onto my knees I hear a swishing sound in the sky. It's like a huge propeller, but not as loud as a helicopter. A drone?

There's a flicker of movement above me. I squint my eyes at the sky, but all I see is shimmering white. Steady gusts of air lick at my clammy skin. Whatever it is, it's found me, circling above as if I'm its prey. I start manically scrambling in the opposite direction, searching for somewhere to hide.

It's hopeless. My arms and legs are shaking so violently in a mixture of pain, exhaustion and panic that they won't do what they're supposed to. I feel like I've been burned from the inside all the way out to my skin.

There's a heavy thump on the road behind me and my stomach lurches into my mouth. I turn, defeated, to face my predator. White light illuminates the darkness, and dumb shock replaces the sensations thrashing through my body.

The source of that light appears to be a giant horse. Enormous feathered wings flare from either side of its wither, and its forehead is crowned by a single golden horn.

I gasp, completely freaked out. But strangely enough, it's not the sight of a unicorn that has me so rattled. It's that I've seen it before. The creature before me, this unicorn, has haunted and soothed my dreams for years.

'Get on,' a gravelly baritone commands. Huge ice blue eyes stare down at me through lush eyelashes set within a long equine face. The white beast shakes its spiky mane impatiently. Muscles ripple under his lustrous coat.

Get on? Get on what?

As if reading my thoughts, the unicorn turns to the side and shows me the long, sleek curve of his back.

You've got to be kidding. I don't want to be recaptured by the Agency but I'm not crazy enough to jump onto a mythical flying horse that only exists in my dreams.

Barking and the heavy breathing and snorting of hounds closes in. Men's voices yell as their footsteps thunder towards us.

'Get on,' the beast orders again, frustration in his voice.

I scramble up, before falling down again. The unicorn charges straight at me. I desperately try to roll out of his way, but I'm not fast enough. The animal wedges his nose under my torso and flicks back his head, catapulting me upwards like a ragdoll.

A small cry escapes my lips as I rise about two metres into the sky. Gravity takes over and I cradle my head, readying for impact onto the rocky ground. But it never comes. The unicorn breaks my fall as I thump down, straddling his back.

'Please,' I hear myself squeak, even though I have no idea what I'm asking for.

'Hang on.' The gravelly voice reverberates through me.

I have just enough time to wrap my arms around his neck before we're galloping away from the Agency.

I'm now wide awake. The pain and fogginess have given way to a rush of adrenaline. I feel myself slipping from my mount, so I lean forward and hold on tighter, my cheek pressing against the unicorn's silken coat.

A tickling sensation runs up the backs of my thighs. Looking around, I see the unicorn's outstretched wings fan out and beat rhythmically against me.

They remind me of the wings of a hawk – a giant hawk, powerful and majestic. They make me think of my own wings. I reach around to my back in the hope that they might have sprouted again.

Nothing.

The unicorn's wings extend to their full magnificent span and I realise he is readying to take off. Before I can count all the reasons this is a bad idea, we're ascending, soaring higher and higher, past treetops and power lines. The unicorn lurches to the side, narrowly missing an owl flying directly towards us. I tighten my grip even more, terrified I'll fall off his back.

My ears pop as we climb. Tears stream from my eyes, and the icy air burns my face and lungs. I bury my head in his thick mane. I have no idea where I'm going and who – or what – is taking me there. I don't even know if I'm being rescued or just captured by someone else.

It's not until we're above the clouds that the beast levels out. We're buffeted by changes in air pressure, but the unicorn doesn't reduce his speed. My hair whips around my head.

I wait for him to speak again, but he doesn't. I wonder if I imagined it the first time.

Eventually I muster the courage to ask where we're going and what he's going to do to me. I know it's dumb, but part of me hopes that maybe we could cut some sort of deal. He could drop me off at home. I could give him a couple of carrots or rainbows or whatever it is unicorns eat, and we could call it even.

All I get in return is silence.

Through the breaks in the cloud, which are turning pink with the first light of a new day, I can see that we're flying west out of London, following the Thames in the direction of Windsor. I've stopped shivering; the heat from his body warms the inside of my thighs, radiating throughout my whole body. I relax slightly and wonder if, in other circumstances, I might enjoy this experience. And then I notice his scent – musky and oddly comforting.

The moment of almost-enjoyment passes as, without warning, the beating of his wings slows and they angle back. We're descending.

Fast.

Through stinging, watering eyes, I see the blurry lights cast by houses on the streets below. I close my eyes as the weight of my body pushes forward into the beast's neck so that I fear overbalancing and toppling forward. I cling to him, but the pace of his descent increases even further and I can't stop my body from leaving his back. I'm vertical, upside down, my feet in the air and my arms desperately holding on.

My grip slips and I flip backwards, hurtling towards the ground.

I put my hands up to protect my head, but before I hit, I feel a pair of human arms plucking me from the sky and holding me tight. Lowering my hands, I open my eyes and look up.

The unicorn is gone, replaced by a person.

I stare up at ice blue eyes. *'You?!'*

chapter 11

I struggle free from his arms and stagger away, only to collapse onto the footpath.

'Stay back!' I yell with an arm up. 'Who ... *what* are you?'

Somewhere in the distance, a dog barks. A light goes off in a nearby house. Traffic hums in the distance. Otherwise, the row of terraces that line the street is quiet.

The imposter doctor from the hospital stands in the road. A unicorn?

I stare up at him and am struck again by how beautiful he is, his incandescent skin illuminated by the moonlight. He could be chiselled from marble – not just because of his square jaw but because he's as cold and hard as stone. That flash of warmth I glimpsed in the hospital is gone. I get the sense that he would prefer to be anywhere but near me. But then why did he bother to come and get me?

'You've remembered?' he says.

I'm unable to quell my frustration. 'Remembered what? All I know is that you were at the hospital pretending to be a doctor and then you went all weird and bolted. And now you turn up here … there – wherever we just were – as a …'

His eyes scan my body, lingering on my cuts and abrasions. 'You need help. Come inside if you want it. Or don't. Your choice.' He turns and walks towards a white terrace house. Without so much as a backwards glance, he unlocks the door and disappears inside.

I'm left sitting outside, wondering what to do, as the lights go on in the house.

My head tells me to get out of here. Now is my chance to get away from him and forget that this – any of this – ever happened. But where would I go?

My gut tells me to follow the doctor – or whoever he is – and find out what on earth is going on. He doesn't seem to be a threat. Aside from the rocky landing, I'm pretty sure he just helped me escape from the Agency.

I gingerly lever myself up from the concrete and stagger towards the house, my legs and hips complaining with every step. The front garden is empty except for a dead pot plant with a faded red and green Christmas ribbon tied around it.

The theme continues inside. The most diplomatic way to describe the flying doctor's house is 'lived in'. Shoes line the hallway and I have to step over a sports bag with boxing gloves bursting out of the zip, to enter the living room.

It's polished timber and open plan with a kitchen on one side and a lounge room and bathroom on the other. There's a staircase with tattered beige carpet on the far side of the lounge room. A fruit bowl containing a couple of oranges sits on the kitchen bench, along with a collection of remote controls and a hospital ID tag that is so obviously fake I can't believe I didn't spot it at the time.

He's at the stove, cracking an egg into a fry pan. He looks up as I walk in.

'I hope you like your eggs scrambled,' he says. 'It's my specialty and you need food.'

Of all the things that have happened tonight, this scene of domestic normality strikes me as the most surreal. Minutes ago I was being hounded by government agents before being flown across London on the back of a unicorn – a unicorn who's turned into a guy who is now offering me scrambled eggs.

He motions towards a leather jacket sitting on the bench. I'm about to decline but I'm cold so I take it. I can feel his eyes on me as I shrug into his jacket and zip it all the way up to the top.

I'm relieved when he turns back to the stove. Just like in the hospital, I can't tear my eyes away from him and I don't want him to see that I'm staring. His jeans are ripped and he's not wearing a belt. His t-shirt is fraying around the neck and it has a faded logo on it that reminds me of the Celtic symbols I saw in Iridesca. His triangular frame – broad shoulders, thin waist – suggests that those boxing gloves in the hall get used pretty regularly.

Turning off the stove, he gestures towards the stools lining the kitchen bench. All three are piled high with medical journals, dog-eared novels and political biographies. I shift the pile off one chair to make room to sit down.

He grabs a knife and slices an orange in half in one swift motion. I stare at his enormous hand as he massages the orange on a juicer. For a tiny moment I wonder what that hand would feel like on me. Then I blush and look away. I have no idea where that thought just came from.

I watch out of my peripheral vision as he scoops out the orange pulp and sucks it off his fingers. He washes his hands under the tap and dries them on his t-shirt. He pours me a glass of juice before dishing the eggs onto a plate, seemingly having forgotten the toast.

'I want to know who you are. *What* you are,' I correct myself.

'Eat,' he says, ignoring my question.

Suddenly I'm ravenous. I can't remember the last time I ate. He silently watches me shovel eggs into my mouth. If I wasn't so hungry I'd be feeling self-conscious right now.

'Come over into the light so I can examine you,' he says after I scoop up the last of the eggs.

My fork clatters to the plate. Coming inside might have been a big mistake.

'First you tell me what just happened out there. The whole flying horse, disappearing thing.' I can't bring myself to say the word 'unicorn' out loud. Talking about unicorns or fairies in the same way you talk about people, pot plants or planes means actually admitting they exist. And if I do that, I fear I will have totally lost my grip on reality. I'll never get back to my normal life.

He looks at me, judging whether I'm being serious. 'I didn't disappear. I transed.'

'You what?'

'Transed. You know, change from one form to another,' he says matter-of-factly. 'Didn't you trans when you flew out of the Agency?' His eyebrows rise but he doesn't wait for an answer. 'And I'm quite sure you also know that I'm not a horse. "Unicorn" is the word you're looking for. *Equus unus cornu*, if you want to be scientific.'

I open my mouth to ask whose science, but he exhales a frustrated sigh. 'Look, you're hurt. You need medical attention.'

Instinctively I fold my arms over my chest.

'I'm a doctor, not a pervert.'

'You can't possibly be a doctor,' I challenge.

'I am,' he says. 'Just not from around here.' The corner of his mouth tugs upwards and I find myself staring at his dimple. 'I entered the Guild of Master Healers when I was fourteen,' he explains. 'Where I studied, everyone has a role according to their natural aptitude. We start our training earlier than what you're used to. And then we progress according to merit rather than years.'

I raise my eyebrows, glancing at the fake ID.

'I was worried,' he says, serious again. 'I wanted to make sure you were okay.'

Against all reason, I find myself giving him the benefit of the doubt. I slowly slide off the stool and walk over to him in the kitchen.

He washes his hands again, this time more like a doctor than a guy, and then examines the stitches on my temple. Satisfied, he slips his jacket off my shoulders. I gasp as he touches the tops of my arms. Even though I'm pretty sure he's not going to hurt me, my body responds the way it always does when someone gets too close. It freaks out. I close my eyes and try to calm my breathing.

'Your skin. It's clammy,' he says. 'Classic flight response. You're scared of me.'

'No, I'm not.' I wish I hadn't said that so quickly.

He raises an eyebrow and gently stretches out one of my arms, carefully inspecting the abrasions on my wrist from the handcuffs.

My skin's tingling, partly from his touch, but mostly from the intensity of his gaze. I want to flee – not from him, but from this whole situation.

But I don't. More specifically, I can't. My feet have turned to lead. I swallow hard as he checks my other arm, then squats in front of me, checking my legs. The top of his head is now level with my belly button.

He touches a bloody gash on my knee. Tiny surges of heat radiate from where his finger strokes my leg, all the way up to my core. And for the briefest and most mortifying of moments, it's not a doctor's touch. It feels sensual.

I must be in shock because for the first time in never, I actually want a guy to look at me, appreciate me. At the same time, I wish the ground would open up and swallow me whole. My cheeks grow hot from the crazy and unwelcome thoughts rushing through my head.

Fortunately, he seems oblivious.

'It's okay,' he says, tracking his finger over the wound. 'Not deep enough to need stitches.' He stands and moves around behind me. As he opens out the torn pieces of fabric of the back of my dress his knuckles skim along my exposed back. He shifts my hair to one side so he can see my neck. 'What on earth …?'

My hand instinctively covers the right side of my neck and my body visibly shivers as I recall Westerfield's taser and his delight in using it on me. Now that Tom has drawn my attention to it I'm acutely aware of a burning, throbbing pain coming from my neck.

'Let me see,' he says, prying my fingers away and leaning in to examine it. I feel his breath on my cheek as he takes my jaw in his warm hand and gently angles me towards the light. 'What happened to you?'

I say nothing, unsure how much to divulge.

'Chess, you can trust me.'

It's the first time he's said my name since the hospital.

'How can I?' I say.

Tom's quiet for what must be a whole minute, his face full of meanings that I can't decipher.

'I lied to you before. You do know me. We met long before the hospital,' he says finally, in a voice that is surprisingly gentle. And then, almost to himself, 'I've thought about you every day for years and you don't even know who I am.'

My mind reels as he treats the burn on my neck, trying to hold back a lifetime's worth of memories that are threatening to break through. I'm pretty sure we didn't know each other as children. Kids in my neighbourhood don't grow up to become medical professionals. But I'm getting that feeling again, the warmth and familiarity I felt when he was near me in the hospital.

After he's finished, he rubs his hand through his spiky fringe and looks directly into my eyes.

'I have a story to tell you. Get comfortable.'

I walk back around to the stool on the other side of the kitchen bench and sit down, although 'comfortable' is probably the last word I'd used to describe how I'm feeling.

'The story is about a girl. A girl who was alone and sad.'

Sickness wells in the pit of my stomach.

'She was so desperately sad,' he continues. 'But she was also funny, strong and courageous and warm and' – he looks across the bench to me – 'beautiful. She was so beautiful.'

I bite my lip, unsure of how to react. It feels like I'm strapped into the passenger seat of a car that I know is about to plough into oncoming traffic, but I can't do anything about it.

He holds my gaze. 'And she could transcend her body.'

'Go on,' I whisper.

'One night when she was floating free …' He pauses, and my heart beats so loudly I swear I can hear it. 'With her helpless body lying below —'

The spell is broken.

'How could you?' I splutter, and push back off my stool, sending a pile of books and magazines flying onto the floor. A violent wave of nausea crashes down on me and I run to his bathroom, slamming the door and locking it behind me. I kneel down in front of the toilet and brace myself.

Hot tears sting my eyes. A cold trickle of sweat runs down my back.

I know what's coming.

When there is nothing left in my stomach I lay my head on the cool bathroom tiles to recover and wonder yet again if I'll ever be able to leave my past behind.

Tom knocks on the door and jiggles the handle. 'Chess, let me in.'

'Get away from me,' I try to yell but it comes out as a pathetic little whimper. I know that I carry wounds that will never heal, but he has no right to make them fester.

'I'm an idiot.' His voice sounds pained. 'I didn't mean to hurt you. I didn't think about how you'd react.'

I pull myself up and look into his bathroom mirror. I'm that little girl again and all I can see are bruises and shame. I hate that I let myself be a victim. I was pathetic then and I'm pathetic now.

'Open the door,' I hear Tom say. 'Please.'

I splash water on my face, but it doesn't help. Some things can't be washed away. After a long time, I take a swig of his mouthwash sitting on the vanity and unlock the door. Tom reaches out to take my hand but I slap it away.

'Don't touch me.'

He nods and then asks me to sit on the couch. I can't stop shaking. I curl up in a ball and hug my legs against me, trying to still myself.

'Drink,' he says, handing me a glass of water.

I take the glass and turn away from him. My stomach feels raw and I don't want him to see me like this.

'Drink it,' he orders. 'You need to keep up your fluids.'

I take a sip of the water. It's all I can manage.

'Who are you?' I whisper.

'Deep down you know who I am,' he says seriously, almost desperately. 'And what I am. Your memories have been hidden from you. But you might have found them again in your dreams.' He sits down on the couch. 'Have you, Chess? Have you found me in your dreams?'

I shake my head. 'No, no. It wasn't real. It was just a dream. A stupid, childish dream.' I scamper to the far end of the couch. 'Leave me alone.' I cover my face with my hands. I want to shut him out. I want to shut everything out. My world is spinning too fast and I want to get off.

I feel him peel my hands back from my eyes.

'I came to you every time you called me for almost a year. We'd fly through the night sky together.' He looks at me, his ice blue eyes pleading.

Fresh tears well in my eyes as I recall the photo of the boy in Agent Eight's folder. The boy who grew up and is now sitting next to me.

Tom reaches for me. He wraps his arms around me and pulls me close. I stiffen at first but then melt onto his shoulder. The way he strokes my hair, his musky smell, the familiar thud of his heart, returns me to the time when he was the light in my darkness.

It was real. All of it.

I stumble upon hidden memories, one after another. He would meet me at my window night after night. Sometimes he came as a boy and we'd hover on my ceiling and just talk.

104

Other times he would change – *trans* – into a unicorn and I would clamber onto his back and we'd gallop into the night sky. He made me smile, something I did so rarely as a child. He was so confident and bold. I remember his beautiful face.

I pull him closer, my head nestling in. I clutch onto him, fearful of letting him go, of losing him all over again.

'In my dream you were my best friend,' I say softly. 'If it was real then why did you stop coming?'

He sighs and tightens his embrace, but I push out of his arms.

'Why did you abandon me?'

'I had to disappear for a while. After Larry …'

As soon as he says Larry's name, I feel like I'm going to be sick again.

A minute passes in silence. I look at Tom, searching his face. He stares down at his feet.

'Did you kill Larry?'

'No, no. At least, not in the way you think.'

'You either killed him or you didn't. Murder isn't a matter of perspective.'

'Larry killed Larry,' Tom snaps.

'Larry's body was found floating in a drain,' I say flatly. 'The police said he had a steel pipe wedged in his gut.'

Tom runs his hand through his fringe and gets that look again, the one where he's going to say something he knows I'm not going to want to hear.

'One night … It was the night of your eleventh birthday.

You begged me to help you. You couldn't bear it any longer. I knew you weren't just asking me to distract you from the horror, to go on another crazy adventure across London. You wanted me to stop Larry so he wouldn't hurt you anymore. Ever again.'

'But I didn't ask you to kill him,' I say, horrified.

'Well, not outright —'

'Not at all,' I say emphatically. 'I would never. Don't you put this on me.'

Tom rubs his chin. 'You needed my help so I helped you. End of story.'

I stare at him, speechless. Who is this person I used to know? Such cold brutality.

Taking advantage of my silence, he continues. 'I conjured a spell to induce hallucinations and paranoia. My sister is an apothecary fairy; she helped me with it. My guess is that Larry thought he was a small animal like a frog or a rat, being hunted by a predator – a bird or a fox or something. People who fall under this particular spell inevitably do something stupid. In fact, the spell holds until they do.'

I raise an eyebrow in disbelief.

'He must have jumped onto something sharp and impaled himself before he drowned.' Tom shrugs dismissively. 'What do you care, anyway? He deserved to die.'

I open my mouth to say something in defence of ... well, not Larry, as such, but against killing in general. But nothing comes out. I look at Tom, trying to work him out. He looks back at me, as if I'm the weird one for having a problem with murder.

I had every reason in the world to want Larry dead, but I would never have actually gone through with it.

Tom chooses his words carefully. 'It was decided that I should live in Iridesca for a bit, until things calmed down and the authorities lost interest in the case. I joined the Guild of Master Healers as soon as they'd have me. I came back home last year; by then I looked nothing like the kid the Agency was looking for. I didn't want to leave you, Chess. Honest. But it was the only way.'

I sense the seriousness of his words and wonder if I can believe him. Did he really regret leaving me?

I walk over to the kitchen on unsteady legs to refill my glass. My mouth is as dry as a desert as I prepare to tell him that his plan didn't work. Tom is obviously 'the boyfriend' Agent Eight is referring to. 'The Agency has joined the dots between the two of us.'

'The Agency's the least of our problems,' Tom says. He pauses in a way that tells me I'm not going to like what he's about to say. 'You can't be here with me,' he says. 'I'm more dangerous to you than you could possibly imagine.'

Okay, now I'm completely lost.

'The magic I used on Larry altered the natural balance of life and death. To perform magic that powerful requires a sacrifice of a similar magnitude.'

He looks at me, and I stare back blankly.

'You must forsake that which you desire most,' he says. 'That's why all your memories of me were hidden. Giving you up was the price I had to pay for saving you.'

It takes me another moment before I catch on. *I'm* what

he desired most? I can't look at him so I stare down at my hands, clasped around the glass. No one has ever felt like that about me.

'I looked you up when I got back. All I wanted was to see you again. Just once. Well, perhaps a few more times than that,' he adds sheepishly.

I sneak a peek at him. He's grinning and I see both dimples for the first time.

'I kept my distance,' he continues. 'But then, when you were hurt … I had to … to make sure you were okay. But now I have to get as far away from you as possible. We can't be together. Ever.'

I'm shocked by what I see on his face. He doesn't look embarrassed or vulnerable or even regretful for exposing so much of himself to me. He looks strong.

'What happens if we're together?' I ask, my voice faltering.

Tom gazes out the window. A slow, deep breath escapes him.

'I've never crossed the natural laws before, so I don't know exactly how, or what, or when it happens. All I know is that nature will enact its revenge to restore the balance eventually.'

Goosebumps spring to life up my arms.

'Death?' I ask.

He nods slowly.

'Whose death?'

A moment passes, then his eyes lock with mine. 'Yours.'

chapter 12

I slam the glass down on the bench and a hairline crack snakes up the side.

'You're risking my life by bringing me here, just so you can play the hero again?'

'What?' Tom splutters.

'First you use me as your excuse to act out your murderous fantasy, and then you steal my memories and risk my life with your stupid spell, without consulting me.'

'I did it for you!'

'You did it for *you*,' I snap.

He swears under his breath. 'Did your life get better after that bastard got what he deserved? Did it?' he repeats, staring at me, challenging me.

'Yes,' I concede.

'Well then, what's your problem? Why are you roasting me for helping you?'

'Because you didn't ask me!' I grip my fingers on the edge of the bench. They're tingling with an acute case of pins and needles. I must be angrier than I know. 'You're just another person trying to control me, thinking you know what's best for me. Well, let me tell you, you don't.'

'Chess, your hands ...'

'Huh?' I look at my hands, furious.

Light.

There's shimmering light coming from my hands. This is no ordinary pins and needles. Sparkling wisps of fine dust are trailing from the tips of my fingers and the sides of my palms. I lift them in front of my face. More wisps of fine, sparkling dust trail off my skin, momentarily suspended in the air before winking out like dying stars.

I shake my hands, which only seems to make it worse.

'What's happening to me?'

Tom is by my side in an instant. 'It's the spell,' he says, holding my fingers towards the light. 'It's beginning. You need to get away – far away – from here. From me. You shouldn't be here now, but I couldn't just leave you to those dogs in the middle of the night.'

He starts shoving things into a bag – a bottle of water, his medical kit – then there's a knock at the front door.

We look at each other.

'We must've been followed,' I say.

'Go upstairs to my bedroom and stay there until I come to get you.' He reaches for his mobile phone, gripping it like it's a weapon, and walks slowly towards the door.

The knocking continues, faster and louder, as I race up the stairs. My heart's pounding and I feel like I'm going to be sick as I run into his room. The bed is unmade, his sheets tangled. I note that there's only one pillow, which pleases me more than it should. I remind myself that there are way more important things to worry about right now and check my hands for sparkling dust. The weird effect seems to have slowed, but not stopped entirely, and the tingling sensation is still there, as strong as before. But for now, the terror of being locked in one of Agent Eight's cages overrides the thought of my hands turning to dust.

I should hide, but where? The cupboard is stuffed so full the doors won't close. I consider climbing out the window, but I worry that the noise of opening it will tip them off.

Is this it? Is this where I get locked away in a cage for life?

Muffled voices float up from below – Tom's and a woman's. They're arguing. I can't make out what they're saying, but something tells me it wasn't the Agency at the door. They'd have tasered him by now. Or he'd have done whatever it is unicorns do when they're backed into a corner. I can't make out sentences, but catch brief snatches of words. Words like 'danger' and 'duty'.

If I didn't know better, I'd say Tom is being lectured.

He is still refusing to let the woman in. 'It's not a good time,' he's saying. 'Come back later.'

'I know she's in there.'

Then it hits me. The woman's voice. I know it – I know her – but it can't be who I think it is. I plant an ear against the door and still my breathing so I can hear her more clearly. The voices grow louder. They must be in the kitchen.

'Step aside right now, young man,' she bellows, 'or I'll have words with your mother.'

I break into a smile. Tom seems a little old for that sort of threat.

Even though I could be in imminent danger, I'm not scared anymore. There's something about that voice that puts me at ease. It always has.

As I creep out of the bedroom to the top of the stairs, I'm relieved to discover that my fingers have returned to normal and the tingling sensation has completely gone. One flight of stairs must be enough of a distance from Tom to keep the Spell Enforcer, or whatever it is, placated. For now at least.

I try to catch a glimpse of the visitor but Tom's back is blocking my view. He's like a bouncer trying to keep a punter out.

And then she calls my name.

'Gladys?' I reply, stepping back down the stairs.

Gladys sweeps her ancient frame across the floor, moving with an agility that belies her years.

'Thank the Goddess you're safe,' she says, enfolding me in a hug and squishing my face against her soft, worn cheek. 'When the Protectorate could not locate you, the Chancellor recklessly authorised an alert to all Fae in London. It could have ended very badly.'

She looks over to Tom. 'Thank you, young man, for being the first responder.'

'What are *you* doing here?' I step out of the hug and take in her oversized kimono in red tartan flowing over black leather pants and military-style boots. Waves of white ruffles ripple out from between the black satin trim of the kimono, contained by a wide leather belt with a thick gold buckle. Compared with the faded pastel housecoat she gets about in at the laundromat, it looks like she's going to a costume party. Although what the theme would be, I can't even imagine.

'If you want something done properly you have to do it yourself,' she says simply. 'I came straight from Iridesca. I didn't have time to change.' She pulls a hairpin from her grey bun and, with a slight grimace, she swishes it in the air. I stare at her, speechless, as the kimono melts away and is replaced with a homely peach twinset and pearls. 'Are you really so surprised, dear?'

'Surprised?' I say. 'I didn't have a freaking clue who you were! In fact, I still don't.' I hope the shock in my voice is masking my feelings of betrayal. Why didn't she tell me who she was? More to the point, why didn't she tell me who *I* was?

'You know the Luminaress?' Tom asks me.

'The what?' I say, more confused than ever.

'Teacher, dear,' Gladys explains softly. 'Keeper of Fae wisdom.' And then, more sternly to Tom, 'Of course. I've been charged with her training.' She looks at me with a degree of pride that seems wildly misplaced.

'Training?' Tom says, frowning at me. 'You're training with the Order? Who are you?'

I'm as surprised as he is. The only thing Gladys has ever taught me is how to starch collars. It also dawns on me that Tom hasn't a clue who I am. All these years, he must have assumed I was just an ordinary fairy girl. If a fairy could be ordinary, that is.

I'm about to tell him that I'm apparently Princess Francesca Raven, but the look on his face tells me that he just worked it out for himself.

'You're ... *her*?' He stares at me as if analysing every pore on my face. 'How could I not have seen it? You're the spitting image of your mother.' He drops to one knee and bows his head. 'Your Highness. Forgive me. I had no —'

'Oh, for goodness sake, get up!' I say. 'Things are weird enough right now. The last thing I – we – need is you treating me like I'm a princess. Cut it out.'

Tom peers up at me cautiously, suddenly unsure of what to do. I'm half amused, but only half. If everyone's going to go down on one knee when they see me, the novelty of being a princess is going to wear thin pretty quickly.

Gladys watches Tom's revelation with detached amusement. 'Now that we all know each other,' she says, surveying the room, 'practically every member of the Fae is out looking for you right now, dear. Half of them want to protect you, the other half want your blood. And there's no telling who's who. And then there's those Agency people we must deal with.'

'You know about the Agency?' I ask Gladys.

'Of course, dear,' Gladys says, without the slightest sense that she needs to elaborate.

I stare at her, trying to reconcile the woman I've known for most of my life with the person standing in front of me. She fed me when I was starving. She helped me with my homework and hugged me on those few occasions I needed it, even though at the time I insisted that I didn't. I knew she was eccentric; one moment she was as tough as nails and the next she'd go all Earth Mother. And the songs, the bizarre, rhyming ditties she's always singing as if life were a musical. But to learn that she's a fairy – and, to judge from Tom's reaction, an important one – is just too much.

'Why didn't you tell me?'

'Would you have believed me if I had?'

The answer is no, but that's hardly the point.

'I didn't think so,' Gladys says, walking over to Tom's couch and sitting down as if she's an invited guest. 'You were not ready to hear the truth.'

She pats the seat next to her. 'Events are fast overtaking us. The throne has been vacant too long and already the enemy forces have made their move. Your uncle is moving more quickly than we anticipated, and since your meeting with the Chancellor was a complete disast— misunderstanding, I've been asked to intervene. Nature abhors a vacuum. It's time for you to come out of the dark into the light. Much is riding on it.'

I assume she's talking about me becoming the Fae Queen. I take a deep breath and steady myself. It pains me to disappoint Gladys but she needs to know the truth.

'I can't be the person you want me to be.'

Gladys reaches over and squeezes my hand. She looks almost sad, but not for herself or the Fae who are relying on me. It's like she can see straight through me, into my hopelessness.

'You need to stop waiting for someone else to save you, dear.' She tucks a strand of wayward hair behind my ear.

'That person you've been hoping will come along and make things right, all these years? It's you.' She points her long, bony finger at me. 'Once you find the courage to accept that *you* are the one you've been waiting for, you will find your power.'

Tom's phone beeps. His expression hardens as he reads the message and then reaches for the TV remote. He switches on the TV and flicks through the channels to the twenty-four-hour news station. I'm greeted by an image of myself – my mugshot from when I was done for stealing Gladys's pills, with the word 'WANTED' at the bottom of the screen. Agent Eight didn't waste much time making good on her promise to open Larry's sealed murder investigation.

The next image is one of Tom wearing medical scrubs. It's a grainy shot that looks like it was captured from CCTV footage. The newsreader says we were last seen at Chelsea and Westminster Hospital; Tom was trespassing and I was a patient who fled without being discharged. And that we're both wanted for questioning in relation to a suspicious death, and presumed dangerous.

Gladys clicks her tongue. 'Fake news. It astounds me, the rubbish humans believe.'

Tom and I exchange a glance. It's clear Gladys has no clue about our history. And Tom doesn't seem to be in any rush to tell her.

The news bulletin cuts to an interview with a nurse outside the hospital fretting about how she shouldn't have to work alongside killers. The reporter interjects with the word 'alleged' before Tom turns off the television and slams the remote onto the bench. It shatters and the batteries fly across the room from the force.

The oxygen drains from the room as I stare at Tom. He's as still and cold as stone but his fists are clenched. He's seething with rage. Whatever connection we had re-established before Gladys arrived has gone. Yesterday he was free to move between the realms. Today he's an outlaw. And it's all because he thought I asked him to murder someone for me. For a horrifying moment, I wonder if perhaps I did.

'There must be something we can do,' I say, my voice thin. 'Surely we can explain …' I have no idea how to finish the sentence. *Explain what?* I think to myself. Knowing what I know now, explaining things would be about the worst thing we could do.

And who would we explain it to? The police would think we were crazy if we started talking about magic, hallucinogenic potions. And the Agency isn't about to let up until I give them some key which I'm still clueless about.

I rub my hands through my greasy hair, trying to think through this methodically, like breaking a system. But I don't have all the parameters and variables. And the ones I do know don't make any sense. I still have no idea what I've stumbled into here. Or what I'm supposed to do and be.

'Perhaps I could talk to Marshall,' I start again, clinging to the world I know. 'He has contacts.'

'Not the kind of contacts we want,' says Gladys quietly.

Her response is predictable. Gladys has never approved of Marshall. She wasn't thrilled when she found out I was getting the drugs to help her from Marshall's company. Her only comment was that it was poetic justice, because 'his lot' were thieves anyway. Then, when he was the only thing standing between me and prison, she called him a do-gooder trying to make amends for past crimes.

But after what the tour guide said at the V&A, I begin to see Gladys's prejudice against Marshall in a new light.

'You're not seriously holding a grudge against Marshall because of the old legend about stealing the Luck of Edenhall, are you?'

'It is not a legend. It is history. *Your* history.'

'Whatever,' I say, dropping it. 'It's not like we can afford to be choosy about our friends right now.'

'Better to be friendless than to choose friends who should not be,' she mutters.

'You're being completely unreason—'

'Dear, you can never go back,' Gladys interrupts.

Hesitantly, I look at Tom. He stands, jaw clenched in a frosty rage, and says nothing. He's so angry he won't even look at me, the perfect picture of someone who wishes he'd never met me. He must blame me for ruining his life. And in a way, he's right.

I have the first moment of clarity since all this craziness began. What Gladys said is true: there's no life for me here anymore. Hiding and hoping that things will resolve themselves has never worked for me. I'd be stupid to think it would this time.

And unless I find the key for the Agency there'll be no life for Tom either. As Princess Francesca, I will have a shot at appeasing the Agency and clearing Tom's name. As Chess, it would be impossible.

I turn to Gladys. 'Okay. So if I accept all of this, what now?'

'You have a war to stop,' she says with a confidence that sounds completely delusional.

Tom raises his hand, signalling for us to be quiet. He cocks his head to one side, listening. I swear his ears prick up ever so slightly.

I can't hear a thing. I don't think Gladys can either, but the tensing of her posture tells me that she believes that Tom can.

And whatever it is, it's not good.

chapter 13

Then I hear it: sirens, in the distance, joined now by the rumble of what sounds like low-flying helicopters.

'Come, dear, this way.' Gladys is all business, acting as though Tom isn't here. She's taken control of the situation.

Tom grabs his keys, readying to leave, when the house is rocked by vibrations. Worst-case scenarios rush through my mind, like being trapped in another cage or being separated from Tom and losing him all over again. I take the bug from the interrogation room out of my pocket and, without him noticing, slip it into Tom's. I wasn't sure what I was going to do with the bug when I lifted it, but this seems like a good use for it. If we get separated again, I should be able to find him by triangulating the bug's signal. And then we can work out a hack for that stupid spell.

Gladys is halfway up the stairs. I go to follow, when the front door smashes in, battered clean off its hinges, large splinters flying. Men in black commando gear storm in, stomping over the fallen door. At the rear, I spy Agent Eight.

'Don't even think about it,' she says, drawing a gun level with my chest.

Gladys turns around on the stairs and Tom takes a step towards me.

'You won't kill me,' I say with stupid confidence. 'If you do you'll never get your hands on your precious key.'

Agent Eight's face breaks into a sinister smile. It's the first time I've seen her teeth. She's a smoker, I'd bet.

She lowers her gun and for a split second I think I've called her bluff. A moment later, there's a blast and I'm sprawling on the floor. I'm cold and numb all over, except for my leg, which is burning. I look down and see blood – my blood, pooling on the floor.

Tom is by my side. He rips his t-shirt off and ties it around my leg as a tourniquet, his athletic arms and shoulders working with effortless efficiency to stop the gushing blood. He's not looking at me. I can't tell if he's still furious with me for ruining his life or if he's just in doctor mode.

'Unprovoked violence is a violation of the Treaty,' Gladys says, outraged.

Agent Eight shrugs. 'After what she did at our facility, nobody will dispute that it was self-defence.'

She orders her guards to cuff us.

Tom lunges at the guards as they approach. He doesn't stand a chance. Three meatheads pin him to the ground while Agent Eight kicks him in the ribs.

I try to get to Tom but my leg is burning and throbbing, and my body is unwilling or unable to do what my mind tells it.

With surprising agility for someone who looks just shy of 100, Gladys bounds down the stairs, clamps a hand around my arm and lifts me into a standing position.

I make another attempt to move to Tom, but Gladys has other plans. Waving her hairpin like an orchestra conductor, she traces out the shape of a square in the air, then grabs the back of my dress and shoves me headfirst into the wall.

I close my eyes and put my hands up protectively, bracing for impact. But I fall forward and keep falling, well past the point where I should have hit the plaster.

I open my eyes. The wall has opened into a tunnel. Gladys is behind me, propping me up and pushing me forwards. Looking back, I make out the room we just left, receding from view as a slow-moving, thick mist envelops us. Before the room fades from sight entirely, I see Agent Eight running her hands along the wall, trying to follow us. But whatever door or portal Gladys opened is closed. Behind Agent Eight, Tom is being shackled by the guards.

'Tom!' I scream, before slamming face-first into ... grass?

Dewy grass.

I twist around. My leg is killing me and I cry out again as I thrash about, clenching my jaw so much that it hurts, and clinging to my wound. My hand is slick with warm, sticky blood. I bite down on my lip.

Gladys lands gracefully on her feet beside me. She kneels at my side, inspecting my leg. Her twinset is drenched with blood. But it's not all from me.

'Your nose is bleeding.'

'Yes,' she says simply. She holds me tightly in her arms. 'Don't worry, dear, help is on its way.'

I feel lightheaded. 'Tom – we've got to go back and help Tom!' I try to sit up, sending another bolt of pain through my leg and body.

'Later, dear. You're in no condition. We have other priorities now.' And then she adds, 'He's more than capable of looking after himself.'

I want to insist, but nausea washes over me and I know I would be no help to Tom like this.

'Send someone else. Do something!' I say helplessly.

'Help's coming,' Gladys repeats as she tightens her grip around me.

We're in some kind of clearing but I feel too faint to look around. Through a haze of pain, I hear the distant rumble of an engine. A motorbike. And then I see it, racing towards us, grass and mud flying off the wheels.

For a moment, I forget the pain at the sight of a rider in leathers and a passenger seated behind in what looks to be a ball gown the colour of buttercups. A long skirt billows out behind them.

The bike screeches to a halt, sending grass and moss into the air. The one in the leather suit leaps from the seat of her bike and removes her helmet. It's the same woman as at the V&A.

Jules.

The one in the dress removes her helmet, revealing a mop of blonde curls and a heart-shaped face. She looks a few years older than me and I wonder vaguely how she feels about the mud splattered all up her dress.

'Bullet,' Gladys says.

The blonde strides over to me and yanks off her necklace, detaching what looks to be a tiny wooden treasure chest charm from the chain. She places the chest on the grass beside me and reaches into her boot, retrieving a metal wand, inlaid with grooves and swirls.

She touches the charm with the wand, releasing delicate, shimmering dust. Immediately the lid of the charm unfolds and then folds back again, and again, expanding in size each time. It quadruples in size and then quadruples again until it has the dimensions of a small chest. If I wasn't already moaning from pain I would yelp from the surprise of it.

The wooden lid of the chest creaks as the blonde pries it open. More iridescent dust appears on the inside of the chest as wooden dividers materialise and then slide into a chessboard pattern. Tiny glass vials of multi-coloured liquid and powders sprout like mushrooms after summer rain.

White-hot pain runs down my leg. I shiver; the rest of my body suddenly cold. From what I can make out, we're in a park. Nowhere near a doctor, I imagine.

'Hospital?' I croak at Gladys.

Jules and the other woman exchange quizzical glances.

Gladys squeezes my hand. 'It's okay, dear. Abby is a master apothecary.'

Jules unwraps Tom's bloodied t-shirt to reveal my wound. *What's happened to Tom?* I wonder. What has Agent Eight done to him? I need to fix the mess I've created for us.

For him.

The blonde, who must be Abby the apothecary, stares at Tom's t-shirt, seemingly more interested in the Celtic symbol on it than in my bullet wound. She looks at me, then at the t-shirt again, and then back to me with an expression so lethal that I momentarily forget that I'm in pain.

'Your first duty is to the Apothecary Guild,' Gladys says in a tone that instantly puts an end to whatever Abby was thinking.

Abby mutters something under her breath before returning her attention to her chest of vials.

'You better not bleed on my dress, Princess,' Abby says as she retrieves a pewter dish from the chest. She measures out three pinches of a green power, a splash of black liquid, two drops of a red serum and what looks like an ordinary leaf from an oak tree into the dish and stirs it all together with her wand. After sniffing the concoction like a pretentious wine connoisseur, she tosses the dish into the air. But instead of falling back onto the moss, it hovers, suspended above the ground. Abby points her wand at the dish. Golden light streams out, illuminating it. Wisps of smoke rise from the mixture, accompanied by a sweet, pungent aroma. The dish gently lowers from the air onto the moss, seemingly all on its own. Abby collects the contents in a vintage amber eye-dropper.

'This'll save your leg,' she says to me, 'but it's going to sting so much you'll wish I let you bleed out and die.'

I barely have time to take in her words when she releases one drop of the potion onto my wound.

I scream, my yelps of pain echoing around the clearing. It's as if a thousand fire ants all stung me at once. I instinctively curl to the side in preparation to get up and run away, but Gladys forces me back, flat on the ground.

Abby inspects my bullet wound, which has started to blister from the potion.

'Perfect,' she says, clearly satisfied with her work. 'You're going to have to suck it up, Princess, because that wasn't even the worst bit.'

Without warning, she squeezes out the remaining potion onto my wound. My back arches, my teeth clench and my eyes water. The pain takes me to the brink of unconsciousness before changing into a tingling sensation. My skin turns hot and tight, and the bullet slug pops out of my leg. Jules catches it mid-flight with one hand.

There's more tingling and the skin itches and tightens even more. I watch as sinew and skin knit back together, all trace of the wound disappearing before my eyes. Abby turns her attention to the cut on my temple, then the burn on my neck. There are more potions and more pain. I rub my hand along my neck and feel only smoothness.

The instant she's finished, Abby stands up and straightens her gown, which is now flecked with as much blood as mud. With a flick of her wand, her chest of potions begins to fold, collapsing in on itself until it has returned to its original miniature size. She reattaches it to her necklace and faces Gladys.

'I have discharged my duty,' she says, and after a brief

glance at Jules, Abby spins around on the heel of her boot and stalks off into the forest.

Gladys impassively watches her go. I stand, gingerly transferring my weight onto my bad leg.

'I counsel that we do not linger, Your Highness,' Jules says.

Gladys nods her agreement.

I take a tentative half-step, half-limp, and wait for the pain. But it doesn't come. My leg seems to be completely fine. It's hard to get my head around being completely pain-free only minutes after being shot.

I take a better look at my surroundings. We're in a mossy clearing in a glade. The air is cool and crisp. I'd guess we're in the English countryside, the kind you see in tourist brochures, but I've never seen any English countryside where the enormous tree trunks are planted into the ground like the legs of giants, with leaves the size of car tires, and butterflies so big they should be on a leash.

Iridesca.

I'm back in Iridesca.

Surprisingly, it feels like home.

chapter 14

'Nice house,' I say as we emerge from the forest and an enormous stone castle comes into view. Jules is pushing her motorbike on one side of me and Gladys is on the other. They both seem to know where they're going.

We're greeted by a pebbled path meandering towards the castle. A marble fountain filled with impossibly crystal-blue water sits halfway along the path. Water tinkles from the mouths of sculpted mermaids fanning out from the centre of the fountain. Four paths fork out from the fountain, each lined with shrubs the size of delivery vans.

'What now?' I ask, staring at the flowerbeds filled with overgrown roses with thorns the size of shark fins.

'Inside,' Gladys says matter-of-factly.

'Inside? Who lives here?'

Jules looks at me, her face lined with confusion.

'You,' Gladys replies. 'Windsor Castle is your family's primary residence.' She strides towards the castle with the ease of someone popping around to a friend's house for a cup of tea and a biscuit.

Primary residence? Mind. Officially. Blown. The immensity of the castle is overwhelming; it projects its grandeur almost like a silent rebuke to the enormous trees that dwarf it.

Gladys looks back at my bare feet. 'That will never do,' she says, pulling her hairpin out of her bun.

'I want *my* shoes,' I insist, before she has a chance to magic up something to her taste. With her laundry-lady dowdy and bizarre fairy matriarch aesthetics, who knows what I'd get.

'You are Princess Francesca of House Raven now.'

'I'm still Chess.'

'Very well,' she concedes, conjuring my trusty old commando boots. She slips her hairpin into her bun and continues towards the castle.

'Did I really live here? In a castle?' I say to Jules.

'You do live here,' she says with a quick smile, motioning towards the massive banners attached to the castle.

Knowing that I am the girl on the banners, and not her doppelganger, makes the sight even creepier than before. And the words 'Our Salvation' in big bold letters does nothing to settle my anxiety.

Guards stand to attention on one side of the castle. On the other side are horses.

I do a double take. They're not horses.

Like Tom, they're bulkier than horses, and their horns make them look like gentle mystical creatures but dangerous at the same time. Two of them are midnight black, another two are white as snow and the final one is a rusty red colour.

They're all wearing gold breastplates embossed with the same insignia that Jules has pinned to her uniform – a unicorn in a circle. My guess is that the red unicorn is in charge. He's wearing a chain bridle made from big golden loops, but it looks more decorative than functional.

'If I may be so bold, Your Highness?' Jules says beside me, her voice hushed.

'Sure,' I say, unable to tear my eyes away from the unicorns.

'Not everyone will be happy you've returned. The unicorns in the Protectorate, they're not to be trusted, Your Highness. Since the – since your mother was …'

'Killed,' I finish for her.

She looks mortified. 'No, I mean, I mean …'

'It's okay,' I say gently.

'As you wish, Your Highness,' she says, her eyes downcast. 'But you must be careful. The palace is full of spies.'

'I'll keep that in mind,' I say, wondering – not for the first time – what I'm getting myself into. 'And Jules?'

'Yes, Your Highness?'

'Stop calling me "Your Highness". I think we've moved far beyond these formalities. From now on, you can look me in the eye and call me Chess.'

'Yes, Your Highness.'

I approach the entrance to Windsor Castle, unsure if Jules is messing with me or if she's just ridiculously rule-bound. Gladys leads the way. Watching her ambling up the high stone steps, I wonder again, *Who is this woman? And why didn't she tell me about any of this?*

At the entrance, the red unicorn with the gold chains stiffens to attention.

'All hail Princess Francesca of House Raven,' the unicorn growls. 'Rejoice, for she has returned.' The other unicorns stand to attention.

I don't know where to look. I've always hated being the centre of attention. I prefer to fade into the background. Perhaps it's self-preservation, or maybe it's professional pride. The whole point of being a hacker, after all, is to remain invisible. In my experience, attention always leads to trouble.

I bite my lip and stare at my shoes. I probably should have polished them once or twice in the last two years. I clasp my hands together in what I hope is a royal pose. And then, because it feels silly, I unclasp them, letting them fall by my side. That seems wrong too.

'Um, thanks,' I say to the parade of unicorns. 'At, um … at ease,' I say, hoping that's what people say in these kinds of situations.

'That is Second Officer Wynstar of the Protectorate,' whispers Jules.

'That must make you his boss,' I whisper back, concluding that a First Officer must outrank a Second Officer.

Jules stands in front of Wynstar expectantly. He stares back at her and I wonder if I'm the only one feeling awkward about the silence stretching out. It's like watching a duel, not knowing who is going to draw their weapon first.

Eventually Second Officer Wynstar bows his head to her. The gesture is perfunctory, devoid of respect, but I could swear the tiniest hint of a smirk flashes across Jules's face. I suppress the urge to give her a high-five.

My attention is drawn to one of the white unicorns. He looks almost exactly like Tom, except he has duller blue eyes, and a meaner vibe.

Tom. I wince at the memory of him lying on the ground as Agent Eight laid into him. I just hope that was the worst of it, that they're not hurting him even more now. He must have known he was hopelessly outnumbered.

'That is Loxley,' Jules whispers as we walk past the white unicorn. 'Another officer, and one to be cautious of.'

Loxley hisses softly as we pass. I guess he doesn't like me much.

We step through the enormous doors and into a grand hall. Inside, the castle is a hive of activity. Some women rush around in crisp white and, to my eyes, impractical, flowing gowns. And there are other women, dressed like Jules, standing to attention in every doorway. Everyone stops what they're doing as we approach and turns to look at us. Some gawk, while others give a quick sideways glance and then pretend they saw nothing. I stare right back. It's hard not to. I've never seen so many sets of impressive cheekbones in one place before.

A hush falls over the grand hall as a woman dressed in soft folds of cascading silver begins to descend the huge staircase.

'This is the Supreme Executor, dear,' Gladys whispers

into my ear. The deference in her tone is not Gladys's style, but if she was going to be intimidated by anyone I guess it would be this woman. The Supreme Executor looks like she's used to getting her own way.

'What does she do?' I whisper back.

'Think of her as the prime minister of Albion. The one in charge.'

'I thought that was the Chancellor.'

Gladys's eyes twinkle. 'Oh dear Goddess, no. He is our diplomat. One who thinks he is a good deal more diplomatic than he actually is.'

The Supreme Executor reaches the bottom of the stairs and glides over to me. The lines on her face tell me that she's seen a lot of life. The austere look in her eyes tells me she doesn't approve of much of what she's seen. And I get a feeling that I'm no exception.

She bows and I notice that she has long metal hairpins in her hair, just like Gladys.

'Welcome, Princess Francesca Raven,' she says in a tone that makes me feel anything but welcome. 'We have waited many moons for your restoration.'

I turn to Gladys, my eyebrow raised. 'My what?'

Gladys steps forward. 'Princess Francesca thanks you for your patience and your allegiance. She will not disappoint.'

'We shall see,' the Supreme Executor says, before sweeping through the hall. The silence remains until she's out of sight and then everyone returns to what they were doing.

I frown at Gladys. What's she signing me up to? I don't owe these people anything; I don't care how long they've waited. That was their choice. It had nothing to do with me.

A flock of staff moves into action, rushing about us with clockwork efficiency. There's a lot of curtsying and bowing going on in my direction. I feel like the new kid on my first day at some prestigious school. With no idea how to respond – do I curtsey or bow back? – I give something between a nod and a bow in reply. It's not very princess-y. Anyone looking on would probably think I'd been overcome by a spasm, forcing me to stoop awkwardly. I feel like I'm making a complete idiot of myself and just wish we'd get to wherever we're going.

Jules and I trail behind Gladys as we cross the hall. A gigantic mosaic of a flying unicorn is tiled on the floor. Waiting on the other side of the mosaic are two girls about my age, both dressed in those impractical white flowing gowns that seem to be a uniform. They look at me with wide, expectant eyes, as if they're queuing for an autograph from their favourite pop star. I'm more comfortable with the cool appraisal of the Supreme Executor. I prefer to do my disappointing upfront.

'Welcome home, Your Highness,' the girls say in unison as they curtsey to me.

'This is Brina, your first maid,' Gladys says, gesturing towards the one who has managed to replace her enthusiasm with professionalism.

'And Callie, your second maid.'

Callie seems to be taking a little longer to get her emotions in check.

I smile at them stiffly and wonder if now is a good time to mention that I won't be needing any maids. These people dumped me in foster care, giving me no choice but to look after myself. It's a little late to make amends now.

'To Princess Francesca's chambers, please,' Gladys says to them, and I wince at the formality. 'Princess' is a big leap from 'dear'.

'As you wish, Luminaress,' Brina says.

Gladys turns back to me. 'You'll need to be rested for tomorrow.'

'What's tomorrow?'

She smiles and then glides up the stairs after the maids, leaving Jules and me to follow. I pretend not to notice as Callie whips around to take another peek at me. We walk through a long corridor lit by candle chandeliers suspended from the ceiling. The walls are covered with oil paintings, all of them portraits of women, framed in gold leaf. The styles of the painting and their frames change, but the subjects are all wearing the same necklace with an enormous ruby dangling from it.

'Your chambers, Your Highness,' Brina says, stopping in front of a closed door.

Pastel-coloured letters spell out my name. I run my fingers over the top of the wooden 'F' in Francesca and wonder if this room has been used in the thirteen years since I left it.

Brina flings open the door, and I fight back tears as I step back into the childhood that was taken from me.

It looks like a child's fantasy bedroom featured in a glossy interior design magazine. The four-poster bed in the middle of the room has a bedspread with rainbows and stars, and a canopy to match. The toys and furniture show signs of use but there's no obvious fading or wearing. The rocking horse in the corner and the wooden puzzles and blocks look new.

I half expect a child to come bounding through the door, having returned home from kindergarten or a day at the park. And then I remember that I'm the child. This is my room. Fragments of a long-lost childhood flit through my mind – familiar colours and scents, the way the light falls, the shape of the windows – with a vividness that makes them impossible to deny.

There's a seat underneath the bay window that faces out onto a garden of giant tulips and daffodils. I sit down and rub my fingers through the thick plush seat covering. I recognise the feeling instantly. I've sat here before, my legs tucked up under me while I drew swirly patterns in the velvet. Someone sat with me, reading me stories, but I can't remember who.

'Your wardrobe has been filled with new clothes, Your Highness,' says Brina from behind me. 'Everything else is as you left it.'

I walk over to the dressing room, which is about the size of my flat above Gladys's laundromat. A full-length mirror fills the end. One side is stuffed with puffy, frilly little-girl things, and the other side is packed, floor to ceiling, with garments in silk, velvet, leather and lace.

I run my fingers along the clothes. It's strange to think they all belong to me. It's a fantasy, a dream come true, to own so many clothes. For most of my childhood I owned one dress. One faded blue dress with torn frills on the hem. Even now, I can only afford to buy my clothes from charity stores.

Why didn't Gladys, who was supposed to be looking after me – and all these other people who seem so pleased to see me that they're hanging banners on buildings – bother to ensure that I had the most basic things, like clothing? Like food?

Like safety?

Raw emotion swells inside me. I try to push it back down. I can't go there. Not now.

'You don't expect me to wear this?' I say, pulling out a navy blue silk gown with a sweetheart neckline and a huge flouncy skirt. I hold it out in front of me as if it were a smelly rag rather than haute couture.

Gladys takes the dress and stretches the boned bodice across my torso. 'It's a perfect fit.'

'You've missed my point,' I say. 'It's just not very … um … Chess.'

Gladys thrusts the gown back into my hands. 'It is very Francesca of House Raven.'

Out of the corner of my eye I catch my maids exchanging an awkward glance.

Replacing the gown on the rack, I pull out another dress. It's champagne coloured and flouncy, and just as over the top as the other one. I note a little hidey-hole in the back of the gown and look closer. The back bodice is not a single piece of fabric, but two pieces sewn into the side seams and overlapping at the centre.

Wings.

It must be for wings. Does this mean my wings will return?

I shiver with anticipation as I turn to Gladys to ask about them. But as I do, she pushes on the mirror and it swings open to reveal a bathroom on the other side. It's all marble and mirrors. There's a huge shower adorned with mermaid statuettes that I bet never runs cold, and an enormous bath with a row of carved wooden swan and unicorn bath toys sitting on the ledge.

The opulence makes me feel like an imposter. At the same time, I can't wait to have the longest, hottest shower of my life. I don't know how long it's been since I bathed. Or slept.

Gladys tells me to clean up and get some rest before lunch. My head's full of questions about my childhood, my wings and, most of all, about Tom. Anticipating them, Gladys just says, 'Questions later. Rest now.' And with that she bustles to the door, shooing Jules out with her.

I rest my forehead against the mirror of my dressing room and take a deep breath. What have I done? What am I about to do?

Hands grab me from behind – one on my shoulder, the other on my back. I scream in fright and swing around, narrowly missing my attacker's face.

Jules bursts through the door, landing in the centre of the room in some kick-arse warrior pose. She relaxes her stance when she sees Callie cowering on the floor.

'She attacked me,' I say, wrapping my arms around myself.

Callie just sits there in the middle of a marshmallow of white fabric, staring up at me in shock.

In one smooth movement, Jules reaches down and helps Callie to her feet.

'She was assisting you to undress, Your Highness,' Brina ventures.

'Well, then … don't,' I say. 'If you'd just get out and leave me alone then this wouldn't have happened.'

'But it is our duty to —'

'Go!' I say firmly, feeling increasingly ashamed for almost decking my maid and wanting this embarrassment to end.

The maids scurry out of the room and I could swear Jules has the faintest smirk on her face as she follows them.

The door clicks shut and I'm alone. I'm used to being alone, but not like this. Without warning, a crushing feeling descends upon me like an oppressive cloud. This sort of alone isn't just the absence of people, it's gut-wrenching loneliness. It's an ache that only comes from knowing precisely what – or who – you're missing.

I curl up on the bed and think of the boy who risked everything to save me when I was a child. He should not have made the decisions he did without consulting me, but he was the one person who cared when everybody else looked the other way. And that counts.

Long-lost memories flood my mind. The first time Tom came to my window. It was a night so terrible I truly wished I were dead.

I was ten years old, lying on my bed in a faded yellow nightie as silent tears streamed down my face.

Larry was there.

Something broke inside me that night. But it wasn't a bone or any part of my physical body. It was my spirit, I guess. A bright flash filled the room, my back arched and I felt my whole centre of consciousness rush through the pores of my skin, the way water explodes from a burst water balloon.

I remember swallowing a scream, before I started reeling backwards – no, it was upwards. I stopped when I hit the ceiling.

Peering out from behind the auburn wisps of my fringe, I stared down at my young body a metre below where I was hovering. The 'me' lying on my bed below was staring right back at the 'me' above.

It was me, but it was separate from me.

I remember forcing myself to focus on my floating self, even though I was terrified of what I might find. Of course, I'd heard that people have souls, but I'd never really thought about whether they wear clothes or have bodies. I inspected my new weightless self. As far as I could tell, both of me looked the same.

And then I got the feeling someone else was up there with me. Just outside my window, on the top floor of our council high-rise, there was movement. It was too big to be a bird, and even the strongest – or the dumbest – kids on the estate couldn't scale that height.

'Who's there?' I whispered.

Silence.

'Hello?'

The window creaked open just a little; a shaft of golden light shot through. A lustrous white unicorn leaned into my room, too perfect to be real, but too solid to be imagined. He asked if I wanted to go flying with him, as if it were the most normal thing in the world. I don't know if it was his confidence or the fact that I was a kid and already having an out-of-body experience, but without giving it a second thought, I said 'yes'.

Tom didn't just save me on the night he killed Larry, he saved me every time he came to my window. He gave me friendship, and he gave me hope. Even when his spell made me forget that my friend was real, my dreams of him made the intolerable tolerable. I owe him a life debt, and despite Gladys's assurances that he can look after himself, rescuing Tom from the Agency is what I must do to repay him.

I look down at my dress, still covered in grime and blood, and my thoughts drift to Tom rescuing me from the Agency. I guess flying on the back of a unicorn was a little harder to come to terms with as a sixteen-year-old than it was as a kid. I think of his powerful body flying me to safety. I can still feel his warmth and strength penetrating my skin. I want to fly with him again, but this time I want to enjoy it, rather than being freaking terrified.

And I want to feel his human body next to mine again. The way he wrapped his arms around me on his couch and made me feel so safe and no longer alone. I want to feel that again. I need to feel that again.

I vow that, whatever it takes, I will rescue him.

chapter 15

The bed shakes beneath me and I'm awake.

The windows rattle in their frames. I let out a yelp and, with only the barest idea of what I'm doing, slide out of bed and crouch on the floor.

An earthquake? Here, in London? Or whatever they call this city in Iridesca – Trinovantum?

I hear an explosion. And then another.

I peer up and see morning sunlight pouring through the windows, seemingly at odds with the echoes of the boom still reverberating around me.

My bedroom door bursts open and Jules flies towards me, followed by the thundering boots of what must be twenty other people all dressed in the same armour-like clothes.

Guards.

'Are you alright, Your Highness?' Jules crouches by my side, hovering over me protectively while the others form a circle around me, peering out the window.

'What was that?'

'Rebels,' she answers. 'It's unlikely they breached the warded perimeter. More than likely a warning to get our attention.'

'Well, they got my attention.'

'Nothing to worry about, Your Highness. They've hit closer than this before, but we don't like to take chances.'

'Before?' I ask. 'You mean this sort of thing happens regularly?'

Jules gives me an odd look.

'Oh yeah, the war and all that,' I mumble.

A few minutes pass, and when it's clear that there are no more bombs, the guards trek out. Jules is the last to leave my room, replaced by Brina and Callie, standing tentatively in the doorway.

'Would Your Highness like her breakfast?' Brina suggests.

Seriously? We were under fire a minute ago and now we're talking about breakfast? I'm about to say as much but Callie shrinks when I look at her and I officially feel like the worst person in the world.

'Sure. Breakfast would be great,' I say, realising that I must have slept through lunch. And dinner. No wonder I'm starving.

Callie gingerly places an empty tray on the bed, making a bridge over my legs. She pulls a thin piece of metal decorated with what look like intricate Celtic symbols from her boot and swishes it. A boiled egg in a chicken-shaped cup and five thin slices of toast appear on the tray.

I jolt back in fright, staring at the food.

'I'm sorry, Your Highness. I was told eggs and soldiers were your favourite.'

'When she was three,' sighs Brina.

Callie's cheeks flush crimson. She's probably worried I'm going to try to hit her again. I dip a toast soldier into the egg and stuff it in my mouth to make her feel better.

'Would Her Highness desire more toast?' Callie asks when my plate is empty. 'Or something else, perhaps?'

'Definitely. What else have you got?'

I'm delighted when my empty plate is magically refilled with toast, some pastries and an apple so red and succulent it could have come straight out of *Snow White*.

I take a deep breath. 'We got off on the wrong foot yesterday and I'm sorry. I'd like for you both to call me Chess,' I say. They both look like I've asked them to drown kittens, so I add, 'Um, that's a command. Please.'

Brina opens her mouth but nothing comes out. I suspect that getting rid of the formality around here is going to take a while.

After eating I get up and go to the bathroom, Brina and Callie following me.

'I can get undressed on my own,' I say.

'Yes, Your Highness,' Brina says, but doesn't move.

'So, um … what are you still doing in here?'

'You may require assistance while you bathe.'

'I'm pretty sure I won't,' I say, pointing to the door.

The shower is wonderfully hot, but I can't relax. The muscles of my neck are knotted and my breathing shallow. I realise that my body is on high alert, waiting for another nasty surprise. Another explosion or attack or something. And it's not just here in Iridesca. I think of the trouble I'm in back in London. People think I'm a murderer.

I need to see Marshall again, to explain everything. I have no idea what I'll say but he's done so much for me; I need him to know that it wasn't all for nothing. That the stories about me that he's bound to have heard by now aren't true.

I'm not a murderer. I did deserve my second chance.

I step out of the bathroom wrapped in a white fluffy robe, and see Brina and Callie waiting obediently just outside the bathroom door. Brina asks what I'd like to wear. Apparently it's her job to get my clothes for me, which strikes me as ridiculous. How hard can it be to pull something off a hanger?

My wardrobe contains enough clothes to rival a department store but I can't find anything I'd feel comfortable wearing. It's between figure-hugging bodysuits, much the same as Jules's uniform, or long, flowing gowns.

'I'll put my own dress back on.'

'But it's dirty, Your Highness,' Brina says.

'Can't you clean it with magic or something?'

'It's torn in the back.'

'I'm guessing if you can magic up a buffet breakfast you can fix some torn fabric, yes?'

Brina looks uncertain for a moment and then acquiesces with stiff formality. 'As you wish, Your Highness.'

The limited selection in clothes also applies to shoes. It's a choice between boots, boots or boots. I choose boots.

Again, I opt for my own over the new stuff.

When I finally emerge from the dressing room, my bed is made and Gladys is sitting on it. She takes one look at my dress and a pencil-thin eyebrow shoots up to her hairline.

'You must learn to pick your battles, my dear,' she says, swishing her hairpin.

I gasp as my dress disappears and is replaced with a blood red gown with a full skirt and a corset that is stupidly tight. I'm about to protest but I'm distracted by the black velvet box Gladys hands me. I trace my finger over the lid embossed with a unicorn's head inside a circle. It's the same symbol I saw on Jules's uniform and the other Protectorate officers'.

'That is the insignia of House Raven,' Gladys says. 'It's your family seal.'

I open the box to find a ruby pendant inside, identical to the one worn by all the women in the corridor paintings.

'The Amulet of Ascendancy,' Gladys says, walking over to the window seat. 'It belonged to your mother and her mother before that. And now, as Queen in the Ascendant, it belongs to you.' Gladys's blood-stained twinset from yesterday has been replaced with more red tartan. This time it's a full skirt matched with a crisp white shirt and a brown leather vest.

'Put it on,' she instructs.

As I slip the pendant over my head I worry that we're going to spend the day playing dress-ups. I don't have time to play.

'I'm grateful for this, Gladys. Really, I am. But we need to talk about Tom. He needs our help.'

Gladys looks unmoved. 'A rescue mission is out of the question,' she says. 'Too dangerous. We cannot anticipate what your uncle will do next. You must understand the magnitude of his power; he draws it from your family line.'

'My what?'

'In war, there are casualties,' she continues, ignoring my question. 'This we must accept. You are not used to this world and the stark realities we face. In time you will see that, regrettable thought it may be, nothing is to be done for that boy.' As an afterthought, she adds, 'We will honour him.'

'*Honour* him?' I say, outraged. 'We need to help him!'

'First, we need to finish the training we've started. Then perhaps we'll talk more about this young man,' she says, although it's clear to me that she has no intention of discussing Tom ever again. Was Gladys always this obtuse? Eccentric, absolutely – but this new fairy version of Gladys is infuriatingly opaque, her words containing more layers than an onion.

'Started? What have we started?'

'You'll see.' Gladys gives me a smile that I don't feel like returning. My temper is rising, and I'm straining to hold my tongue as I follow her out the door. I don't understand why she insists on maintaining the pretence that she's been training me all these years.

We walk along a wide corridor, past door after door, all of them closed, until we finally come to one that opens into a huge, circular room. Leather-bound books line the walls in a kind of orderly chaos. They look ancient but well kept, and they're stacked so high that it's impossible to read the spines of the books on the top shelves. I would have loved to sit in a place like this when I was a child, to be surrounded by the calm certainty of books. Two tawny leather couches face one another in the centre of the room, with a coffee table sitting in between.

'Now,' says Gladys, settling into one of the couches, 'a cup of tea's in order. Be a dear?'

'Tea?' I ask, not even trying to disguise my frustration. It's not that I mind making a cup of tea. I've made Gladys hundreds – thousands, even – and I know just how she likes it. But I don't have time for this. I need to get Tom back. 'Can't we just get on with the lesson?'

'This is the lesson,' Gladys replies, her eyes sparkling.

'Ok-a-a-a-y,' I say, getting more and more annoyed. 'Just so we're clear, when you say "cup of tea", you actually mean a cup of tea? Black, watery, milky stuff? Or is "cup of tea" a secret code for something else? Because if it is, I've completely missed it.'

'Always needing Gladys to spell things out for you,' she says, sighing. 'Use what Gladys has taught you.' She pulls a silver metal bar from her boot and hands it to me. Intricate patterns swirl along the length of the wand's shaft. It's similar to the one Callie used to conjure my breakfast, except this wand is tapered at one end, like a screwdriver. 'That belonged to Ada Lovelace.'

I remember learning about Ada Lovelace at school.

That was one lesson I paid attention to. She was a genius who essentially invented computer programming way back in the 1800s. Long before any men thought of it.

'Ada Lovelace was a fairy?'

Gladys nods. 'Your relative, also. Ada was the sister of Queen Josephine, which would make her your distant aunt. She was the most brilliant neoteric fairy in the history of the Fae.'

'A *neoteric*,' I say, mostly to myself. That's what Gladys called me when I fixed the washing machines at the laundromat.

'Yes, dear. A bringer of new ideas, new ways. It's your guild. Think of it as your club or tribe, the people who share the same skills and outlook. Neoteric Fae light the path forward,' she says with weighty expectation. 'Now, put Ada's instrument to good use and summon my cup of tea, please.'

'What? Out of thin air?'

Gladys sighs again. 'Do you remember my song, "Oh Cometh to Thee"?'

'Of course I do.' It's one of the many tuneless songs she's sung for as long as I can remember. It's so deeply etched into my mind that I don't even hear the words anymore, like wallpaper you no longer notice because you've looked at the pattern for so long.

Gladys begins singing:

> *Oh, cometh to thee*
> *O'er land, o'er sea*

Deliver my desire
With haste and safety

An ornate china teacup painted with a floral pattern and a matching saucer start to materialise on the coffee table in front of Gladys. At first it's just a blur of colour and light, and then, as if forming atom by atom, it emerges as a hot cup of tea.

Gladys picks it up, lightly blowing steam off the top. 'I summoned this cup from the Palace China Room. The milk, tea and water from the kitchen. Now you try,' she says, indicating that I do something with Ada Lovelace's wand.

'How? I can't —'

'You can,' Gladys cuts me off sharply. 'I have spent years training you. Not to fall at the first hurdle, mind. No, that will never do.'

'Again with the training!' I say, throwing the wand onto the table. 'When did you train me to do that?' My voice is pierced with anger. 'In the past three days I've been kidnapped, tasered, locked in a cage, named as public enemy number one for a murder I didn't commit, catapulted through a roof, sprouted wings and, just to top it all off, I got shot. And suddenly I find out that I'm loaded, when all this time I've been destitute. And all these people now say they need me. Well, where were they when *I* needed *them*? Where were *you*?'

Gladys's eyes widen in surprise but I plough on.

'The one person who saved me has been captured and no one seems to care. People keep treating me as if I'm some brave general who's going to lead them into battle, but I've got no idea what I'm supposed to be doing. *None!* And now I'm supposed to magic up a cup of tea – *a cup of tea!* – out of thin air, using nothing but a song with really bad rhymes? Okay, then, let's have a go, shall we? Let's fight a war with crockery.'

I'm unable to keep the sarcasm from my voice as I reel off Gladys's stupid verse in a sing-song voice.

'There! See? Sorry to disappoint *but I don't do tricks!*' Tears of anger and anguish wash down my cheeks.

Then I notice Gladys's face. It's lit up in childlike wonder.

'What?' I snap.

I slowly turn around a full 360 degrees and take in the scene before me. On every spare surface, and floating in mid-air around the library, from the ceiling to the floor, are hundreds of steaming hot cups of tea. The cups and saucers are in every design imaginable – a floral design here, gold leaf there, every colour of the rainbow, all exquisitely painted. Each is surrounded by a shimmering haze of sparkling dust, lighting up the whole room.

'Oh my ...' I manage to get out, before the cups crash to the floor, most of them smashing and sloshing tea on the carpet.

Gladys is completely unfazed. 'We'll need to work on your presentation, dear. But you've got the idea.' She settles back into the couch and takes a sip of her tea, a satisfied smile calmly spreading across her face.

chapter 16

'Spells?' I stare, disbelieving. 'You've been teaching me *spells*?'

Gladys smiles proudly. 'Ever since you came into my care. But your powers are unheralded. I've never seen anyone perform the Art without a channelling instrument.' She looks down at Ada Lovelace's wand, lying idly on the table. 'It shouldn't be possible.'

You'd think she'd be pleased by this, but apparently not. The lines around her eyes crinkle into deep gullies of worry.

'Untrained, you are a hand grenade. Without the pin.'

A moment later the concern has vanished from her face as she begins singing another familiar song, restoring the room to its former state. The teacups glisten, evaporating from view in wisps of odourless gas.

As I look on, still amazed that solid objects can just materialise – and dematerialise – in front of my eyes, she turns her attention to a huge book sitting about halfway up the bookshelf. She whispers another song I know by heart.

From there it sails and floats on high
Dancing a journey through the sky
Gently it rests and comes to lie
The place I claim with mine eye

The book shuffles from where it sits on the shelf, levitates upwards momentarily, before gracefully floating down and landing in my outstretched hands. It looks like an ancient, well-thumbed encyclopaedia. I sneeze as dust puffs up into my nose.

'*The Book of Artifice,*' Gladys says. 'The foundation of every spell that can be conjured can be found between its covers. If you've been paying attention all these years, you should know every single spell in this book.'

I sit down opposite Gladys and open the book. Its pages are soft and smooth, more like fine cotton than ordinary paper. As I leaf through it, I see what Gladys means: I know them all. All the strange ditties she has always sung around the laundromat are here, laid out in careful script.

'With more practice in the Art, you won't need to say the words aloud.'

'What is the Art?'

'Humans call it "magic", but that always sounds so vulgar to Fae ears. The words of the Art are just there to help focus your mind and direct your energy. And as you become more adept, you can develop your own spells, using the book as a foundation.'

I turn to the spell for transferring between realms.

'You have conjured that spell before,' Gladys says.

'When?'

'When you transferred back to Volgaris in the middle of your meeting with the Chancellor. Exasperating though he may be, dear, you really must learn to control your temper. And now you know what can happen when you neglect to visualise your target destination during a transfer spell.'

'That's how I wound up unconscious in the middle of Kensington High Street?'

'Correct.'

'I used my own magic when I came back to London?' I say, amazed.

Gladys nods.

'But how did I do it?'

'Only you know that, dear,' she says. 'And in time you will learn to harness it.'

Her lips purse and her forehead tilts forward. I've seen that look before and I know she's about to deliver a warning.

'Every time the Fae practise the Art in Volgaris, there is a price to be paid,' Gladys says. The more serious the spell, the higher the price. Most often we pay in pain, sometimes excruciating and debilitating pain. With more practice you can choose to pay for the Art with the loss of precious memories. I do not advise this. Conjuring a transfer spell in Volgaris comes at a very high price. That's why we only travel between realms when we absolutely must. Far more experienced Fae than you have transferred to Volgaris and have been unable – or unwilling – to pay the price to return.'

'But you transferred me to Iridesca,' I say, recalling the way she rammed me into Tom's wall that then disappeared right before impact. 'What did you pay for that?'

'A fair price.'

I recall that Gladys's nose was bleeding just after the transfer. 'You paid in pain.'

'Correct,' she says, in a way that doesn't invite further questions.

'How do you know the price for each spell?' I'm wondering what I will have to pay if I use magic to rescue Tom. If I can use magic at all, that is. The only thing I know for sure is that I can cater for a tea party, but that's not much use against Agent Eight.

'You'll know the price in the moment between intent and action, as sure as you see me here before you. It's as clear and forceful as a clap of thunder. What did you pay when you escaped from the Agency?'

I think of the bone-splitting pain that hit me when I was suspended in mid-air, my wings flapping for the very first time.

'Rather unpleasant, you'll agree,' Gladys says. 'A self-regulating system, ingenious as it is dangerous. It is to ensure our ways do not impinge on the humans.'

I ponder this for a moment. 'Why didn't you just cure yourself of the blood disease? Surely any price would be worth it?'

'That would require a cataclysmic spell – a spell that alters the balance of life and death decreed by Mother Nature. There's no more serious business,' she says solemnly.

156

Goosebumps spring up along my arms as I realise that this must be the same type of spell that Tom used to kill Larry, the one where he had to sacrifice what he desired most. *Me.*

Gladys tells me that in Iridesca, anybody can use the Art whenever they like. It's as normal and accepted as the law of gravity. The only spell that carries a cost in Iridesca is a cataclysmic spell.

'Life and death are universals and have universal value,' Gladys says. 'If I were to perform a cataclysmic spell to save my life, I would have to sacrifice that which I desire most – my life. Quite a paradox, you see? To save my life I would have to sacrifice it.'

'Well, then ask someone else to do it for you.'

Gladys shakes her head. 'I could not ask someone to sacrifice their greatest desire in all of the realms for me.'

As her words sink in, I'm struck by how alone Gladys is. She doesn't have anybody who cares enough to save her. And I realise that I know next to nothing about her, or nothing that really matters anyway. Nothing about her family or her life before I met her. Maybe, like me, her family is long dead. It never came up and, if I'm being honest, I never really thought to ask. Gladys just is. I can't ever recall her socialising with anybody. Except me. Sure, she made small talk with regulars at the laundromat, but there was no one she'd have a deep and meaningful conversation with.

Am I her only friend?

I flick through the book until I find the cataclysmic

spell, and then make sure that I remember all the words correctly. If Marshall's pills stop working, I will perform this spell for her. I don't care what it costs me. Until I rescue Tom, Gladys is all I've got. And I owe her.

'There's no reason to save me,' Gladys says, crashing in on my thoughts. 'My wellbeing is of no matter where the survival of the Fae is concerned.'

This does nothing to make me feel better. Does she not think she's worth saving? Or is this just the same fatalistic coldness I saw when she was dismissing Tom as a casualty of war?

'Why don't Fae value life the way humans do?'

'A lioness fights to the death to protect her pride because the pride's survival depends on it, no? But she will not extend a single claw to save any other lion. It is the law of nature.'

That seems screwed up to me. In my experience, whenever someone justifies something as part of the 'natural order', they're just excusing their own negligence.

'Isn't that the definition of evil?'

'Not at all,' Gladys assures me. 'Granted, nature is amoral, but that's not the same as evil.'

She pulls another hairpin out of her bun and waves it, conjuring a water fountain in front of the bookcase.

'Observe. Water. Is it good or bad?'

'Good, of course.'

'Ah, but water can be deadly. Tsunamis destroy whole villages and towns.'

At her words, the still water in the fountain rises into a

rolling wall, reaching to the top of the room. I instinctively raise my arms, anticipating its force as it comes washing down, but it breaks over us, then pools around the library. Water laps at my waist, chilling my legs and soaking my dress. The couches and books float around us.

'Floods wipe out crops and property. Water enables bacteria that transport disease, killing millions.' She waves the wand again and the water vanishes as quickly as it appeared, leaving no trace. I run my hand down my gown and find it bone dry. The books and furniture are returned to their rightful places, and Gladys is at my side as if the whole thing had been an illusion.

'The truth is that we project good and evil onto water. But water just is. It is not good nor evil – it is amoral.' Gladys watches me closely. 'You are Fae and that is our way. Neither good nor bad, but beyond both.'

I'm lost in thought for a moment. Amorality might work for water, but something still doesn't add up. What about intention and free will? Surely we're not all just blown by the wind, at the mercy of nature. And not all Fae are so heartless and indifferent. Tom cast a cataclysmic spell to save me when I was a child, but he didn't do it because the survival of the Fae was at stake. He wasn't motivated by saving the heir to the throne, because he didn't even know who I was. To him, I was just a kid trapped in a bad situation. Why would he do such a thing, if doing good wasn't in his nature?

I decide against pushing this further. I figure the less Gladys knows about Tom – and my debt to him – the better. Gladys knows me well enough to guess what I'll do, and I can't afford to have her try to stop me.

'Imposing moral values on that which is neutral makes humans weak,' Gladys continues. 'It makes them suffer guilt and shame, feelings that can only exist in a moral context. The Fae are spared this fate. In nature, there is no remorse. Everything is as it is.'

I bristle. I know what it's like to grow up in a household with no morality.

'So you think humans should just forget right and wrong and not care about who they hurt?'

'On the contrary.' She leans towards me and whispers as if she's about to impart a state secret. 'Human morality is core to our existence.'

I wait for further explanation.

'Fairies and unicorns would not exist if not for humans,' she says. 'The source of the Art is energy – energy created by human moral action. When humans act morally they release energetic vibrations. It is that energy that unicorns are able to channel through their horns, and fairies or unicorns in their two-legged form channel it through a metal called chromium.'

She turns her hairpin over in her palm. 'Hairpins, walking sticks, even phones. They all contain chromium and make useful instruments for channelling the Art.'

Now I get the Agency's precautions – all that wariness around my watch and shoes, even the teaspoon in the hospital. They must have been expecting me to use something containing chromium as a weapon.

Gladys raises her wand and a flame bursts from the top of it. Golden light dances across her face.

'The Art is nothing more than intense energetic vibrations, and human moral energy is the flint that starts our magical fires. No morality, no Art. It's as simple – or complex – as that.' She extinguishes the flame with her fingers and then settles back into the couch. 'But, as in all nature, everything has its opposite. Just as the Art is ignited by chromium, it is extinguished by graphite. This is why human prisons are now made of graphite. They're designed to hold humans and Fae alike.'

I think back to the cage Agent Eight imprisoned me in. She must have been sure it would hold me because it was made from graphite.

'But I produced enough magic to explode my way out of the Agency's cage,' I say.

'Unfortunate,' Gladys says, making a tutting sound. 'Necessary but unfortunate. If the Agency believe they cannot contain you, they will arrive at only one conclusion.'

'They'll want to kill me?' I say weakly.

Gladys purses her lips. 'No more questions,' she says. 'Now is the time to practise.' Nodding towards *The Book of Artifice*, she says, 'Gladys has taught you more than enough to be going on with.'

I go back to the book, finding a spell for dematerialising objects. I say the words out loud while focusing on making Gladys's teaspoon disappear.

Nothing.

The spoon just sits there on the saucer.

'Use your wand,' Gladys urges.

I try again.

Nothing. Not even a wobble.

'Articulate the words clearly,' she orders.

I try again. Nothing.

'Stand up straight. Relax your body. Clear your mind. Feel your power.'

But nothing happens. No matter how hard I clasp my wand or ready my muscles or will my thoughts, I get nothing.

Zilch. Diddly squat.

Gladys has me try to levitate the spoon instead. It's supposed to be easier. Basic, she claims.

No dice.

'Maybe I used up all my magic with the teacups,' I say, only half joking.

'Nonsense,' says Gladys. 'The Art cannot be used up. So long as there is human morality the Art can be channelled.'

I try again and again. The hours tick by, my limbs feel heavy and my head aches. The room has grown dark and I'm ravenously hungry. But the only thing I have managed to conjure is my frustration and Gladys's puzzlement.

'Perhaps food will help,' Gladys says optimistically as she conjures a plate of potato scones.

It doesn't.

Defeated, I slump onto the couch. 'Looks like you were wrong about my special powers.'

'It will come,' Gladys says with a confidence I don't share.

'What if you've all been backing the wrong horse all these years?' I say, unable to hide the edge of despair in my voice. 'Everyone wants something from me, and I keep falling down. I saw what we're up against – those creatures that attacked me in the V&A. What were they, anyway?'

'Pycts.' Registering my confusion, she adds, 'You probably know them as pixies.'

'Pixies? Aren't pixies supposed to be cute little creatures in kids' movies?'

Gladys shakes her head. 'Agency propaganda. Pycts are not the stuff of children's movies. Don't be fooled. They are dimwitted but deadly.' She leans forward, resting her hands in her lap. 'There are rumours that your uncle Damius is building an army to bolster the rebels, but we did not foresee that it would be an army of pycts. Pycts are extinct, you see. Well, they were.'

'A whole army?' I ask. I'd only seen four of them at the V&A.

'It is only a rumour.'

'Well, I'm no match for that.'

'Come,' she says, rising. 'There are some people you should meet.' She ushers me out of the library and back out into the corridor, stopping at the portraits. 'The royal line. Your forebears. All of them masters of the Art. All of them leaders.' She nods towards the paintings. 'You'll take your place in time.'

'Looks like the family business stops with me,' I say glumly.

'Stuff and nonsense,' Gladys chides.

'But I —'

'Enough buts,' she says impatiently, and I know I'm in for a session of tough love. 'You think you know something of sacrifice? Giving up before you even begin, eh?' She's off again, bustling down the corridor. She stops at a portrait about halfway along. 'Queen Signe, your great-great-great-great-grandmother.'

The woman in the painting has emerald eyes and long wavy blonde hair. I search for a family resemblance but find none.

'Before her reign, the humans and the Fae existed in an almost constant state of war. The humans were terrified of the Fae. And they were right to be. For a long time, the Fae would creep into cottages in the dead of night and steal human young. They were ripped from their cradles and brought back here to power the Art.'

'Changelings?'

'And much trickery and bad behaviour besides. Some of it aimless, much of it ruinous – to humans and Fae alike. Fairies were routinely rounded up and killed by the humans. And the Fae unleashed terrible plagues on the humans or seduced them to their deaths. A more pleasant way to go, but gone, nonetheless.

'Queen Signe broke the cycle of terror by forging a peace treaty with King James. The King allowed members of the Fae to take up permanent residence in Volgaris. They began channelling moral energy into Iridesca so there was no longer any need to relocate human children. And Queen Signe curbed the use of the Art in Volgaris. You might say that she clipped our magical wings in Volgaris by locking away the unbridled Art that we wield in Iridesca.'

'That's why magic is essentially free in Iridesca but when you conjure a spell in Volgaris you must pay a price,' I say, trying to keep up.

Gladys nods. 'Queen Signe confined the unbridled Art in a chalice devised by the King's alchemists – a chalice whose power could be unlocked only by a fairy possessed with moral sense. Impossible to break. As a gesture of goodwill, the chalice was located in Volgaris itself. King James's alchemists were satisfied that unbridled magic would be beyond reach in Volgaris for all eternity – humans can't unlock the chalice because they are not fairies, and fairies can't unlock it because they are not moral. Quite an elegant solution, you'll agree.'

Gladys's eyes are downcast. She looks like she is recalling the events of the Treaty like they happened only yesterday. If I didn't know better, I'd have thought she was there.

'A high price our queen paid for her troubles, too. Many Fae – even her closest kin – would never again trust her. She was charged with all kinds of nonsense: perverting the natural order; imposing limits where none should be. She went into self-imposed exile and suffered an untimely death.'

Gladys looks at me, making sure I'm paying attention. 'Queen Signe brought a peace that has lasted these past 400 years, but she was destroyed by it.'

Okay. Point taken. I'm chastened and humbled by Gladys's words.

'If you are to become a leader,' she goes on, her eyes boring into me, 'first you will need to master something far more powerful than the Art. You must master yourself.' Her voice softens. 'For 400 years, the Art in Volgaris has been contained and peace between humans and Fae has prevailed. Your birth has put that at risk. Your mother's fairy blood mixed with your father's human morality means you, and only you, are a moral fairy. You alone, possess the power to unlock the unbridled Art in Volgaris.'

'No way,' I say. 'How can I be the only moral fairy? Surely my parents aren't the only fairy and human to get it on in 400 years.'

'They are the only ones to have produced a fairy. All the other recorded unions produced unnatural abominations. Which is why inter-realm procreation is strictly forbidden. But what is done is done,' Gladys says dismissively. 'For some Fae – dissenters of the Treaty, for the most part – you are vindication that the natural order will right itself. Limiting power, so it is said, would never last. Just as water wears at stone for aeons to create a great estuary, so nature will find a way to overcome the restrictions placed on the Art.

'And there may be some truth in that,' she sighs. 'Your birth not only threatens the Treaty, it is also perilous to the very survival of our realms. Whoever unlocks the chalice will decide how the unbridled power is channelled. Will it be returned to nature as it once was, or will the power fuel heinous ambition? Along one path lies the continuation of the peace your forebear forged. Along the other path lies

166

unending violence, pain and the destruction of our worlds if the unbridled Art is released into the hands of someone who will misuse it.'

She looks me squarely in the face, appraising me. 'You, and you alone, have the power to decide along which path we shall travel. All of us. Fae and humans alike.'

She turns and continues up the passage a short way as questions swarm around my head.

'The chalice of unbridled magic,' I say, as the pieces of my life's puzzle start to slot into place. 'It's the Luck of Edenhall.'

Gladys gives a single nod and continues down the stairs. I linger a moment at the painting of Queen Signe, thinking back to Marshall and the story about his family I heard from the tour guide at the V&A. How much does he know about the chalice and its provenance? He sure was sensitive about the topic. Does the Luck of Edenhall mean more to him than injured family pride and a lost fortune?

I hurry after Gladys, but stop as a realisation almost crumples me to the floor. The key to the Luck of Edenhall is my one bargaining chip. It's Tom's and my Get Out of Jail Free Card – literally. But, assuming I can find the key, how can I just hand it over to Agent Eight now that I know what it will unlock? I assume she'll lock the key away in some dusty government vault for safe-keeping. But what if it ends up in the wrong hands? Nobody should be trusted with that amount of power. The only safe place for the key is where it currently is: lost.

But how can I *not* trade the key for Tom's freedom?

Tom sacrificed so much to save me; surely I owe it to him to do anything and everything in my power to do the same.

I'm breathless when I catch up to Gladys. She leads me out of the grand old castle and into the gardens. If she senses my distress, she doesn't show it. We walk in silence past a dozen unicorns trotting in formation around the grounds. I try not to gawk, but I can't keep my eyes off them, especially Loxley, who stares straight at me. I feel like he's challenging me, but to what? A race? A fight? The throne itself?

Jules's warning about the Protectorate unicorns echoes in my ears. My feeling of foreboding intensifies as I wonder if everyone is happy about living under a matriarchy. All the rulers in the hall of portraits are women.

'Why, in all those centuries, have there never been any kings?' I ask Gladys.

'Female genes are dominant so our queens produce more daughters than sons,' Gladys explains. Then, lowering her voice as if she doesn't want the unicorns to hear, she says, 'Which is fortunate, because men do not do well in positions of power. A male heir is a last resort. We have not had violence in the Royal House for generations. And for the first time in recorded history we have a man vying for the throne. And how does he plan to do it?' She curls her lip as if she has a bad taste in her mouth. 'By shedding blood.'

She walks on, seemingly oblivious as to whose blood Damius is trying to shed.

We pass the fountain and walk along the path away

from the castle. The huge trees grow thicker, their interweaving branches denser, and the garden grows darker and colder. Overhead, the sky has turned to a slate grey, threatening rain.

We reach a ramp constructed from moss-covered stones, rising steadily up a hill. At the end of the elevated ramp stands an archway fashioned from rows of trees, their tops thatched together to form an alcove. It's dark and noticeably colder in here, the thatched trees blocking the light. Through the alcove sits a stone building with a high arched roof, mirroring the thatched trees. It's covered in thick moss and ivy, but gives the impression of being ancient and solid. It's so deeply nestled into the trees that from a distance you wouldn't know it was here.

'What is this place?'

'The Temple,' says Gladys without further elaboration.

'I didn't know Fae were religious. Seems odd if you're all amoral.'

'We worship the laws of nature and the universe that provides,' Gladys replies, weaving her way through the trees towards the building's door. 'The Temple is a sacred place where we go for spiritual reflection. And practice. The magical energy from the hundreds of thousands of spells that have been conjured in here over centuries should awaken the Art in you. It's the perfect place to practise using your instrument.'

Gladys flicks her wand and the thick wooden doors creak open. I shiver as I adjust to the unexpected warmth inside.

Inside, the building's arched windows are a dark red colour, making it impossible to see outside. What little light penetrates through the trees outside reflects off hundreds, possibly thousands, of red stones lining the walls. I take a closer look – I swear they are rubies. Each one of them contributes to the blood-red gloom that chokes the space.

Bench seats line both sides of the Temple, making it appear like a gothic church. An altar sits up the front, covered in more rubies arranged in celestial patterns. Between the altar and the bench seats is a circle about a metre in diameter, marked out on the floor in yet more rubies.

My skin prickles with a sense of danger. Before I can work out why, a flash of golden fire shoots out from behind the jewelled altar at the front of the Temple, directed straight at me.

chapter 17

Gladys is in front of me in an instant, blocking the energy and redirecting it to a window.

I drop to the ground as another flash flies towards me. Gladys again deflects the flaming gold; it hits the ruby-studded wall and is absorbed with a crackle and a singe. She lowers her wand and makes a 'tut-tutting' noise, the kind you'd make to bickering children.

'Show yourself,' Gladys orders.

I lower my hands from my face and see ... Abby. The apothecary. She's changed her dress. This one is covered in so many rose petals it looks as though Valentine's Day threw up on her. The playfulness of her dress is at odds with the sneer on her pretty face.

'That's enough mischief, my dear,' Gladys says. To my amazement there's the hint of a grin at the corner of her mouth.

'Mischief!' I protest, standing up. 'She just tried to kill me!'

Gladys fixes her wand back into her bun. 'If she'd been

trying, dear, you'd be dead. Since you're here, Abby, you can stay to help.'

'Help her? Again? Never!' Abby says, her words dripping acid. Her delicate features contort so much that her ice blue eyes look cross-eyed. I can't decide if she's furious or completely unhinged – or both.

Gladys raises her eyebrows at Ms Psycho-Walking-Floral-Arrangement. 'What specifically are your accusations against Princess Francesca?'

My attacker points her trembling finger at me. Despite her girly appearance she looks utterly terrifying. 'She ruined my brother's life. Twice.'

My jaw drops and my legs go weak. She's Tom's sister.

'Twice?' Gladys whirls to me, her eyebrows arched questioningly. I realise that, despite her air of omnipotence, she doesn't really know anything about my life that happened outside of her laundromat. She clearly doesn't know that Tom cast a cataclysmic spell to save me. Or that he had to go into hiding after it.

I cross my arms defiantly. She has no right to demand full disclosure when she has withheld so much from me for so long. Besides, if Gladys had helped me all those years ago, Tom wouldn't have had to perform that spell, and we wouldn't be having this conversation.

An unwelcome thought resurfaces: if Gladys was my protector, why didn't she *protect* me?

I close my eyes and push the thoughts back down. I can't go there. When I open my eyes again, Gladys is still staring at me but her expression has changed. It's a look I've never seen on her face in all the years I've known her. It's not probing or angry or concerned. It's just, well, blank.

Abby walks around to the front of the altar and pulls herself up onto it. 'I'll stay for the show, but I'm not helping. I've already done more for her than she deserves,' she says, looking pointedly at my perfectly healed legs.

Gladys directs me to stand in the centre of the ring made out of rubies laid into the floor. 'Rubies contain chromium,' she explains, 'so the Fae consider them to be sacred and spiritual.'

I rub my hand over the amulet dangling from my neck. I guess that explains why it's a ruby.

Gladys demonstrates by shooting little sparks out of the tip of her wand. She tells me it's the magical equivalent of practising scales on the piano and it's supposed to be simple.

Except it's not. Not for me, anyway. I faithfully follow her instructions, visualising the moral energy channelling through the air, into my core, and then up through my torso and arm and out through the wand. But the wand is unresponsive, just like in the library. Nothing happens.

'She must take after her father,' Abby says to Gladys as if I'm not there. And then to me, she says, 'What a disappointment you turned out to be.'

Gladys ignores her. 'Open your mind, child, welcome the energy into your body and then expel it out through your wand.'

I try. I strain, I grunt and I sweat from the effort. I try to work out what I did – how I felt – locked in the cage at the Agency.

I'm about to throw the wand on the ground in frustration, when there's a slight tingling feeling at the tips of my fingers. Looking down, I think I see a glimmer of blue light radiating from my hands. But then it disappears and the tingling fades.

Laughter erupts from the altar. 'There's so much magical residue in these walls that a lobotomised frog could activate a channelling instrument if it tried hard enough.'

Gladys makes no attempt to silence Abby. In fact, her eyes twinkle with amusement.

'The only thing regal and powerful about her is the amulet dangling from her neck,' Abby continues.

Irritation kindles in my gut as I watch them share a joke at my expense. Isn't Gladys supposed to be on my side? Heat rushes through my veins. My hands grow so hot and stiff that the wand tumbles from my grasp and clatters onto the floor.

Before I can stop it, a searing bolt of blue surges from the ends of my fingers.

Abby shrieks and dives to the floor.

She's too slow. The stream of fire connects with her skirt. I scream as flames race up Abby's dress, filling the temple in thick smoke.

The fire is extinguished just as quickly. I turn to see Gladys standing calmly, hairpin in hand. With a slight swish of her wand, Abby's dress is completely restored. Her sense of humour is going to take longer to recover.

'She just tried to kill me!' Abby shrieks, looking even more furious than she did when we first came into the Temple.

Now it's Gladys's turn to laugh. 'If she had, dear, you would be dead.'

Touché.

'In all my years,' Gladys murmurs, taking me over to a bench seat. 'To channel flames without an instrument ...' She stares at me in awe and wonder.

I'm barely listening as I sit down next to her. It feels like I just had a massive static electric shock, only a hundred times more intense. I inspect my hands, expecting to see burns and blisters. But despite the heat and the pain, the skin is unbroken. Aside from a residual tingling, there's nothing wrong at all.

'Even I could not imagine you would have such extraordinary power,' Gladys continues.

I don't share her excitement.

'But, but, I don't even know how I did it,' I say, my voice trembling. 'I really could have killed her.' And the worst bit is that I don't know how *not* to do it again.

'You are still fearful of your power so your body tries to suppress it. It only surfaces when the anger wells up inside you and you lose control. Embrace your power and you will control it, just as a rider guides her steed.'

I watch my wand rise from the floor at Gladys's command, float over to me and settle in my palm.

'And you must learn to hold on to your wand,' Gladys says.

We're interrupted by the sound of someone clearing his throat. I turn towards the entrance of the Temple to see the Chancellor, looking as pompous as I remember. He lowers his head and does some sweeping gesture with his arm that looks like an elephant's trunk, but which I suppose is a bow.

'Your Highness, forgive the intrusion, but I wanted to share my great pleasure at seeing you in Iridesca again.' He shuffles towards us, beaming a warm smile. 'By the authority of the Order of the Fae, I have set in train preparations for your big day.'

I lift an eyebrow. 'Big day?'

'Why, your coronation, of course,' he says, a self-satisfied smile crossing his face. 'Surely you did not expect to take the throne without proper ceremony?'

'No,' I say, trying to play it cool. I've been so focused on learning enough of the Art to rescue Tom that I'd almost forgotten about the whole crown thing. 'It's just so soon.'

'Ah, the luxury of time,' he says, as if recalling some fond memory. 'Regrettably, it is one we do not have. The date is set for the next full moon. Nine days hence.'

I look at Gladys in horror. How could she have forgotten to mention that I'm supposed to be a queen and ruler in just over a week?

'I can barely manage my own life, let alone lead an entire realm,' I whisper to Gladys.

But the Chancellor hears. 'Technically it's three realms, Your Highness. The Fae in Volgaris and Transcendence are your subjects as much as those here in Iridesca.'

'We really need to talk about this,' I say through gritted teeth.

'I fear that will have to wait, Princess,' says the Chancellor, turning to Gladys. 'I must claim the Luminaress for urgent business. The Order of the Fae has convened a crisis meeting to discuss reports of' – he looks at me and then Abby, choosing his words – 'recent mobilisations.'

Gladys stands to leave and I go to accompany her. If I'm supposed to be Queen, I'd better start learning about Fae politics.

The Chancellor wags a jewelled finger at me. 'Until you have sworn your oath at your coronation, you are not permitted to enter the Circle of the Order.'

'Keep practising with your wand until I return,' Gladys instructs. She steps through the door of the Temple and then turns back to Abby, who has been observing us silently from the altar.

'I know your mind, my dear, and I counsel you to let it go. Persuading anyone to save your brother will be a long and fruitless task.'

It's a good thing I'm already standing because Abby runs towards the bench seats and kicks the first one in the row. Her kick is so forceful that the seat flies forward and smashes into the seat in front, creating a domino effect of crashing pews. When the last seat in the Temple has collapsed, Abby falls to the ground. She cradles her foot in her lap and tears stream down her face.

She looks utterly exhausted. Defeated. My heart breaks for her and I don't care anymore that she was horrible to me or that she may or may not have tried to kill me. I understand her devastation. I would cry too if I thought I would never see Tom again.

I keep a safe distance in case she wants to do to me what

she did to the chairs. And I wait until the torrent of tears slows to a trickle and then dries up. It kills me to know that I'm responsible for her distress. I want to say something to comfort her but I can't find the right words.

'I'm going after him,' I say eventually.

Abby looks up at me. 'What?'

'That's the only reason I'm here, trying to learn to use this stupid thing.' I nod at the wand. 'As soon as I've learned enough, I'm going back for Tom.'

She stares at me, incredulous. 'You think it'll be that easy, do you? And you think the Order will let you?'

'I'll find a way.'

'You're not what I expected,' Abby says, smoothing out the folds of her gown.

'What did you expect?' I say, wishing I didn't suddenly feel so self-conscious.

She shrugs. 'I thought you'd be more like a fairy.' She flicks her wand again and a photo appears in her hand. It's in a ceramic photo frame in the shape of a dragonfly. 'This was taken the day Tom went into hiding in Iridesca. I didn't see him for two years after that, until I was able to move here to join the Apothecary Guild.'

I stare down at the photo of a gangly boy trying to look braver than he feels. He has his arm flung over Abby's shoulders. I begin to realise just how much Tom gave up for me.

'How old are you in this photo?'

'We were thirteen.'

We? It's a sucker punch to the gut. I broke up a pair of

twins. The last remaining resentment I've been feeling towards Abby evaporates. No wonder she wanted me dead.

Abby sighs as she clasps the photo. A tattoo of a passionfruit vine winds around her fingers.

'I know it's not really your fault,' she says.

My eyes mist over. I would give anything for those words to be true. If I hadn't asked Tom for help, he would not have lost years of his childhood and Abby would still have her brother.

'One thing I know about my brother is that he's his own person,' Abby says, her pride dressed up as exasperation. 'He makes his own decisions.'

'Why did he do that spell for me?'

'My family's wondered that for years. He didn't tell us you were Princess Francesca.'

'He didn't know. I didn't know.'

She taps her wand on the photo frame and it vanishes. 'Tom didn't explain his reasons. Never has. Probably never will. But as far as I can tell, he's never regretted it.'

I wish I could believe her, but the look on Tom's face after he saw the news report tells a different story. He was so angry with me he couldn't even make eye contact. I guess even he has his limits, and being wanted for murder all over again and having his face splashed across every TV and newspaper in the country is a bridge too far.

We sit in silence for a minute. I suspect we're both thinking about Tom. He needs me. He needs me to get better at the Art so I can save him.

'How did you learn to use a wand?' I ask Abby.

She scrunches up her nose, looking slightly puzzled. 'I don't remember. It just happened.'

'Is that the way it is for all fairies?'

Abby nods and looks at me like I'm a loser.

'Why won't it just happen for me, then? And where are my wings? Aren't fairies supposed to have wings?'

'You have wings. Didn't you use them when you escaped the Agency? Everybody's talking about it.'

'I did. But that was the first and last time. They've disappeared and haven't come back.'

'Well, you have to want to fly,' she says, amused. 'They'll only appear when you want to get somewhere. It's like walking. You don't consciously think about walking, do you? And your legs and feet aren't constantly moving, are they? You want to go somewhere, you just walk. It's the same with wings – except they're tucked away until you need them.'

I reach around to touch the centre of my back, but feel nothing. I'm not convinced by Abby's explanation. I mean, I can at least see my legs when I'm not walking.

Before I can voice any of my doubts, Abby is up on her feet. With a mischievous look in her eye, she grabs my hand.

'Let's go.'

My vision blurs momentarily, then refocuses and the Temple is gone.

chapter 18

Razor-sharp pellets of icy rain buffet us.

The wind is so strong I'm sure the next gust will sweep us away.

I look up at three enormous spikes fashioned from thick glass soaring to the sky, the kind that has a greenish hue.

The Shard.

We're at the top of London's – and Trinovantum's – tallest building. Without a safety harness. I take a step backwards, putting as much distance as possible between me and the precipice.

The city stretches out 300 metres below us. It's the London I know, only this version looks like it's been rebuilt with medieval technology and has a serious weed and flower problem. From where we stand, I can see the extent of the damage from the fighting. The V&A and Albert Hall weren't the only casualties; St Paul's dome has been reduced to a crown of thorns. The familiar shape of the Gherkin remains, but it's a skeleton. The glass has gone. One of the towers of Tower Bridge lies in the Thames, as if a child has kicked half a sandcastle version over and hasn't finished the job. The bridge itself is a tangled mess of cables, wood and steel. The clock face of Big Ben is an empty, blackened socket, while the brickwork of the tower is pockmarked by gashes and what looks like the carbon residue of fire. The walls of the houses of parliament are mostly intact, but even from up here, it's clear they're ruined, wrecked shells. Overgrown flowers with stems as thick as tree trunks push their way through the roof.

Not a single building appears to have escaped some kind of damage.

The streets look deserted, but you get the feeling there's life – just not out in the open.

Looking across the horizon, long columns of smoke climb into the air. My guess is that they're cooking fires; people trying to eke out an existence amidst the carnage. At least, I hope they're cooking fires and not smoking ruins of recent battles – or worse, funeral pyres.

Abby appears unmoved by the scene of desolation below. I'm not sure if it's because she's seen all of this before and it's old news, or if it's the same fairy indifference to the wellbeing of others that I've seen in Gladys.

'Why did you bring me here?' I shout at Abby. I'm struggling to even hear myself over the howling wind.

'You wanted to fly, didn't you?' she says, stepping perilously close to the edge. She gives me a smile that reminds me of Tom.

Is that a smile of friendship? Or deceit? Something more sinister?

Is she daring me to jump, knowing full well I'll never survive?

'I don't know how,' I say.

Abby moves closer to me. 'Like I said, your wings will appear when you need to fly.'

Jules's words of warning ring in my head. I need to be careful. Not everyone is happy with my return to Iridesca. I have no idea where Abby stands. Is this payback for what I've done to her brother? A ploy to get me out of the way? I want to use my wings again so desperately, but couldn't we start with a low branch on one of the enormous trees that litter the ruined cityscape below? My wings stopped me from hurtling to my death when I escaped from the Agency but that wasn't exactly flying. At best, it was a controlled crash.

Abby stretches out her arm, motioning for me to take her hand again. Still smiling that same mischievous smile, she tells me to stop worrying.

Unsure how else I'm going to get down from here, I take her proffered hand. It's warm and her grip is strong. She pulls me with a force that I don't expect. I let out a gasp, and we're running – running towards the edge of the building.

As we reach the edge, a gust of wind forces our hands apart, but it's too late to stop.

We jump.

Or rather, Abby jumps and I am pulled along after her. For a split second the momentum of our leap keeps me suspended in mid-air alongside Abby. Her two enormous wings flutter out behind her like a butterfly's, reflecting the dusk light of the sky. From the enormous smile on her face to the tips of her pointed toes, she looks euphoric. In this moment, she looks so much like Tom.

My wings. Where are my wings?

And then it hits me.

I'm going to die.

I'm flailing, falling, plummeting.

My heart's pounding and the rushing air forces my screams of terror back down my throat. Tears stream from my eyes, instantly dried by the air. My dress is billowing up around my face and I'm hurtling towards the deadly stones below.

I claw at the air, trying to find something to hold on to.

Abby zooms towards me, her wings folded close to her body. Her mouth is wide with shrieks that I can't hear. Is she trying to save me? Or finish me off? Whatever her intent, she's too far away; she won't reach me in time. I twist my body in panic and my mind empties of everything but one single thought.

Tom.

And then, finally, there's an itch between my shoulder blades. I recognise the feeling instantly. The itching turns to burning, but it's happening too slowly.

Enormous poppies on tall stems rush past me as I hurtle towards the ground. Reaching, I snatch at the flower stems with both hands. I miss and lunge again. This time I clutch one, my hands tightening around the thick neck of the flower. The stem is wet and cool and soft. Tendrils sink into my skin, helping me get a grip, but I'm not slowing quickly enough and my hip and knee slam into the glass of the building, the force catapulting me outwards as the poppy stem bends under my weight.

But it holds.

I swing in the breeze, clinging tight, dangling just too far off the ground to jump.

Abby reaches me just as my wings burst out of the back of my dress. I look back at them as they unfurl, just as wondrous as the last time. But there's no peace or joy like before. Just an overwhelming sense of inadequacy.

My wings failed me. If I hadn't grabbed the poppy to break my fall, I'd be dead.

'Ohmygod, ohmygod, ohmygod,' Abby says again and again. 'Are you alright?'

I can't tell if she's sorry that I almost died or sorry that I didn't.

I release my vice-like hold on the poppy and flutter down to the ground. My hands are red raw from the friction. The rain is harder now and my wings droop with the soggy weight before folding back into my body and disappearing.

Abby watches me warily for a moment.

'You —' I begin, but Abby peers around, sniffing the air like a dog. 'What?'

She grabs my arm and yanks me, running towards an alley. Any trace of concern or guilt about almost pulling me to my death has vanished.

'What are you —?'

Abby lifts a finger to her mouth, signalling for me to hush. She stops abruptly as she nears the alley. I slam into her. Her eyes narrow slightly as she strains to listen. I hear nothing, except for the rain and a far-off crack of thunder.

Then I hear it: a rumbling of drums. No, not drums. Marching. Hundreds, even thousands, of feet, stepping forcefully and precisely in time.

We creep into the alley and peer around the corner, back into the street. In the distance, row after row of bodies in tight formation stretch along the street as far as I can see. The same creatures that Jules saved me from at the V&A.

'Pycts,' I whisper, trying not to gag from the putrid smell that wafts around us.

'P-p-pycts?' Abby whispers back, her voice breaking. 'But they're extinct.'

'Evidently not.' I can't take my eyes off them. An entire army of walking carcasses. Spear-like wands swing in unison, clasped within bony hands with over-long fingers and talons at their ends. My stomach clenches as I remember how it felt to be touched by them.

'I guess Damius's army is no longer just rumour,' I say, wondering what Gladys will make of this.

I draw breath as the front of the parade gets closer. We back into a tiny alcove. Abby pushes her hand against my body, squishing me into the doorway. I try not to breathe in the fresh waves of stench assaulting me as the rows start to move past.

A moment later, there's silence.

The marching has stopped. The army has come to a halt

in the road, just metres from us. They're standing in neat lines, poised, waiting.

I press myself further back into the alcove, keeping an eye on the pycts, willing them to leave. My heart is beating so loud I'm certain it will give us away.

'We need to get back to Windsor,' Abby whispers.

She reaches down to her boot for her wand. Her brow furrows.

'Well, what are you waiting for?' I whisper, panic rising in my voice. 'Transfer us back.'

'I can't.'

'What?'

'My wand. It's gone. It must have fallen out when I was diving to save you.'

She says this as if it's all my fault. As if I'm responsible for falling off a tower that she pulled me off and for losing her wand.

One of the decaying soldiers lifts his chin and sniffs the air, his snub nose crinkling up like a pig foraging for truffles. He stretches his neck to the side and looks in our direction, scanning the walls with his rat eyes.

Abby hunches her shoulders, trying to make herself smaller.

A second soldier starts sniffing the air. How they've managed to detect our scent over their own foul smell is beyond me. More and more of them scan the alley, their little red eyes peering towards us, their pointed ears twitching.

The first creature breaks formation, snarling as he takes a step towards the alley.

'Any time you want to transfer us back, Princess,' Abby whispers.

'Me?'

'If you can escape from an Agency cage, transferring back to the palace should be a cinch.'

'But I have no idea how I did it,' I gulp.

Abby lets out an irritated sigh. 'Well, give me your wand and I'll do it,' she says, holding out her hand.

'I … I left it at the Temple.'

More pycts leave their marching lines and slowly fan out into the alley, sniffing the air and the ground and peering into windows. It's only a matter of time before they're upon us.

I turn back to Abby in a panic. 'What are you going to do?'

She raises an eyebrow. 'So it's my job to save you, is it?'

Gladys's words come rushing back. *Once you find the courage to accept that you're the one you've been waiting for, you will find your power.* The snappy little slogan is all well and good in theory, but it's not much use to me now. And it wasn't much use to me when I was hurtling towards the ground with no wings.

'According to the legends, their magic is supposed to be weak,' Abby whispers. 'It's like they cast mud instead of spells, but there are too many of them to fight. I need to find something I can use as a wand.'

We look around the alcove but there's nothing. Just stone and wood. From what we can see of the lane, there's no chromium anywhere.

'The station. We can find something in the station,' says Abby. She slips into the lane, ordering me to follow her and to stay calm. 'If they smell your fear, they will attack. Don't look back,' she murmurs, walking quickly but casually in the direction of London Bridge train station.

This feels like a bad idea but I follow anyway. I'm not about to stay here by myself. In my mind I chant, *Show no fear, show no fear, show no fear.*

I get about four steps before giving in to the urge to look at the snarling creatures behind us. Incredibly, none of them has moved. They're all looking intently in our direction, watching us like a pack of dogs, their heads cocked. The front pycts look to one another uncertainly, as if waiting for some kind of explanation.

I look back around and continue behind Abby.

Show no fear, show no fear, show no fear.

For a moment, I allow myself the luxury of believing that, incredibly, impossibly, we're pulling this off. Abby's strategy of nonchalantly walking out into the open as if they pose no threat to us has thrown them. It's crazy brave, but we seem to have landed on the right side of brave.

As we reach the entrance to the London Bridge train station I let out a breath and take one last look over my shoulder at these creatures.

My eyes lock with those of a pyct wearing tatty overalls. His nostrils flair and his mouth opens into a snarl, revealing sharp, yellowed teeth. I momentarily forget my show-no-fear mantra and let out a full-on, freaked-out scream.

The pyct's snarls rise into a shrill shriek, echoing around the city.

'Run!' Abby yells, and she bolts.

I need no encouragement, sprinting after her. I hear a thunderous beating on the cobblestones as the herd rushes towards us. We take the steps by threes and fours down into the train station, more sliding than running. They're behind us, closing in fast. While most of them are about our size, they're faster and look stronger. Not to mention that they outnumber us many times over.

We reach the bottom of the stairs. Through the gloom I make out the familiar signs of dilapidation that have taken over the rest of Trinovantum. Smashed tiles and broken glass litter the floor.

'Chromium. We need something with chrome plating,' Abby says between heaving breaths. 'Railings. Door handles. Beams. Tools. Anything you can find that might contain chromium.'

I spin around, wildly scanning for anything that looks like metal. Some of the doors have been removed and lie smashed and broken on the floor, their handles removed, leaving scarred sockets. All that remains of the stair railings are jagged holes in the walls. Evidently, we're not the only ones who have been to the station scavenging for chromium.

There are people down here; children, dirty and desperate and wearing rags. They bundle up their scant belongings and run ahead, jumping off the platform and disappearing into boltholes. Doors for maintenance tunnels slam shut. *Where are their parents?* I find myself wondering.

If we manage to get out of this alive, there is so much I need to learn about my new home.

Abby turns sharply and sprints down the corridor. I follow her. The wall tiles are a blur. My chest heaves, my lungs burning with the exertion. But the galloping echo behind us spurs me on. The whole place is quaking, like the roof and tunnel could collapse on us at any moment.

We reach the end of the first platform and stop.

A dead end.

The pycts stream onto the platform, their rumbling feet echoing in the confined space. Some topple onto the tracks, pushed by the oncoming mass of decomposing flesh. Undeterred, they simply get up and keep running towards us.

I'm struck with feelings of awe and horror, all at once. And then I'm struck by a flying object, right on the collarbone. I look down and see a brown muddy patch on the neckline of my dress. It hurts enough to leave a bruise but it's not going to kill me. *That's it?* I think. This isn't a fight, this is paintball.

Then another clump of mud flies from the wand of a pyct and hits me in the side of the head, followed by one on my neck, knocking me to the ground.

'Get up or you'll be buried alive!' Abby yells.

I look up and see that her rose-garden dress is starting to look like a muddy compost heap.

'Any time you want to jump in, Princess, feel free,'

'What do I do?' I stagger back onto my feet while blocking more mud pies with my arms.

Abby turns to face more pycts who've jumped onto the tracks and are leaping and bounding towards us like wild dogs. They bound off the curved tiled walls of the tunnel, sending a wave of mud crashing down on our heads.

'Do what you did at the Temple! Channel your energy!'

'I don't know how I did it!' I scream. 'I have no control over my magic.'

'Well, about now would be a good time to get some control.'

The pycts are closing in. Their stench mixes with the hot air of the subterranean station.

We move back against the far wall and I realise we're fast running out of platform. I raise my arms in front of me, trying to harness my magical energy, but nothing happens.

Nothing. Not even the faintest tingle.

I lift my hands again and beckon the Art. Did I just feel a tingle? I can't be sure, but there was something.

'Abby?'

'A little busy right now,' she says. Sweat is pouring off her as she ducks and dodges incoming pixie blasts. 'How's that control coming, Princess?'

'*Abby!*' I scream. 'Behind you!'

Abby turns her head and catches a glimpse of more vile creatures advancing towards us. The pycts pound us with muddy blasts from all sides, knocking us to the ground. The stinking mud piles around us, then begins to cover us. Darkness surrounds me; the air is thick and stale. I turn to see Abby raise her head. She's seen something. A way out? She kicks desperately at the mounting mud, her feet skidding against the floor before she pushes her way forward. She scrambles free and crawls towards a doorway, towards the pycts, who seem oblivious to her. Their sole focus appears to be burying me alive in a muddy grave.

Abby reaches the doorway and reaches out to touch the hinge hanging from the door. She turns back and smiles at me.

'Time to find out what you're made of, Princess.' She mutters the transfer spell and is gone.

Just like that. She abandoned me.

And, worse, she used me as a distraction. The pycts didn't stop her from reaching the chromium hinge because they were too busy pummelling me.

Another pyct blast crashes down on me, blocking off my air, and I realise that outrage and self-pity are not going to help me get out of here alive.

The weight of the mud mound squashes my lungs and is gooey and sticky on my eyelashes. I try the Art again, and this time something clicks. The briefest connection between my intent and the tingling at the tips of my fingers.

I try again, and feel the tingle again, stronger this time. The power rises within me, but it feels different. Every other time it's felt like a bolt of lightning – powerful but momentary, far beyond my control and over so quickly that I have no idea what happened. This time, it builds and builds, coursing through me, awaiting my direction.

My senses go into overdrive as I lever myself to my feet and burst up and out of the muddy mound. I am everywhere. I see and hear everything with a kind of acute, crystalline clarity. For a few seconds, I remain in a fugue-like state of wonderment at my own powers. Timeless. Still. Surveying all that is before me.

And then a group of pycts jumps at me, and with what I can only describe as calm detachment, I unleash the full force of my power.

Reality folds in on itself and a pulse bursts around me, followed by a flash of blue light. In my state of heightened awareness, I experience everything at once, the whole scene in high definition and from every conceivable angle. Their shrieks and screams reach a shrill crescendo and then abruptly terminate.

Every single pyct explodes in a cloud of ash that drops unceremoniously to the floor.

Quiet settles around me; the only sound is the humming of air through the tunnel.

I'm hot. Too hot. I'm burning from the inside out. I let out a gasp, exhaustion mixed with terror.

I feel myself swaying, my vision blurring and my legs crumpling beneath me.

The last thing I hear before I hit the floor is the sound of galloping hooves.

chapter 19

I'm alone.

Moonlight floods the room, casting shadows in an eerie stillness.

Somewhere in the distance a clock chimes, but I'm not listening closely enough to count the strokes.

I'm in the palace. I don't know how I know, and I don't remember getting here. But I know that I'm in the palace, in my room. And I'm clean. Someone has washed the mud off me and changed me into my night gown.

Something has happened to me. I feel different. I am different. Power courses through me, an acute awareness. Unbidden, memories from the previous night fill my mind.

Magic. My magic. I controlled the Art. Without a wand.

I can still feel it: a power and sureness I've never had before. Something snapped and something came back together, forged stronger than before. For the first time in my life, I feel whole. The Art is no longer a series of songs in an ancient book. It's living and breathing in me. Now I understand what Gladys was getting at: the Art is *will* – magnified, amplified, intensified.

My will.

I *am* the one I've been waiting for.

My door creaks open, and Jules pokes her head around. She opens it wide. Brina and Callie stand behind her.

'It is pleasing to see that you are awake, Your Highness,' Jules says, and it's clear that she really means it. 'Inform the Luminaress,' she orders Brina, who promptly scuttles away.

A memory of the pycts falling to the floor as dust flashes through my mind.

'I killed them.'

'Your Highness?' Jules says, stepping into my bed chamber.

'The pycts.'

'They'd have thought nothing of killing you,' she says, sounding like a seasoned battle commander.

'But … but … they're dead. All dead,' I say.

'There was only one path for you to travel. You acted as you must; you are our hope, our future. You were barely alive when Wynstar found you on that train platform.'

'Wynstar?' Wasn't he the one Jules told me to be wary of when I first arrived?

'Second Officer Wynstar of the Protectorate,' she says, before adding, 'It was a surprise to us too, Your Highness – a welcome one, of course.'

Brina returns and clears her throat. 'The Luminaress has asked that you join her in the garden as soon as you're ready.'

Good, I think, springing out of bed. I've learned how to wield the Art just as Gladys asked, so now she can help me rescue Tom. Or I'll do it without her.

I walk over to the wardrobe and Brina and Callie follow me across the room expectantly. They want to dress me but I don't have time for all their fussing right now. I've got rescue plans to make.

'Don't you have somewhere else to be?' I try to say it casually, but it comes out more sharply than I mean it to.

Both look uncertain. Callie looks like she's about to burst into tears. Jules stiffens and is suddenly intensely interested in nothing in particular on the floor. I've broken protocol. Again.

I look at the two women standing there in their perfect white gowns – two girls, actually. They could even be younger than me. They're just trying to do their jobs, just trying to help me. And I'm being a stuck-up princess. Literally.

'You may go,' Brina says to Callie with a hint of protectiveness, presumably giving her an opportunity to compose herself.

'No,' I say, feeling like the worst person in the world. I've made no attempt to get to know anything about these two girls who feed me, dress me and respond to pretty much any request. Yes, I'm eager to rescue Tom, but what sort of person am I if I can't spare five minutes to show some respect and kindness?

'Do you want to sit?' I say, walking over to my window seat.

'On there?' Brina looks like I've just asked her to club a baby seal.

'Why not?' I say.

She perches on the edge of the seat, back straight, lips pursed. Callie is more relaxed, shuffling back towards the window and then crossing her legs. I sit on the matching velvet footstool. Jules remains standing between my bed and the door.

'I'm sorry about before,' I say sheepishly. 'And before that. And before that. I don't have a good excuse for my behaviour and I'm not going to insult you by coming up with a bad one.'

Neither maid speaks but I notice Brina's posture relax ever so slightly.

It occurs to be that I'm the only one who's going to break the silence. I really wish I weren't so socially awkward. I rack my brain, thinking of something, anything, to say.

Eventually I come up with 'Where do you live?'

Callie's eyes redden as if she's about to cry again. I silently swear at myself. Clearly I'm making things worse.

'The palace,' she says hesitantly.

'But your family? Do you have a home outside Windsor Castle?' I push. 'Where do you go on your days off?'

A tear winds its way down Callie's pretty cheek.

It surprises me when Jules steps forward and answers. 'Callie lives with the other maids – well, what is left of them – when she isn't working. Her home was destroyed in a rebel attack. Her family, also. Retribution for their loyalty to the Crown.' Jules tries to present it as a commander giving a battle situation report, but there's sorrow in her voice.

I don't really do physical contact. Occasionally I let Gladys hug me, and I liked it when Tom hugged me on his couch. I liked it a lot. But in this moment, it's the only thing I can think of to do. I reach out and hug Callie.

'I'm sorry,' I whisper. Words have never felt so inadequate.

'May I suggest something in silk, Your Highness?' Brina says tightly, rising from the window seat and walking towards the wardrobe.

'Sure,' I say, deciding not to protest about the clothes. It now seems like such a silly fight. And I don't utter a word of complaint when Callie sits me down at my dressing table and braids my hair all around the top of my head so it looks like I'm wearing a feathery auburn crown. I'm surprised to discover that I even quite like the jewelled butterfly clasp she uses to secure my braid. I draw the line at make-up, opting to apply my own eyeliner and a swipe of mascara.

Jules, Brina and Callie escort me as far as the front door of the palace, passing me to a pack of unicorns I don't recognise with Protectorate emblems on their bridles. I guess they've amped up my security after my disappearing act with Abby. The unicorns trot alongside me until we reach Gladys, sitting by the fishpond. Actually, it's more like a lake with fish in it. Hundreds of fish in rainbow hues swim through the water lilies. Dragonflies buzz and frogs the size of puppies croak and hop along the surface.

'Ah, there you are, dear. You had us worried,' Gladys says, patting the stone next to her for me to sit down. 'Your body raged with fever. An intensity that I have not seen in all my years. I suspect you were only moments away from incinerating yourself the way you did those wretched pycts.' She squeezes my hand. 'There will be no more magic from you, my girl, not without the supervision of your Luminaress. Gladys must monitor every spell you conjure until we understand what happened to you, and how to ensure it does not happen again.' She smiles softly, a picture of serenity, as if we have not a care in the world.

It pisses me off.

'There are children squatting in the train station!' I blurt.

'Yes, dear.'

'I saw Trinovantum – or what's become of it – from the top of the Shard. And in the streets. It's a wasteland out there. Even the palace staff have lost their homes, their families … Why should I be living in this luxury when the rest of Albion is a bomb crater?'

'Because you are nobility,' she says matter-of-factly.

I look at her, astounded again at her cold-heartedness.

'Indulging in luxury while others suffer? That doesn't seem very noble to me. Even if I do manage to make it to the throne without Damius knocking me off, I'm going to be Queen of a pile of rubble. What point is there in being a queen if it makes no difference to them out there, beyond these walls?'

'You will be Queen in a week; the restoration of the royal line will be the first step in rectifying matters.' Her eyes sparkle as if she's having a private little joke with herself. 'Your mother shared a similar interest in, shall we say, political matters.'

I whip around to face Gladys so fast that I almost topple into the pond. 'You knew my mother?'

'Of course, dear. I was Luminaress to her, too.'

'Tell me about her.' I suspect she's deliberately raising my mother to change the subject. But I don't care. I need to know more.

'Walk with me,' she says, rising from her seat. 'Gladys is too old to be sitting on cold, hard surfaces.'

I follow her around the pond and past vegetable beds, where a gardener is tending a lush strawberry patch.

'Cordelia was young, too, when she took the Crown,' Gladys begins. 'Your grandmother, Queen Gelda, bore a son when she was forty-seven – your uncle Damius. We all assumed, your uncle included, that for the first time in 2000 years, the throne would pass to a male heir. But on the eve of Gelda's fifty-seventh birthday, she announced that she was expecting a daughter. We all rejoiced that there was to be another queen.' She pauses. 'Well, not everyone rejoiced.'

'Damius must have been royally pissed to be passed over like that.'

'Yes, dear. I believe your uncle has never fully accepted the situation,' Gladys rephrases primly.

'Where is he now? And why don't you just go and arrest the guy?'

'Believe me, my dear, we have tried. And we are trying. Damius fled after his failed rebellion – the one that claimed your parents – and we have not been able to locate him since.'

Gladys extracts a hairpin from her bun and uses it to levitate a strawberry off the ground and into her palm. She pulls off the stalk and pops the strawberry into her mouth.

'You try,' she says, handing me her hairpin. 'Gently, slowly.'

'I don't need a wand,' I say, beginning to sing the summoning spell.

> *Oh cometh to thee*
> *O'er land, o'er sea*
> *Deliver my desire*
> *With haste and safety*

The welcome warmth of the Art ignites inside me. It feels calm, natural even. A strawberry detaches from its bush and floats up to my palm, and a smile spreads across my face.

'Good,' is all Gladys says.

Out of the corner of my eye I see the gardener plant her hands on her hips and shake her head.

'Some members of the Order thought they could exploit your mother's youth,' Gladys continues. 'They assumed she would be a puppet, easily intimidated and manipulated.' She gives a nostalgic chuckle. 'My word, did she prove them wrong. Your very existence shows just how headstrong your mother could be. She was determined to marry your father despite the most vocal objections. And so she did.'

'Perhaps it would have been better for everyone if she hadn't,' I say, thinking of Callie and all the other Fae who must have equally tragic stories. 'This war would never have happened if I hadn't been born.'

'Your uncle would have had a harder job to recruit rebels without his nonsense propaganda about pure blood, but he was never going to give up his ambitions for the throne without a fight.'

Gladys walks on, pointing out landmarks along the way: the stables, the Protectorate barracks, the thirteenth-century Curfew Tower that houses a dungeon.

'Have you decided what you will do with the key to the Luck of Edenhall?' she says, trying to be casual.

'Gladys, I don't even know where the key is.'

'You do, dear. All that you seek is already within you.'

I open my mouth to ask her to be a tad more specific, but then stop. If Gladys hasn't given me a straight answer by now, I figure she never will. I almost wish we were back in the laundromat, where the mundane occupied our days. There were never any mysteries or riddles when it came to steaming and ironing.

'First,' I say firmly, 'Tom. We need to talk about Tom.'

The faintest flicker at the edge of her eyes is enough to betray her annoyance. 'I promised we will honour him. And, when the appropriate time comes, we shall.'

'That is not good enough.'

'Nature has no regard for individuals,' she says stiffly. 'We're all to play our part.'

'Nature might have no need of individuals,' I say. 'But *I* do.'

She stares at me for a moment. 'Impossible child!' she says, a mixture of exasperation and admiration in her voice. 'Just like your mother. You must do what nature demands of you.'

'You're right,' I say, an idea – and a plan – forming in my head.

chapter 20

With the excuse that I need to rest, I make my way back to the castle, my Protectorate unicorn guard keeping a watchful eye on me. They take their leave and four women in Protectorate bodysuits escort me back to my room. I am certain that the Protectorate's role is to monitor me as much as it is to protect me.

Gladys said I need to be true to my nature. Well, every fibre of my being tells me I need to save Tom.

I need to find out where he's being held, and anything else about the Agency that might help me free him. And since hacking is in my nature, that's exactly what I'm going to do. But first, I need my laptop.

If I can summon teacups, then why not a computer? I visualise my laptop where I left it – on my unmade bed above Gladys's laundromat – and chant the summoning spell. I keep my voice low so as not to alert the guards outside my bedroom door.

With a slight ripple in the air and a shimmering of dust, my laptop materialises on my dresser. I instantly feel calmer, more in control. Picking it up, I give it a little hug, like it's a long-lost friend. I remove the hair brush and hand mirror and gently place my laptop on the temporary workspace. If I ever make it to Queen I'm going to treat myself to a coronation present and get a proper desk.

I check my email and text messages. There's only one. It's from Janine the Labeller, asking for my whereabouts. She seems genuinely concerned for my wellbeing after the 'terrorist attack' at the V&A. Nobody else seems to be. I can be wanted for murder and effectively disappear off the face of the earth and there is not a single person in my life who cares enough to contact me. Most days I don't mind too much that I don't have any friends or family. Today is not one of those days.

Which is one more reason I have to rescue Tom. He's the only person who understands me. The only one who's ever understood me, cared for me, and hasn't wanted anything in return.

Time to test how these realms are connected. The Chancellor said they share the same atmosphere, so logically that means we're on the same bandwidth.

I launch a little app I devised for borrowing other people's wi-fi. I don't see it as stealing, so much as creating an opportunity for people to share their good fortune with others. Like me, for example.

The networks in range in Volgaris begin popping up on my screen. I can see them, but can I connect to them from Iridesca? I try Harry's private network. He doesn't strike me as the sort to tolerate slow speeds.

A few seconds later the wireless icon on my laptop blinks to life at full strength. I re-route through a virtual private network and log in to the Government Secure Intranet, the UK government's official network. From there I jump onto GCSX – the Government Secure Extranet – and search for the Council for Inter-Realm Affairs. Nothing. I try all kinds of alternatives and variants but get nothing relevant.

I search for 'Agency', 'Treaty', 'Signe', 'Cordelia', 'Chess', 'Raven' and 'Francesca', and even try 'unicorn', 'fairies' and 'pycts'. Nothing. This can't be right. Even a department as secret as the Agency must have some sort of digital footprint. But everything I try brings up irrelevant content or 'Your query found 0 matches'.

I realise I've lost track of time when Brina and Callie appear at my door to dress me for dinner with Gladys and a few select members of the Order. We're supposed to be discussing plans for my coronation. I tell my maids that I'm not feeling well and to please pass on my apologies. They seem to buy my excuse because Callie manifests a tray of food for me to eat in my room.

Munching on a dinner roll, I decide to focus on Agency staff records. Since I don't know Agent Eight's name, I tap in 'Westerfield' and search the entire network and sub-nets, hoping the agents were dumb enough to use their real names.

'Thank you, Agent Westerfield,' I say under my breath as a dozen or so matches appear on the screen.

I discount many of the search results immediately as

they have women's first names. Surely he must be here. Top-secret government agency or not, he has to get paid, after all.

One Westerfield jumps out at me: Westerfield, Gordon, listed against the Aberdeen Coastguard operations centre. Aberdeen, Scotland? Either 'Scotland' is code for all things Fae-related, or it's a coincidence.

I try Westerfield's full name, but it returns the same result. Then I try 'Aberdeen Coastguard operations centre'. This looks more promising. I'm no marine expert, but there seems to be a lot of encryption for dealing with fishing boats in distress.

I bypass the encryption and I'm in.

A search on 'Tom Williams' turns up nothing. I try 'Thomas Williams' and then 'Mr Williams'. I even try 'Dr Williams', smirking at my memory of teasing him about not being a real doctor. Again, I get nothing. They must be using a code name for him.

I give up on Tom and instead look to see if there's more in there about my past. At the very least, I'll find out more about the Agency's operations.

I trawl through folders, but most of it appears to be routine monitoring of the realms and the Fae, until I find some folders with a second level of encryption.

I bypass it again. The files seem to be internal records on the Agents themselves: clearances, background notes, staff records.

Interesting.

I find a listing for 'agent_08'. Very interesting. According to the file, Agent Eight's name is Felicity Tunbridge. She was educated at Oxford before starting her career in the Home Office, then transferring to MI6 and then to the Agency.

Most of it is written in a mass of acronyms and jargon. A lay reader wouldn't guess that it has anything to do with fairies or unicorns. 'Inter-realm affairs' could be a reference to the United Kingdom. Then I find a file labelled 'LoE Project'.

The Luck of Edenhall. It must be.

Agent Eight – *Felicity* – was assigned to the project two years before I was born. She was to produce a 'half-blood daughter' by 'partnering' with the Prince of Albion.

So I'm not the only human-Fae child? Then it occurs to me who the Prince of Albion is. Agent Eight and Damius? *Eww.*

The report includes a picture of a baby. I zoom in, but the image is too pixelated to see much. I read on: '... effort to sire a child possessing the powers and moral energy with potential to unlock the LoE ... Progeny incapable ... Discovered to be scaevus ... Progeny discarded.'

The shock and disgust takes a moment to sink in.

Agent Eight had a child with Damius in an attempt to unlock the Luck of Edenhall. And when the child couldn't do it, they killed her?

And Agent Eight accuses *me* of being a monster?

And what on earth is 'scaevus'?

The rest of the documents are a mass of acronyms and tables I can't make head or tail of, except for the final document. It's a brief, unsigned letter from a 'Director of Operations' on official letterhead, expressing 'concerns about the observed development of emotional attachment to the child and father' on the part of Agent Eight, and then, 'Decision: LoE Project shuttered.'

I run searches on 'LoE' and 'Luck of Edenhall'. But there's nothing more – or at least, nothing that means anything to me. I search again on Tom's name but come up blank.

Pondering my next step, I remember the listening device I slipped into Tom's pocket. It might still be on him. My ribs are still a little tender from the bodyslam I did to retrieve it from the desk in the interrogation room. Maybe the bruises weren't for nothing.

I recall the serial number that I read off the top of the bug and enter it into another app on my laptop. Hacking listening devices isn't something I do every day, but I figure the encryption engine and geolocation will work pretty much the same on any device. It's a low-power device with hardly any processing power, so it's likely there's almost no security to speak of.

I wait for the map to load.

And wait.

And wait.

It must be a weak signal.

I wait some more. And some more.

The map is loading one excruciatingly slow pixel at a time. I calculate that at this rate it's going to take about half an hour for the map to load. *Dammit.*

I stand up, stretching my stiff neck from side to side and rolling my shoulders. My head is fuzzy from staring at the screen too long. I need some fresh air.

Not wanting to deal with the unwanted company of a Protectorate detail, and the subsequent fallout when they report back to whoever's orders they're following, I creep out of my bay window.

The moon breaks free from the thick cloud, creating enough light to see shadows in the gardens. The moon will be full in a matter of days. And I am expected to be Queen. The thought of it makes my head hurt. I walk over to a stone bench to sit down and wonder how much time I have in peace until I'm discovered. A squirrel scurries out of the bushes and stops in front of the seat. It looks up at me, tilting its furry head. Startled by approaching footsteps, it continues on.

'Your Highness?'

'Don't bow,' I say to Jules, stopping her mid dip. 'If you're going to watch me then you may as well sit.' Even in the dim light I can see the confusion on her face. I pat the bench seat beside me. 'Don't make me command you.'

'As you wish, Your Highness,' Jules says, stiffly lowering herself onto the seat.

It's amazing how Jules can be so graceful and confident when she's being a warrior and then so awkward and unsure when she's doing life.

'What do you do when you're not guarding me?' I ask.

'I train,' she says in a tentative voice, as if she's worried it's a trick question.

'Anything else?'

211

'I sleep, of course. If you are suggesting that I'm in need of additional skill development I will action your request immediately.'

'I'm not suggesting that,' I assure her. It's probably a good thing that it's too dark for her to see the bemused expression I'm unable to keep off my face. 'You're already awesome. I was just wondering what people did around here when they're not working.'

'I am always working.'

'Why?'

'The Protectorate is my home and my family. It is what I am,' she adds with a little quiver of emotion.

I let out a quiet sigh. 'It must be nice to really belong.'

'You have no reason to envy me, You Highness.'

I'm struck by the raw honesty in her unguarded tone, something I haven't heard from anyone since I arrived in Iridesca. It's so different from Gladys's cryptic responses to everything.

'Jules, can I ask you one more thing?'

'As you wish.'

'What does "scaevus" mean?'

Jules sucks in a long, jagged breath, followed by a couple of short ones. When she's composed herself, she spits on the ground.

'An abomination,' she says.

'What is it?'

Jules looks around like she's making sure we're alone, then whispers, 'A female who cannot fly in her two-legged form, but can trans to unicorn.'

'But that sounds pretty cool,' I say. 'I'd love to be able to change into a flying horse.'

'No, Your Highness, you would not. It is a violation of nature. To be scaevus is a death sentence.'

'Seriously? People surely aren't killed just for being born different?'

'There is a scaevus in the dungeon at this moment. She is to be executed at first light.'

The blood drains from my face. 'You're joking.'

'Your Highness, I would never.'

'Take me to her.'

'Your Highness, I counsel that you —'

'Now, please.'

We walk across the manicured lawn towards the dungeon. Who are these people? They'll allow all manner of cruelty and sit idle when they could change things because it's supposedly what nature has ordained, but then conveniently forget all the natural philosophy stuff when they come across some people who aren't like them?

I thought I was on the side of the good guys, the side that is enlightened and abhors violence. Gladys hinted as much. But the more I learn, the more I think the Fae are just a different species of barbaric. Worst of all, I'm expected to fight for these people. I'm beginning to wonder if Damius and this lot all deserve each other.

By the time we reach the tower my body is racked with fury. The dungeon at Windsor Castle was built in the thirteenth century – and it looks like it. They didn't care much for natural light and ventilation back then.

Two hulking male guards step in front of the spiral staircase. I guess they need to rely on brute strength for security in the dungeon since the graphite bars stifle the Art down here. But it's patently clear to me that, just like at the Agency, graphite does not dampen my magic. Magic swells along with rage and disgust in the pit of my gut. It's molten, it's building, it's begging for release.

'Out of my way,' I order the two guards blocking my path.

'Your Highness, I am not permitted —' says one guard.

'*Now!*' I command, without breaking my stride.

'We cannot —' starts the other.

A blazing bolt bursts unexpectedly from each of my hands. I gasp as the bolts collide with the guards, slamming them against opposite sides of the stone archway. Their eyes roll back and they slump down the walls like potato sacks.

Jules doesn't appear half as shocked as I am. 'They will awake with headaches,' she says, checking their pulses. 'But that will pass.'

I silently hope Jules is right as I step around the guards' unconscious bodies and race down to the cells, collecting grime and all manner of nastiness on the hem of my gown. Jules follows me in silence.

The air is thick and foul. From the dim flicker of torchlight I can see moisture dripping down the walls. The energy changes as I descend. It's heavy and dark, as if I've just walked into depression incarnate. It feels like I'm inhaling despair with each breath.

Two more guards greet us at the bottom of the stairs. They look towards Jules, presumably asking for guidance or help. She offers none.

'We can do this the easy way or the hard way,' I snap.

One guard puts his hands up in surrender, and the other one holds out a ring of keys.

'Leave,' I say. But I'm talking to their backs; they're already scurrying up the stairs.

I peer into the first cell and stop abruptly. A girl, filthy and scrawny, is curled up in the corner. She couldn't be more than twelve years old. How could a child do something so terrible that she deserves to be here?

She slowly raises her head and looks at me. Her face is tear streaked, her eyes wide with fright.

'It's okay,' I say gently. 'I'm not going to hurt you.'

She doesn't reply.

'What's your name?'

'Maria.'

'Why are you here, Maria?'

She says nothing, but I can see her teeth chattering from cold. I conjure the thickest, warmest cloak from my dressing room around her shoulders and repeat my question.

'I am scaevus,' she says, in a voice croaky from not being used.

'You're in prison because you can become a unicorn?'

She pulls the cloak tighter and looks into dead space.

'Where are you parents?'

A tear drops from Maria's eye, turning the dirt on her cheek to mud. 'I do not have parents anymore. They

215

disowned me. And then alerted the Protectorate.'

I spin around to Jules, who is standing a pace behind me. 'You do this?'

'It is our duty,' Jules says.

'It's your duty to lock up children?' I say, incredulous.

'Yes, Your Highness.' Something flickers in Jules's eyes, but it's gone before I can decipher it.

I turn back to Maria and unlock her cell. 'Do you have anywhere else to go? Anywhere outside of Albion? Family or friends who will hide you from these, these ... monsters?'

'I have kin in Serenissima.'

'Where?'

'Venice, Your Highness,' Jules says.

I begin chanting the transfer spell I learned while folding socks at Gladys's table. I bet she never imagined I'd be using her songs to undermine her laws and rescue prisoners.

'Your Highness, your health,' Jules interrupts. 'You should not conjure without the supervision of the Luminaress.'

'And you should not lock up innocent children,' I snap, before beginning the spell again.

> *My heart, my mind, my soul*
> *The window of realms in harmony*
> *Space and time in my control*
> *I am both the lock and key*

The dank wall behind Jules begins to shimmer and the stones peel back on themselves like the lid of a can of sardines, revealing a dark tunnel behind. I visualise what I've seen and know of Venice at the end of the tunnel. The rush of magic and power feels glorious.

Until it doesn't.

A burning, aching sickness starts to build within me. 'Go now,' I say. 'Quickly.' I'm unsure how long I can hold open the portal before I pass out.

Maria steps into the tunnel tentatively, as if this is some sort of trick. Then she gives me an uncertain smile and runs to freedom.

As the stone portal closes behind Maria I lean against the cold, damp stone to catch my breath and steady myself. Jules is looking so pale she could be ill.

'Are there any more scaevus girls locked in this hellhole?' I demand.

A conflicted look flickers across her face. 'No, Your Highness.'

As we reach the top of the dungeon stairs I watch Jules's posture change. Her neck lengthens, her shoulders square and her jaw locks into her kick-arse expression.

'You four, line up against the wall outside,' she orders the guards.

It's a relief to see that the two I knocked unconscious are now awake.

Jules requests to address the guards in private. I move further away from the prison and can't hear what she's saying to them – although I see golden light radiating from her knuckledusters.

As Jules escorts me back to my room, she says, 'I regret

to inform you that a prisoner has escaped from the dungeon, Your Highness.'

'Oh?' I say.

'It's the first escape in over a hundred years.'

'Really.'

'I have interrogated the prison guards and not one of them witnessed the escape or saw anything out of the ordinary. Two of them have sustained minor head injuries, however, which might account for the memory loss. I will document that in my report.'

'Good idea,' I say with a smirk. Then I add, quietly, in case anyone else is about, 'But this isn't over.'

chapter 21

I'm consumed with rage and disgust about the treatment of Maria. The callous disregard for people is bad enough, but the one consolation I have had is that the enemy is worse. Much worse. I thought I was on the side of good. I've been clinging to that. I needed that.

Now I see I've been naive. And betrayed.

I should have seen it coming. The indifference about Tom's fate and the willingness to chalk him up as a casualty of war was a big flashing red light about the true nature of 'my people' that I chose to ignore. Then there's the lack of concern about the wellbeing and safety of those beyond the walls of the palace, while we play dress-ups and make plans for a coronation.

Sure, it rankled, but I accepted the explanation that we're living in a time of war and nothing is to be done. What would I know about war, anyway? I wanted so much to believe in something, something good, that I bought into the simple explanations. But Maria has opened my eyes.

'Locking a girl in a dungeon is not amoral,' I whisper to Jules as I climb through my bedroom window. She climbs in after me, her shoulders tense. 'It's not neutral, either. It's evil. Pure and simple. And it's being done in my name. I will not succumb to this.'

I'm so over all the Fae talk of superiority and the laws of nature. I know what's right and now I'm going to fight for it, starting with what I should have done when all this began.

Save Tom.

Jules stands in the centre of my room, looking at my computer. The map has finished loading; there's going to be no more delaying.

The docks. Tom is at the docks. Well, his jeans are, at least. Presuming the bug's still in his pocket.

'You cannot go, Your Highness,' says Jules. 'Master Williams is immaterial to the maintenance of the Treaty. Nor is he necessary to the survival of the Fae.'

'Have you been reading my mind?' I say, sounding angrier than I am.

'I would never, Your Highness,' she says, blushing. 'You must believe me. It's just that your concern for Master Williams has been clear since you came here.'

'Am I really that transparent?'

'Officers of the Protectorate are trained to detect signs of dissimulation.'

'So that would be a "yes" – I really am that transparent.'

Jules looks down, embarrassed. I'm about to ask her how she can be so cold about Tom before I realise there's no point. My sense of obligation to Tom is grounded in morality. To Jules it's either incomprehensible or a human weakness that is to be overcome.

'I am going to find Tom,' I say, in a voice that I hope sounds authoritative, 'and you're not going to stop me.' And then for good measure, I add, 'As your Princess I command you to return to your post and say nothing of this to anyone.'

Conflict registers on Jules's face. 'I cannot do that, Your Highness.' She bows her head in contrition and I try to work out what to do. Do I go in heavy and demand compliance? Pretend to go to bed and then do the transfer spell when she's not around?

'For your protection, it is my duty to accompany you.' Jules lifts her gaze to meet mine and I could swear a conspiratorial grin flashes across her face. I'm guessing she's broken the rules only twice in her whole life. And both times have been tonight. Because of me.

'Thank you,' I say. 'But I have one condition. You are not to use the Art in Volgaris. You will not make any sacrifices on my account.'

She says nothing.

'Jules?' I say sternly.

'I will endeavour to do as you wish, Your Highness.'

'You will leave the Art to me.' I'm hoping I sound more confident than I feel. Maria's transfer took it out of me but Gladys told me that was a heavy-duty spell. Perhaps smaller ones will be okay. And I'll worry about how I'm going to manage transferring Tom, Jules and me back to Iridesca when the time comes.

I use the Art to shorten the hem of my dress to above the knee and remove the sleeves. This gives me a rush of energy rather than pain. I take that as a good omen.

Inspecting my reflection in the mirror, I see more of a normal teen going through an emo phase than a fairy princess.

'What is the target destination?' Jules asks.

I enlarge the map to show her the Agency's site at the docks. Her knuckledusters flicker and a portal materialises on my bedroom wall. A foghorn signals somewhere in the distance, sounding more like a warning than a greeting. We step into the tunnel and the portal vanishes behind us.

Through the thick, early morning fog I can make out a chain-linked fence topped with razor wire. On the other side of the fence is a long stretch of shipping containers. Some containers are stacked sky high like building blocks, while others stand alone like discarded toys. Cargo cranes tower above them. I was expecting a compound, or some sort of building at least, but this seems to be an industrial storage facility. Why would the Agency need shipping containers?

Some sort of trap, perhaps?

Jules tilts her head to the side, listening. She steps in front of me like a shield and readies her knuckledusters as a security guard approaches in all-black commando gear, a gun strapped over his shoulder. He looks to be on high alert, as if he's expecting trouble rather than just completing a routine perimeter check.

Something's here that's out of the ordinary. You don't protect a yard full of regular shipping containers with G.I. Joe.

As the guard nears us I push past Jules. Using the cover of the fog, I brace for the pain and blurt:

Where you look, you have not seen
Where you go, you have not been
Your tongue in knots, will not encumber
Your memory shall forever slumber.

Recognition briefly flickers on G.I. Joe's face as he reaches for his gun. But before he can raise it, he fumbles, his jaw slackens and his eyes roll back in his head. He crumples onto the dirt with a thud.

I cover my mouth as I gasp. That wasn't supposed to happen. It was a memory-wiping spell; I thought he'd just walk past, with no memory of ever having seen us. My hands start to shake, the beginnings of an anxiety attack. I'm so out of my depth.

'He will recover, in an hour. Or two,' Jules says, bending down to inspect the motionless lump of a man at her feet. 'No more than a day.' She tears off a square of fabric from the front of the guard's uniform and hands it to me. 'Your nose is bleeding, Your Highness. You should have let me deal with him. You paid for that spell with blood vessels.'

'I know,' I say, taking the fabric. 'It hurt like hell.' I slump onto the ground and rest my forehead on my knees.

'Your Highness?'

'I thought I could do this but I can't,' I say miserably, gesturing to the unconscious guard.

'Do what, Your Highness?'

'The spell – all of it. I could have killed him.'

Jules squats down in front of me and, for the first time since we met in the ruins of the V&A, looks me squarely in the eye.

'You conducted your spell faithfully,' she says. Then, after a pause, she adds cautiously, 'If I may make a suggestion?'

'Go right ahead.'

'Next time, perhaps use a little less emphasis on the word "slumber".'

She bursts out laughing and it's so unexpected, I can't help but laugh too. Feeling slightly reassured, I rise to my feet and scan the length of the fence. I spot a hole that's been stitched with new wire.

Jules untwists the tightly wound wire with her bare hands, effortlessly pulling it apart as if she's unlacing a shoe. The friction of wire rubbing against wire creates sparks as it unfurls. She climbs through the hole, oblivious to my look of amazement at her raw strength. I'm about to follow her through the fence when, without turning, she says, 'A moment, Your Highness.'

Two dogs come bounding around the corner of the shipping containers, straight towards us. German shepherds. By their snarling, I'd guess they're not happy to see us.

'Uh, Jules,' I say, backing away from the hole in the fence. She's already registered the dogs, but seems unconcerned. Her body relaxes as she fixes her gaze on the dogs flying towards her, their growls and snarls becoming ever more threatening.

'Jules!' I say again, but she's totally calm.

I watch in wonder as the dogs slow under her gaze. They're suddenly uncertain. With a couple of metres to go, they pull up and stare at Jules.

I hold my breath as I watch the standoff, wondering if my spells would work on animals. Are they just sizing her up before they savage her?

After what seems an eternity, the dogs' snarling becomes less threatening, and then stops entirely. They drop their heads and pad curiously towards her outstretched hand.

Jules turns her palm up and the dogs sniff and lick at her hand. Crouching on one knee, she scratches one of the dogs around the collar as if it's a family pet. The other nudges her leg and licks her hand. It looks like she's whispering something in their ears. Both enormous beasts turn around and pad off in the opposite direction.

'I thought we agreed you weren't to use magic.'

'I didn't use magic,' she says. 'Animals find me quite charming. I've always found them to be better company than Fae. More accepting.' She watches the dogs for a moment, then holds out her hand, ushering me through the hole in the fence.

I scan the mass of shipping containers before me. 'Okay, what now?' If I hadn't knocked out the guard we could have interrogated him.

'Stay here,' Jules says, studying the ground like a tracker. She walks off in one direction and then returns, before taking another path, and then another.

'There are two containers with fresh footprints out

front,' she says when she returns. 'And one is equipped with more security than the other. I counsel that we begin with that one.'

I follow her to an olive green container at the far corner of the compound. A weathered and rusty padlock and chain is wrapped around the door handle and a security keypad and panel is bolted next to the door. This level of security reminds me of my time in juvenile detention.

I pull my wand from the inside of my boot.

'Your Highness, no more magic,' Jules warns.

'I don't need the Art to pick a lock,' I say with mock offence. I slide the tapered end of the wand into the barrel of the lock until I hear a satisfying click. I pull it out and use it to smash the protective screen on the security panel. I wonder if Ada Lovelace would be turning in her grave or cheering for me. Maybe she picked locks for kicks like I do.

I rewire the security panel and then wait as it cycles through random number combinations. When it hits on the correct number sequence the shipping container door pops open.

It's completely empty. No shelving, no goods. And no Tom. Nothing.

Jules nods towards the far end of the container, and I make out what looks like a small recess in the floor. She walks over and pulls up a rusty lever. Dim light floats up, casting faint shadows on the wall.

A hatch?

I gently close the heavy metal door behind me and walk over to the hole in the floor of the container. I peer down at a staircase. It looks like an underground bunker of some sort, hidden below the shipping container. I give Jules a silent look before going first; she follows close behind. At the bottom of the stairs the bunker opens out into a space about the size of a basketball court. Water drips from overhead pipes and through the rock wall. The air is moist and musty.

At the far end of the room I spy a cage. No bed, no blankets, no food or water.

Just Tom.

His hands are fixed to the overhead bars. I gasp at the sight of him hanging in the air, his legs dangling about a metre from the ground. He's naked except for a pair of grey shorts. His jeans are folded alongside a bottle of water and a couple of chocolate bars on a table just out of reach from the cage. So close, yet so far. I wonder how long it's been since he's had anything to eat or drink. I think of the endless smorgasbord of food I've been enjoying while he's been trapped down here.

He's facing away from us but from the triangular shape of his torso I'm certain that it's him. There's a ripe bruise on his back, stretching around his side. I feel sick as I realise it must be from when Agent Eight kicked him while he was creating a diversion so Gladys and I could escape.

A low grunt of pain escapes his body. Seeing him like this almost brings me to my knees. They didn't just capture him; they've been torturing him. I'm filled with regret and self-loathing. I should have come sooner.

Then I notice he's moving, slowly, up and down. The

muscles in his back and arms ripple and flex with each movement. A light sheen of perspiration covers his skin from the effort.

The grunt isn't pain. It's exertion. He's doing chin-ups.

Jules clears her throat. 'I now understand your motivation to be reunited with Master Williams, Your Highness,' she deadpans.

I blush. When did my straight-laced bodyguard turn into a smartarse?

'I'm repaying a debt to an old friend, that's all,' I say without conviction.

Tom must sense our presence. He jumps down from the bars and slowly turns to face us. The look of defiance on his face melts away as soon as he sees me, but then his eyes harden.

A million thoughts rush into my mind as I run towards him. I want to apologise for what I've done to his life. I want to know if he's okay, if the massive bruise from Agent Eight is as bad as it looks. If he's hungry or thirsty or hurt. But all that tumbles out of my mouth is, 'You're not wearing any clothes.'

He turns to Jules. 'Get her away from me.'

It takes a moment for me to make sense of his words.

I open my mouth to reply. But I've got nothing. I'm too pissed off. Is Tom just as heartless as all the other Fae? Does their amorality make them incapable of gratitude and kindness, even love?

It's not that I was expecting gushing gratitude and a triumphant reunion. Okay, maybe a little. At the very least,

I'd thought he would be pleased to be rescued.

Just not by me, it would seem. How can I have got this so wrong?

The lock on his cage isn't any more complicated than the one on the shipping container. I insert my wand and twist it. The lock clicks over and I push the cage door open. I take a step towards Tom, and he takes two steps in the opposite direction, further back into the cage.

'Seriously?' I say, straining to hide how annoyed I am. 'Would you prefer I just left you here to rot?'

Before he can answer, heavy footsteps thunder down the stairs and four guards run towards us, screaming for us to get on the ground.

Guns. They have guns.

I shudder, recalling the sting of the bullet wound. But I don't move. I can't. Fear freezes me.

Jules is off, running towards them. She takes out two guards with a series of lightning-fast roundhouse kicks. A third trips over his fallen comrade, but manages to free his weapon. Jules rears back and kicks his hand, sending the gun flying. He cries out in pain, gripping his hands and swearing before Jules silences him with a quick karate chop to the back of the neck. The fourth guard raises what looks like a taser, aiming it directly at me. I just stand there like an idiot, staring at him.

He fires. The bolt of electricity shoots through the air in slow motion. I'm falling out of the way, the electricity missing me by inches as Tom flies out of the cage, knocking me out of the line of fire. I smack into the wall and watch helplessly as the blast hits Tom right in the heart. He crashes to the ground, convulsing.

'*No!*' I scream, scrambling to my feet. I'm about to unleash on the guard, but Jules beats me to it, flattening him to the ground with another karate chop.

She rushes over to me.

'I'm fine,' I say breathlessly, even though I'm not. My head aches from the impact and I can't focus properly. 'Tom. Get Tom.'

Jules bends down over Tom's body, sprawled, unmoving, on the ground.

This can't be happening. *No, no, no.* This isn't how we end.

Finally, she stands. 'I'm sorry, Your Highness. I'm unable to revive him.'

chapter 22

Sickness sinks into the pit of my stomach.

Tom's dead. Because of me.

'We must depart, Your Highness. *Now!*' yells Jules. She hoists Tom onto her shoulder in a fireman's carry in one smooth movement.

At the edge of my attention, footsteps echo in the staircase. I look over to see Agent Eight running through the doorway, weapon drawn.

A moment of clarity. We need to get back to Iridesca. The least I can do is get Tom's body back to Abby. I don't even want to think what Agent Eight and the Agency would do with him. As tears stream down my face, I begin chanting the transfer spell while carving out a portal on the wall.

> *My heart, my mind, my soul*
> *The window of realms in harmony*

'Your Highness, we should not transfer,' Jules says, but there's no other way out.

Space and time in my control
I am both the lock and key

I welcome the pain that accompanies the spell. It's brutal. It's excruciating. It's what I deserve.

The portal opens as agents stream down the stairs and into the room. Jules pushes me into the portal and then follows right behind, carrying Tom's lifeless body.

We're sucked into the nothingness of the portal and I panic. In the pain and confusion, I didn't think about where we were going. I try to visualise a destination. *The palace library. No, the gardens. No, my bedroom.*

Before I can develop a clear picture in my mind, the dank bunker is gone and we're …

Looking at a street sign that reads 'London: 140 miles'.

The transfer failed. We're still in Volgaris. In the middle of a busy highway.

A truck screams past me on the other side of the road, so close I can see the tyre tread. A horn blares and I look up to see a car hurtling towards us.

For a second, I'm too stunned to move. The car is closing in too fast and I'm too slow. My feet give out from under me as I'm thrust across the gravel and tar.

Jules.

She grab-tackles me off the road and we tumble down the embankment.

I roll over and see Tom slumped on the ground. I realise all over again what I've lost.

The connecting thread to my childhood. Gone.

My future. He was supposed to be in it.

Plans and hopes that I wasn't even conscious I had made unravel in an instant.

And it's my fault. That shot was meant for me. I double over in pain, my heart aching from a hole that could only ever have been filled by Tom.

Jules seems unaffected. All guts and no heart. Damn Fae amorality. The Agency just killed one of her own, and she's completely unmoved. She scans our surrounds, alert to danger and already planning our next move.

I cradle Tom's head in my lap, stroking my fingers along the hairline of his beautiful face. There's so much I wanted to say to him. I needed to thank him for saving me all those years ago. He sacrificed so much for me – his family, his childhood, and now his future as well.

I ruined his life. Twice. Just like Abby said.

I wish I had the chance to take it all back, to tell him how sorry I am for everything.

And then I realise that I can. My reality is different now. I have the power to change it.

Why didn't I think of that before?

'Show me how to do a cataclysmic spell,' I say to Jules. I can remember the words of Gladys's songs but, after what I did to the security guard at the docks, I want Jules to talk me through it so I don't make a mistake. It's not something I can afford to get wrong.

Jules scrunches up her face. 'Your Highness, you cannot perform such a spell.'

The heat of anger and desperation courses through my

veins. 'Don't tell me what I cannot do!'

'Your Highness, you cannot —'

'Why are you stopping me?' I fling my arms out in desperation and frustration. 'If I'm as powerful as everyone seems to think then this should be a cinch.'

'Your Highness —'

'Just tell me how to do it!' I yell. Blue sparks shoot out of my fingertips.

Jules covers her face protectively, making no attempt to fight back. The long grass nearby catches alight.

'Sorry,' I say, astonished. 'I didn't mean for that to happen. It's just, I'm so sick of everything being out of my control.'

Jules calmly stamps out the blaze with her boots. 'Your Highness, you cannot perform a cataclysmic spell because Master Williams is not dead.'

'*What?*'

'Cataclysmic spells alter the natural order of life and death —'

'I know that already. But you said ... you said you couldn't revive him.'

'Correct. Master Williams must wake in his own time. There is nothing I can do to expedite the process.'

I lean forward and place my hand on Tom's bare chest. A moment later I detect the lightest movement. He *is* alive. I close my eyes and savour the moment. It's one of those rare occasions when fate has smiled on me instead of slapping me down. I've just been gifted a do-over and I'm not going to waste it.

'Let's get him home,' I say, beginning the transfer spell again. I'm determined to concentrate and get it right this time.

'Your Highness, I counsel that we do not transfer Master Williams when he is not conscious.'

'Why?'

'An unconscious person may lose their grasp on their life force during the transfer. It is possible that you will only transfer his body back to Iridesca and his life force will be left in Volgaris. Lost.'

'That doesn't sound good.'

'I am quite sure it is not, Your Highness.'

'And how long until he wakes up?'

Jules looks uncertain. 'Perhaps an hour. Perhaps a year.'

The burst of hope I just received is sucked out of me like water down a drain.

'Well, we can't just stay here waiting for him to wake up,' I say. 'Tom and I are wanted criminals. And the Agency is sure to be tracking us. We need to find somewhere safe to go.'

Jules nods as if I just gave her a command and strides to the side of the road. She peers at the traffic like she's looking for something. Or someone. A minute goes by and she holds up a hand, flagging down a van.

To my surprise, it screeches to a halt and pulls over, stopping right in front of us.

Lucky.

The driver gets out and walks towards us.

'Don't I know yer from somewhere, then, luv?' he says.

My breath catches in my throat. He must have seen the news broadcasts or the 'Wanted' signs. But then I notice that he's not looking at me, or at Tom. He's talking to Jules.

'Don't tell me, don't tell me. Wonder Woman? Nah, yer don't 'ave no cape. Cat Woman? Wiv a brown suit.' He laughs so hard his belly shakes, just like Santa. He looks a bit like Santa too. White beard. Kind eyes. And most importantly, not from the Agency.

I smile awkwardly, relieved that he doesn't seem to know who Tom and I are. Then he notices that Tom isn't moving.

'Oh. I'll call for 'elp.'

'No,' Jules and I say in unison.

'Alright,' he says slowly, nodding his head in understanding. He seems remarkably calm for someone who's just come across a body that looks like it's dead.

'Can you take us into London?' I say. There's only one person in the world who's capable of helping me at this point. I just hope he's still willing. Jules looks at me uncertainly, but says nothing.

'Sure, right, get in,' says Santa, turning and heading back to his van.

Jules carries Tom into the back of the van and lays him down next to a ladder and a variety of paint tins and brushes. Reluctantly I agree to leave Jules in the back with Tom. The back of the van is windowless, completely cut off from the front cabin. It's not like there is anything I can do to help Tom right now, but I'd like to be there when he wakes up. *If* he wakes up. But I need to sit up front to give directions. While

I can't fault Jules's combat skills, going incognito is a whole other ballgame. I figure it'd take about five minutes before she did or said something weird to make Santa suspicious.

I clock a fire extinguisher attached to the door, right next to my foot. A potential weapon if Santa turns out not to be as nice as he looks.

'Must 'ave been quite a party,' Santa says as he guns the engine and pulls out into the flow of traffic. Chit chat is the last thing I want to do right now, but it feels like the price I need to pay for the ride.

'What are you doing out so late?' I ask.

'Not late. Early. Got a paintin' job first thing. Work starts soon as the sun comes up.' He takes a swig of chocolate milk and then offers me the carton. 'Want some?'

I shake my head, noting the food crumbs around the rim.

'Suit y'self,' he says, and takes another swig.

I rest my head against the window. It's cold and the vibrations on my forehead are uncomfortable. I stare out at the lights of the oncoming traffic, and count all the different ways I've screwed up. I ruined Tom's life amongst the humans and then almost killed him. And now he's going to spend goodness knows how long unconscious.

Abby's face haunts me the most. I know she abandoned me with the pycts, but I promised I'd save her brother. I'm sure putting him in an indefinite coma is not what she had in mind. And I'm seriously questioning my ability to keep all three of us safe, fed and hidden.

Gladys and the rest of them shouldn't have put their faith in me. I was stupid to start believing I was worthy of it. A fairy princess to bring peace and hope? What a joke. I can't even keep my friends safe. They're pinning their hopes on the belief that I'll be as powerful as my mother, or as clever as my father.

They're all doomed.

I notice Santa watching me out of the corner of his eye. I stare down at the fire extinguisher, trying to estimate how fast I can grab it. He has one hand on the wheel and the other one in a bag of crisps. After a quick check in his rear-view mirror he lunges across at me.

I freeze, my fingers digging into the seat. He *is* a psychopath after all. The fire extinguisher seems so close but also so far.

He fumbles with the catch on the glove compartment, the van swerving slightly as he drives with one hand on the wheel. My mind skips through all the things that could be in there – gun, knife, bloodied crowbar.

The leather-bound book of poetry he tosses into my lap is the last thing I expect.

He leans back over and plants both hands back on the wheel, straightening the van.

''ave a look,' he says, nodding at the ancient-looking volume.

I run my fingers over the binding. The book is not old, even though it's trying to look it. The faded patches of leather look tacky, as if they were applied by the same machinery that makes designer faded jeans.

I open the book at the page with the folded corner and start reading.

'*And the day came when the risk to remain tight in a bud was more painful than the risk it took to blossom.*'

'Know what that means?' he says.

I shrug.

'Nah, me neiver. But it impresses the ladies. Works every time. Right.' He laughs but then his eyes grow serious. 'It means you can't give up when fings get rough. You've got to come out swingin', luv. Even if you're scared. Especially when you're scared.'

He turns to me. I wish he'd just concentrate on the road.

'You fink it's 'ard to keep fightin'? Well, it's a lot 'arder to spend the rest o' your life cowerin' in the bloody corner o' the bleedin' ring, right, Princess.'

I sit bolt upright. *Princess?* Does he know who I am, or does he call all young women 'princess'? I search his face for signs of recognition but he just smiles at me, creases deepening around his soft eyes, and then turns back to the road.

We drive on in silence.

Santa seems content to leave me with my thoughts. Somewhere beneath my massive pile of hopelessness a tiny ember of purpose sparks to life.

I think about Tom lying in the back of the van. It's not too late for me to clear his name. Maybe by the time he wakes up, his life will be able to go back to normal, to what it was before I came along and ruined it. Backing down or running away isn't an option for me. I owe it to Tom to make things right, and fight whatever battles lie ahead of me.

As we near London I give Marshall's address to Santa.

His callused hands tense on the steering wheel and the sparkle fades from his smiley eyes.

'Sorry, princess, Musgrave lands ain't for the likes o' me.'

From the look of revulsion on his face I guess that Santa must really hate rich people. I don't want to press the issue so I just ask him to drop us as close to Marshall's house as he's willing.

He stops his van two blocks from Marshall's Bedford Square residence. Most of the townhouses have three windows across. Marshall's has six.

It's just past five in the morning, but the lights are on. Marshall must be an early riser. Or his staff are.

I thank Santa for the ride and hop out. As I walk to the back of the van and unlatch the door, I'm hoping I'll find Tom sitting up. My heart sinks as I take in his motionless body. Jules jumps down from the van and I see that she's tense. She sniffs the air and scans the quiet, well-ordered street as if she's expecting danger.

'I am not convinced that coming here is the best course of action, Your Highness.'

'Neither am I, but do you have a better plan?' When she offers nothing, I say with an edge of frustration, 'We have nowhere else to go, Jules. The Agency will be crawling all over Tom's house and the laundromat. The police will be at the V&A, trying to arrest me for murder. Believe me, I don't want to ask for Marshall's help any more than you do. It's humiliating. But we don't have the luxury of being choosey right now. And I think he was trying to tell me something important, something that might help us.'

Jules concedes with a curt nod as she lifts Tom's body from the van and effortlessly folds him over her shoulder.

The van's engine rumbles to life. Santa drives off as we walk in the direction of Marshall's townhouse.

I press the buzzer on the solid front door and the intercom rustles to life.

'Yes?'

'I'm a friend of Mr Musgrave,' I say, trying to sound convincing. 'I really need to see him.'

Silence.

I look at Jules with Tom slung over her shoulder, and realise that it might have been smarter to come to the door alone. The three of us look like criminals who've forgotten to take off our Halloween gear. I sense that security cameras on us.

'Name?' the voice says eventually.

'Chess. Chess Raven.'

'And your associates?'

'Friends of mine. We need to speak with Mr Musgrave urgently.'

More silence.

My stomach sinks as it dawns on me that my plan isn't going to work. Marshall may not even be home. There's no way his security detail is going to let us in. I imagine the security guy is calling the police, conferring with someone right now. And just as I'm about to tell Jules that we're going to bail out, the intercom crackles.

'Someone will be down shortly,' says the voice. The door unlatches and swings ajar. I smile hopefully at Jules as we walk in, relieved that at least something I've done tonight has worked. She gives a weak smile in return.

I'm almost knocked over by how posh the house is. The foyer is a chessboard of spotless black and white marble tiles that terminate at a closed door. Oil paintings and large mirrors in gilded frames hang on white walls. To one side there's a staircase with a strip of red carpet running up the middle; on the other side are three doorways leading to other rooms, but their heavy wooden doors are blocking my view so I can't see inside them.

We wait for a moment, then the door at the end of the foyer opens and a man in his thirties with slicked-back hair appears, wearing a suit and tie. From the way he walks, I'd say he's ex-military. An ex-military butler? For a man in Marshall's position, it figures, I guess. Close behind the butler are two more men, who look like they're still in the military. One of them has a Rottweiler on a leash. Despite her dog-whispering abilities, I can tell by Jules's tense body language that the snarling Rottweiler isn't helping to allay her concerns about Marshall's trustworthiness. None of them seem remotely concerned about Tom's body slung over Jules's shoulder. Or even amazed that Jules is able to carry such a weight so effortlessly.

'If you'll just come with us,' says the man in the suit.

'Where's Marshall?' I say, growing uneasy.

The man ignores me. 'Bring them,' he orders the guys in uniform.

Out of the corner of my eye I see Jules raise her knuckledusters. But before she has time to fire off a spell I grab her wrist and shake my head. It's no wonder they're suspicious of us, but Marshall is my sponsor. He's all I've got here in Volgaris. The last thing I need is someone getting hurt. Not to mention the explaining I'd have to do about the magic.

One of the uniformed guards takes advantage of the distraction and slams Jules up against the wall while the other manhandles Tom off her shoulder. The butler pushes me towards a doorway under the stairs.

'Marshall!' I scream. '*Marshall!*'

I'm too late. The guards push Jules and me through the door and down a short flight of stairs. Tom is thrown in after us. Jules and I do our best to break his fall but I wince as his shoulder hits the concrete floor. The door slams behind us and I hear a heavy bolt shift into place on the outside of the door, plunging us into pitch blackness.

chapter 23

I fumble around in the darkness until I find a light switch.

The light flickers to life and I'm greeted by a sight that almost makes me forget that we've just been locked in Marshall's cellar.

Tom's eyes flutter open and he rolls over onto his side. He looks around the cellar and then at me directly. My heart does a little flip-flop. I rush over to him, but he shuffles out of my reach.

It's like he just died all over again.

'Where are we?' he says, his voice laboured. He's mustered enough energy to look annoyed, though. Annoyed with me. Again.

'At Marshall Musgrave's house,' I say. 'He's sort of a friend of mine.'

'You've got to be joking,' Tom says. 'I'd rather be a prisoner of the Agency than a Musgrave.'

'We're not prisoners. There's just been some sort of misunderstanding,' I say, but there is not nearly as much conviction in my words as I had hoped.

'What have you done?' Tom says.

'What have *I* done? I just rescued you from a freaking cage. I was the only one who wasn't going to just leave you there to die. You're welcome!'

He shakes his head in frustration. 'You don't get it, do you? I'm bad for you, Chess. You need to stay away from me.'

'Is this about the stupid spell? I don't care about that.'

If I'm being completely honest, I am actually freaked out by the cataclysmic spell thing. Being told you're going to die because of some ancient voodoo will do that to a girl. But I'm not about to admit that to anyone, least of all Tom.

He looks at me as if I'm being completely unreasonable.

'What was I supposed to do?' I continue. 'You're the only person who knows me – really knows me. You were the only one who cared enough to save me. I couldn't just turn my back on you.'

He gets to his feet, looking remarkably well for someone who's just woken from a coma.

'I didn't save you, Chess. All I did was make your life worse.' He lets out a bitter laugh. 'You're now wanted for murder because of me. But none of that will matter if you don't keep away from me. You'll be dead.'

'Tom,' I say, raising my palms for him to stop. 'You're the only one who didn't look the other way. You *did* save me.'

'But I didn't. What you said back at my place was right. I wanted to be the hero. I wanted to be *your* hero. I didn't think about the consequences.'

Without thinking, I step forward and wrap my arms around him. My head nestles into his neck, with my chin resting just above his naked, hard chest. He hesitates for a moment but then wraps his arms around me.

And it feels, well, right. I don't sense his anger anymore, or even coldness. It's more like sorrow.

'Can you ever forgive me, Chess?' he says softly.

'I'm the one who should be begging for forgiveness. The only reason we're still in this mess is because I can't work out where the key to the Luck of Edenhall is, even though I'm somehow supposed to know.'

He looks down at me with the faintest of smiles that pushes away all the sadness that creeps into my heart whenever I recall my past. I'm very much in the present, acutely aware of the heat of Tom's body. As I stare up into his pools of blue, I feel safe. Even though I'm trapped in a cellar with no idea what's going to happen if I can't get us out – or even if I can – I am somehow confident that as long as we are together, everything will be okay.

Jules clears her throat, puncturing our little bubble. She's staring intently at her boots but I can still see that she's embarrassed by our public display of affection. Without looking up, she says, 'Something is not as it should be, Your Highness. We can't transfer. We are trapped.'

I scan the room, registering that it's bigger than I first realised. Clean, whitewashed walls give it the appearance of a wine cellar. But there aren't any bottles of wine.

Jules goes over to the wall and rubs it with her hand. She knocks on it.

'Graphite,' she says. 'The walls are coated in graphite. It's as good as bars on a cage to us.'

Tom swears. 'You can never trust a Musgrave.'

'This must be a coincidence,' I say, the certainty leaching out of my words. Marshall kept me out of jail. He saved Gladys's life. Why would he turn on me now?

'Coincidence?' Tom scoffs. 'A Musgrave who just happens to have an unused cellar with walls painted with graphite paint? Wake up, Chess. What do you really know about him?'

Jules interjects with a calmer voice. 'If I may, Your Highness, the Musgrave family has never been a friend of the Fae.'

'Look, I know his family history with the Luck of Edenhall. But that was a long time ago,' I say desperately.

'The Musgrave luck ran out,' Tom says. 'It was the price they paid for claiming the Luck of Edenhall, which didn't belong to them. A Musgrave should not have the power that Marshall now wields. He wants something.'

I roll my eyes. 'That's just a lot of prejudice built on fairytales.'

'And his interest in you is all kinds of wrong,' Tom says.

I look up at Tom, wondering what he's insinuating. That Marshall's keen on me? That's crazy. My mind races over our past meetings, searching for signs that Marshall was in any way attracted to me.

There was the time he took me to his country estate to ride his horses. He'd explained it would be a good way to get to know each other a little better, in a more relaxed environment, away from the formality of the Second Chances program. Despite our present predicament, I find myself smiling briefly at the memory. The day was a complete disaster. My horse bolted, I went tumbling and ended up in the Emergency Department. Marshall insisted on driving me to the hospital and waited with me the whole time until I was discharged. And then he drove me home.

Certain that Marshall is not, and has never, hit on me, I'm relieved to dismiss the unwelcome thought.

'I counsel that we focus our attention on present matters,' Jules says urgently.

I take a deep breath. 'Well, now that you're awake we don't need Marshall's help anyway. Let's just get out of here.'

If the Agency couldn't keep me in a graphite cage, I figure that a bit of paint isn't going to stop me. I motion for Tom and Jules to step back. I have no idea what's going to happen; the last time I did this the roof exploded. But just as I start to gather my thoughts and focus my mind, there's a sound at the door. The bolt unhitches and the handle begins to turn.

Jules steps protectively in front of me.

'Chess,' calls a familiar voice down the stairs. 'I'm so sorry.'

A warm smile spreads across Marshall's face but it doesn't have the same effect on me as usual. He's wearing a suit but his hair is wet, as if he just got out the shower.

'I owe you and your associates an apology. My guards.

They're good, very good, but, shall we say, a little overzealous where my personal safety is concerned.'

Marshall stops at the bottom of the stairs. He barely reacts to seeing Tom half-naked. He's slightly less composed at the sight of Jules, his jaw tensing briefly before relaxing again as his eyes lock with hers. I guess it's not every day he finds a woman dressed as a superhero in his cellar.

Marshall orders the man who met us at the door to take Tom and Jules into the kitchen and get them something to eat. 'And find some clothes for the gentleman,' he adds. 'Chess and I can talk in private.'

Jules and Tom object in unison.

'I'll be fine,' I say, with more confidence than I feel. I can't waste the opportunity to find out what Marshall really knows about the Luck of Edenhall, and anything else that might help me. Marshall and I can have our private chat and then we can be on our way back to Iridesca in no time. 'Go. Eat,' I say to Tom and Jules.

Neither looks pleased. Jules passes Tom one of her knuckledusters and he slips it onto his hand. He tells me to call if I need him.

My gut's churning. I've never been able to relax in Marshall's presence but this is different. I don't know where I stand with him anymore. Seeds of doubt are starting to take root.

I brush aside my misgivings, and follow Marshall into what looks to be his office. It's about four times the size of the house I grew up in. The room is surrounded by solid bookshelves, full of neatly shelved books.

A large desk sits just off the centre of the room. Its contents are a mix of old and new. Right next to the laptop – a model I'd kill to get my hands on – is a Montblanc fountain pen, a paperweight and a letter opener. I wonder if Marshall actually reads these books or uses this stationery, or if he just displays them the way other people might display art or flower arrangements.

He motions for me to sit down in a leather-upholstered chair, the type that curves around your body like a glove. But I can't relax. I can't even pretend to.

Marshall leans against the desk in front of me with his hands on his hips, his body tense. The warmth from before is gone and I feel like I'm in the principal's office.

Tick.

Tick.

Tick.

'Want to tell me what's going on?' he says, eyebrows raised. 'You need to tell me the truth, Chess. All of it. I can't help you unless you do.' He must know I'm about to deflect his question because he adds, 'I'm not just your sponsor. I care about you.'

Part of me does want to tell him everything. It would be a relief to spill my worries to an ordinary person. My life has veered far indeed from anything resembling normal when *Marshall* is the most ordinary person in it. But what he's asking is impossible. The truth is not an option. I don't even know if I can trust him.

'I can't,' I say.

'You need to help me help you. Your face is plastered all

over the media. They're saying you broke into a military installation and attacked government officials. And that you're working for a domestic terrorist organisation.'

I focus on the grandfather clock standing against the oak-panelled wall while I wait for his rant to end. I figure I'll be able to ask my questions sooner if I don't interrupt.

'And that you're a murderer. You're not, are you?'

I don't know how to answer that question. Do pycts count? What about Larry?

'Those other two – how well do you know them?' he probes.

'Well enough,' is all I can say. The truth – that I've only just met Jules, and that Tom is a childhood friend that had been totally blanked from my memory – is unlikely to put Marshall's mind at ease. It doesn't even sound good to me.

He walks over to the cabinet sitting underneath his portrait and pours himself a cup of black coffee from the steaming decanter. He offers me one but I decline. He downs his coffee, then pours himself another before settling into the leather chair opposite me. It strikes me how different we are. He wears the power that Gladys tells me I'm supposed to harness like his favourite suit. And he looks good in it.

'I can clear your name, make all your troubles go away,' Marshall says. 'We can work together, help each other to get all the things we've both always wanted.'

Now he has my attention. He's offering a clean slate.

I could have my life back, maybe even change my identity and forget about Damius and the Fae throne, put the Agency behind me. I'd be lying if I said I wasn't tempted. I've been on my own for as long as I can remember; I'm so tired of being scared and desperate all the time. Is it so wrong to want someone to protect me, to care for me, to make all the pain stop?

'When we first met, I saw something in you,' Marshall says. He takes a sip of his coffee, holds it in his mouth and swallows it slowly, as if he's savouring a memory as well as the taste. 'Something special, something I'd been searching for, for a long, long time. Back then, I wondered if you even knew how remarkable you were.'

He tilts his chin slightly and studies my response with unblinking eyes. He's waiting, hoping I'll say something. But I'm lost.

'Now I am quite sure that you do know what you are, what you can unlock with the extraordinary power you possess.'

I sit up straight in my chair, my blood running cold. He's talking about unlocking the Luck of Edenhall. Tom was right. I can't trust a Musgrave. Just like his ancestors, he's trying to steal the unbridled Fae power in the Chalice. My stomach curdles as I think about his greed. Doesn't he already have enough power? What on earth would he do with more? Nothing good. I'm certain of it.

'Yet you continue to play your little games,' Marshall goes on. 'Holding out on Agent Eight. The Order. Even the old woman.'

My mouth drops open. He takes a sip of his coffee but keeps his eyes on me. I can't decide if I'm feeling like a prize or prey.

'Over the years, people have called you difficult, petulant, even naive. But now I wonder if you had us all fooled, and instead you have been shrewd. Perhaps you have been waiting all this time for a better offer.'

He leans forward in his chair and I swallow hard.

'For *my* offer.'

'This really is all about the Luck of Edenhall?'

'Of course,' he says with a shrug. 'Hasn't it always been about the Chalice? Why you sought out a connection with me by stealing the old woman's meds?'

'That was a coincidence,' I say, as my heart thumps against my ribs. 'You can't possibly think that —'

He holds up his hand as if he's trying to push my words back down my throat and then continues to talk over me. 'It's why you've been stringing me along with your adorable, yet obviously confected, cluelessness at our meetings. How many opportunities did I give you to raise the subject of the key? But you continue to toy with me.'

He's a totally different person from the one I've known these past months. His sureness with the world now comes across as naked arrogance. His words are controlling rather than confident. There's a hardness and coldness that I've seen in flashes but always put down to my own issues.

'For years I've been watching you. Waiting. And then you came to me. Do you expect me to believe that was a coincidence?'

I take a breath and feel like I've just sucked in a mouth of sawdust.

'That's why you assigned me to data entry at the V&A?

To keep an eye on me? To keep me close to the Luck of Edenhall?' It's not really a question. I know the answer. But a small part of me is still hoping that I'm wrong, that this is a misunderstanding.

He simply nods.

I stare at him. I never figured Marshall and I were going to be besties. But I thought he was on my side, that he cared enough about me to want to help. But he's no different from all the other people in my life who just saw me as something to exploit.

He flashes a winning smile but it's too late for that. The controlled softening of his features unnerves me. I could always see through his charms, but the fact that he made an effort was somehow part of the charm. Now, it just seems manipulative, orchestrated to get me to do whatever he wants.

'It's time to deal, Princess Francesca of House Raven. Tell me what you want in exchange for the key.'

My stomach clenches. He's clearly known my real name longer than I have.

'Marshall,' I begin, trying to find the right combination of words. 'You've got me —'

'Wrong? No. No, I'm quite sure I haven't.'

'I would never —'

'Name your price, Princess. Enough with the games.'

'Marshall —'

'Stop wasting my time.'

'You can't have it.'

Silence.

I suck in a steadying breath. 'I will not give you the key.'

'Yes, you will,' he says, standing and invading my space. 'Perhaps not today' – he leans forward and I press my body as far back into the chair as possible – 'but you will.' And then through perfectly white gritted teeth, he says, '*I. Do. Not. Lose.*'

A deep rumbling envelops the house. It sounds like the earth is convulsing.

Marshall steps back from me. I look up at the windows and stand, instinctively preparing myself for what's coming. A chill slithers down the length of my back and the hairs on the back of my arms rise. The Art sparks to life in my veins. If it's another attack of ravens, this time I'm ready.

Or ready-ish. At least this time I know there's more in this world than what I see in front of me.

Marshall's office windows rattle in their frames, and shockwaves reverberate through the room. The whole house is creaking and shaking. The air is shifting.

But it's not ravens.

Thick cords of smoke stream from the air vents around the top of the ceiling and spew up from the carpet. The plumes twist around each other like snakes in a deadly dance.

Suffocating smoke fills my lungs. I have to get out of here.

I turn back to Marshall. But he's gone.

I suck in too much smoke and start coughing as I flee the office. Thick smoke fills the hallway but rather than filling the entire space, it converges, swirling in a single place.

A head forms from the churning smoke. Green eyes I've seen before. Short auburn hair, and a maniacal smile.

The smoke solidifies, revealing a man's body clad in a studded jacket, a leather kilt and commando boots. A glistening, ruby-encrusted dagger is clasped in one of the man's hands.

'Ah, Francesca,' he croons. 'I do so love family reunions.'

chapter 24

Damius.

I should run, but I can't.

I can't tear my eyes from the being who's materialised from the cloud of smoke billowing in front of me.

He's ... he's the spitting image of the paintings I've seen of my mother. The same eyes. The same cheekbones.

His face transports me back to a place and time before words, before judgement, before guilt. I'm engulfed with a sadness and longing that is even stronger than my fear.

My head is certain of the danger I'm in, but my heart is torn in two. He's the only family I have, the only connection to my mother.

Footsteps thunder down the hall behind me as spears of golden light shoot past my ears towards Damius.

My uncle casually holds out his hands, flicking the light back as if it's no more than a minor irritant.

I hear Jules and Tom both calling at me to duck but I've lost my capacity to respond.

I just stand there, staring at the only family I have.

Frozen by the confusion of what I want, compared with what is.

Damius's return fire is so close it singes my hair.

'Playtime is over, my dear niece,' Damius hisses. 'You may have destroyed some of my army, but I have watched you and learned. It will not happen again. It's time for you to pick a side. I warn you, I can be very persuasive.'

He throws a flame towards me, skimming my body and singeing the hairs on my forearms.

I'm so terrified I don't even scream. I just watch the aura of flames outline the contours of my body.

Tom incants, firing off a spell that smothers the flames surrounding me, and Jules simultaneously unleashes another blazing volley from her knuckledusters.

Damius bats Jules's blasts away like they're mosquitoes. He raises an arm, palm flattened, taking direct aim at me.

I watch as the space around his open palm warps with radiating heat.

'No!' Tom roars as he lunges to push me out of the line of fire.

Another volley from Jules.

Damius flicks it away again, but it's enough of distraction for Tom to drag me from the room. Marshall's goons are in the hallway. Tom raises his free hand, but before he can do anything they turn and run. They might once have been professional soldiers, but they've seen and heard enough to know when they're out their league.

We run through the house, a blur of tasteful and very expensive furniture, paintings and sculptures. We're moving so fast that I swear we're going to smash into a wall, but Tom takes each turn with such certainty and sureness that we narrowly miss each time. Even in human form, he has the speed and dexterity of a unicorn.

I hear Jules behind us, firing off blasts as she runs. Turning my head to look behind, I see Damius striding towards us.

'Outside!' Jules yells.

We dash past the door to the cellar under the stairs and through the front door and back onto the footpath. Tom releases me as Jules begins carving a portal into the road.

She leaps into it, pulling me down through the ground. Tom's body slams into mine as we tumble down into blackness. Looking up, back towards the mouth of the hole, I see Damius standing over the portal. Right before it closes he slices his dagger through the air in front of his throat.

I shiver at the violence in his eyes.

The hastily carved portal is a bumpy ride. It's like being sucked through a long, dark wind tunnel. I feel like I'm suffocating, as if I'm being buried deeper and deeper underground.

We fall over each other through open air, a jumble of arms and legs.

A hand, large and sturdy, tightly clasps my wrist.

Tom.

And then there's golden light. The end of the tunnel.

Jules slams onto the floor. Flat on her back, she lets out a groan as she reaches up towards us, cushioning our fall with a spell. There's a gentle thud as if I've just collided with a giant balloon in the air.

Jules looks winded. Blood smears her face, leaking from her nose and her ears. Her face scrunches with exertion as she lowers Tom and me onto a rug. A familiar rug.

My bed chamber in Iridesca.

Tom's hand is still clamped around my wrist. He releases his grip and sits up against the side of my bed, breathing heavily. He touches the blood leaking from his ears and then uses Jules's knuckledusters to clean it away with a spell.

I'm shaking, adrenaline coursing through me. I roll up, supporting myself with one hand.

Jules staggers to her feet. 'You'll be needing your rest, Your Highness,' she says, between gasps of breath. 'The castle will be stirring soon.'

'Jules.' I stand to go after her, but she simply bows and slips out the door.

Tom reaches up and pulls me back. 'Allow her to recover in private,' he says quietly. 'It's a matter of honour for an officer of the Protectorate. Trust me.'

I lie flat out on the rug, my breath still short, my heart still racing.

Tom lies down next to me and props his head up on his hand. He's so close his light breath caresses my cheek.

'Thank you, Chess,' he says after a time. 'I know the risks you took for me.'

I like the way he just said my name – as if it's delicate and succulent, like a ripe mango you can't help but sink your teeth into. I lick my lips and a butterfly takes flight in my stomach.

'Don't thank me. It's the least I could do. I needed some way to make up for what I've done to your life … What I keep doing to it.'

'You have nothing to apologise for.' He says it with such conviction that I almost believe him.

Lying next to him in the first light of day, I get a strange sensation. It's warm and bright and energising, something I haven't felt in a long time. Despite everything that has happened, and all that is about to come, in this one precious moment, I feel happy.

'Take me to Transcendence.'

Tom looks me straight in the eyes. 'Now?'

'Just like when we were kids. I want to leave my body and fly with you.'

A mischievous smile spreads across his face, deepening his dimples. A flash of golden light bursts from his body. Shimmering particles merge together on the ceiling, forming a perfect, weightless image of Tom above me. His corporeal body lies still beside me.

'Come on,' he says from above me.

'I don't remember how.'

Tom crosses his legs, hovering above me like a floating statue of Buddha.

'There are a few ways to leave your body,' he says. 'Sometimes, when you're in great physical or emotional pain, you can literally jump out of your skin. That's probably what happened the first time you did it.' He pauses for a moment, presumably to check my response. I suppose he's worried that I'm going to rush into the bathroom and heave my guts out again.

I reassure him that I'm okay.

'It can also happen when you experience intense pleasure.'

The words hang in the air between us until I look away, trying to disguise my embarrassment.

'Is there a third option?

'Meditation can work too. I'll guide you through it.'

Tom tells me to relax and take deep breaths. I close my eyes and feel myself sink deeper into the rug.

He moves down so that he's next to me, interlocking his little finger with mine. My eyes spring open. It feels more like a soothing stream of energy than physical touch.

'Close your eyes again and focus on the rhythm of my voice.' He tells me to visualise the energy centres in my body, starting with red at the base of my spine. I imagine a red swirling ball of energy filling me with light and power.

Next is the orange energy of my sacrum, followed by yellow for my stomach, green for my heart and blue for my throat. When we get to violet, between my eyebrows, he tells me to imagine stopping the swirling ball of energy.

'Your third eye is for intellect and thinking. That won't help you transcend. You need to feel, not think, your way out of your body,' he says.

It takes a few goes but eventually I imagine that the swirling purple ball has transformed into a calm lake. We move on to the white energy centre at the top of my head.

'This is your pathway for supreme light,' he says. 'Take a deep breath, and as you exhale, gently push your energy up and out of your white centre. I'll be waiting for you.'

I do as he says but nothing happens.

'Try again,' he says, his voice distant, as if he's talking to me from behind a wall. 'You're more powerful than you know.'

My body starts vibrating with sensation and it feels so familiar, as if my body has remembered what to do, even if my mind hasn't.

There's a flash of light, a rush of air and then I'm floating. I remember the feeling of warmth and comfort as if I felt it only yesterday.

Love.

I am love.

Opening my eyes, I look down to see my body, lying still, yet peaceful. It's shocking to see my body when I'm not in it. But it's not nearly as surprising as it is to see Tom's body – or more specifically, to see the way Tom is looking at me. Unmistakable longing glistens in his eyes.

'Over here,' he says.

I follow his voice and I'm confronted by the most beautiful sight I've ever seen. A luminous unicorn, standing proud and strong, looks up at me from my bay window.

Tom swishes his tufty mane and I float down to him. I reach my hand out. I want to pat him, but then I remember that this isn't just an animal, it's Tom. I quickly withdraw my hand, embarrassed.

'You used to run your fingers through my mane all the time,' he says, reading my thoughts.

That was before we knew what we were doing, I think but don't say. I tentatively reach out and touch the white hair on the top of his head. A spark of energy flickers between us on contact. I flinch, but then, realising – no, remembering – there's nothing to be worried about, I slide my hand down his soft mane.

Climbing onto his back, I lean forward and whisper in his ear, 'Take me high.'

Tom lifts his nose and snorts and we're rising, his enormous wings outstretched and beating rhythmically against my legs, moving us to the doors of the bay window. I clutch his mane instinctively, wondering how we'll get outside, when we pass right through the wood and glass of the door. It's been rendered insubstantial.

'How …?' I say, as we emerge on the other side.

'Everything is energy. We are particles of energy. We are one.'

I look down and see for myself.

This isn't Albion. And it isn't London.

It's everything.

The best way I can describe it is a combination of both realms; the wild gardens and gothic oaks of Iridesca overlay Volgaris, filling it with brilliant colours and light.

The cool breeze of a perfect, mild English spring morning caresses my face as Tom's feathered wings pull us upwards, above the palace pathway and gardens. His wings beat faster, and I feel the rush of air as we're pushed upwards. In the predawn, the trees are filled with the cacophony of birdsong and insect hums.

The sounds pass through me, becoming part of me. It's the strangest sensation, feeling utterly whole, grounded even, but at the same time experiencing the weightlessness of oneness with everything around me.

We swing wide over the palace, out above the green countryside and waterways below. Cool air eddies around us as we pick up speed, darting amongst the foliage. I tighten my grip around Tom's warm body as we lift even higher.

The view takes my breath away all over again. Early morning dew glistens in the sun's first beams of light curving over the horizon.

Far beneath, I spy Heathrow in a clearing. Planes circle below us; others sit on the tarmac like discarded children's toys. The outer suburbs in the distance are alive with possibility. The buildings are lit like crystalline structures, auras. Even the plainest of architecture is a marvellous crystal palace, surrounded in haloes of incandescent light.

Descending rapidly, we scream along the snaking tail of the Thames. We're almost in the city; Tower Bridge comes into view, whole again. Rather than the brackish sludge I know so well, the water is a vibrant greenish blue. It's so clear that I make out my features in the reflections glistening off the water.

I don't know if it's the speed we're travelling at or a trick of the early morning light, but the face staring back at me is almost unrecognisable. It's not just the particles of light energy streaming from my hair and playing off my face. I see something I haven't seen before.

I see hope.

I see strength.

I see someone I like.

Tom turns with the bend of the river, and the speed of his wings throws up a fine mist from the tributary, hiding the reflection. He subtly shifts the angle of his wings, and we're climbing again. He banks left and then a sharp right, and then, sweeping his wings back, he slows us. We come in to land on the roof of the western-most walkway of Tower Bridge, Tom's hooves touching down surely. He canters to the centre of the roof, before slowing to a complete halt.

I dismount and stand beside him. He catches his breath as I wrap my arm under his head to place my hand on the soft hair of his face. He nuzzles his head closer in to me and we stand together silently, staring out at the city before us, a sea of sparkling energy particles playing off the river, trees and buildings like a dense mass of fireflies.

The Tower of London is a magical wonderland.

St Paul's is complete again.

The Gherkin is whole.

The Shard is resplendent

Everything looks – and feels – exactly right.

The sight summons memories from a lost childhood. This vista I saw in dreams, and then forgot, was real after all. I have been waiting my whole life to return to this place, a place before pain and sadness and destruction. A place outside of time.

'Can we stay here forever?' I say.

'Yes and no.'

I look up, waiting for him to explain.

'Transcendence isn't a place in the normal sense. It's more a state of mind. One that we can take with us wherever we go.'

We stand in contented silence, taking in the beauty. Eventually, Tom shifts his head again, extending his wings, gesturing to leave. I climb onto his back and he canters to one end of the walkway roof and turns. I tighten my grip as he stamps a hoof and jolts forwards, working up to a furious pace before launching us into the air. His wings catch the air and we climb higher. We sweep back around behind the Shard, then rejoin the path of the crystal-clear river towards Windsor. Before long, the trees get thicker and we're nearing the deep green of the palace grounds.

We're both laughing with exhilaration as Tom bounds through my bedroom window. He stops abruptly in front of my rug and lowers his head. I topple forward off him and fall straight into my body. A light sensation of attraction, like the feeling of two magnets connecting, sends tingles through me as my body and soul eagerly re-embrace.

Opening my eyes, I stretch as if I've just woken from a deep sleep.

Tom blinks, opens his eyes, and shoots me his grin, served up with a side of dimples.

An unfamiliar flame ignites somewhere deep within me.

I try to smother it with a voice of reason but I cannot.

His lips are centimetres from mine, inviting me closer. I feel his eyes on me.

I'm terrified by how much I want him. It's a desperate, insatiable wanting that I've never experienced before. I watch my body as if it's somebody else's, moving closer to his, the gap between us dissolving.

I feel his warmth and see every single eyelash framing his eyes. He's staring at me with an intensity that robs me of breath. Gently, he traces his finger around the outside of my lips.

'There isn't anywhere in the world I'd prefer to be right now.' His voice is husky and I bite down hard on the inside of my cheek.

A single kiss will open the floodgates. I'm not sure if I can cope with where that will lead.

'Don't look so worried,' Tom says softly. 'I have no expectations.'

'Oh,' I say, suddenly feeling foolish. Did he just reject me?

He slowly runs his finger along my shoulder and down my arm, my skin tingling from the tiny electric pulses irradiating from his touch. It's tantalising. I want more, so much more, but I also know I shouldn't.

I can't.

'Have you ever been with someone, Chess?'

Mortified, I bury my face into the rug, willing it to swallow me up. Sometimes I wonder if I'm the only sixteen-year-old in the world who's this naive.

It would be easiest to say I've never found anybody I was

interested in. Which is true. I've never felt any burning desire for anyone. Not like I feel for Tom right now. But for some reason the whole awful, unedited, truth tumbles out of my mouth before I can censor it.

'Sometimes I feel like I'm damaged goods.' I try to steady my voice, but fail. 'If anyone gets too close, they'll know how broken I am.'

With one hand on my shoulder, he looks straight into my eyes. 'What you've been through doesn't define you. When I look at you, that's not what I see.'

'What do you see?'

I brush his hand aside and curl up into the fetal position, hiding my glistening eyes.

'I see a smart, witty, beautiful woman with untapped passion and power. Someone who has no idea what she's capable of.'

'Don't talk like that,' I say, unable to look at him. 'That's not who I am. It's just what you expect me to be because I'm Queen Cordelia's daughter.'

'You're wrong. You enchanted me when I was a kid and you mesmerise me now.'

He pushes my legs down from my chest with firm hands and shuffles his body closer to mine, blocking me from moving back into the fetal position.

'Chess, you don't need to make yourself small anymore.'

It's the weirdest, nicest, most insightful thing anybody has ever said to me. I close my eyes to stop the swell of emotion from breaking its banks. But when I feel his lips brush against my eyelids, I am lost.

All the sensible reasons as to why I shouldn't kiss him are trampled by an urgent, unquenchable desire.

I thread my fingers through his hair, drawing him closer to me. He responds to my invitation, parting his lips, allowing my tongue to penetrate his mouth and taste him.

It's not enough. I want more.

I need more.

His eyes burn into mine.

A faint tingle of pins and needles starts up in my hands and arms. I ignore it, focusing instead on the ripples of muscle on his chest as he pulls me closer to him. I feel like we are merging.

And then his hands are still and he pulls away.

I reach to pull him closer, but he peels my hands off him. 'This is a really bad idea.' His voice is hoarse.

'But I want to,' I say breathlessly. It's like someone has just turned off my oxygen supply.

Effortlessly, he lifts me off him and rolls away to the other side of the rug, looking at the ceiling.

Pins and needles course through my body.

I sit up, wondering what I did wrong. A rush of nausea washes over me. I *am* broken.

He sits up hurriedly. 'Don't get me wrong, Chess. I want you; you have no idea just how much I want you.' In a steadier voice, he says, 'But we can't.'

My stomach feels hollow; all the breath leaves me, as if someone just punched me.

Suddenly annoyed, I say, 'You don't get to decide what's best for me.' He lets out an exasperated sigh but I keep going. 'You stick your tongue in my mouth and then pull back because you suddenly decide that *I* can't handle it?'

'Well, technically it was *your* tongue, *my* mouth.' And then he has the audacity to flash a dimple at me and I can't decide if I want to slap it or lick it.

I feel the heat seep out of my argument but I'm not quite done yet.

'If you don't want me then just be honest and say it. Don't make this about what's right for me.'

'Believe me, Chess, I want you – in every sense of the word.'

I look over at him, surprised that I do believe him.

'Well then, what's there to argue about?'

'Look what's happening to your hands,' he says. I look down and see tiny light particles forming a ghostly aura around my hands and arms, sparkling dust floating off my skin. 'Intimacy is the ultimate union.'

I don't know whether to laugh or cry. After years of avoiding any close contact, I finally find someone I want to be with more than anything but I can't – because of a spell.

'There must be something we can do about that stupid spell.'

'There is only one thing. But it's a sacrifice that I could never ask of anyone.'

'Another death,' I say.

He nods. 'Someone else would have to correct the balance.'

A silence falls between us. Not awkward, or uncomfortable. Just silence.

I can hear Tom breathing, the steady rise and fall of his chest, as I stew in the injustice of wanting the one thing I can't have.

I search for the words, words that might make things better. My words, which I now know can command forces beyond imagining, opening unseen worlds and rendering reality a plaything, seem useless. Whatever power I possess, I cannot undo what has been done.

'What does this mean for us?' I say eventually.

'I have friends in Iridesca,' Tom replies, standing up. 'I'll stay with them until I figure out what to do.'

'At least stay for breakfast,' I say. Watching my hands slowing turning to dust is freaking me out, but I can't bear the thought of losing him again so soon.

He shakes his head, his eyes full of sadness and resignation.

'The obliteration in your hands will spread until it reaches the point of no return.'

He leans close and kisses my eyelids, before disappearing into the empty morning.

The pins and needles vanish with him.

chapter 25

Hooves *clip-clop* outside my window. Bright light pours through the gap in my curtains.

It takes me a moment to remember where I am.

This morning comes flooding back.

My head aches from a vulnerability hangover. I feel disconnected from my body. I wish I could block it all out.

I'm stripped bare.

This morning I needed Tom to stay. Now I'm relieved he didn't. How could I face him?

I was so stupid to expose myself like that. I dropped my guard. I lost control. I didn't just share my body, but my deepest secrets.

And my heart.

I try to think of something, *anything* other than this morning. But the more I try, the more intensely I feel him on my skin, taste him in my mouth.

And I hate myself for having liked it.

I hear a knock at my door and freeze as though I'm about to be sprung by my parents for sneaking a boyfriend into my room. Immediately I realise how ridiculous that is. Still, my stomach is cinched in a tight knot of anxiety and my cheeks are burning with shame.

Brina bustles into the room in her crisp white uniform.

'Sorry to disturb you, Your Highness, but it has just gone past midday.'

She's followed by a maid I don't recognise, a redhead with a long plait down her back.

'Where's Callie?' I ask.

The two maids look at each other for a beat and then Brina says, 'She's gone, Your Highness.'

'Gone where?'

'Anastasia will be your second maid from now on,' Brina says simply as she pulls open my curtains.

It's clear they don't want to talk about it and I don't push it – there's plenty I don't feel like talking about today either.

Anastasia places the empty tray over my legs.

'The Luminaress requests that you eat and dress quickly, Your Highness,' she says. 'There is an urgent matter she must address with you.'

'That doesn't sound good,' I say with a humourless smile.

My mind races through all the unpleasant reasons why Gladys would be in such a hurry to talk to me. And, of course, I get stuck on Tom and the time he spent in my bedroom.

'Is it anything to do with … um … this morning?' I figure that service staff see and hear everything so if they don't know Tom was here, then Gladys might not know either.

Brina bites her lip, clearly torn between her duty to me and her instructions from Gladys. But the giggle that escapes from Anastasia's mouth is answer enough.

'He is quite something, Your Highness,' she says as she waves her wand and conjures eggs and toast. Scrambled. No soldiers this time.

I'm about to say that nothing happened, this isn't what it looks like, but there's no indication that either of them are shocked or embarrassed. Then I remember: fairies don't do shame.

I choose to skip the flouncy dresses and wear a black bodysuit, patterned with the grooved armour that looks like muscle fibres. It doesn't help my mood any. I may as well be naked, given how exposed and vulnerable I feel.

Gladys must have been waiting right outside my door because as soon as I'm dressed she appears in the middle of my room. Her face is a picture of disapproval.

'You've been busy,' she states in a tone that has the maids scurrying out of the room.

I figure offence is the best defence. She's never had any interest in my private life before. She has no right to pry. But before I can get a word out she pulls me into a hug.

'You could have been killed. You took an awful risk, sneaking off to rescue that useless boy.'

'He's not useless,' I protest. 'And besides, it worked out.'

Gladys shakes her head and the lines around her eyes crinkle with concern.

'There's something you don't know,' she says, walking over to the window seat. 'I only realised it myself after your battle with the pycts. After you nearly died because of your own magic.'

I sit down on the edge of my bed, sensing that whatever she has to tell me, it's not going to be good.

'You recall that our kind use chromium to channel the Art?'

'All of you except me,' I say. I can't get Ada Lovelace's wand to do anything except pick locks.

'You're half human,' she says. 'Chromium is a trace element in human blood.' For a moment Gladys's eyes light up in wonder, making her look almost childlike. I must look blank because she continues.

'You don't need a wand, dear – you *are* a wand. You are your own power. Inside of you lies a deep reservoir of unlimited power. All that you require is already flowing within your life force.' The wonder has gone from her eyes, replaced by concern. 'But you are not yet disciplined enough to cope with the power that you have. You must exercise it with purpose rather than fear. You lost control when you performed that spell on the pycts and it almost set off a chain reaction within you. Fainting and collapsing was a mechanism of self-preservation. Your mind shut down before you overwhelmed your body.'

The full meaning of her words dawns on me.

'So if I end up having to battle Damius, my magic won't kill him. I'll kill myself.'

'Your strength is your greatest weakness. Your power is unprecedented. Our stories contain no records of such powers. Until you learn to conquer your fear, you must restrict yourself to small spells that your constitution can withstand.'

She walks over to me and takes my hands. 'You must understand this, Chess. Your unauthorised rescue mission of that inconsequential unicorn could have cost you your life and cost the Fae and humans their only hope for peace.'

I bristle at her dismissal of Tom as inconsequential.

'But what's done is done,' she goes on, the matter already forgotten. I guess that's the other side of being amoral: no time spent ruminating over how other people might have failed you. 'Events are moving faster than we had anticipated. Your uncle has marshalled forces far greater than we had feared.' Gladys walks to the door. 'Come. It's time you met with your Council.'

'Council?'

'Your Council of War, of course. You didn't think we were going to leave you to face the threat alone, did you?'

We wind through the corridors of the palace. I can feel every pair of eyes boring into me as we pass. In some faces I see awe, in others fear. But the reaction I notice most is faintly muted disapproval.

I'm unsure what offends them. Is it that I succeeded in harnessing my magical power to kill the pycts when they were hoping my mongrel blood would fail? Do they distrust me for leaving the palace to rescue the 'inconsequential unicorn'? Or are they just pissed that I didn't die in the process?

With me out of the way, Damius could take the throne without obstruction, or the Order of the Fae could carry on running its caretaker government. After thirteen years, why would they want a monarch back? Some would say that I'm no longer needed.

And I can see their point.

Or perhaps everyone I walk past is simply reflecting back the humiliation I feel over what happened with Tom this morning. The fear and disapproval I think I see in their faces are my own feelings about the way I disgraced myself: revealing too much, begging him to stay.

My stream of destructive thoughts is brought to an abrupt halt when we stop in front of a wooden double door with the unicorn emblem of House Raven embossed on either side. Two officers of the Protectorate stand guard. They bow and salute us. I nod back awkwardly and make a mental note to ask Gladys about the proper etiquette.

Gladys pushes open the heavy doors to reveal what looks like a ballroom that's been temporarily turned into a meeting hall. About the size of two basketball courts, its walls are panelled in rough oak and covered with portraits and landscapes hung in gilded frames. The high ceiling is decorated in a mural of fairies, unicorns and mermaids in a garden with a fountain. The largest chandelier I've ever seen hangs from the centre of the room; its crystal-encrusted tendrils span out across the space.

The room buzzes with the voices of the assembled Fae. Helmeted men, well over six foot, tower above me as I pass. A week ago I would have assumed that so many tall men in the one place must be a basketball team dressing up for an end-of-season bash. Now it strikes me as obvious that they're unicorns in two-legged form. Other people are dressed in variations of Jules's uniform, with pins and medals that I assume denote differences of seniority. I compare my own bodysuit, and feel like an imposter. Judging by its decorations, I outrank the lot of them. I feel like a little girl playing dress-up soldiers.

The throng of people parts as Gladys and I move through the room, their conversation dampening. Some offer thin, grudging smiles, while others beam at me. I'm uncomfortable with both reactions. Their hum of conversation picks up again as soon as we pass.

At one end of the room I spy three golden thrones elevated on a red-carpeted platform. Each throne has a red velvet cushioned seat and rubies encrusted in intricate swirling patters.

I suck in a jagged breath when I see the footstool at the base of one of the thrones. I remember it. I used it to climb up into the enormous chair to sit next to my mother and father. A memory of music and dancing flashes through my mind. I sat right there in that chair, watching all the people dance. I wanted to climb down and join in. My mother looked over and smiled at me. She reached down and took my tiny hand in hers. With her other hand she traced the shape of a love heart into my palm.

The memory is so vivid, so potent, that I can feel her warmth. Her softness. I can feel the love of my mother's touch. My eyes prickle with tears and my heart aches – literally, as if its essence has just been gouged out and all that remains is a hollow shell.

'Not now, dear,' Gladys whispers gently. 'There will be time for nostalgia later.'

She takes my shoulders and spins me away from the thrones and back into the present. At the head of a long oval-shaped table on the other side of the room sits the Chancellor, dressed in his sapphire cloak, his fingers weighed down with rings. Next to him sits the Supreme Executor.

'Your mother was never much good at following protocol either,' she says as I approach the table. Her lips stretch into a smile that is more reproof than fondness.

'And all have paid the price for it.'

I look towards the source of the snide remark. It came from a man standing to the side of the table. His blue eyes blaze with contempt.

I recognise him immediately. Well, sort of. The face is different and his mop of blond scruffy hair is cut shorter than I was expecting, but his nastiness is unmistakable. The Chancellor, clearly embarrassed by the man's outburst, introduces him as Loxley, Officer of the Protectorate. In two-legged form.

I smile at one of the men at the table as the chatter restarts around us. From the rust-coloured skin and row of gold loops snaking up each ear I identify him as Wynstar. He stands and bows to me. I want to thank him for saving me after the pycts, but this isn't the right time.

Across from us stands Jules. I quickly scan her for injuries from this morning and I'm relieved to find no sign of any. She gives me a brief nod and then looks away, her smile gone. I follow her gaze to see who she's staring at.

Loxley.

He sends back a malicious grin.

The woman next to Jules shakes her head disapprovingly at Loxley. She's introduced as the head of the Protectorate, General Sewell. The General looks considerably older than Jules, but I'm not fooled by her cropped grey hair. The sureness of her posture and the muscle definition beneath her bodysuit makes me think she's earned every one of those medals pinned across both sides of her chest.

I catch a glimpse of familiar blonde curls in the crowd. She has her back to me but I'm certain it's Abby. What's she doing at the Council of War meeting?

I look beyond her to the person in the doorway and my heart stops.

chapter 26

He's here.

At the far end of the room.

Tom.

Beautiful, dressed in a khaki kilt, leather jacket and unlaced army boots.

I tune out from the buzz of chatter around me, unable to concentrate on anything else.

He looks directly into my eyes with such single-minded intent that I feel like we're the only two people in the room. All I can think about is that the only person who's ever made me feel happy and safe is still here.

But then my memories from this morning assault me with such force that I grab hold of a chair to steady myself.

The truths I laid bare.

All that I shared.

I dropped my guard, lost control. Why did I have to ruin everything?

My mouth is parched, my palms wet.

I was never going to see him again. That thought

devastated me but it was also a comfort. At least I wouldn't have to face him. Yet here he is.

His head cocks to one side. A half-smile creeps across his face, flashing a dimple at me. My desire to flee is as strong as my compulsion to run to him. But I'm bolted to the floor.

Abby squeals as she spots Tom across the room, startling those closest to her. She weaves her way through the crowd to embrace her brother. He returns her hug and whispers something into her ear.

Even from the far end of the room, I see tears in Abby's eyes. I'm genuinely happy for her, happy for them both. And for the briefest of moments I'm proud of myself. I told Abby I would save her brother, and I did.

Tom's eyes return to mine over the top of Abby's head. Searching.

Penetrating.

Probing.

I look away, too embarrassed to meet his gaze. It's a relief when Gladys guides me to my chair.

Tom and Abby move around to stand behind Jules and the General. I'm so attuned to Tom that the scent of his masculinity intoxicates me from where I'm sitting.

I really wish that it didn't.

Abby catches my eye across the table, and mouths, 'Thank you.'

She abandoned me to a pyct army and now we're supposed to be friends? Fortunately, the Chancellor calls the meeting to order so I don't have to respond.

A hush falls across the room as some of the assembled Fae take their seats. Others remain standing around the perimeter of the inner circle.

'Ours are extraordinary times. They will test us all,' the Chancellor begins dramatically, and I fight the urge to roll my eyes. I could swear he's enjoying his moment as the centre of attention.

'Our queen is lost to us. Our princess is under threat.' At this he beams at me. 'And our own kin are being turned, against their will, into pycts, to form an army whose very purpose, we must assume, is to destroy us and all we hold dear.'

Loxley lets out a deep, gravelly, equine snort. 'You don't know that all are unwilling.'

'Of course they are,' snaps the Supreme Executor. 'The pycts have been extinct for generations. No Fae in their right mind would choose a form so vile. But as we have learned from Apothecary Abby Williams, the pycts have now amassed in the hundreds.'

I feel the blood drain from my face.

'The pycts were Fae?' I whisper to Gladys.

'We believe so,' she replies.

'But I killed them.'

'Yes, dear,' Gladys says matter-of-factly. 'But there are more. Many more we must deal with.'

Blood pumps in my ears like the beat of a drum. My chest tightens and my hands begin to shake as I think about all the people – my people – I murdered. I'm part of this bloodshed, of the killing I was supposed to stop.

'I don't understand,' I splutter. 'How can a fairy or a unicorn turn into a pyct?'

'We believe Damius has created a virus,' Gladys replies in a hushed voice, but by the way the room falls deathly silent, it's clear that everyone is listening.

The Supreme Executor capitalises on the silence and conjures an image above the table. My best guess is that it's a single-strand genome of some sort. I should have paid more attention in biology.

'This is the RNA virus that is causing the pyct infection,' the Supreme Executor says as the molecular structure rotates above us. 'The virus triggers a genetic mutation in Fae DNA, flipping the exact genetic sequence to turn Fae into pycts.'

'But that's not possible,' says Abby as she stares intently at the genome. 'Making such a structure would require genetic material that does not exist in our kind. Unless … unless …'

All eyes shift to Abby.

Abby's eyes settle on me.

'Unless *what*?' the Supreme Executor says, her eyes shifting between Abby and me.

'Nothing. I spoke without thinking,' Abby says, in a way that seems completely out of character.

'All we know is that the virus is highly contagious,' the Supreme Executor continues. 'It starts with corporeal weakness and pain, followed by the loss of mental faculties. In a short time the transformation is complete and another Fae is lost to Damius.'

'Even our strongholds are not immune,' says the Chancellor. 'Under this very roof, one young maid succumbed and responded to Damius's call.'

A knot tightens in the pit of my stomach. He must be talking about Callie. That explains Brina and Anastasia's reticence.

I can't breathe. The room spins. It could have easily been Callie in that pyct army. If she had turned into a pyct one day earlier, or if I had fought them one day later, I would have murdered Callie. Who did I kill instead? Hundreds of lives cut short because of me.

My trembling hands fly to my chest as I try to suck in air.

A golden hue radiates from a hairpin Gladys has removed from her bun. She conjures a glass of water and orders me to drink.

I gulp down the water, this time not at all surprised by the taste of raspberries and honey. The tightness in my chest eases ever so slightly. I can breathe again, but the meeting is a blur. It's not until I hear Tom say my name that my focus is ripped back into the room. He and Jules are giving a report about Damius's attack on me at Marshall's house.

As I listen to their retelling of events, something occurs to me. I was an easy target for Damius. But his flames went around me. Even I would have better aim than that. If Damius is as powerful as he's supposed to be, surely he would have been able to hit me.

The Chancellor thumps his hand on the table. 'The unprovoked attack on our princess cannot go unanswered.'

'Annihilating Damius's pyct army is a proportionate response,' says the Supreme Executor in agreement. She instructs General Sewell to draw up battle plans for the attack.

'*No!*' I blurt.

The room goes quiet as all eyes turn to me. I fight the impulse to sink low in my chair.

'I mean ... You can't just kill the pycts. They're innocent.'

A brief moment of indecision follows as the Chancellor and the Supreme Executor exchange glances. Neither says a word. Instead, they both turn to Gladys, waiting, demanding some kind of explanation. Gladys sits back in her chair and coolly returns their glare.

'Your Highness,' begins the Chancellor, with the smile of someone explaining a basic point to a child. 'They are pycts. This is our way.'

'It's not my way.'

A deeper silence envelops the room as everyone stares at me. My cheeks burn and I can feel the crimson rash snaking up my neck. I'm not used to this sort of attention and I can't decide if I want to burst into tears or vomit. Or both.

But I can't back down.

'They're your friends, your family. Our maids,' I say, trying to hold my voice steady. 'You cannot kill them in cold blood. Our fight is not with the pycts. Our fight is with Damius. Killing innocent people to punish Damius accomplishes nothing and makes us just has bad as him.'

The Supreme Executer leans forward. 'My dear princess, Damius tried to kill you – the heir to the Fae throne. We cannot tolerate —'

'Damius did not try to kill me.' I shoot Tom and Jules an apologetic glance for contradicting them. 'Damius was toying with me, menacing me. He was sending a message. He didn't kill me because he wants what everyone else wants: the key to the Chalice. And he needs me alive in order to get it.'

I decide not to mention the small detail that I have no idea where the key is or how it could possibly unlock a glass cup that doesn't even have a lock. But I figure if they don't know what I don't know, I might as well use that to my advantage.

The Supreme Executor turns to Tom and Jules, both of whom are looking uncomfortable.

'What Chess – excuse me, Her Highness – says about Damius's attack is possible,' Tom says in a considered tone.

I see Loxley's eyes narrow at Tom's slip-up with my name.

'We can use the key as bait to drag Damius out into the open,' I say. 'Then you can have your battle with him if you choose. But no more killing innocents.'

Wynstar is on his feet. 'You have the key already?' A beat later, he adds, 'Your Highness.'

I'm taken aback by his sudden interest and forcefulness. 'No.'

'But you know its location?'

'Not exactly.'

'But you can find it?' Wynstar prods.

'I, um, well …' I hesitate, feeling my plan beginning to unravel.

Loxley tosses his hands into the air. 'You plan to bait Damius, Princess, but you do not have the bait?'

'I'll get it,' I say, hoping I sound more confident than I feel. 'Give me time to get it and stop the senseless killing.'

Glances are exchanged across the table. I'm not sure who, if anyone, I have convinced with my plan. I turn directly to the Supreme Executor with my final appeal.

'Innocent Fae are dead. My mother is dead. My father is dead. Many of their supporters are dead. If we keep going at this rate, this war will kill us all.' Emboldened, I continue. 'You say it's not your way. Well, look at what your way has caused.'

Silence.

I look around at the faces of those seated and then to those standing around the room. Some are clearly shocked into silence. Others seem interested, unsure how to respond, and still others look irritated by my interruption, at having to indulge their naive princess.

I look at the only person who really matters to me and see his eyebrow rise quizzically. His head tilts slightly as if he's considering something, then he folds his arms across his broad torso.

No one speaks, so I continue. 'I've been outside the walls of this palace. Beyond this island of privilege and luxury lies a wasteland, a land in ruin. You sit here planning a war, planning the destruction of hundreds, even thousands, of your own as if it's nothing more than a minor inconvenience. For all your planning and councils and talk of war, you're isolated, cut off from the very world you're trying to save. And you pretend it's nature taking its course. But it's not. You have done this. All of you.'

My words are met with collective gasps. Appalled looks are exchanged across the table, as if I'm the foul-mouthed mongrel who was let in by mistake. But I'm not quite done yet. I don't know where my boldness is coming from but I ride its wave, the way I have so often done with my fear.

'My people, the people you claim to be fighting for, are suffering. And what do you give them? Pretty banners and distractions. Well, not in my name.'

I wait to be put in my place, but no one says anything. There's nothing except an awkward cough and the shuffling of feet.

All eyes turn to the Supreme Executor for her response. It would seem she's been making most of the important decisions around here since my mother's death. And my little speech isn't going to break that habit.

'You have until midnight tonight to summon your uncle,' she says finally. Then she orders General Sewell to use every available resource to locate the pyct army. 'If Princess Francesca fails, then you are authorised to eradicate the enemy.'

Chairs scrape as the people around the table stand; others bow in my direction and then disperse. I watch as Loxley slinks out, looking contemptuous.

Tom moves towards me but Gladys blocks his path.

'You are no longer required, young man,' she says, and the full meaning of her words is perfectly clear.

Anger flashes across Tom's face but he doesn't object.

He gives Gladys a curt nod and turns towards the door. Without even a glance in my direction, he's gone.

Feeling numb, I make my way towards the door, trailed by Gladys and Jules. The remaining crowd parts around me, a sea of pity and concern, perhaps even amusement.

What was I thinking, making a deal like that with the Supreme Executor?

How can I possibly find the key to the Luck of Edenhall in one day? Where do I even start looking? It's surely not an ordinary key, because there's no lock on the cup for it to fit into. I don't even know what I'm looking for.

I wanted to save the pycts, but I've just made it worse for them by forcing the Supreme Executor to set a deadline for their 'eradication'. All because of my stupid, audacious, impossible plan.

Callie's face appears in my mind. She put her trust in this lot and lost her family because they were loyal to mine. And now that she's a pyct, she'll die unless I can work out how to stop the retaliation.

When we're a safe distance from the Council, Gladys hooks her arm through mine. 'I hope you know what you're doing, dear,' she whispers. I see doubt in her face for the first time, almost like she's unsure of who I am, who I've become. And it kills me.

Reaching my chamber, I rack my brain for something to say to reassure her, to reassure myself. But I've got nothing.

'I need to be alone right now.' I shut the door on her and scrub my eyes with the heels of my hands.

I need time to think. To plan.

'That was quite a speech,' a voice says behind me.

I whirl around to find Abby standing with hands on her hips. She must have been behind the door.

'The Great Princess Francesca of House Raven. "She will return",' Abby scoffs, presumably quoting the ridiculous banners hanging all around the ruined city. 'Bet they're all having second thoughts about you now. Did you see the looks on their faces? Priceless! They're livid.'

'At least I'm trying something different,' I say, annoyed. 'It's not like any of the military geniuses out there are making things better.'

'Calm down. I agree with you.' She walks over to the window, and her gown, covered in red and yellow poppies, fans out behind her. 'Finally someone's talking about taking the fight to Damius. What's the plan?'

I say nothing.

'You *do* have a plan, don't you?'

'Well …'

'You don't have a plan? I don't know whether to laugh or cry. You know they're going to be calling for your head – especially when they join the dots and realise that the pyct virus is your fault too.'

'What?'

'That RNA virus could only have been created with fairy DNA with the trace element chromium.'

I'm not following.

'Blood!' Abby says, with exaggerated exasperation. 'Do I have to spell this out for you? Fairy blood doesn't contain chromium. That virus could only have been made from fairy blood that also contains chromium. And there's only one fairy with blood like that.'

Her words are like a punch to the gut. 'But how could Damius get my blood? I only met him last night.'

'I don't know. When you were a baby, perhaps? What I do know for sure is that if it weren't for you, pycts would still be extinct and all those Fae would be unharmed.'

'You're enjoying this,' I say, as my shock and guilt ferments into rage. 'Just like when you abandoned me in the Tube station. I bet that was your plan all along.'

'Chill, Princess,' she says. 'What did you expect me to do? I'm an apothecary, not a warrior. And anyway, I helped you.'

'Helped me? How?'

'By forcing you to stop being such a bloody coward.' She sits down on the window seat, her dress covering most of the velvet. 'You should be thanking me,' she adds, suddenly sounding bored with this conversation.

'Get out, Abby.'

'As you wish, Your Highness.' She stands and swishes over to the door. 'I guess you don't want the message Tom asked me to give you.'

I all but run after her.

She hands me a small envelope sealed with wax imprinted with a unicorn crest. When she's gone, I rip it open and read the note.

They're lying to you. Meet me at the butterfly house. Alone.

293

chapter 27

'Were you followed?' Tom says without looking up.

'I snuck out my window,' I say, closing the glass doors of the butterfly house behind me. 'Not very princess-y, I know.'

The air is humid and thick with the scent of blooming flowers. I don't know why it's called a house; it's the size of a football stadium, packed with butterflies of every colour and size surrounding a large pool of crystalline water speckled with huge lily pads.

Being surrounded by such beauty feels abhorrent when I think of the devastation just outside these walls – and the bloodshed that's hours away if I can't find the key.

Tom skims a stone along the surface of the bubbling stream. The stone hops along the water before coming to rest in the lush greenery, and butterflies burst out in an explosion of fluttering colour.

Tom picks up another stone, smooth and grey, and turns it over in his hand.

The same hand that held me this morning.

My cheeks flush with colour.

He picks this moment to look at me.

One corner of his mouth tugs upwards. I'm embarrassed and furious all at once and I wonder if unicorns can read minds.

I instantly regret coming. I almost didn't. I didn't want to give him a private audience to my humiliation. But my curiosity was stronger than my pride.

I can't look at him. Instead, I study every intricate swirl on the sandstone tiles beneath my boots as if my life depends on it. I'm afraid that if Tom looks into my eyes he will see the desire in me that I'm so desperate to hide, even from myself. I will not make myself vulnerable.

'Will talking about it help?' he says casually.

'There's nothing to say.'

I can feel his eyes on me but I refuse to look at him.

'We shared ourselves with each other. And now you can barely look at me. I think there's plenty to say.'

I cringe as his words form images in my mind. I try to lift my gaze to prove him wrong and restore some dignity, but my eyes are weighed down with a toxic mix of emotions.

'This morning was a mistake,' I blurt.

Out of my peripheral vision I can see a thin smile forming on his lovely face.

'You forget you're talking to a unicorn. I can sense your desire as clearly as I can smell your fear of it.'

Not a mind reader, then, but the next best thing.

He tosses the stone into the stream. 'You don't have to pretend with me, Chess. Intimacy doesn't have to be about power. There doesn't have to be a winner and a loser.'

As if by instruction, a butterfly flutters over and lands on my shoulder.

'Besides,' Tom continues, 'if anyone has lost their power in this situation, it's me.'

I force myself to look him in the eyes, trying to make sense of what he just said. I didn't expect him to look as emotionally exposed as I feel.

'You must know what you do to me. What you've always done to me.' Sadness creeps into his beautiful features. 'Not that it matters, anyway. I still have to honour the bargain and leave you. I stayed for the Council meeting because the Supreme Executor commanded me to report on our encounter with Damius. And the only reason I'm still here is because there's something you need to know – something the Order is keeping from you.'

He sits down on a mossy log next to the steam, and motions towards the wrought iron chair opposite.

'You're going to need to sit down for this.'

My stomach is a raw knot as I fan the butterflies off the chair and sit. I'm not sure how many more surprises I can take right now.

Sighing, Tom rubs his hand through his fringe and clears his throat. But he doesn't speak. His hesitation is agonising. Whatever he has to say surely can't be as bad as this suspense.

'Just say it,' I snap.

He nods briefly. 'Your mother,' he says. 'She's not dead.'

My eyes widen. I stare at him, trying to decide if he's telling the truth or if he means something else.

'She's not dead,' he repeats.

'But the Chancellor said Damius killed my mother,' I say forcefully. 'He told me that the first time I met him. It's not a conversation I'm likely to forget.'

'Did he actually say Damius killed her?'

'I … I can't remember if those were his exact words. He probably softened it a bit, but he left me in no doubt.'

'Words are important. They don't always mean what you think. Your uncle took your mother's life but he didn't kill her. Damius stole Queen Cordelia's life force and has imprisoned it. Where, I don't know. The Order has searched for it and hasn't found it. But her body lies here in Windsor, very much not dead.'

I so desperately want to believe what he's telling me. But false hope is too painful.

'How do you know about all of this if it's a secret?'

'I didn't have a lot to do when I was hiding in Iridesca as a kid. I was out looking for trouble one night and discovered her catacomb. Over time I pieced the truth together.'

'You know where her body is?'

'I can take you there.' Tom stands and walks to the back of the butterfly house. He strides across a small rockery carpeted in moss. Behind it, there's a stone wall thick with ferns. A waterfall bubbles down the wall, feeding the pool of water at the centre of the butterfly house.

'Careful,' he says as I take a tentative step onto the mossy rocks, then he crouches down and disappears behind a fern.

I bend down to follow, but I'm met with solid sandstone. Tom seems to have slipped directly into the stone. He must have used the Art to transfer, but I didn't detect any dust residue.

Then he appears again. For a moment, I think he's somehow part of the rock. And then I understand: there's no magic here. It's a small opening, but the inside wall blends seamlessly to the wall outside, creating the illusion that it's a continuous flat surface.

'Clever, isn't it?' says Tom.

I crouch down and squeeze through the hole in the wall. We're in a little alcove at the top of stone steps. The air is cold and the air moist. Tom lights the way with magic gleaming from his watchband. I follow him down three flights of steps and turn into a cavernous room with a domed roof. My heart pounds in my chest and a lump forms in my throat.

The walls are covered with ivy interwoven so thickly it seems to be part of the structure. Tall white lilies stand to attention around the room. I look up to see refracted light streaming through the pond in the butterfly house that's directly above us. Reflections of water and lily pads bounce around the walls.

My eyes track along the path of smooth stepping stones nestled in the lush moss, forming a path to a glass case in the centre of the cavern. A woman's body lies inside.

I reach out for Tom, steadying myself. Being told I'm a fairy princess is nothing compared to the shock of hearing that my mother isn't dead.

I know she's not fully alive but that's so much better than being dead.

I take another step forward and a bubble of anxiety explodes in my gut. I feel ill, I feel clammy. I've been alone so long I can't get my head around being anything else.

'Will she know I'm here?' I ask Tom.

'I don't know for sure. She may be able to sense our presence. She may even be able to hear us. But she may not. My guess is that it's a bit like being in a coma. As far as I can tell, no one really knows how Damius's dark magic works.'

I can't even recall how many times I've fantasised about meeting my mother. But I never dreamed it would be quite like this. I push through the sickly mix of trepidation and excitement, and approach the glass case. Ivy sprouts around its legs and a bunch of fresh violets rests on top. My mother's hands are clasped together on top of her emerald gown.

A tear creeps from the corner of my eye as I see the shallow rise and fall of her chest.

She really is alive.

I'm not sure what I thought my mother would look like in the flesh, but I'm certain it wasn't this. For starters, she is so clean, almost translucent. The parents of the kids I grew up with wore the harshness of their lives like stains. Since meeting Marshall and working at the V&A, I've seen what privilege looks like: unblemished complexions, silky hair, white teeth, manicured hands. But those people seemed like a different species from me.

As I stare down at my mother I see parts of myself. I have her bone structure – high cheekbones and a pointy little chin. Her hands are daintier than mine. Looking at them summons a memory of her stroking my hair, so vivid I swear I can feel it. I probe for more memories of her but am unable to recall anything else. The desire to know her pierces me so deeply that I shudder. I run my finger along the edge of the glass case.

'Why didn't Damius just kill her?'

'Some say that even Damius would not be so bold as to shed blood in the Royal House.'

I sense uncertainty in his voice. 'What do you say?'

'Damius has unprecedented magical abilities for a male Fae. One explanation is that he has violated your mother's life energy, drawing on it to fortify his own power. That's why he kept her body alive. To use her.'

'I'll kill him,' I say, my tone so harsh that I barely recognise my voice. 'I want him to suffer for what he's done. To pay. To know what it's like to lose everything.'

Tom stares at me, clearly surprised by the venom in my words.

'When I agreed to take the throne, I only did it to save you. When I made the deal to bait Damius with the Supreme Executor just now, it was to save the pycts. Now I want revenge.'

'I understand,' Tom says, his voice soft.

'Why hasn't anyone told me the truth about my mother? Why are they keeping this from me?'

'Politics.' He rubs his hand through his fringe again and

lets out a sigh. 'Damius can only exploit your mother's power while her body is alive. The Order would be able to weaken Damius's power if they killed your mother.'

My blood runs cold. 'Never. I'd never allow it.'

'Precisely,' he says, 'which is why it's easier for them if you think your mother is already dead.'

'And my father?' I ask. 'Is he really dead?'

Tom squeezes my hand. 'His body was never recovered after the rebel attack. I'm sorry.'

'I suppose it was too much to hope that I'd discover I had two "not dead" parents in one day.'

'Your father was a brilliant physicist,' Tom says. 'He's the only human to have worked out how to pass between the veil of our worlds without assistance. Certain factions of the Order considered him a threat to Fae security and wanted him executed. Your mother spared him. She wanted to discover how Samuel Maxwell had simulated the Art. And then, fortunately for me,' he says with a smile, 'you happened.'

He pulls me into a hug and I sink into his arms. All the awkwardness from before has gone. He feels so good.

So right.

After a moment I look up and ask the question I keep wondering about.

'Why did you perform that cataclysmic spell for me?'

'Because I love you, Chess,' he says simply. 'I always have.'

No one has ever said those words to me. I'd always expected them to feel abrasive, to mistrust them, to fear them. As if the person uttering them would be manipulating me, asking too much from me.

Instead, I hook my arms around his neck, look into his beautiful eyes and kiss him. It's a thank you, an apology and an invitation.

But as he holds onto me and kisses me back, as if savouring every sensation, committing it to memory, I know it's also a goodbye.

chapter 28

The air shifts around me.

Goosebumps prickle my skin.

There's a presence, malevolent and cold.

I step back from Tom.

The light in the catacomb has changed; the sunlight streaming through the pool is gone.

It feels like death is descending.

Tom swears as colour drains from his face. 'It's happening.'

'What is?' I manage to say before a bolt of pain through my spine has me crumpling onto one knee.

I clutch my head. It feels like I'm caught between a vice.

Tom tries to pull me up towards him, but moving makes it worse, so much worse. The ground around me sizzles; cracks snake along the rock and moss.

'Run,' Tom urges as he pulls me around the deep chasms that are beginning to form in the ground.

But I can't move, much less run. The shimmering dust has returned to my hands.

He picks me up and carries me back the way we came. We reach the top of the steps and we manage to scramble back through the opening and out into the butterfly house.

The mass of butterflies has fled, the few stragglers rushing to conceal themselves behind leaves and flowers.

My throat constricts, blocking my oxygen supply. I'm being assaulted from within.

'I can't breathe,' I splutter as Tom lays me on the ground.

Tom's watchband is gleaming, as is the wand he's pulled from his boot. He's chanting, cursing, apologising.

And calling for help.

I look up, my vision clouding. A second figure comes into view.

Gladys.

She's kneeling beside me. She grabs my wrist, lifting my hand towards her, inspecting it. I follow her gaze and see the impossible. My hand has completely gone, replaced by a cloud of shimmering dust.

I'm disintegrating, disappearing.

Stony coldness creeps up my arm.

I look to Gladys, pleading with my eyes for her to stop it.

But she yells at me. 'Is this the price you paid for rescuing this useless boy?'

'It wasn't her magic,' Tom says gravely. 'It was mine.'

The vision in front of me is switching.

One moment I see Gladys's face, her eyes wide, her teeth clenched.

I blink and she's gone.

Everything is quiet.

I'm in a school hallway.

It's deserted, deathly quiet.

I'm starving.

In front of me stands a row of pegs on the wall with school bags hanging off them.

I watch my hands taking a sandwich from a lunchbox that isn't mine.

I feel bad. Stealing is wrong. But my body aches with hunger.

I take a bite; it's jam.

I can't taste anything except shame.

I blink again.

The lunchbox has disappeared.

I'm trying to walk. I'm about to fall, but just manage to stay upright.

I look down at my feet. They're tiny. Baby feet.

I'm clinging to the finger of a man. My whole hand wraps around one enormous finger.

'You can do it, Chess,' the man is saying, pride in his voice. I look up and try to make out his face, but the sun streaming through the window behind him blinds me. A woman is clapping encouragement.

Another blink.

A woman's voice.

'Stop pretending. Try harder.'

We're seated on an upholstered bench seat. A glass case is in front of me.

A cup. It's pretty.

But I'm scared of it. It's alive, but not like a person or an animal. It's aware.

There's something I'm supposed to do.

I don't want to be here.

The woman sighs. 'This is pointless,' she says, and stands to leave.

Blink.

A dank, featureless room.

My bedroom.

Larry and Sue's house.

I'm crouched in the corner; the door is shut. I'm staring at the closed door, wishing – willing – it to lock.

Someone's trying the handle and there's yelling on the other side. But no matter how hard he tries, he can't get in.

I'm begging and hoping to die.

But I don't really want to die. I just want the pain and fear to stop.

Blink.

'I want to live, I want to live,' I hear myself splutter.

'What did you do to her?' Gladys says, but her voice is oddly distorted, slowed. 'Tell me you didn't barter her life with the Art.'

'I did.'

The cataclysmic spell.

I'm going to die.

'Fool! She's our one hope.'

My feet are numb, the cold slithering up my thighs.

'It was my fault,' I say through the fog. 'Larry. He saved me from Larry.'

My vision clouds again. The view in front of me is blurring, fading to white. But I can just make out Gladys's face turning pale as she peers at me through haunted eyes.

Is it guilt? In a fairy?

And at that moment, even through the haze, I realise that she knows what I went through. I had wanted to believe that she didn't, but now I can see that she knew all along. She was supposed to be my protector but she did nothing.

Gladys's face hardens as she grabs my shoulders with both hands. 'Do not let anyone distract you from your true purpose,' she implores. Her eyes bore into Tom and then flick back to me. 'Or you will ruin everything we hold dear.'

Springing to her feet with the litheness of an athlete, Gladys clutches her hairpin. She spins it above her head like a drummer spinning a drumstick. The hairpin becomes a blur, and her chanting becomes louder and louder, but I can't make out what she's saying. It sounds like some ancient language transmitting through a detuned radio.

The air prickles with static. Hard droplets of rain pelt from above us through the broken panels in the roof. The wind rumbles, slowly at first, then building to the roar of a jet. As the storm gathers speed, every pane of glass in the butterfly house shatters, and shards of glass rain down all around us. I can barely make Gladys out for the leaves and flowers and rain spiralling around her. She is the eye of a cyclone, summoning the fury of nature to her. Lightning shoots upwards from the ground. The leaves and flowers and rain explode.

And then … stillness.

Quiet.

My lungs fill with air. I suck it in.

The pain recedes.

The chill subsides.

I grab my hands together; they're fleshy and whole.

I'm not going to die.

I let out a little cry of relief. She's freed us; me and Tom. She knew how to fix the cataclysmic spell. She didn't save me when I was a child, but she's saved me now.

'Gladys,' I say, leveraging myself up on one arm. I know we can't put off the conversation about my past for too much longer. I'm going to have to confront her at some point. But for now, I just want to thank her.

Tom gets to his feet. He must have been knocked over by the force of Gladys's spell too. His eyes are wide, his features taut with horror.

I follow his gaze to where Gladys lies in a crumpled heap on the ground.

'Gladys! No!' I stagger towards her.

The realisation slowly dawns. She's rebalanced life and death.

'Take it back, take it back!' I scream. 'You will not die for me!'

I roll her towards me. Blood leaks from her nose. Her eyes are glassy.

'A power unbridled can only be unlocked by a power unbridled,' she says with a raspy breath. She closes her eyes and her head falls back.

'Gladys! Don't leave me.'

I cradle her in my arms, tears streaming down my cheeks and begin to chant the words of the cataclysmic spell. I don't care about the cost of this magic. I will pay anything to bring Gladys back.

I make this vow upon my soul
Life and death I will control
No return, and no remorse
As I alter nature's course.

The path of Gladys be undone
Leave unfinished what has begun
Cataclysmic, I pay the price
My most desired, I sacrifice.

Nothing.

'It's not working!' I scream at Tom. 'Why isn't it working?'

I frantically chant the cataclysmic spell one more time. And then another.

Tom's hand is on my shoulder. I can hear him saying my name but I chant the spell again, this time louder and faster. I do exactly what Gladys taught me: focus my mind, channel my energy. It must work.

'Chess.' With firm hands, Tom pulls me back from Gladys. 'Chess! She's gone.'

I push him away and turn back to Gladys. 'It has to work. I just have to try again.'

Tom lifts me off the ground and drags me back. 'She's gone,' he says again, taking my face in his hands. 'Once a life force has crossed over, it cannot be enticed back.'

I look at Gladys, her body now a shell, devoid of life, light and energy.

I flop onto the ground and howl, wrapping my arms around my legs and rocking back and forth, sobbing hysterically.

What have I done?

Death follows me, surrounds me and destroys anyone close to me.

Tom is beside me, silent, holding his head in his hands.

There's a crunching sound of broken glass behind us. We turn towards the door of the butterfly house.

Wynstar approaches, his black, red and gold kilt drenched from Gladys's storm. A group of Protectorate unicorns gather behind him, swishing their manes and sending droplets of water flying.

Wynstar's eyes are cold, hard malice. 'She should have let you die. It would have saved me the trouble.'

Tom is on his feet.

I stare at Wynstar for a moment, trying to process what he's just said.

'There will never be a mongrel on the throne.' He spits in my direction. 'Your mother was a whore and a disgrace to the Fae. If she had any sense of duty she would have executed Samuel Maxwell. Instead, she contaminated sacred Fae blood with an abomination – you. There is only one man remaining who is worthy of the Crown.'

Damius. Wynstar is in league with my uncle.

'But ... but ... the pycts. You saved me. Why didn't you just let me die?'

As soon as I ask the question I realise the answer.

'The key. Damius wants the key. You had to keep me alive to get it.'

In an instant, his contempt is replaced my amusement. He chuckles to himself, as if enjoying a private joke.

'You just lost your great defender, Princess. With the old woman gone, there's no one to protect you.' He levels me with a calculating stare, then gives a brief nod to the pack of unicorns behind him. 'Get the girl. And kill her pony.'

chapter 29

Tom's chest and thighs expand, straining against his shirt and kilt.

Just when I think the fabric will surely tear in two, it vanishes in a cloud of iridescent dust.

Emerging from the shimmering haze is Tom, transformed into the form of a hulking unicorn, towering above me. I stare up at him in awe. His horn glows and his nostrils flare as the Protectorate unicorns close in.

I take a running leap, grabbing his shoulder and swinging my leg over him in one practised move. I've done this before, many times. Muscle memory kicks in and I wrap my legs tightly around his body.

We rear up, and I see golden light shoot from his horn. Tom's fiery blast stuns and scatters the Protectorate unicorns long enough for us to bolt out of the butterfly house and into the grounds of the castle.

Tom's powerful legs pump the ground faster and faster. I shift my weight to match his stride, and turn to see the Protectorate unicorns storming after us.

If they've noticed Gladys on the floor, they don't seem to care. Loxley stomps right on her face, and it almost looks deliberate.

'Gladys!' I scream above the thundering of hooves. 'Tom, we've got to go back!'

'We can't,' Tom says as we continue to gather speed. He veers right, dodging the scorching blaze coming from the horn of a unicorn behind us. It's as if he has eyes in the back of his head. My thighs press into his body, and my fingers dig into his mane to keep from slipping off.

He parries again, this time finding cover behind a thicket of trees.

A barrage of fiery bolts narrowly misses me, hitting the trees ahead and exploding into flames. Fire races along the leaves and branches, igniting the neighbouring trees.

A perfect ring of fire blazes around us.

Tom snorts, circling around, taking in our flaming prison.

We're trapped.

Heat and smoke snake down my throat, making my eyes water. Tom snorts again and then we're sprinting towards the flames. I feel a tickling flutter on my thighs as his wings sprout from the sides of his body. They beat rhythmically and, just when I'm sure we're going to be consumed by the flames, his wings fold back, catching the air, and we're rising off the ground, soaring sharply up and over the burning trees. I bite back a cough and rub at the soot stinging my eyes.

A blast collides with my shoulder and I slam forward,

screaming in pain as I tighten my grip on Tom's mane. With my other hand I reach around to feel where I've been hit. My bodysuit is scorching hot but not burnt and, aside from the pain, I'm unharmed. I'm going to have an impressive bruise there tomorrow.

If we live that long.

Tom swears as he flies towards the Temple.

Turning back, I count twelve fierce unicorns swooping towards us like eagles hunting prey. More bolts fly from their horns. Tom lurches to evade them, weaving in and out of trees. But even with his speed and aeronautics, there are just too many blasts. And they're coming so quickly.

As we reach the outer walls of the Temple, Tom's breathing becomes laboured. I feel the heat from his body and his sweat dampening his coat.

I swivel further around on Tom's back to face our attackers. My eyes lock with Loxley's. The image of him trampling on Gladys ignites a primal heat within me. It tears through my veins. My whole body vibrates with delicious energy. The Art calls to me, begging me to unleash the full fury of my power. But Gladys's words hold me back: *You are not yet disciplined enough to cope with the power you have.*

Untamed, my magic could kill me. I can't risk incinerating myself like I almost did when I was fighting the pycts. It takes all my self-control to contain the power coursing within me. I stretch out one hand, clutching Tom tighter with the other. The air ripples with heat around my fingertips and, warps for a moment, before forming into a pulse of air just powerful enough to deter rather than destroy. The blast of air collides squarely with Loxley's horn and knocks him to the back of the pack.

I fire another, and another.

More blasts rain down on us from the unicorns and I do my best to deflect them, but one hits Tom's back. He groans and his body shudders as the bolt burns through his coat into his flesh. I reach forward and smother the blaze with the sleeve of my suit.

Tom spins around as wildfire erupts from his horn, forming a protective dome around us.

I swivel back to see the blasts from the Protectorate unicorns collide with Tom's blazing shield and then ricochet off. But each impact nudges us backwards until Tom is trapped up against the wall of the Temple.

'I can't hold much longer,' he shouts, the strain fracturing his voice. 'Jump onto the roof of the Temple and get to the castle.'

'What about you?' I yell back over the roaring blasts.

'Do it!'

'I'm not leaving you!' I scream. I won't let anyone else sacrifice their life for me.

I climb to my feet and somehow balance on Tom's back. I spread my arms wide and summon hate.

Hate for Larry, for giving Tom a reason to cast that cataclysmic spell.

Hate for Damius, for destroying my parents and stealing my childhood.

Hate for Wynstar, for calling my mother a whore.

315

Scorching, insatiable rage ignites within the core of my being, streaming into my chest, and rising into my throat.

And I welcome it.

It feels rapturous.

After years of silence – with social workers, teachers, police, everyone – I can finally let out all the pent-up feelings I've never been permitted to express.

The delicious heat courses along my arms to my hands, waiting to explode.

'Chess,' Tom warns. 'It'll consume you.'

I ignore him. I've made my decision.

'Gladys died so you could live. Don't make her sacrifice count for nothing.'

Blue flames dance along my fingertips, begging to be released.

'No, Chess,' Tom pleads. 'Don't make me live without you.'

'You won't have to,' I yell back as I rip my mother's pendant from my neck. I steady my breath and still my mind. Holding the pendant above my head in one hand, with the other hand outstretched, I release an intense, controlled spike of magic straight into the ruby.

The gemstone comes to life, each particle absorbing and multiplying my power. The power builds and builds until the ruby can no longer contain it. A magnified blast of molten energy propels straight out of my mother's pendant and through Tom's protective field.

Lightning surges and flickers across the sky. The Protectorate unicorns yelp like wounded dogs, cowering as my flames lick their bodies.

In the panic, smoke and confusion, Tom launches us skyward once again. We swoop over the castle. The Windsor grounds recede into the distance. I clutch Tom's mane once more, scanning the air behind and the ground below us for any more of Wynstar's unicorns, but for the moment we're safe.

Adrenaline rushes through me. I'm tipsy in the knowledge that I saved us.

It doesn't last long, as the image of Gladys lying dead on the ground of the butterfly house crashes into my mind, smothering every spark of joy. I fix my mother's amulet back around my neck and flop onto Tom's mane. I don't hold back. My whole body shakes with gut-wrenching sobs.

Yes, Gladys was prickly at times. Yes, she let me down when I was young. And she was not always truthful. But she gave me sanctuary. She was my friend, my guide. And she's dead because of me.

I'm sucked so far into the abyss of despair that I barely notice when, in mid-flight, Tom channels the Art through his horn and carves out a portal in a cloud.

Then we're in London, in Volgaris, joining seamlessly to where we were in Iridesca. The buildings are familiar in their triumph over nature. The air here is thicker with smog and the smells of industry. I nuzzle my face back into Tom's mane until he lands softly and whispers my name.

I look up. We're in the middle of lush woodlands. A robin chirps in the distance and, closer by, a mother duck calls to her ducklings. A light breeze carries the sweet scent of lilacs and roses. But my heart is so full of anguish that even this beauty can't move me.

Tom slowly lowers his head to the ground and I tumble forward down his neck. A carpet of moss cushions my fall and I curl up into a ball.

There's a fluttering sound and Tom's enormous feathered wings fold forward to cradle me.

'I'm sorry, Chess. I'm so sorry Gladys is dead.' He wraps his wings tighter around me in an angel's embrace. 'But I will never be sorry about the cataclysmic spell. You were worth saving all those years ago and you were worth saving in the butterfly house. Gladys knew what she was doing.'

'How can I keep going?' I mumble into my sleeve, which is slippery with tears. 'How can I ever be enough to honour her sacrifice?'

'Because you are you.'

I slowly move out of his silken hold so I can see his face. His magnificent wings nestle perfectly into his body. Despite my guilt and grief, I'm struck by the sight of his strong and commanding frame standing amongst the oak trees. But it is his faith in me that takes my breath away. Only now do I realise the value of such a gift.

I reach out to him. My palm glides down the side of his nose in long, deliberate strokes.

He stares at me through thick, long lashes.

The sounds of the garden fade into the background. The air becomes a thick blanket, enveloping us in a private moment. Something passes between us that feels timeless and permanent, a bond forged from our shared struggles, joys and dreams.

I step back and break our eye contact, overwhelmed by the intensity. 'Where are we?'

'Her Majesty's private garden.'

I raise an eyebrow.

'Buckingham Palace,' he explains. 'Thirty-nine acres of woodland in the centre of London for one woman and a few corgis. We're unlikely to be disturbed – by the owners, at least. As for the Protectorate unicorns, I can't be sure. Without Gladys's influence, we can't be sure if the Order will hold strong against the rebel guards and the growing number of dissenters or buckle to them.'

His eyes travel slowly up my body. 'I didn't know what state you were going to be in. I thought you were going to incinerate yourself back there and I was going to have to try to put you back together. We can rest here for a bit, but we're not in the clear yet.'

Tom shakes his head, a look of wonder in his eyes. 'Mind telling me how you managed to fight off the entire herd of Protectorate unicorns with barely a scratch? I've never seen anything like it.'

'Your sister gave me the idea. She laughed at me when I couldn't handle a wand back at the Temple. She couldn't believe I was unable to summon the Art, with all the energy that the rubies on the walls have absorbed over years. It got me thinking – my mother's amulet must have absorbed powerful magic from Fae queens for centuries. I figured I'd only have to use a little of my own magic to direct the spell without killing myself, and the power of my foremothers would do the rest.'

'You're incredible,' he says, laughing, and then winces.

'You're hurt.' I step closer, inspecting him. I find an angry patch of blisters and welts across his coat.

'Don't,' he warns, as I prepare to summon a spell. 'We're in Volgaris now. You'll have to pay for it. And you've lost enough today.'

I shake my head and speak the incantation. A picture of two paths forking out forms in my mind; one is for pain, the other is for memory. Since my poor body has endured so much over the last few days, I choose to pay with a memory.

An image of my past flashes before me and my gut clenches as I respond emotionally to the memory. But the image disappears before my mind has time to register what it is. I don't even know which memory I'm looking for.

I recite a healing spell and Tom's burn turns golden before closing over. An angry red mark remains underneath the white coat, which begins to grow back over. It's not a great job, but it will have to do until we can get to an apothecary or healer.

The muscles in Tom's face relax, and I'm pleased that at the very least I've stopped the pain. But a moment later, he's frowning again.

'What did you just pay for that spell?'

'Nothing. A memory.'

'Don't ever give up your memories,' he says seriously.

'There are plenty of memories I'd gladly give up.'

'No, Chess, your memory is what orients you in time and space. Memories make us unique. All your experiences piece together to make you who you are. They show you where you've been and guide you to where you need to go,' he says. 'Lose too many and you lose yourself.'

I stare up at him, his words sinking in as I recall the childhood memories that flashed through my mind back at the butterfly house.

Memories of my hunger at school and the moment I became a thief.

A man who must have been my father.

My terror of Larry.

Being asked to unlock the Luck of Edenhall.

In one way or another, all of these experiences have led to this moment.

And that's when I know what I must do to find the key to the Chalice.

chapter 30

Wind howls in my ears as we soar above the centre of London.

Tom manoeuvres between buildings, turning sharply. I wrap my arms around his neck.

'What if people see us?' I say, leaning into the space behind Tom's ear to be heard above the wind.

'What are they going to do? Put us on the Wanted list again?' Tom's wings beat powerfully, swinging wide over Hyde Park. 'Fly with me.'

My body tenses at the mere suggestion of it.

'It'll be quicker,' he urges. 'The longer we're out here, the more we're exposed. Fly with me, Chess.'

The memory of my flailing wings at the Shard has me tightening my grip.

'But last time —'

'Last time you didn't know your power.'

Attempting to fly on my own right now feels crazy stupid. But with all that came before and all that is about to come, living fearlessly in this moment is suddenly more important than clinging to what I know.

Or, at least, what I thought I knew.

Finger by finger, I release my grip and loosen my clenched thighs from around Tom's body. My heart's in my throat. I do my best to ignore it. Tom slows and then hovers as I climb onto his back. I tilt my head towards the heavens. My hair whips around my face.

'Will you catch me if I fall?'

'I won't have to.'

I feel the power in me, like an adrenaline kick to the heart but surer, more stable, more lasting. My mind screams at me that this is insane.

I go with my heart, leaping into the nothingness.

My stomach plummets as I wait and hope for my wings to appear.

Time slows.

My head aligns with my heart. I'm done with waiting and hoping.

Up until now, my wings have chosen me.

This time, I choose them. I command them.

My wings burst from my back in an explosion of iridescence. I catch the breeze, slowing and then halting my descent. I flex my wings as surely as a muscle, feeling them slice and scoop the air in smooth, steady arcs. Long-dormant muscles awaken, extending and contracting as I feel myself lift gently into a hover.

The breeze is cool on my skin, but in the exhilaration of the moment I feel warm.

Turning, I gasp at the sublime grandeur of my wings,

gracefully beating in the breeze.

My wings are part of me. They are me.

Still hovering, I turn a full 360 degrees, each beat of my wings becoming surer and easier. My breath settles and I feel at home. I squint in the bright sunlight as I take in the view over London. It's stunning, nothing like the view from a building or Google Earth. So open, so free.

I laugh and cry at once.

A moment later I soar upwards, overtaken by pure joy. At first, I'm surprised by how fast I travel. I race through the thermals, then slow myself, spiralling to meet Tom. He looks back at me, his head held high and his ears pointing forward.

'You're the bravest person I've ever met, Chess Raven,' he says, eyes shining with pride, and for a moment I forget how to breathe.

'Race you to the V&A,' he yells, and speeds away.

Now that's a challenge I can't refuse.

Instinctively, my arms arch in front of me like a swimmer's, then cut back through the air in one swift propulsion. My wings take over, beating effortlessly. The wind is cold on my teeth, and I realise that my mouth is open because I'm grinning.

I fly level with Tom and then zoom past him, looking over my shoulder.

'Thought I'd give you a head start,' he calls.

'That was a mistake,' I yell back.

I expect him to laugh but his ears fold back and his neck arches.

'Watch out!'

I spin around.

The sky tears apart in front of me with a bolt of blinding light and a deafening boom.

A white unicorn hurtles through the punctured sky like a missile.

I'm the target.

I shoot upwards but the unicorn adjusts his course. He's so close now that I recognise the golden horn trained on me like a loaded gun.

Loxley.

I summon the Art but I'm too slow. Loxley howls and his face contorts in pain as flames shoot from his horn, screaming towards me.

Time slows as I watch the distance between me and Loxley's blast collapse. My powers are building, I brace for the pain or conjuring a spell, but the blast is coming too fast. Tom flies towards me but there's no way he'll reach me in time.

From nowhere, a piercing screech of nails down a blackboard deafens me. The air sizzles with sparking particles. A blackish-brown blur bursts across my field of vision and I'm propelled through space, out of the blast's range.

I steady my wings, hovering in the sky and trying to work out what's going on. A cloud of singed black feathers explodes in the air around a brown unicorn. He lets out a guttural roar as the remaining feathers on his wounded wing shrivel and drop off, leaving nothing but exposed bone. I've never seen this unicorn before but he just protected me. He pushed me out of the path of Loxley's bolt, taking the full brunt of the attack himself.

A blonde fairy hovers nearby, raising her arms and unleashing a torrent of fire on Loxley.

Abby? From out of nowhere.

Tom joins his sister, reigning down molten fire on Loxley. Both their faces contort and strain from the pain of conjuring the Art in Volgaris.

My attention goes to the brown unicorn. His eyes close and his head flops forward. His injured wing droops, before recoiling into his body, followed by the other wing.

A shimmering cloud of particles explodes around him and the brown unicorn transes into …

Jules.

chapter 31

She's dropping like a stone.

I contract my wings, smoothing them as close to my body as I can. I pull my hands back at my side and speed down towards Jules, straight at the ground. The rush of air pierces my eyes and the friction burns my cheeks. My hair is tight against my scalp, as if it's being plastered back.

I will myself to accelerate as the concrete rises up to meet us.

I will not let her die.

With less than 50 metres to go, I snatch her limp hands and extend my wings to their full span to slow myself. We come to a halt with only metres to spare.

I cradle Jules's semi-conscious body in my arms. She doesn't feel as heavy as she should; it's more like the weight of carrying a person buoyed by water. I launch skyward, warily at first, anxious how Abby and Tom are faring with Loxley.

Abby comes hurtling towards me with Tom behind her. I quickly scan for injuries. They're sweaty and bloody from fighting with the Art in Volgaris but I don't see any serious wounds.

'Is she alright?' Abby asks, placing a hand on Jules's forehead. She doesn't seem at all surprised to discover that the black-brown unicorn just transed into my bodyguard.

'I don't know,' I say. 'Are we safe?'

'He fled to Iridesca,' says Tom. 'We need to hurry. He might return with backup.'

'We need to get her somewhere I can treat her,' Abby says, wiping the blood from her nose with the back of her hand.

'The roof of the V&A,' Tom says, pointing to the dome in the distance. 'That's where we were headed.'

We fly upwards, Tom leading as I carry Jules, followed closely by Abby.

We touch down and I carefully lower Jules onto the part of the glass-panelled roof of the V&A that isn't smashed. Blue tarpaulins are stretched over large sections of the roof. I'm guessing we have the ravens to thank for that. My wings draw back into my body. I feel them inside me as a comforting presence, waiting for when I need them. It makes me wonder how I could have lived with such power inside me for all these years and never have realised.

Tom transes back into human form, his kilt and leather jacket reappearing.

Abby's wings retract and disappear as she crouches beside Jules, examining her like a paramedic. Jules groans and rolls on her side, curling into a ball.

Abby produces a small vial from her armoured bodysuit

and places it to Jules's lips. She whispers something that I can't make out. Some fairy alchemy, I figure.

Jules swallows the potion, grimaces, coughs and splutters. She's hurt but alive. She pushes Abby away, setting her off balance.

'Leave me,' Jules says with a murmured groan.

'I'm just going to check you over,' Abby says.

'I do not need medical attention,' Jules says, curling back into a foetal position. A sob escapes her. It's not pain.

It's gut-wrenching, uncontrolled, torment.

Shame?

Shame at being scaevus?

I don't get it. Everyone keeps telling me fairies don't do shame or guilt. The Fae say it makes them superior to humans. And humans say it makes them evil. But then they go and do stuff that makes me doubt it.

It's not the first time I've seen humanity in Jules. When I first met her, she gave the last pyct that was attacking me a chance to live. I'm no expert, but as far as I know, nature doesn't show mercy.

I stand there like an idiot, overcome by the magnitude of what Jules has just done. She revealed herself, essentially risking her own life – in more ways than one – to save mine.

I bend down and rest my hand tentatively on her shoulder.

'I don't care that you're a unicorn,' I say. 'In fact, I think it's pretty cool.'

'You should care, Your Highness,' she says, her voice rough with emotion.

'Well, I don't. You could trans into a slug and it wouldn't make any difference to me.'

'I am outside of the natural order, an abomination. I am not worthy to serve you.'

'You're my friend. And you've saved my butt more times that I care to mention.'

'I will tender my resignation immediately.'

'To who?' I almost laugh, looking around the empty roof of the V&A.

'You must accept it, Your Highness. It's your duty to enforce the way.'

'Nope. It's not *my* way. I'm not doing it.'

Jules's tear-streaked face turns towards Tom. 'Then the duty falls to Master Williams to report me to the Protectorate.'

In my best impression of a stern royal, I say, 'What Master Williams witnessed today was First Officer Jules of the Protectorate bravely risking her life to save the heir to the throne. Isn't that right, Master Williams?'

I stare imperiously at Tom, awaiting his answer. Instead, he addresses Jules directly.

'You are what you are, and you are exactly who you're meant to be.'

At that moment I know for sure that I am totally and utterly in love with him.

'Listen, Jules,' I say, standing up. 'I'm about to do something that's most probably dangerous and certainly ill-considered, and there isn't anyone I would want to watch my back more than you. So, when you're feeling up to it, on your feet, soldier. I need you.' I look at Tom and Abby. 'I need all of you.'

Abby helps Jules to her feet. She's still cowering, but whatever alchemical potion Abby gave her seems to be working its magic.

We make our way around a hexagonal glass dome that forms part of the roof, jumping over raised pipes and air ducts. I examine the lock on the rooftop exit. It gives way easily, with a bit of help from the pin from Tom's kilt.

Inside, we weave through the lunchtime crowd towards the Medieval and Renaissance Room.

It feels like a lifetime ago that I walked this exact corridor on my way to meet Marshall for my birthday lunch. I have to remind myself that it's only been a few days. When Gladys told me in Tom's house that I could never go back, I had no idea how true those words would turn out to be.

And now I wouldn't want to go back, even if I could. My life before was bleak and lonely, but it was all I had ever known. I made the mistake of thinking that the unhappy familiar was preferable to the risk it would take to change it. I was wrong. My reality and belief in what is possible will never again be so limited. If only I could have understood this without losing Gladys.

I push the grief and guilt down deep. I need to find the courage to be the person she wanted me to be. If I can't, I'll never be able to live with her sacrifice.

The museum is crawling with tourists, and I'm acutely aware that every one of them has probably seen the news reports about Tom and me. Not to mention that three women in bodysuits and a guy in a kilt aren't likely to blend in. One phone call to the police is all it will take for it to be over.

But I don't have the luxury of waiting and being cautious. We only have half a day left to find the key to the Luck of Edenhall so I can use it to draw Damius out of hiding. Then the Protectorate can capture him and I can stop this war with the pycts.

I just wish I had more of a plan for locating the key. All I have to go on is that Agent Eight brought me here as a child to find it. Perhaps she was trying to awaken some wisdom she knew to be innate in me.

It's not much, but it's all I have right now.

As soon as I step into the Medieval and Renaissance Room I can tell that something is wrong. Something about the energy in the room.

Jules and Tom sniff the air, much like you'd expect unicorns to do. It makes me wonder why I didn't see it in Jules before. They both tense, scanning the room for danger. It's not just me being jumpy; whatever it is, they sense it too. Abby walks over to Leonardo da Vinci's notebooks but her eyes are also darting around.

At the far side of the room sits the cabinet that holds the Luck of Edenhall. A middle-aged couple is standing right in front of it, blocking my view.

Jules is out in front and Tom flanks my right like a bodyguard as I take another step towards the Chalice.

A huge, calloused hand clamps down on my left shoulder.

Jules pivots, somehow sensing the contact.

'Don't move,' a raspy voice whispers into my ear.

It's Tony, the security guard for the Medieval and Renaissance Room.

A weak smile tugs at my lips. We've become not-quite friends over the past few months. He's even shown me photos of his kids. I'm hoping that will be enough for him to look the other way while a wanted felon is in his patrol area.

But he doesn't return my smile.

My heart races. Tom tenses, readying for a fight. I hear Abby suck in a breath. Jules stares pointedly at Tony's hand on my shoulder.

'You shouldn't have come back,' Tony says, hastily removing his hand. 'Princess,' he adds after a pause. He scans the room to see if anyone is looking and then lowers his head in a discreet little bow. If you didn't know better, you'd think he was stifling a sneeze.

My mouth drops open. 'You're Fae?'

Another slow nod.

'And you knew about me?'

'I had a pretty good idea,' he says. 'The way you kept coming back to this room. It was like the Chalice was calling to you.'

'You were spying on me?'

Tony stiffens. 'My responsibility was to keep watch over the Luck of Edenhall,' he says defensively.

'Was?'

He nods towards the cabinet. 'Gone. Stolen. Last night.'

I peer around Tony. Sure enough, the glass case is empty, replaced by a small sign that, even from this distance, I can read: 'Exhibit temporarily being restored'.

'Stolen? By who?'

His leathery brow crinkles. 'You.'

He says it with such certainty that I don't know how to respond. But before I can say another word, I sense a shift in the air, a change in the room's energy.

It dawns on me what's wrong.

Schoolchildren.

Normally at this time of day the V&A rings with the sounds of excited children yabbering and the not-so excited ones complaining that art is boring.

But not today. Today it's only adults.

This is a trap.

'We need to get out of here,' I say. 'Fast.'

I grab Tom's hand and whirl around to retrace our steps towards the exit. We make it a few paces when an imposing figure emerges from the crowd that now seems to be deliberately blocking our path.

'Hello again, Francesca.'

chapter 32

Agent Eight.

I turn to run but the middle-aged couple in front of the Luck of Edenhall cabinet step in front of us. Both reach into their jackets.

Guns. Automatic, I'd say. With a dull metal finish.

I recognise the floppy jowls and apologetic smile on one of the agents. Agent Weekes apparently still wants to make friends with me. But it's a little late for that, especially when he's pointing a gun at my head.

I scan the room as every single person draws a weapon of some kind. Thirty, possibly forty weapons are trained on us. Agent Westerfield holds a taser. Probably the same one he zapped me with in the hospital. Tony steps back and pulls his gun as well. I look him in the eye but he avoids my gaze, confirming his betrayal.

Agent Eight stares at Jules, her Lego hair unmoving as she looks my bodyguard up and down, appraising her from head to toe. It's like she's sizing her up before a fight. Jules's face remains impassive, but I can see the tension in her body. She's ready for anything. Agent Eight wouldn't stand a chance, gun or no gun.

Agent Eight whips her piercing stare to me and stalks closer. Each clack of her heeled stilettos on the marbled floor tightens the knot in my gut.

But the knot unravels as the Art awakens in my veins. A warm calmness pervades my being. It's a relief to be free from the anxiety but I have no idea what I'm going to do with the power that's building in me. I don't want to unleash the full fury of what I know I possess. Now would not be a good time to incinerate myself. And since I'm in Volgaris, I'm not sure I could withstand the pain of using so much magic anyway. After Tom's warning about my memories being essential to who I am, I'd only be willing to trade pain for magic.

But I refuse to let Agent Eight lay one manicured talon on my friends.

And I won't be caged like an animal again.

Ever.

'Where is it?' Agent Eight demands, invading my space.

I roll my eyes. 'Haven't we had this conversation before?'

She sighs. 'Let me explain how this works, you little delinquent.' She's standing so close to me that I can smell the stale coffee on the hiss of her breath. 'You're going to give me what I want, or you and lover boy and your new gal pals are going to spend the rest of your lives wishing you'd learned how to cooperate.'

'Does it look like I'm hiding anything in this bodysuit?' I say, tapping my waist and thighs.

Her hand flicks upwards as she moves to strike me across the face.

With my powers cascading through me, it's as if she's moving in slow motion. I grab her hand mid-air and crush her fingers back into the palm of her own hand.

Wincing in agony, she wrenches her hand back. I tighten my grip. Her knees buckle but she manages to stay on her feet, an icy stare boring into me.

The surrounding agents glance sideways at one another, seemingly uncertain of what to do next. Muzzles of guns are readjusted against shoulders, readying to fire.

I release Agent Eight's hand. She shudders in relief and massages her crushed fingers. Straightening up, she shifts her hair out of her face.

'Nice trick,' she says, taking a step back from me. 'But you're surrounded. And you already know I won't hesitate to use lethal force. Let's start again, shall we? We know you have the Chalice and we've already established that you have the key. Give me both. Now. Or your horsey boyfriend over there pays.'

She levels Tom with a dead stare. I'm guessing his escape made her look bad.

'I didn't take the Luck of Edenhall,' I say.

'Wrong answer.' Nodding to the agent nearest to her, she says, 'Finish them. Make sure the Princess is unharmed.'

In an instant, Jules takes out three guards with a series of kicks and I don't know what. Tom knocks the guard closest to him to the ground with a fist to his jaw. Abby ducks behind a statue.

But it's not enough to contain the situation. Not even close.

My senses burst into overdrive as all hell breaks loose.

The air around us explodes with energy pulses and bullets. I can pinpoint the explosion of each gun barrel, distinguish them from one another. I see the air warp, can trace the tiny heat signature tailing behind each bullet. They're coming from all directions, converging on my friends.

I don't think.

I do.

I clasp my mother's amulet, holding it out in front of me.

An image of me as a child snuggling into a soft, warm body flashes into my mind. A memory of my mother. It's the price of my magic. A price I will not pay. I choose pain instead and grit my teeth for the onslaught.

Power pours out of me and into the amulet.

Blue light fills the room and connects with laser precision on each individual blast.

The bullets stop, hovering in mid-air on their trajectories like lethal insects buzzing in front of my friends' heads and over their hearts, before bursting into clouds of simmering dust.

I cry out; I'm burning up from the inside. But I can't stop. The agents reload their weapons and prepare to take more shots.

I push through the agony. Just one more burst of power and this will end.

I conjure the spell for heating metal. Agents gasp and swear as their weapons turn to molten metal and drip onto the floor in scorching puddles.

My legs are jelly and I stumble to the ground. I try to get up but my head's spinning and I'm having trouble focusing.

Heavy boots slam into artefacts and bodies. I see Jules deliver a series of roundhouse kicks and karate chops, flooring more agents stupid enough to come near her.

From behind, an agent lifts a marble statue above her head.

'Jules!' I manage to cry out.

Tony, the security guard, lands a huge hand across the back of the man's neck and knocks him to the floor. He turns to me and winks.

Westerfield rushes towards me but Tom blocks his path, trading blows in a pub brawl.

Abby pushes over the marble statue she's been hiding behind, taking out two agents.

I wipe the trickle of blood coming from my nose. But it it's not a trickle, it's a stream.

Over the sounds of shouts and groans, glass and marble smashing, I feel, then hear, vibrations.

The Art.

The veil between the realms is being rent apart. A pack of unicorns dressed in armour emblazoned with the Protectorate's insignia tear through the arched entrance.

The four unicorns leading the attack break away and run directly towards me, jumping over smashed masterpieces and pushing agents from their path. I put up my hands to defend myself, weakened but not prepared to give up.

But the unicorns surround me protectively. The rest of them fill the room's perimeter. A group of around twenty female Protectorate officers, led by General Sewell, strides into the room after the unicorns. Sewell scans the scene with the authority and invincibility of a commander leading an advance party against a smaller, weaker opponent.

Which is exactly what the Agency is, I guess.

Some agents stand in awed wonder. Others whip their heads from right to left, panicking like cornered animals. A few bolts of magic from me and some hand-to-hand combat is one thing. Being hemmed in on all sides by unicorns and warriors is completely out of their league.

'What is the meaning of this?' Agent Eight says to Sewell with a steely gaze. 'This is an illegal occupation, in gross violation of the Treaty. What's more, you are interfering with a legitimate policing operation.'

Credit where it's due – either Agent Eight's a natural actor, or she really believes what she's saying.

'This Fae' – she spits in my direction – 'and her accomplices have been engaged in a series of unauthorised operations.'

General Sewell looks her up and down. 'Spare me the legalities,' she says. 'As you well know, your Agency has perpetrated many more and far graver breaches of the Treaty between our two peoples, not the least of which is the incarceration of the Queen in the Ascendant. We are here merely to protect her and ensure her safe passage.'

'I know no such thing,' Agent Eight lies through her teeth, a picture of calm. 'What I do know is that these Fae have stolen the Luck of Edenhall. King James himself stipulated that the Chalice must remain within the care of humans at all times. By taking it, they have put the status of the Treaty in question.'

'You would question the proprietary of the Queen in the Ascendant?' counters Sewell without so much as a glance in my direction. 'Have you evidence of this theft?'

Agent Eight clearly has nothing, and I consider the possibility that this was all a setup. If the Agency could pin the theft of the Luck of Edenahll on me, they could legally detain me and, under the Treaty, the Fae would be powerless to stop it.

'I thought as much,' says Sewell. 'As you are obviously incapable of ensuring her safety – in fact, you're endangering it – our presence is entirely legitimate.' She turns to me and says, 'Come now, Your Highness.'

I should be cheering at the General kicking Agent Eight's butt like this. But instead I'm pissed off. At both of them.

General Sewell's treating me as if I'm an incorrigible child who needs to keep quiet, get in the car and do as I'm told. It's like every meeting with a social worker, doctor or lawyer I've ever had. They don't even pretend to care about what you think; they talk about you as if you're not there.

'Do I get a say in any of this?' I say. 'I know I'm just the Princess and "Queen in the Ascendant", or whatever.'

Both Agent Eight and General Sewell stare at me.

Behind them, a mischievous smile creases Abby's face. Jules examines her feet, looking uncomfortable. Tom is somewhere in the middle. Pride shines in his eyes but I can tell he's concerned about where this will lead.

General Sewell walks towards me and, in hushed tones, says, 'Your Highness, there are your duties to consider.'

'I was given until twilight to stop senseless carnage,' I say, with the confidence and authority of my title. 'I expected the Council to honour its word.'

'That was before you were attacked, Your Highness,' she says, gesturing to the assembled agents. 'My orders are to secure your person and return you safely to Albion at once.'

She turns and gives a nod to the unicorns flanking me. Apparently the matter is decided.

'Whose orders?' I challenge.

Her eyes widen at my resistance. 'The Supreme Executor's.'

'The Supreme Executor can overrule the Queen in the Ascendant?'

'No, of course not. But when it comes to the protection of the Crown ...' She reconsiders. 'If I may, Your Highness, this conversation would be best had far from prying ears.' Lowering her voice, she says, 'Yours is a precarious position. Your safety and duties are paramount.'

'I'm not finished here,' I say, stepping in front of the unicorns guarding me. General Sewell opens her mouth, but I push past her to where Agent Eight stands, her arms folded.

'You know I don't have the Chalice. So you can stop using that to threaten the Treaty and to justify your little vendetta against me.'

She opens her mouth to speak but I cut her off.

'Let's talk about my uncle, shall we?'

The colour leaches from Agent Eight's face and, for the slightest moment, her features crumble into panic. She darts a guilty sideways glance at Westerfield.

It's all I need to confirm my suspicions that she's a double agent.

Damius isn't ancient history; he's not some past assignment that didn't work out. My bet is that she fell in love with the monster she was sent to manipulate.

She collects herself and steps forward, examining me, inspecting me. 'We have been keeping busy, haven't we?' she taunts. 'I see you haven't learned from your mistakes. Still snooping around in things that don't concern you. Poking your nose in where it's not welcome.' And then, from behind me, she whispers in my ear, 'If we're going to make it personal, let's talk about your mother.'

I spin around to face her. It might just be her clumsy attempt to change the subject from Damius, but I don't care. If she knows anything about my mother I have to find out.

'What do you know about my mother?'

Agent Eight laughs. It sounds more like relief than amusement.

'You really don't know, do you?' Nodding towards the General, she adds, 'I bet *she* knows all about your mother.

343

But why would anybody rush to save such a – how shall I put it? – *problematic* queen. No, better to wait for her daughter, her stupid, compliant daughter who can be made to dance at the end of a string.'

General Sewell shakes her head defiantly. I'm not sure what charge she's denying – that she knows something about my mother or that she conspired not to tell me. But I don't call her on it because I need to know what Agent Eight knows of my mother.

'All this time your own mother's life force has been right here in the V&A and you had no idea,' Agent Eight says.

My heart stops. 'Where?'

'Follow me, and perhaps we can come to an arrangement. You give me what I've always wanted and I'll let you in on a few secrets,' she says, looking malevolently at General Sewell.

Jules and Tom step towards me; so do my unicorn guards and General Sewell's officers.

'Uh-uh,' Agent Eight says. 'The Princess comes alone or not at all.'

'Your Highness, I must advise —' General Sewell starts.

'No,' I say, holding up my hand. 'I go alone.'

'It's a trap,' Tom says under his breath.

'I know,' I mouth. But no sound comes out.

chapter 33

I follow Agent Eight out of the Medieval and Renaissance Room and along the corridor, a trail of my blood falling behind me.

'Where are you taking me?' I demand.

'You'll see.'

We walk out of the building and across the grassy internal courtyard. There's a bounce in her step that makes my chest pound.

I can no longer feel pain for casting the heating spell, but from my unsteady feet and the blood still gushing from my nose, I'm sure it hasn't gone. I'm just too busy focusing on my mother to register it.

'The Poynter Room?' I ask as Agent Eight leads me towards the cafe.

I take her silence as a 'yes' and push past her, running towards the door.

The Poynter Room is cordoned off with orange tape and a sign that reads 'Closed for Restoration Work'. The room itself is shrouded in gloom, the windows replaced with boards. But aside from the windows, it's as if the attack of ravens never happened. The tables and chairs have been pushed neatly to one side, the broken glass and plaster swept away. I can make out a thin crack in the ceiling but, for all I know, that could have been there before.

'Where is she?' I say to Agent Eight, who's standing in the doorway with a grin that I want to rip off her face.

But it's not her who speaks.

'Are you ready to stop playing games now?'

I slowly turn towards the voice that uttered those exact words to me a few days ago.

'Marshall?'

He's seated at a lone table on the far side of the room, a bottle of wine and one glass in front of him.

'You've come to your senses,' he says.

'What? No,' I say, looking at him closely. There's something different about him. His navy pinstripe suit and red tie are impeccable as usual, but the boyish glint in his eye has gone, replaced by something harsh. He looks tired, distracted. A vein pulses in his neck. The little finger on his left hand quivers.

He points to the chair opposite. It's a command rather than an invitation.

I stay standing.

'You've been far less forthcoming than I'd hoped. It's time we talked openly.' His mouth twitches at the corner. The tremor in his little finger has spread to the rest of his fingers.

A cold shiver shoots through me. Every instinct in my

body is screaming at me to run, but I have to see this through, to finally work out what's really is going on.

I catch a glance exchanged between him and Agent Eight. They know each other?

'Wait, you work for the Agency?' I say to Marshall. 'Has all this been some elaborate recruitment exercise?'

Agent Eight laughs. 'I told you the dumb act wasn't all an act,' she says to Marshall.

'I do not work for the Agency,' Marshall says calmly. The twitching in his fingers is becoming more noticeable, like he's having a seizure.

'There's more at stake here than you realise, Marshall,' I seethe.

'Oh, I know what's at stake, my dear. And you've already given me more than you know.'

As I watch the manufactured warmth drain from his face, I wonder if he's actually insane.

It's his eyes that change first. They switch, shade by shade, melding from brown to green. Like an autumn leaf, his hair gradually turns to auburn. His cheekbones re-form, sharpening and stretching the skin as though he's undergoing a sudden growth spurt. His forehead lengthens to create perfect facial symmetry.

My wings flare from my back, readying to flee.

Reaching down, he pulls a familiar dagger from his boot. The encrusted ruby glistens as he flicks it. His suit is replaced with a black leather kilt and a long leather coat, opened over a white shirt with a ruffed collar. A bulbous ring of amber sits on his little finger like a tumour.

Damius.

'What … what have you done with Marshall?'

'I am Marshall,' he says. 'Have been for these past thirteen years. Musgrave didn't put up much of a fight in the end. Last of the Musgrave family line. And good riddance, too.'

I stare at him in horror, forcing breath back into my lungs.

'It's the perfect disguise, don't you think? The Order tore the realms apart looking for me after the rebellion. And here I was, all this time, hiding in plain sight. The Fae have skirmished with the Musgrave family through the centuries. It was the perfect place to wait for the right moment to claim the throne that should always have been mine.'

He smiles at me and signals for me to join him at the table. It's a gesture you'd expect from a friend, not the monster who has ruined your life many times over.

'It didn't have to go this way. You could have just given me what was mine and been spared all of this. But your mother's lapdogs and those fanatics in the Order with their misplaced loyalties put paid to that. I gave you every opportunity to come to your senses. But you insist on being difficult.'

My clenched fists itch to strike something as fury pumps through my veins.

'Now I ask myself, why just take the Crown when I can have everything?' he says as he conjures the Luck of Edenhall onto the table.

So the theft was a setup. I glance back at Agent Eight. She shrugs.

The power vibrating from the Chalice repulses me. It's wrong; every cell in me shudders. Every fibre of my being warns me not to get too close.

'Now,' Damius says. 'Where is that key you've been withholding all these years?'

'Where's my mother?' I counter through gritted teeth.

He points towards the tiled wall behind me. I turn to look at a spot I've walked past dozens of times. Through the dim light, I make out what used to be the tile painting of the Statue of Venus. It's now a gouge in the wall.

My chest aches as I run over to the empty wooden frame. She was trying to tell me. All these years, she was waiting for me to save her. And on some level, I knew. I just hadn't learned how to believe it.

Crumpling to my knees, my hands leave streaks of blood on the wood and tiles either side of where my mother's life force used to be. I flop my head forwards on the cold hard tiles and liquid anguish streams down my cheeks.

'She's quite safe,' he says. 'I've relocated her somewhere nice and cosy, somewhere she can make herself useful without getting in the way.'

She's been trapped in the tiles for years, with Damius draining her power like a leech. I sat at the table right next to her just days ago, when I was having my birthday lunch. She was trying to tell me with her beckoning hand in my peripheral vision. Perhaps she was trying to warn me about Marshall. But I wasn't able to make sense of what I was seeing. I just thought I was imagining things. Or that I was losing my mind. And Damius sat there the whole time, watching my mother's futile attempts and my cluelessness.

'Come now, let us not dwell on the past,' he says. We can help each other.'

I turn back to the table. I hate Damius so much I don't just want to kill him once; I want to make him suffer and then kill him over and over and over again.

'Felicity delivered you to me. And so shall you deliver me the key,' he says as I approach.

He and Agent Eight are looking at each other and my stomach turns. Agent Eight is gazing at the man she loves, but he's looking at her like she's staff, an employee. Clearly she hasn't moved on since they tried to make their moral fairy baby. It would break my heart – if I didn't hate her guts. She betrayed me with false promises about my mother to lure me here. And she's betrayed the Agency too. She doesn't want the key to keep if safe from anyone who'd misuse it; she wants it for my uncle.

Damius looks kindly at me. 'You and I are so similar,' he says, his voice softening.

'I am nothing like you,' I spit.

'Oh, but you are,' he says, standing up. 'Consider the symmetry. Our childhoods – both soured by meddling Fae. I am just as much a victim of their perverse rules as you. I was just a boy when I was discarded, abandoned – robbed of all that was promised to me.'

He pivots, turning his back to me and walks in a small

circle, like a scholar demonstrating a proof to a prized student.

'For most of your life you've been an embarrassment to the Order. Of course, they flatter you with titles now, but where were they all those years ago?' He lowers his voice, looking straight into my eyes. 'Think about it, Francesca. You were next in line to the throne, but they abandoned you as a child. They sent the old woman to look over you and teach you a trick or two just in case they might one day need you. But it's hardly the way to treat royalty, is it? I've seen household animals treated better. You know it's true.'

My small crack of uncertainty widens into a gaping crevice.

'Do you really think they will ever accept a half-blood like you? Come, Francesca, don't be so naive. To them, you are nothing more than a puppet. Of course, they'll dress you in beautiful costumes and put you on show now and again. But they will never relinquish their hold on the strings. Does anyone ever think to ask how a puppet feels? What it needs? What it *desires*?'

Tom's face flashes in my mind.

'You already know the answer. They have no use for you besides being a tool, to misdirect people's attention, to keep me off the throne, and to maintain their own grip on power. No doubt they'll provide you with every luxury, as they tried to do with me. But that's all the better to control you, in your gilded cage. You'll want for nothing – except your dignity and self-determination.

'Ask yourself, what do you really know of those who

claim to be your friends? The Chancellor? The Supreme Executor? They have asked much of you, but what have they given in return?'

He pauses again, his eyes boring in to me.

'I have been dealing with the royal household far longer than you, dear niece, and I know how they work. They feel entitled to run your life, telling you what you can and cannot do, pretending all the while that they know best. But what say did you have in this? In any of it?'

He walks slowly back to the table and sips his wine.

I say nothing. I don't want to admit it, and I know he's trying to push my buttons, manipulate me, but part of what he says is true. I'm watched everywhere I go. I have to sneak out of my window like a rebellious kid just to get some privacy. They wouldn't allow me to find Tom. They have treated me like a child. And they hid the truth about my mother from me.

'Even the old woman —'

'Leave Gladys out of this,' I say, my voice cold as stone. There's so much about what Gladys did and didn't do that I don't understand. And now I never will. But she died for me. She cared for me so much that she sacrificed her life so I could live. I will not hear anyone, especially not my uncle, say a bad word about her. Any enemy of Gladys's will always be an enemy of mine. 'I will never help you.'

'Oh, but you already have. Together we have built an army.'

My blood runs cold. 'What?'

'After your little *accident* on the horse I found what I'd

352

been searching for. Your DNA: half human, half Fae, and containing the perfect combination of molecules to engineer a little RNA virus to recreate pycts.'

Abby was right. The pyct virus exists because of me.

'Ironic, don't you think?' he says, running his finger along the tablecloth. 'Your blood – the very reason the royal house will never truly accept you – is the foundation of my new power.'

My stomach clenches in sickness.

'Together we have created an army that will deliver me three realms,' he says triumphantly.

'You're mad. You're both mad,' I say, backing away from him and looking at Agent Eight, who is lapping up every word from the doorway. 'You'll destroy all of us.'

'You need not worry yourself, my dear. The virus was made from your DNA, after all. You are immune. And I took the precaution of immunising myself – and those closest to me,' he adds like an afterthought. 'A reward for past loyalties. Our next joint venture, Francesca, is unlocking the unbridled power of the Chalice.'

'I will not,' I say with steely resolve.

'Have it your way. I had hoped you'd see reason after you understood that the Order are using you, but clearly you need some more incentive.'

With lightning-fast speed, Damius is in front of me, blocking my path. He raises his hand, the amber ring swirling as though it has liquefied. As the amber gathers speed like a hurricane inside a snow globe, so too does the air around us.

My hair whips about my face.

Tables and chairs overturn and clatter to the ground.

I bend my knees and brace against the floor to stop from toppling over.

Agent Eight holds fast to the door, her shoulders hunched and head drawn in towards her collarbone. It's the first time I've seen her look unsure, scared even.

Streaks of amber light burst from his ring, smashing the boards on the windows into splinters in an ear-splitting crack. I cover my head protectively, watching for signs of pain on Damius's face. Surely a spell of this size in Volgaris would be too painful to maintain for long. And once he's weakened from using the Art, I will strike. But there's not a grimace of discomfort or a trickle of blood to be seen. He looks emboldened and invigorated and he doesn't stop. A horrifying realisation dawns. He's using my mother's power. She is paying the price for his magic.

I run to him, to tackle him to the ground, to make him stop hurting my mother. But before I reach him he stretches his arms wide. Light slashes across the sky and I feel, then hear, an enormous boom. The force of the explosion knocks me to the ground. There's a shrieking of twisting metal and smashing plaster overhead. A panel from the roof plummets towards me.

My wings begin to beat, levitating me off the ground and out of the way.

And then the ceiling cascades down in a deadly storm of debris.

chapter 34

Shrieking alarms pierce my skull, broken only by the squeal of emergency vehicle sirens echoing through the streets.

Dust stings my eyes and fills my throat and lungs.

I cover my mouth with my sleeve, but I still hack and cough like I've got a twenty-a-day habit.

I stumble to the relative safety of the doorframe as parts of the roof continue to collapse, smashing and cracking the tiles below.

Peering through the dust, I make out Agent Eight's body pinned underneath a section of plaster cornicing. I lift it off her and check she's breathing.

She's alive but out cold. I roll her over on her side and leave her there.

Damius remains stock-still, unharmed and seemingly unmoved by Agent Eight's state. Untouched by the destruction he unleashed, he stretches out his arms again, pointing them to the sky.

Through the gaping hole, where daylight is partially obscured by the plumes of dust from the destroyed roof, I can see an ominous black cloud. But it's different from any normal cloud. Small sections of it tear off, swirling and gaseous, as they streak down to the ground.

Hundreds – no, thousands – of dark swirls, lit by a backdrop of lightning, fall to the ground. As they near the earth, they take form.

Pycts.

Wave after wave of infected Fae land in formation inside the Poynter Room, kicking up the dust and debris. And judging by the sounds of people screaming and stampeding, they're in the surrounding building and grounds too.

More pycts thud to their landing like a war drum.

Agents run for their life, seeking escape from the ruined building. They may be familiar with Fae and the Art, but Damius's display appears to evoke a sense of survival over duty.

Looking at the damaged building, as the dust begins to clear and the debris settles, I realise I've seen this before: the half-destroyed roof, the jagged edge of the collapsed wall. The smashed tiles below. It's the very same pattern of destruction in the ruins of the Poynter Room I witnessed when first I came to Iridesca. The outlines of the ruin are unmistakable. The only difference is that everything there was overgrown with trees, flowers and moss.

The war that ravaged Trinovantum has come to London.

I was supposed to stop a war. Instead, I've ensured it will be replayed on a new battlefield, with higher stakes and more casualties.

Tom, Jules and Abby burst into the room, followed by General Sewell and the rumble of hooves.

Taking in the devastation, Abby's wings bloom and Tom transes to his unicorn form. Jules remains in her two-legged form but I notice she now has two swords strapped across her back.

The pycts greet their presence with a chorus of shrieks and stomping, but they remain in place like good soldiers.

'Fan out,' the General orders as the Protectorate officers and unicorns line up against the pycts.

'Ah, how good of you to join us,' Damius says with a smirk. 'Sewell, isn't it? Haven't you risen through the ranks? Such a shame that your career will be cut short.'

Damius has played me from the start.

He's not only orchestrated this war, but has chosen the battlefield. The Protectorate might have had a chance in Iridesca, but in Volgaris they'll basically be confined to hand-to-hand combat. Despite their superior skills there's no way the Protectorate can hold out against an entire army of pycts.

I stare at the faces of the nearest pycts, wondering if I know any of them. Or if they know me.

And still they come. Swooping from the sky like a mass of tormented paratroopers, snarling and growling, they land with thud after thud after thud.

Tom, Jules and Abby are at my side.

Tom leans over, keeping one eye on the pycts. 'We need to transfer. Now.'

'Your Highness,' Jules urges, 'we are outnumbered.'

I look from Jules to Tom.

Steadying my trembling hands, I'm racking by brain for a way out of the mess that I've created.

I can feel General Sewell's eyes boring into my back, ordering me to flee.

I think through my options.

Running isn't one of them. To run is to lose. I will lose any chance we have at stopping Damius and finding my mother. I will lose the faith that Gladys put in me. And I will lose my chance to prove that I am nobody's puppet.

The Art rallies in the pit of my stomach. It dances with delight along my veins, waiting for release. My senses sharpen, my heart is buoyed with power and hope. Just like in the train station, all it would take is one glorious spell and Damius's pyct army would be dust.

But I can't. They are Fae, my people, enslaved by Damius. They're innocents. I cannot vaporise them. And just in case I was still undecided, the price of the spell flashes into my mind. Using the Art in Volgaris to take out an entire army would cost me my life.

The pycts form a thick, deep semi-circle around the room and outside, a seething mass of snarling, grunting and gnashing not-quite human forms. Their unholy stench almost overwhelms me. Some of them go down on all fours, baying at me like ferocious dogs.

Baying for blood.

My blood.

Damius steps closer.

'One last chance, Princess. The key.'

My only option at this point is to use a smaller spell that my body can withstand to destroy Damius. Without their master, the pycts may not attack. I hope against hope that I can control my power. And that it doesn't kill me before I'm done.

I clasp my mother's pendant around my neck and hold it out in front of me, readying to channel my powers.

But before I can conjure my spell, the pedant is wrenched from my neck and propelled through the air, straight into Damius's outstretched hand.

He regards it curiously, stroking it like a favourite pet.

'Such an impulsive child,' he says, then crushes the pendant in one hand.

I watch in horror as the glinting, fine ruby powder drifts to the floor.

Damius turns on his heel. He walks slowly back to stand at the head of his snarling army. The assembled pycts stream around him to form a protective shield.

I turn to Abby and Tom. 'Go. Please.'

'Not a chance, Chess,' Tom says, without taking his eyes off the pycts.

Abby winks at me. 'Not this time, Princess.'

Jules draws one of her swords and tosses it to Abby, who catches it with the litheness of a cat.

'The Princess,' Damius says. 'Deliver her to me. Destroy the rest.'

The pycts swarm forward. They flick their wands but, unlike in the train station, no mud flies from them. The pycts look as surprised at this as I am. Perhaps their magic is too weak to work in Volgaris.

Jules draws her remaining sword and charges into the fray, picking off pycts from side to side. Tom, using his horn like a sword, impales the approaching pycts and tosses them to the ground. The Protectorate charge, meeting the pycts head-on, throwing the snarling creatures aside like ragdolls.

I watch pyct blood pool on the ground and am sickened by the final proof of my failure.

A horde of pycts circles around me, trying to herd me towards Damius. Their stench and the pus sores on their skin make my stomach curdle. I don't want to hurt them so I keep them at bay with short sharp blasts from my fingertips. I think I'm the only one relying on the Art. But I have to. I wouldn't stand a chance in hand-to-hand combat.

The Protectorate is vastly outnumbered, but the pycts are untrained, lacking the discipline for coordinated attack. The Protectorate is a battle machine. Officers take to the air, while those on the ground push back the horde.

But the Protectorate's aerial advantage doesn't last.

The pycts improvise, bounding off the walls with their powerful legs and leaping at the fairies, dragging them back to the ground.

The place is a chaotic mess. Through the remains of the wall, I watch the battle spreading throughout the building. A few remaining agents and tourists are caught up in the fight. They run for their lives, pursued by monsters from another realm.

Three pycts leap at a Protectorate officer from different directions, grabbing and slashing at her. They pull the fairy to the ground and beat her like street thugs.

I lift off the ground above the pycts circling me and reluctantly fire off rapid blasts of magic, sending all three pycts flying. I'm too late. The fairy remains on the ground, motionless.

A pyct swipes at Abby, knocking her to the ground. I go to fire off another blast but Jules is there in an instant, impaling the pyct with her sword in one hand and helping Abby to her feet with her other.

And then it gets worse.

The thunder of hooves echoes through the building. I turn to see horned creatures charging forwards behind the pycts, clouds of dust following them. But these aren't unicorns as I've come to know them; they're more like a cross between a woolly mammoth and a rhinoceros, right down to the armoured plates that cover their bodies, battering and smashing walls and tiles. Small tufts of coarse hair poke out between the joins in their hardened plates. Fairies, unicorns and pycts scatter or are trampled and crushed by these brutal creatures.

Tortured shrieks fill the air. One officer of the Protectorate after another falls, the beasts' claws slicing through armour as if it were cheap linen. The Protectorate officers use the Art on the approaching beasts but they're too weakened, their spells seeming to only enrage the animals rather than injure them.

At the far end of the room, Damius watches the unfolding slaughter with pleasure.

Then, amongst the chaos, something changes.

There's a lull. Groups of pycts step back from the killing. The trampling of hooves, the clashing of swords, is dying down.

I look around, trying to work out what's going on.

The remaining officers of the Protectorate have dropped to their knees, flailing about on the ground, howling in agony or curled in balls of pain.

Tom cries out to me. He's transed back to his two-legged form and his face is contorted in pain. I push and kick past pycts and run over to him, having trouble breathing.

Jules and Abby writhe on the ground as well. Their hands are beginning to curl into rigid crooks. Hair sprouts between the open sores forming on their skin. Their eyes turn crimson.

The RNA virus is taking hold. Their transition to pycts has begun.

I scan the scene. The same metamorphosis is overtaking all the Fae.

Tom pushes me away. He screeches and starts swiping at some imagined predator. I'm not sure if he's hallucinating from the virus infecting his brain or from the pain of the transition.

And then I know what I must do.

chapter 35

'I'm ready to deal,' I say to my uncle as I approach him.

Pycts stare at me like quizzical dogs, trying to work out whether I'm friend or foe. They yap and claw, but clear a path. The thunder and stamp of their feet echo around the room, only just drowning out the cries of Fae being turned into pycts.

'This will be amusing,' Damius chuckles.

'The antidote to the virus ...'

Damius tilts his head back and looks down his nose. 'In exchange for?'

'Me.'

'*No!*' It's Tom's voice. I can just make it out above the snarling pycts and the groans of pain and agony.

I don't look at him. I can't.

'Take me,' I say. 'Kill me, do whatever you want with me. Just reverse this virus.' I know not all Fae want Damius on the throne. In fact, I'm willing to bet most don't. But surely anything would be better than turning into pycts.

'You are in no position to bargain,' Damius hisses. 'As arrogant as your mother. And just as naive.'

'I'm the reason for your Fae rebellion. With me gone, you eradicate my mongrel blood and you can take the Crown. Undo what you've done, and you can do with me what you will.'

'You flatter yourself, dear niece.' He kicks a broken beam across the room, flattening a row of pycts. 'You're weak. Crippled by morality. You've got nothing inside you except fear and shame and uncontrollable rage. A disgrace to your bloodline. You're nothing more than a genetic accident and you've only lived this long because I have allowed it. If you didn't possess the key I would have killed you thirteen years ago. You had your chance. Now my patience is at an end.'

He pulls the Chalice from inside his coat and thrusts it into my hand. 'Open it.'

I hesitate.

Damius lifts his arms, aims his ring at General Sewell and fires off a golden blast. The bolt hits her in the heart. She gives a yelp of pure pain then turns to dust.

There's a collective gasp from the Protectorate. But I swear Jules's voice is the loudest.

'Who's next?' Damius says, looking around the room.

'No, no. Stop, please!' I beg.

'Open it.'

'Okay,' I say. 'Just stop killing people.'

Even though it repels me, I wrap my fingers around the Chalice. My hands grow hotter and hotter. The blue, green, red and white swirls that pattern the cup begin moving, slithering around the glass like coloured serpents. I've awakened something in it. I stare down at it, entranced by its power and beauty, desperately, silently imploring: *Where is your key? And what is it? Tell me what to look for.*

It sickens me that I'm actually trying to give the key to Damius. But what choice do I have? I cannot be responsible for all this death, for the destruction of the Fae.

'Forgive me, Gladys,' I whisper, and close my eyes, poised to listen to the cup's hidden secret. It's a soft hum at first, growing louder.

I calm my breathing and still myself to receive the message.

Nothing. Vibration and movement without meaning.

What did I expect? Did I really believe I was so special that it would pipe up and give me an answer?

'Tick, tock,' mocks Damius, sounding bored, but his eyes are fixed on the cup.

I can't look at Tom.

Or Jules.

Or Abby.

I'm ashamed to find myself hoping that their transition to pycts has advanced so far that they do not understand I am about to betray all the trust they placed in me, that I'm not the girl they hoped I was.

Damius turns and fires another lethal blast, felling a unicorn whose transition to one of the rhinoceros-like creatures is almost complete.

'No, please! Stop, stop. Please, stop,' I cry.

'You are responsible for this,' Damius says. 'Give me the key and this will end.'

I turn the Luck of Edenhall over in my hand, inspecting it, searching for any clue at all. The pulsating rhythm in the Chalice grows louder, more insistent. It's mirroring my heartbeat. The colours swirl faster, writhing through the glass, combining, breaking apart and recombining in new arrangements.

'One. Last. Chance,' Damius spits through gritted teeth. He aims his ring at Tom and screams, '*Give me the key!*'

'I don't have the key!' I scream back.

Damius levels me with a look of seething rage.

'I don't have it,' I whimper. 'I've never had it. Just stop. Stop it.'

'You just signed your boyfriend's death sentence,' he says, and releases a fiery burst in Tom's direction.

I lunge at my uncle, sending him off balance. Damius's blast misses Tom by millimetres.

Damius recovers quickly, swinging around and knocking me to the ground. I look up at his cold, murderous eyes.

'Without the key you are worthless,' he says as his boot crunches down on my fingers.

I don't fight him. I'm done.

Damius looks almost disappointed by my surrender.

'How could you have saved your people, when you can't even save yourself?'

I can't respond. He speaks the truth.

I look over at Tom, who is now barely recognisable. His muscles have wasted and his flesh is starting to sag off his frame. His fingers have lengthened, his back is hunched. He stares at me as if he's saying goodbye.

'Just get on with it,' I say quietly.

Behind me, I hear Jules cry out. She tries to scramble towards me, but stumbles and curls up into a ball of pain. Abby is writhing on the ground near me, oblivious to what is happening.

'Look at you,' Damius says, crunching down further on my fingers. 'Your humanity sickens me.'

With a smirk, he lands a boot straight to my gut. I whimper as the air is pushed out of me. I clench my jaw against the pain and close my eyes, sinking into the darkness. In the distance, screams of distress from all the Fae I failed form a chorus.

As my mind collapses in on itself in pain and shame, a memory sparks to life. And then another. I claw my way through every agonising, bitter memory, reliving every occasion I was told I didn't matter and believed it. All those times I remained silent, frozen and invisible.

Tom said that memories make us who we are. What do these memories make me?

But he also said that I don't have to make myself small anymore. I've been hollowed out and crushed by smallness; I don't know if I can be any more than that.

You already are. Come.

The voice is muffled but I recognise it.

It's my voice.

I follow it.

An oasis of stillness nestling somewhere between nowhere and everywhere envelops me. I peer into it and the ancient wisdom stares back at me.

Gladys's words echo in my ears. I thought it was just one of her silly riddles, but I was wrong. Everything Gladys ever said to me had a purpose, as if she was planting seeds to bloom days, weeks or years later, when I was ready.

Gladys saw something in me, something more than my broken spirit and my human weakness. Something Damius didn't see. Something I couldn't even see myself.

Until now.

All that you seek is already within you.

Gladys saw the key in me.

And now I see it too.

I'm not the girl who fell.

I'm the one who got back up.

My eyes spring open.

Wide open.

Damius swoops like an angry hornet, readying to launch another kick. I catch his boot mid-air, shock registering on his face. I hold his boot firm and spit the blood from my mouth onto the shiny black leather.

'I am not afraid,' I say, releasing his boot and wiping the blood from my mouth with my sleeve.

'Nice try, dear niece, but it's too little, too late.'

I stagger to my feet. My fear has vanished. I'm not even angry anymore.

With my remaining strength, I summon the Luck of Edenhall into my hands. Holding it out in front of me, I bellow, '*I am the key!*'

Damius's eyes widen. He stares at me in confusion or dawning realisation, or both. Everyone is staring, stunned.

It's as if their agonising transition has been momentarily stalled.

Tom watches me out of his bloodied and swollen eyes. I make the only choice I can make.

I raise the Chalice above my head and cry out:

If this cup should break or fall
Unbridled power heed my call.

With the full force of my body, I slam the Chalice onto the broken tiles of the Poynter Room.

The air echoes with reverberations as the cup fractures into millions of tiny glass shards.

Each shard sets off a chain reaction, shattering again and again. It's impossible, how many shards of glass there are, but still there are more. Coloured shards spread over the chipped and broken ground.

Time slows; fractures.

Breath stalls.

I stand my ground.

I'm the calm at the centre of the blazing furnace. The serenity beneath the raging sea.

I hold out my hands and call the power of the Luck of Edenhall to me, summoning the magic particles lying dormant within each fragment.

A rainbow hue rises up, expanding into space and filling the room with shimmering crystal snowflakes, suspended in the air all around us.

Damius swipes at the iridescent dust, trying to gather

it towards him, to capture it, control it. The power slips through his fingers.

'I am moral, I am Fae. Only I have been entrusted with such power,' I say to Damius.

I call to the power, welcome it, imbibe it.

And, finally, I unleash it.

> *I am power*
> *I am control*
> *I become life*
> *and I become death*
> *Unbridled power, to me obey*
> *Return these pycts back to Fae*

The air crackles as I send the Art out into Volgaris, rushing through every corridor in the V&A and into the grounds outside. Down every street, inside every door and window. Across every garden, field and forest. It sizzles as it collides with each pyct and Fae, undoing the virus. I open portals to Iridesca and Transcendence and send my magic into those realms.

His army gone, Damius lets out a primal howl. Even with my mother's stolen energy, his magic is no match to overcome this. To overcome me.

A black cloud of ravens descends, swirling around him in a cyclonic fog of darkness.

And then he's gone.

All around me, the pycts and half-turned Fae are returning to their normal bodies, shaking themselves as if they have just woken from a nightmare.

Through the sea of bodies I see Callie, looking bewildered but unharmed.

Tom rolls onto his feet. He's bloody but the pyct virus is weakening.

I run to him.

He enfolds me in his arms, squeezing me so tightly that my wounds hurt. But I don't care.

He touches his forehead against mine, and we are still, our hearts beating in time.

epilogue

My hair is swept back in a vintage chignon. Brina has been
fussing with the braided coils on either side for what feels
like an eternity. Callie straightens the train of my dusty
rose raw-silk gown. The bodice is embroidered with gold
thread and the skirt cascades to the floor in a waterfall. It's
the most beautiful dress I've ever seen.

Brina steps back, admiring her work. 'You're the picture
of your mother, Your Highness,' she says for what must be
the thirty-eighth time today.

'You look like yourself, Chess,' Jules says.

My eyes brim with tears at her words. I blink them
away. I had wondered what it would take for Jules to use
my first name. Now I know.

She is kitted out in her formal Protectorate uniform: a
thick grey wool suit with epaulettes and gold buttons. A
collection of ribbons and medals is pinned to her chest. She
itches under her collar and pulls at the tartan sash on her
shoulder.

I'm guessing she'd prefer to be in her bodysuit.

I suck in a calming breath as I step out of the curved arched door of Windsor Castle.

The night air breaks with the deafening roar of cheers and clapping. Thousands of Fae line the path to the Temple, forming an honour guard. The full moon of Albion casts silver light over their faces and I note that all of them are looking straight at me.

I take two steps and my self-consciousness and embarrassment from the attention fade as the path bursts into a bloom of pink. Magenta blossoms, the Fae symbol of gratitude and appreciation, are tossed into the air all around me.

As my satin slippers step upon the blossoms I realise that all of these people have come out at midnight, the time of new beginnings, to celebrate my coronation, and not just because I'm Cordelia's daughter.

I didn't let Gladys down.

After I destroyed Damius's RNA virus, I used the unbridled Art contained within the Luck of Edenhall against itself and destroyed every last shimmering speck of it. There's no power left in the Chalice for anyone to fight over or abuse. The Art in Volgaris remains conditional on payment, so technically King James and Queen Signe's Treaty remains intact.

Not everyone is happy that I destroyed that power. The traditionalists in the Order of the Fae snipe that I ruined their one chance to free the Art in Volgaris. But this is what Queen Signe sacrificed herself for. It's what Gladys would have wanted me to do and what humanity needs to be safe. So as far as I'm concerned: sorry, not sorry.

The Agency's pride is dented after their defeat at the V&A, but not enough to make war. As far as official relations between the realms go, everything is as it has been for the past four centuries. The official explanation for the damage to the V&A is a terror attack. Several commentators have speculated that it must have been perpetrated by the same people who broke into the government facility the day before. That would be Tom and me. Good thing I don't want my data entry job back.

Surprisingly, there weren't that many eyewitnesses to the attack on the V&A. Or perhaps it's not surprising. Those who said they saw mythical beasts descending from the heavens and roaming the halls were described as suffering a mass delusion brought on by the trauma of the day. The people who insisted on what they saw on social media and their own YouTube channels have been portrayed as conspiracy cranks good at making fake news videos – the kind of people who think the world is run by reptile overlords.

As for the Luck of Edenhall, the Agency has already manufactured a replica cup to fool the tourists.

Agent Eight suffered a concussion from the falling plaster, but she's now fully recovered. I'm not totally heartless, though. I did go to the trouble of sending her a Get Well Soon card with a simple message: 'I know. And one day I'll tell.' No doubt this makes her hate me even more. But the way I figure it, Agent Eight and I were never going to be close.

The doors of the Temple creak open to reveal a full house. Rows of pews line both sides of the ornate chamber, a ruby red carpet running up the middle. Fae sit shoulder to shoulder on every pew, sparkling with jewels and shimmering fabrics.

They stand and turn to me as I begin my approach towards the crown sitting atop the altar. The Chancellor and the Supreme Executor stand either side of the altar, their faces solemn. Halfway down the aisle I come to an abrupt halt. Standing there is Santa, the painter with the van and the book of poetry.

'I knew you could do it, luv,' he says quietly.

I reach up on tippy toes and kiss Santa's cheek for nudging me forward when all I thought I was capable of was retreat. His eyes brim with a kind of paternal pride that tugs at my heart. I wish my father was here tonight. It's weird to miss something that you barely remember having.

When I reach the front of the Temple I turn around and scan the crowd. I'm searching for one face only, one pair of ice blue eyes.

And there he is. The one who has made me whole and broken me to pieces all at once.

Sitting in the back corner, a mix of leather, denim, kindness and strength, he is perfection. It's the closest I've been to Tom since we returned to Iridesca. I wish that I'd held him just a little bit longer and a little bit tighter at the V&A before we said goodbye. That I'd taken more time to store away that feeling of completeness, so that I could draw upon it later. Maybe then I wouldn't ache with such emptiness from his absence. Perhaps then I would be able to focus on anything other than his lips, his hands, his words, his everything.

He stares back with an intensity that robs me of my breath. My whole body yearns to close the distance.

But we can't.

Do not let anyone distract you from your true purpose. Or you will ruin everything we hold dear. They were the last words Gladys ever said. They haunt me. I hear those words and see that warning look she gave Tom every time I close my eyes. Gladys died so that I could live to do my duty. I owe it to her legacy, to my mother and to my people to heed her warning. Which means I must find the strength to endure each day without Tom.

Or work out some way that I can obey Gladys's prophecy and still be with him.

But until I figure that out, I cannot risk it.

I realise that I'm staring at Tom when the entire audience turns around to follow my gaze. Soft murmurs and whispers swirl through the room. Tom and I have got to be the worst-kept secret in the three realms.

The Chancellor clears his throat and I turn back to the altar, my cheeks growing red. He welcomes the audience to this 'auspicious occasion'. He was born for this moment.

'Princess Francesca, daughter of Cordelia of House Raven,' he says in his resonant voice. 'If anyone deems Her Highness unfit or unworthy to assume the throne of Albion, speak now or forever hold your peace.'

I look out at my people. There's reverence in some faces, hope in others. I don't miss the occasional look of ambivalence; they're giving me the benefit of the doubt.

For now. I'm going to be watched closely.

After an awkward silence that seems to go on forever, the Chancellor instructs me to kneel before the congregation.

The Supreme Executor drapes the Cloak of Virtue over my shoulders, a thick red velvet with a tartan trim. Next she presents me with the golden Sword of Valour. The Chancellor places the ruby and diamond crown on my head. I register the weight of it, on my head and on my heart.

I foresee a bumpy road ahead, especially when the Order learn that I will not be the puppet they want me to be. I will not shut up, smile and do as I'm told. Far from being a weakness, my morality is the very fuel that ignites my power. I will not smother it.

Rising to my feet, I recite the words I've been rehearsing for the past three days.

'I, Francesca of House Raven, willingly accept the Fae Throne of Albion to rule and serve.'

And then, despite the hours of rehearsal and the Chancellor's firm instructions not to break from the script, I can't help myself. I take a step towards the crowd.

'I will serve as your Queen, but this is not my time. This throne rightfully belongs to my mother, Queen Cordelia. I will be the caretaker until she is able to resume her role. And she will,' I add with absolute certainty. 'I will not rest until I find my mother's consciousness and revive her body.'

My gaze travels to the ice blue eyes at the back of the room, and they lock with mine.

'I will fight every day so that what has been set apart shall be joined together.'

acknowledgements

THANK YOU

ELIZABETH ROSE
PHILIPA ROTHFIELD
REBECCA LOWTH
L-J LACEY
HELEN MILLEN
MEL FITZGERALD
RACHEL SHEEHAN
VALERIE SCANLON
TEAGAN MCHARG
KIRSTIE INNES-WILL
GABRIELA FIORESE
LINDA ANTHONY
DAVID VAZ   ALANNA VAZ   ELISABETH YOUNG
TRISH MILLEN   ALYSON O'SHANNESSY   TRACEY BOWE
ELLIS JAMES
MEAGAN SWEENEY
KATE EDWARDS
JANE HOLMAN
GREG MUIR
JO ROSENBERG
SELWA ANTHONY
CAROLYN MENZIES
MANON VAN STRAATEN
MARISA DI NATALE
SAREA COATES

FRANK SCANLON
DANIELLE LACEY
READERS, REVIEWERS, BOOKSELLERS
TONY PARSONS
HELEN DI NATALE
SONJA EBBELS
JAN EDWARDS
SOPHY WILLIAMS
ANITA GREIG
CAITLIN YATES
CECELIA TODD
MICHAEL EDWARDS
TILLY PARSONS
JULES COLE

CPSIA information can be obtained
at www.ICGtesting.com
Printed in the USA
LVHW051055261121
704491LV00016B/258